The SWORD'S CHOICE

The Sapphire Eruption

The SWORD'S CHOICE

The Sapphire Eruption

I.M. REDWRIGHT

The Sapphire Eruption is a work of fiction. Any resemblance to actual events, or persons (living or dead), is entirely coincidental.

Book cover by James Bousema.

Special thanks to William Oppenheimer for his developmental editing and Scott Alexander Jones for his copyediting and proofreading, the book wouldn't be the same without your amazing work.

ISBN 9788409178414

Visit my website at: www.imredwright.com

To my family, for believing in me. To my friends, for being there. And to any of you fighters, for rising up again, no matter how hard life hits.

Contents

The Fireos, passionate and violent, ruled by the phoenix chosen when the sky turns red.

The Aquos, smart and reflective, a queendom controlled by the royal Dajalam family.

The Tirhans, calm and goodhearted, when the mighty flower blossoms a new ruler rises.

The Aertians, shrewd and indecisive, ruled by those able to hear things others can't.

Four nations. Living in a perpetual state known as the Equilibrium. A perfect harmony. A supposed one.

Prologue

There is a saying in the Fireo Kingdom: *A phoenix is born only when the sky turns red.* The Descendant Phoenix will take the newborn as his disciple until one day, from the ashes of the old monarch, the Ascendant Phoenix will rise and reign with wisdom.

Thommes stood in front of the mirror for only a moment, staring at his old face. His formerly black hair had turned grey long ago, and his brown eyes didn't look quite as alive as when he was young. The right side of his face was burned, as were his torso and his right arm. He had burned himself long ago; he was a fire priest, after all. He had proven the depth of his devotion to the Incandescent, the God of Fire. His appearance would have caused revulsion in any other kingdom, but not in the Fire Kingdom, Firia. In this kingdom, every citizen looked upon any priest of fire with utter respect. For their charred skin symbolized how much the priests worshipped their deity.

The streets were empty, too early for merchants and too late for night owls. The fire priest took such emptiness as a source of relief, because although the ceremony he would soon attend had become routine, it was celebrated with all of the rigor that such an act deserved. He walked as fast as he could, the sound of his staff echoing on the house walls.

Red Sky, a phenomenon that occurred annually, was in the eyes of the people of the Kingdom of Fire, the call from their God to all those born since the last ceremony. The rare event was of great importance, for one of those neonates could become the Ascendant Phoenix, and therefore the future king.

15

The event was led by a priest who carried out the test on each neonate while two soldiers guarded them. The Kingdom of Fire possessed a weapon that represented their God: Distra and Sinistra, the twin swords of fire. Not only did the weapons possess inconceivable power; they were also the weapons that chose the heir to the throne.

Every citizen of the kingdom had been subjected to the test of fire—a cut in the palm by one of the two sacred swords. As the books said, the one who did not bleed would be the one chosen by the God of Fire, the Incandescent, and therefore would replace, upon reaching the full age, the present king. The Fire God was capricious. Much time had passed since Wulkan, the phoenix and therefore current ruler of the Fire Kingdom, had been chosen.

The priest's eyes contemplated the greatness of the palace, a monument made of grey—almost black—stone. A huge wooden gate plated in metal was guarded by two palace guards covered in coal-black armor, armed with spears and shields decorated with two crossed swords and a flaming phoenix in the background, the emblem of the kingdom. Approaching the door, the priest found himself stopped by the guards, although they knew the reason for his visit. The more experienced guard began to speak.

"Tell me, old priest Thommes." A mocking tone was easily noticeable in his voice. "What brings you here at such an early hour?"

"You know why I'm here, Ultramp," Thommes said with a frown while pointing at him with his cane. He was a man whose devotion was surpassed only by his temperament. "And you'd better not waste a second more of my time if you don't want to enrage the Incandescent."

A shiver crossed the backs of both soldiers; the idea of provoking the anger of the God of Fire clearly frightened them. Staring at the priest's burned flesh, as if his charred skin reminded them whose side their god would be on, the soldiers gave the order to open the gate. Behind the door, a single palace servant carrying a candle awaited Thommes, and after carelessly bowing to the priest, he signaled for the priest to follow him. The servant guided Thommes through the different passages of the palace, all unadorned; the king faithfully reflected the simplicity of the people he represented, one of the many characteristics of the Fireos, along with their bad temper and passion for combat. Thommes ran his hand over the thick walls of the palace. The black stone released a certain comforting warmth.

To Wulkan's right lay the throne of his young wife; the throne was empty due to the early timing of the event. To his left, a display case with gold borders was sealed with several locks. On either side of the display case, two guards lay prostrate. These were members of the king's guard, known as the Sons of the Flame.

Thommes bowed to the king, but he was unable to avoid fixing his eyes on the display case. Behind the glass lay the famous twin swords of fire, those weapons whose verdict could anoint new kings and queens and defend their kingdom with unparalleled power. No matter how many years Thommes had been performing the ritual, he still looked with admiration at the case in which the two sacred swords rested.

"My king," Thommes began, kneeling on the cane. "Heaven has spoken. It is time to submit newborns to the trial. It is possible that today the Ascendant Phoenix will emerge, so I ask you to grant me the honor of giving me one of the swords of fire so that I may carry out the ceremony."

The king fixed his tired eyes on Thommes. After a few seconds of silence, he nodded. With a gesture, he ordered his guards to open the showcase. The two guards approached it. Both took a black key from around his neck and proceeded to open the locks in unison. With a loud click, the door of the display case opened. Then one of the guards took one of the cases and carefully offered it to the king.

The king opened the case and took the sword that was inside it with his right hand. As he raised it to the sky, his grave voice echoed throughout the room: "Thommes, priest of Firia, I grant you Distra. May its flame guide your steps and show the word of the Incandescent, thus choosing my legitimate heir."

The choice of Distra caused a slight disappointment to register in Thommes's face. Throughout the many years that he had been carrying out the ceremony, he had always performed it using Distra. Although the twin swords were known to be identical, Thommes had wanted to perform the ceremony with Sinistra at least once; however, it seemed that this would not be possible on this occasion either. The priest supposed that the king's choice was not made by chance, and the fact that the king was left-handed surely had something to do with it.

Fixing his eyes on the sword, Thommes looked at it as if for the first time. The grip was wrapped in a maroonish metal wire. In the dark copper disc pommel was carved a large letter D, inside which was a smaller flame symbol. And the quillons of the bronzed crossguard curved toward the blade. The bright blade. Even for those less knowledgeable regarding the world of weapons, something in the sword allowed them to appreciate that this was not an ordinary sword, despite its simple design.

The king put Distra back in its case and handed it to Thommes.

"Thank you, my king. I will protect the sword with my life."

With a bow, Thommes left the room carrying the heavy case in his arms. Outside, two soldiers of the Sons of the Flame were waiting to act as his escorts. The ceremony would take place in the Lava Sanctuary, named for its proximity to the volcano that was in the north of the kingdom's capital, as had been done since the beginning.

On horseback, Thommes and the two soldiers made their way towards the Lava Sanctuary. Luckily for Thommes and his old bones, it was not a long journey. They would be there at dawn.

"Priest, do you think today will be the day?" said one of the soldiers with a hint of hope in his voice.

Slightly surprised, Thommes turned on his saddle to look at the guards. Out of respect for either the priest or the traditions observed during the other times the event had been performed, the guards did not address him; the ride to the sanctuary was undertaken in silence. He looked the guards up and down. Until then they would have been said to look the same: strong and stupid, like all soldiers. Their blackish armor and helmets barely allowed Thommes to distinguish them; however, after inspecting them more closely, he could see that they were very different. The soldier who had asked him the question was around the age of thirty, and his hickory-brown eyes conveyed enthusiasm. The Sons of the Flame were not only part of the elite army of the Kingdom of Fire; they also used to be its most devoted members, so being part of this ceremony should undoubtedly be an honor for them. The other soldier, however, revealed a lost look in his small, uninterested brown eyes.

"Who knows, young soldier. This may be the day. May the Incandescent bless us with such an honor." While mentioning the deity, the priest raised his hand to the sky, curling his fingers in the shape of a claw symbolizing the God of Fire's flame rising.

After hearing his words, the young soldier smiled enthusiastically as he moved excitedly on his horse.

"That would be incredible!" the young soldier said. "Just thinking I could witness how the new king gets chosen—the Ascendant Phoenix! I get goose bumps!"

The other soldier, who had trailed behind the two men, began to laugh. "More than a hundred years have passed since the last phoenix, King Wulkan, was chosen. Not even this old priest was alive then, and you're thinking you're going to have the chance to live through that moment? Poor naïve man!"

"It is true that many years have gone by since the last king was elected," Thommes added, "but it is not unusual. According to the books, Queen Muramon reigned for three hundred years. Our king is young by comparison."

The soldier, not letting his comrade's comments undermine his enthusiasm, continued asking, "And how will you know who the phoenix is?"

"Well," Thommes said, unsure how to answer. Although his master had transmitted all of his knowledge to the priest, like his predecessor he, his master, had died without having witnessed that moment, as he himself had until now. But, as dictated by the ancient manuscripts, the baby would not bleed. Instead, flames would sprout from his wound. But such a fact was absurd. Without doubt it was a simple metaphor, a mere literary adornment to provide more strength to the story. "All newborns receive a cut in the palm of their hand from one of the twin swords of fire," Thommes told the guard. "If the baby's hand bleeds then he will not be the phoenix."

The three riders could not avoid looking at their palms. On each of them was a scar that evidenced the moment when they had each been submitted to the ceremony—reminders that they had not been chosen.

"On the other hand, if the baby does not bleed, I cannot say for sure what will happen. But as the manuscripts dictate, the phoenix will not bleed and will rise like a king."

Once they had reached the sanctuary, Thommes prepared the room, spreading a white tablecloth with gold edgings over a table on which the sword rested. The sanctuary was a warm place with a musty smell, not a surprising scent given that the sanctuary was a sacred place only visited when the sky turned red. The only decorations in the room, aside from the table, were the torches that hung on the thick black walls. The newborns would pass through the room one by one, being placed upon the table to be submitted to the ritual.

Despite it being so early in the morning, many women had already been waiting with their newborns outside the sanctuary when Thommes and the guards had arrived. Although the laws of the kingdom dictated that every newborn go through this ritual, this was not what moved these mothers to participate in such an act. Fulfilling the wishes of the Incandescent was enough for them. Especially if his desire meant that one of their children would become the next monarch.

The soldiers, having already opened the gates, made each woman go inside one by one. One of the soldiers took a newborn and delivered the infant to the priest while the other closed the door. The ritual required intimacy. The priest, brandishing Distra, made a cut in one of their hands.

With each cut, Thommes stopped breathing for a moment. It was curious how after so many years he did not even hear the cry of the babies when bleeding, and the blood emanating from the wounds deeply frustrated him. This was also reflected in the soldiers and especially in the mother, who saw how her dream of having gestated the phoenix vanished.

During the second day, the sun shone brightly, the sky looking even more reddish than the day before. There was Thommes again, somewhat indisposed by the massive intake of alcohol in line with heated arguments the night before, as the priest liked to drown his frustrations in the tavern. The soldiers, as the day before, rushed to open the doors of the sanctuary. It was time for the ritual, and that day there were fewer women waiting.

When none of the neonates seemed to be the Ascendant Phoenix, mothers interpreted this in different ways, with many of them leaving feeling indignant or even angry, showing the well-known character of the Fireo people. It was late in the afternoon when there was no one else on the other side. Thommes sighed disappointedly.

"It seems that this year is another one without an heir," he said frustrated as he sheathed the sword. "Close the doors of the sanctuary."

While the soldiers listened to the order, a few taps were heard on the other side followed by a baby crying.

"Is it too late?" said the woman, holding her son in her arms, so covered that not even a piece of skin of the child could be seen.

With a gesture, Thommes allowed the woman to go in so that the ritual could be performed on the baby.

The young soldier did not overlook her beauty. She was a young woman with long black hair and light honey-brown eyes that made the soldier frown and get closer to check her pupils to ensure they were not yellow, as this feature that would have proven she was not a pure Fireo citizen, but rather a Fireo-Aertian unickey, a Firtian as they were called, which would prevent her son from being part of the ritual.

The brown eyes and black hair were the typical features of the Fireo people. Each of the other kingdoms had their own easily distinguishable features. Of course, though not too common, there were unickeys, those born from the union of couples from different kingdoms, thus possessing a mixture of features. Curiously, unickeys often appealed to the opposite gender, who were attracted to their atypical features, while conversely the same sex, aware that mixed offspring were usually considered more attractive, did not hide their lack of sympathy—or in some cases, their hatred.

The woman, with a slight bow, extended her son to the soldier. This one could not avoid fixing his eyes on her palms, intent on verifying that she was a citizen of the kingdom. Her mark did not lie.

The older soldier closed the door, while the younger one extended the child to Thommes, and the newborn began to cry while his mother looked at the floor. He began to uncover the baby, laying him on the ritual table.

Thommes, whose hangover headache only deepened due to the endless cries of the child, brandished Distra and began the ritual.

"Thank goodness that today we will finish soon," Thommes murmured while making the cut with Distra on one of the baby's palms. He had decided to go straight to the tavern after the ritual had ended. "Oh Distra, sacred sword that raises kings and queens, voice of God in our domains—show us the way to the eternal flame!"

As was his habit, he took the child to return him to his mother, and only when he saw the faces of the rest of the contestants did he notice something.

"He... He has not bled!" Thommes said in a choked voice.

It could only mean one thing. The cut did not summon a single drop of blood; it only issued an orange flash. But that was not all. Distra, which was lying on the tabletop, had turned into a reddish color, issuing as much heat as it had the day it was forged. Then the sword was engulfed in flames for a brief moment. Then the flames disappeared, with Distra looking like a regular sword again.

Thommes could not believe his eyes. After so much time, so many stories, so many frustrations, there was finally an heir.

"Contemplate the Ascendant Phoenix! Our future king!" roared Thommes, pointing at the little boy who was still crying on the table. He knelt on the ground as he watched with great joy and astonishment how the ritual had finally worked. An heir was chosen after all those years.

The two soldiers, who had been absorbed by the show, finally reacted. The youngest could not avoid setting aside the protocol and jumping joyfully to welcome the new king. It was an honor to witness such an act. The other soldier, however, after understanding the situation, acted quickly, drawing his sword and piercing it into the stomach of the woman, who fell to the ground in a pool of blood. After that, releasing his bloody sword, he approached the table in order to kill the Ascendant Phoenix, but at the last second Thommes placed himself in the middle and was skewered, dying instantaneously. After such a show, the young soldier drew his sword and charged against his mate with fury.

"Traitor! Human waste! You'll pay for this, damn bastard!"

"We have to obey the orders, Lumio!"

Lumio was gaining ground. He lunged forward, thrusting his sword, but the other soldier managed to block the attack. Both blades clashed with a clanky noise. Again, the young soldier lunged, but his enemy parried the attack. His strokes were no more accurate than those of his rival, but they were full of fury.

"Orders?" said Lumio as he thrust with all his might. "No one in his right mind would want to kill the future king!"

Lumio feinted this time, misleading a thrust to his enemy's chest. As his opponent fell into the diversion, he tried to parry the attack once more but discovered too late that the young soldier's sword was in fact not aimed at his chest but at his head. He tried to retreat but it was too late. He could only witness with horror how the blade was getting close to his neck.

The soldier's sharp sword sliced smoothly through the other soldier's neck, his head falling with a thud to the floor while his body collapsed quietly on the ground, blood soaking into the floorboards, creating a pool.

After sheathing the sword quickly, he approached Thommes, wanting to help him. But sadly he found he had already died. When Lumio heard a light sound, he turned to where the woman lay. Was she still alive? he wondered. She was lying on the floor, close to the door. He kneeled down to her. Her clothes were soaked with blood. She would not live long. The soldier tried to attend to her anyways, but she grabbed his hand tightly.

"Take my son away from here," she said in a choked voice. "Please!"

After these words, the woman moaned and stopped breathing.

The young soldier looked at the woman, who had closed her eyes. She had died entrusting her son's life to him. The man got up and began to murmur a prayer for their souls as he made his way to the table where the baby was. The baby watched him with his tiny peanut-brown eyes. They were not as beautiful as his mother's. His pink chubby arms moved slowly. He had come out completely unharmed. The soldier looked at the little one, feeling sorry for him. He had lost his mother and was not even aware of it. The baby had remained impassive to what had happened, totally oblivious to the bloodbath that had occurred around him.

After making sure that the little one was safe, the soldier turned to pick up Distra, which was lying on the floor. The sword was near Thommes' lifeless body. The soldier approached it cautiously, for it had recently been completely engulfed in flames. When he picked the sword up by the hilt, however, he did not notice any heat, so he ran a finger slightly over its edge, discovering with astonishment that the steel of the sword was cold, as if nothing had happened.

The young soldier tearfully took the child and Distra. He left the sanctuary and headed to his horse. He knew what he had to do. For a brief pause, he hesitated. What about his wife and his two daughters? he thought, then he shook his head. The life of the phoenix was at stake. He could take no risks. He had to leave the kingdom.

* * *

Hours later, one of the captains of the Sons of the Flame prostrated himself in front of the king, he was a stout man with dark olive skin. Wulkan was sitting on the throne, the copper crown over his long, straight black hair. His thick eyebrows were arched, and his dark-brown eyes looked worried and severe. He was a tall man with broad shoulders. Despite being more than one hundred years old, he had the appearance of a forty-year-old, thanks to the power of the sacred swords of fire.

"Tavio, tell me you have found Distra?" said the king, his hoarse voice harsh as usual. Wulkan did not like to beat around the bush, especially when his reign was at stake.

"We searched the area. In the sanctuary there were three bodies: a woman, the priest Thommes, and one of our soldiers... Kodul." While mentioning the soldier's name, Tavio could not help looking down. "After examining the scene, everything seems to indicate that Kodul killed the woman and Thommes, then fought the other soldier, Lumio, who killed him. We believe Lumio took the sword, along with the baby..."

"Get him immediately!" said the king violently. "Do not rest until you bring back my sword."

"What about the baby, Your Grace?" asked the soldier.

The king didn't answer. Instead he gave him a fierce look. The soldier nodded and left the place, while ordering his soldiers to immediately capture the fugitive.

1. The Training

Noakhail trained with his father, Lumio, in the art of the sword. Their practice together took place every day, as long as Lumio did not have to act as a personal guard for some wealthy merchant. They lived in Naer, a village in the Queendom of Water, known as the Aquadom, far from the main city, where the palace was located and prudently separated from Firia. The former soldier now had a receding hairline. His hair was dyed dark blond, hiding his naturally grey-black color, and some lines had begun to show across his forehead. Physically, he was still in very good shape, thanks to his constantly training with his son. Noakhail was taller than his father. He was athletic due to his intensive training, and he could not remember a single day when he had not trained.

Lumio carried a sword and a shield while Noakhail brandished two swords. Both fought with fervor, throwing hard cuts that the other had to then avoid or parry. Noakhail's thin lips usually showed a smile, even as he fought with his swords. He had inherited his passion for combat from his father, so much so that his brown eyes shined brightly with each thrust. The steel blades clashed restlessly, thundering over the field. The two men, who practiced daily, took the training very seriously. Noakhail's dyed-blond hair danced as he performed a short quick thrust that he hoped would catch his father unprepared; however, Lumio parried the attack with his shield while making a feint and delivering a strong kick to Noakh's chest, throwing him to the ground.

"Do not leave yourself so exposed!" Lumio reproached Noakh as he urged him to stand up. "Every time you attack, you expose your body too much. You become vulnerable! Use your weapons properly—attack

25

with one, defend with the other. Your fighting technique is too direct and aggressive."

"But Father," the young apprentice complained after pressing his square jaw. "A strike like that would end most fights! Most soldiers would not be able to defeat a strategy consisting of cuts such as the one I just performed."

"It'd be enough if only one of your rivals could do so," answered Lumio, shaking his head. "Noakhail, your life is very important. You have a lot to fight for. Don't let your stubbornness prevent you from achieving victory."

"If my stubbornness gets in my way, I'll defeat it, like I would any other opponent!" he said proudly. "I have decided, Father, I want to be a soldier. I will be part of the Aquadom's army."

Hearing the wishes of his son, Lumio grew enraged.

"Never! Noakhail, you will not become a soldier of this queendom... not while I'm alive!"

"I've made the decision, Father, and even you cannot change my mind!" Noakh said furiously. He had the temperament of his true people; it was in his blood.

"You cannot," said Lumio, his voice faltering. He sheathed his sword and left.

Noakhail did not know how to react, so he stared blankly as his father walked away. This was the first time his father had abandoned a training session—and that meant a lot. No matter how much Noakh might implore his father to end the sessions early because of the pain in his hands, or how hard it might be snowing, they had never stopped training—not for a single day since he could remember. Had his words been so serious as to offend his father?

His father could be so stubborn, the boy thought. He wouldn't even call him Noakh, as the villagers did. He always had to address him by his full name, Noakhail, no matter how much he insisted he preferred to be called simply Noakh. His full name was weird, as most of the children in the village had mockingly pointed out when they had first heard it. He liked Noakh better. It was still an uncommon name, but at least it was shorter and easier to pronounce.

Although there was much he did not understand, he knew that while the rest of the children had played, he had trained with his father tirelessly. His skills with the sword were more advanced than many soldiers in the queendom, despite the fact he was still a young boy. He noticed how his frustration turned into anger. For him, so much training made sense only if he became a soldier. Otherwise, what was the value of learning so much? He had mentioned his decision thinking that it would make his father proud, for being a soldier was the only dignified way to use everything he had been taught in combat. Did his father want him to follow in his footsteps as a bodyguard? It did not make sense. His father kept telling him that it was not the job for him; he always told Noakhail that he had been born for a better life. What else could he use his swordsmanship skills for? The idea of using them to commit robberies made him smile. Perhaps his father wanted him to assault people during the night, he thought ironically.

He looked to the sky. The clouds began to gather, their grey color predicting rain. *If there were a war, I could fight alongside my father. It would be an honor to show him how much I have learned in all these years,* he thought. *He would see how there is no rival to defeat me, not in this kingdom or anywhere else!*

It was true that somehow they were in a state of war. Firia had declared war on the Aquadom almost two decades ago, but apparently, even though the conflict was still supposedly ongoing, there had not been a single attack by the Fireos. Nevertheless, the Aquo Army had increased its numbers, expecting that those fools might attack at any moment. Fireos were an unpredictable people, so for the last twenty years the citizens of the Aquadom had lived in fear of an attack, which right up until today had not happened.

Noakh lay carelessly down on the ground, raising a small cloud of dust. He was in the backyard of his house, a small hut where he and Lumio lived. It was a modest dwelling. They did not have any luxuries. By Aquo standards, they almost lived in poverty. However, they did not need anything other than clothing, shelter, food, and a place to practice their swordsmanship without being disturbed.

A thought ran through his mind: Tomorrow was his birthday. Just thinking about it, he felt a sense of sadness. The moment was supposed to be a joyous time—a time when he was supposed to be with his family. Tradition dictated that the birthday boy had to go to the nearest river and spill a jar of water into it, this being the way in which the Aqua Deus was thanked for its creation.

Although he no longer placed any importance on religion, when he was a child he had not avoided feeling like an outcast. He had been the only one who did not go down to the river with his family to perform the ritual. He once asked his dad about it, wondering why he had decided not to fulfill their religious obligations. But every time he asked, Lumio listened and laughed while completely denying Noakh's request.

As if that were not enough, the rest of the children in town made fun of him, because the tradition stated that the children had to spill the jar of water while accompanied by their mother. Noakh did not even know his mother; his father had told him she died shortly after his birth. Curiously, despite the fact that he could not remember his mother at all, he felt his chest tightened when he thought of her. His father didn't want to talk about his mother, something that had upset Noakh many times during his childhood.

Lying on his back, Noakh heard a low noise, almost imperceptible without the sixth sense of a trained swordsman. He took one of his swords, all of which were still lying on the field, and turning on his stomach while leaning on the ground, he reflexively raised his sword to block a treacherous attack from behind. The two swords collided against each other, causing a loud clang.

Lumio faced him, smiling, his shield held high to parry the next blow.

"I leave for a few minutes—and you're lazing around?" said Lumio.

Noakh could tell that his father was faking disappointment while trying to hide his pride. The boy had been able to parry his father's attack. Lumio had clearly been watching him for a long time, waiting for the proper moment, hoping that Noakh would become distracted so that he could initiate the attack as stealthily as possible. Although his father was still evidently angry at his decision, he seemed to have decided to use that energy in a positive way: to train Noakhail a little harder. He probably figured that doing so would cause Noakh to forget the choice he had made, which his father thought was stupid.

Noakh did not answer. He knew that his father would have skillfully countered any justification on his part. Instead, he decided to make a feint so he could retrieve his other sword.

"Your attack has been too slow, and it followed the wind's direction," said Noakh, confessing how he had been able to detect the attack. "Even a child could have parried it," he mocked.

As always, Noakh's arrogance was answered by a skillful attack from Lumio—a combination of feints with his sword and his shield. Noakh tried to avoid Lumio's attack with the sword, but it served only as a distraction for a much more powerful attack with the shield. The shield impacted Noakh's head sharply. He stepped back, falling to the ground, shocked by the stroke.

Sighing, Lumio helped him get up. Noakh, still stunned, grabbed his father's hand while rubbing the spot where he had been hit. His sight was still slightly blurry. Although Lumio was probably aware that perhaps he had hit Noakh too strongly, he did not apologize. As his father had stated countless times before, Noakh's enemies were not going to show him any mercy from the first moment they confronted him.

"You have never used that move before," Noakh complained, his pride more hurt than his head. He had learned to read his father's movements—useful knowledge, both to prevent a successful attack and to take advantage of a blow.

"In every fight, you have to try something new. Remember yesterday's lesson?"

"Never repeat two blows in a row, unless it's a ruse for an unexpected move," Noakh recited, realizing that was exactly what his father had done. His face turned red with both anger and shame. How could he have forgotten that?

Lumio smiled, seemingly realizing that his son had noticed his strategy. He reached out and began to shake Noakh's blond hair hardily. For Noakh, it was frustrating how his father, one way or another, always managed to defeat him. Even though he realized Lumio was finding it harder and harder to fight him, Noakh was aware his father was still a skillful fighter. He had been a soldier after all, even though his father didn't like to mention it. He had said it just once, and then he had tried to change the subject quickly, but Noakh always remembered being marveled by the idea. That was why he wanted to be a soldier: He looked up his father so much. He wanted to be like him, not only as a fighter but also as a man. But he still had a lot to learn.

They kept talking for a while, waiting for Noakh to feel better. Afterwards, they fought tirelessly, their swords clashing repeatedly—the pupil trying to defeat the master, the master proving the pupil was not yet ready. They fought, no matter if it was so dark nothing could be seen.

2. The fire sword

Today was his birthday. His seventeenth. Noakh got up as usual, as it was not a special day at all—it was just changed by the fact that he would have to go into town that afternoon to buy a good piece of lamb. Somehow, eating lamb on his birthday had become a tradition.

He stood in his room, stretching and yawning. It had always been hard for him to sleep. On the other hand, in the mornings it was even harder to wake up. His room was cramped. There was little space but the bed and an old wardrobe where he stored his clothes—and of course his swords resting on the wall. The planks of his room creaked as he passed through them, unconsciously avoiding the plank beneath the door, which he had stumbled upon more than once.

He looked out the window. He saw that Lumio was already awake: Today was his day off and he was fixing one of the wooden fences in the outdoor courtyard. Apparently some insects had eaten it away. Noakh walked to the kitchen and picked up some bread and cheese for himself from a wooden table and picked up another portion for his father.

As he opened the door, rain started to fall softly. Rain was not unusual in the Aquadom; according to Aquo beliefs, this was the way the Aqua Deus washed away the sins of his followers. Lumio used to joke that, given how often it rained in the queendom, the Aquos had to be sinning all day long.

Noakh approached the courtyard and offered his father his portion of bread and cheese while he was still hammering the fence into place, completely absorbed in his work. He did not even seem to have noticed his son's presence until he raised his arm to take his food, without deviating from his work.

Lumio was more serious than usual. Noakh guessed he was still somewhat annoyed by his words yesterday. Apparently all the additional training they had done had not been enough to calm him down. Reminded of it, Noakh noticed how his shoulders were numb. This always happened when the training lasted longer than usual—and yesterday's session had been particularly long. He decided to let his father keep working, but just then, Lumio suddenly stopped hammering.

"Wait... I guess it's time," he said.

He put the hammer on the ground and stood up. Noakh could not guess what emotions his face expressed. It seemed a mixture of sadness and concern. But what could worry his father in such a way? They had a simple yet pretty relaxed life; also, Lumio was a man who wasn't fond of worrying.

"Time? What do you mean?"

Noakh could not help but show his anxiety as he asked the question. He was somewhat uncomfortable, not knowing what was going on in his father's head.

"It's time for you to know the truth."

With a sigh, Lumio started walking towards his house, leaving Noakh watching him return to the hut. Noakh shrugged, feeling confused, and assumed he should follow him.

Inside the hut, Lumio climbed the stairs up to a small attic without turning to see if his son followed his steps. The attic was where they kept old stuff. Broken shields, wine for special occasions, old clothes, and armor equipment were all over the floor. It was a dusty place, with spider webs covering the walls. There was a small window from which a bit of light came in. Lumio headed to the right corner of the room, where he began moving boxes.

Noakh could not contain himself any longer. "Father, what is happening? What do you mean, 'I have to know the truth'?"

Without a word, Lumio continued to move a box full of armor equipment, after which he set his fingers carefully along the edges of one of the floorboards and carefully removed it. From the opening in the floor, he lifted out an ocher-colored, elongated chest covered in dust. Looking at the chest, he muttered a series of words that Noakh could not understand—something similar to a prayer. Only then did he open it: a long object wrapped in purple velvet. He unwrapped the object carefully, then showed it to Noakh: a sword.

"This sword is your truth, Noakh," Lumio said. With both hands he handed his son the sword. His voice was charged with a mixture of sadness and utter respect.

Noakh examined the sword carefully, trying to solve the riddle. It was apparently a normal sword. It was not a specially ornamented sword. Quite the contrary, it was quite simple in its design.

Evidently seeing that Noakhail did not understand the power encompassed by the sword, Lumio decided to help him to comprehend the sword's significance.

"This is Distra, one of the sacred swords of fire," he said, looking devotedly at the sword. Anyone, he thought, could see how much that sword meant to him. It was the reason his entire life had changed, after all.

"Distra? Swords of fire?" Noakh repeated, confused. He was trying to remember something... something his father had told him. "It sounds like those stories you told me when I was a kid. How did they go? Two swords worthy of kings?"

"Two swords worthy of *choosing* their king," his father corrected him, frowning. "Those are not children's stories at all. This sword is one of the twins of fire, those that choose who will be the phoenix, their future king..."

"And why do you have it?" said Noakh, not understanding anything his father was saying. Why had that sword ended up in the hands of an inhabitant of the Aquadom? Just then he remembered his earlier thought about his father perhaps wanting Noakh to become a robber. Maybe he had been right and his father had been a professional robber himself? "Just looking at this house, it's obvious that we aren't kings... Father, have you stolen it?" he asked in a worried tone.

"Steal? Do not be stupid. Our eye color is different, as is our hair color, no matter how much we dye it. Even our character has little to do with the well-known inhabitants of these lands. Have you never asked yourself about it?"

It was true. He had considered it. In fact, he had even asked his father about it. His father had told him that they had been born different—an explanation that did not make much sense but that had been enough for a child listening to the words of his wise father. They were Fireos.

"Do you remember what the ritual of the Kingdom of Fire was like?"

"If the sword cut the newborn and he bled then he was not the phoenix," said Noakh. With difficulty he tried to remember the other details. "However, if the newborn were to be the next king, flames would emerge from his wound, proving that a phoenix was born..."

"More or less. Now, look." Lumio showed him his left palm. "A scar. Now, look at yours."

Noakh looked at his hand, which displayed his scar. Until now he had not realized how peculiar it was that both he and his father had a scar—a scar from a cut on their hands—probably because he had considered it a typical wound for swordsmen. Lumio had omitted the part of his history about the fire ritual, probably thinking it was obvious enough.

"What does this mean? I do not understand," Noakh said, unwilling to accept that everything he knew about his life was beginning to fade away.

Brandishing the sacred sword, Lumio made a cut in his hand. Blood sprouted from the wound while Noakh stared at him as if he were crazy.

"Now, you take the sword. Cut yourself," said Lumio, handing Noakh the sword.

"What? But..."

"Do it!"

Without understanding what was happening, Noakh brandished the sword. Skeptically, he made a cut in his left hand. Without even glancing at his wound, he stared at his father.

"You see, Father—blood. I do not know what you expected to show, but enough of this silly jo—"

Just then, feeling the heat that emanated from the sword, Noakh looked at his hand. From this did not sprout blood but a reddish flash. He could not say a word. Instinctively, Noakh passed his left hand over the flames of the sword. Noakh gasped. The fire was not burning his flesh.

"It's time you know your story," said Lumio, smiling, satisfied.

Lumio told him everything. How Noakh had been chosen by the sword and had become the Ascendant Phoenix. How the fatal incident at the Lava Sanctuary had led Lumio to flee, leaving behind his wife and two daughters, all in his previous life, to save the heir of the kingdom.

"I decided to escape with you and with the sword... Noakhail, even today I wonder if it was the right decision—but at least it was the decision that kept you alive," Lumio confided. "After seeing my partner attack—and after hearing his words—I assumed someone in the kingdom wanted to kill you. I could not take that risk. There was too much at stake. Who could want to do something like that to a baby? And not just to any baby... to the phoenix? One answer ran through my mind, and today I am even more confident that I was right, no matter how much I've refused to accept it."

"The king," said Noakh, who had come to the same conclusion as his father.

"That's right. Nothing was ever known about that incident, not even about the loss of the sacred sword. Instead, war was declared upon the Aquadom for no reason at all. And despite that, the war is still cold; if they really thought it was the Aquos who took their future king, why has there not been a single attack in almost twenty years? But we, the Fireos? We would fight for fun, and then we get the best excuse ever... and not a single confrontation? Bullshit.

"However, it's just a theory. The soldier I killed at no time mentioned his name. He just said that we should follow orders... I guess he thought that I was involved in their plot, and that at some point I had changed my mind." Lumio shrugged. "I have been thinking about it for years, but no matter the approach, the conclusion remains the same. It had to be the king. Why? I don't know. Wulkan was considered to be a devotee, which was to be expected for the one chosen by the Incandescent itself. Perhaps he had become corrupted after all those years on the throne? Guess I will never know."

Noakh tried to regain control of his thoughts. His mind felt as though it was about to explode after such a revelation. Too much information was being thrown at him at once... too much disturbing reality.

"I hope you now understand why you cannot be part of the army of the Aquadom... It would be, at a minimum, inappropriate," said Lumio, smiling. "But it would be impressive, I must admit—slaying enemies with a fire sword would shock your fellow Aquo soldiers. They wouldn't know whether to cheer you or to run!"

His son wasn't hearing him. Instead he raised his hands, trying to free his head of all the thoughts buzzing like bees around his mind like crazy.

"I... I do not know what to do," Noakh groaned. "Should I claim the throne? Should I assume that as soon as I mention who I am they will want to kill me? Or will the citizens kneel before me? Should I do as if none of this had happened and move on with my life?" Noakh found he was relieved saying out loud some of the many ideas that fluttered through his stressed head. "Father, what should I do?"

Lumio extended his arm and pressed his son's shoulder.

"Your name, Noakhail, has a meaning. In the Fireo language, *akhail* is a word we don't use that much, since it means giving up. I combined it with the word we use in the common tongue for a negation—*no*. As a result, your name means 'Do not give up.'" Noakh would have been shocked at the revealing of the meaning of his name if he hadn't been so perplexed. "Every time I say your name, I remind myself I must never give up. Now that you know its connotation, you shall never forget either, Noakhail. Never give up!"

Lumio then reassured him in a calm voice. "Do not let any of those worries disturb your mind, Noakhail. It's too much information to assimilate." He understood how hard it had to be for his son. He had actually expected him to take it far worse. "I'll leave you alone for a while so that you can absorb all the information. I'll be in the courtyard fixing that damn fence." Lumio descended the stairs, leaving Noakh alone with his thoughts. The boy had a lot to think about.

"The phoenix. A king," Noakh said in what sounded like a whisper. Hearing it didn't make it more real. He still couldn't believe it. Nobody would blame him... Who would react differently if he were suddenly told he was supposed to be the heir to the throne?

Noakh spent a while in the attic thinking, trying to fit together the pieces of the puzzle that, just a few scarce moments ago, his life had been carved into. Little by little, the uncertainty began dissipating, and with it came an inner calm. He understood why his father had hidden something as important as his heritage. That was why he had trained hard, with two swords. That was why his father didn't like to mention his former life as a soldier. Everything made perfect sense. He looked more closely at Distra, his new sword. He could make out a small drawing in part of the copper plating at the hilt. A big D was carved and there was also a tiny flame symbol that was imperceptible except to a sharp eye.

With a slightly clearer head, he decided to seek out his father. Lumio seemed to have finally been able to fix the fence. When he saw Noakh, he got up, assuming that he would like to ask him something, in the best of cases, or perhaps blame him for the choices he had made, in the worst of cases.

Out of everything he had heard, one question kept harassing Noakh tirelessly, over and over. His head felt ready to explode. He had to know the answer to the question, even though he very much feared that answer.

"Father, you left behind your wife and your daughters for a child you did not know," he said while looking at the ground. His voice faltered, as he was unsure he wanted his father to answer. "Don't you regret that?"

Lumio replied by reaching out and hugging him so hard Noakh struggled to breathe. He dried his tears on his father's clothes.

"Never, Noakhail," Lumio said, continuing to embrace Noakh. "I have many things to regret in my life, but you are not one of them... Flarelle and my girls—I pray every day for them to be fine. They were strong. I hope that someday they can forgive me." His voice sounded nostalgic, even though it was true: Not a day passed when he did not pray for his wife and daughters to be safe, but he did not regret his choice.

Noakh could not help gulping. He was aware of all his father had sacrificed. He could have just let Noakh die. Nobody would have known. His life would remain the same. Instead, he had decided to sacrifice his job, his entire family, his home, everything, to save a little boy whom he did not even know.

"What about my parents? Did you know them?" Noakh asked curiously.

"Your mother." Lumio nodded briefly while grimacing. "She brought you to the ritual. She was young and beautiful. She looked at you with so much love. She begged me to save you, I couldn't refuse."

"I see," Noakh said while staring at the floor. A feeling of sorrow invaded him. How could he feel so sad for someone he could not remember?

Wanting to cheer him up, Lumio went to retrieve his sword and his shield, deciding to let Noakh try his new weapon in the backyard of his house, away from prying eavesdroppers. As Lumio had told him, the sword, when in appropriate hands, had great power. A power worthy only of a king.

Brandishing Distra, Noakh began to shake it.

"Well, let's see... So you are Distra. Let's see what you are capable of doing," he said to the sword. A second later he turned red with shame. Why was he talking to a sword? Delivering a couple of lunges into the wind, he saw that the sword did not react. It did nothing that a normal sword could not do.

Lumio was expectant, observing what Noakh would be capable of with such a weapon in his hands.

"Father, this sword does not do anything special," Noakh said disappointedly, even as he continued to thrust the sword into the air.

"She has been asleep for a long time," Lumio guessed. "As told in the books, 'Distra is daring and loves the fight. When it tastes blood, it becomes wrapped in frenzy,'" Lumio recited. He could not remember where he had read those words. Or maybe he had heard them recited by the priest Thommes. Remembering the priest, he could not avoid feeling sad; no matter how many years had passed, that day would be engraved into his mind forever. On more than one night, he had woken up sweating, dreaming about that day's events again. Despite dreaming of it countless times, he had never gotten used to that nightmare—and he never would.

"Does it?" Noakh said, surprised. "You speak as if it were alive, when it's just a piece of metal," he said, staring at Distra, still trying to ignore the fact that he had talked to the sword.

"A piece of metal cannot react as this sword did when it cut you... You know, this sword is different." Brandishing his own sword and his shield, Lumio charged Noakh. "But it seems you're still too weak to use even one pinch of its immense power!" he yelled, trying to both engage and motivate his son.

Noakh parried his father's hard stroke. While dodging the powerful attacks of his opponent, he directed the fight to where his other sword stood leaning against a tree trunk. The technique of fighting with two swords befitted him. Brandishing his two blades, Noakh started his counterattack.

In an avalanche of thrusts and parries, Noakh scratched his father on the cheek with Distra. Blood started spouting. Then the blade began to turn orange and to release heat.

"This heat," Noakh said, surprised. He stared at Distra. "Is it really coming from the sword? It is as if it awoke with the touch of blood!"

"When it tastes blood, it wraps itself in a frenzy," Lumio recited again, then he realized, "Of course! Let's keep fighting."

Continuing the fight, Lumio made a feint, allowing himself to be cut deeply in the torso.

"Father!" said Noakh, startled to see the blood again begin to spout. "Are you okay?"

"Look!" said Lumio, staring at the sword.

Noakh looked at the sword. Distra began to turn more orange, similar to when the metal had first been forged. It grew hotter, but it did not affect Noakh at all.

"I feel its blood thirst... It wants more. *I* want more... It's as if its desire for blood controlled me..."

Lumio looked at Noakh anxiously. "It seems that Distra has awakened." But what was that the blood thirst he was talking about? Wulkan, the Fireo king, had been known for his utter frenzy and bloodlust during combat. But Lumio had always thought Wulkan's lust was simply the lust a Fireo king used to demonstrate his people's passion and love for combat... Perhaps the twin swords had something to do with that?

"That's fine for today," Lumio said. But Noakh instinctively thrust the sword powerfully before him, aiming it at a distant tree. He watched in amazement as a flare erupted from the tip. It struck the tree, engulfing it in flames. Noakh and his father looked at each other, both of them astonished.

"I do not know why I did it. How could I have known? It was like a voice in my mind. But it was not me. Nor can it be..." While speaking, Noakh felt a strong tiredness. It was as if he had been running for hours while carrying a huge load. He could not stop breathing deeply.

Lumio hastened to put out the fire from the tree. He drew a bucket of water from the old well in the backyard, then, approaching the tree, doused the flames with the well water. He looked at his chest, which was bleeding deeply, but that did not matter much after seeing what his son had just done.

"That was... amazing!" said Lumio unable to hide his joy.

Noakh had not only awakened Distra but had already used its power—and this was just the first day! Lumio started to plan his next training sessions, realizing that Noakh now had to adapt his fighting technique to take advantage of his new weapon. This was a bit tricky, though, since neither of them knew exactly how Distra worked. The previous king had trained the heir to the throne, teaching him all the techniques and tricks that the previous kings before him had learned, instructing him how to use the twin swords as effectively as possible. Noakh, however, would have to learn everything on his own.

3. Flames

It was very early in the morning, and the weather was uncommonly pleasant for the Aquadom. The sun had just risen, and a pleasant breeze blew.

Noakh stood in the backyard, wielding his two swords once more. In front of him was a scarecrow. A broom, the pieces of armor they kept in their attic, a metal bucket, and an old shield had been enough to create a soldier on whom to practice. Someone Noakh could wrap in flames. Someone whose destiny he could not feeling sorry about.

Lumio sat in a wooden chair in front of their house. His torso was bandaged. The wound he had suffered after purposefully awakening Distra had been deeper than expected. Despite this, the wound wasn't serious; he would be as good as new in a couple of weeks. However, given that the wound was to his chest, he could not wield either the sword or the shield without reopening the laceration. So Lumio had told Noakhail to train on his own while he watched attentively and shouted out further instructions. On Lumio's left stood a bucket full of water, which Lumio had prepared earlier. This time he would be better prepared for any fire that might suddenly occur. But, if asked, he would not mind seeing his entire house wrapped in a terrible fire if it meant his son could awaken the full power of the sword.

Noakh stood in front of the scarecrow, trying repeatedly to awaken Distra so that he could practice using the full power of his new sword. He tried to focus. He spoke the name of the sword. Nothing happened.

"Damn it," ranted Noakh. "Why can't I get Distra to engulf itself in flames!"

The young man looked at his new sword with frustration. He ran a finger over the edge of the blade in the hopes that the steel was at least

41

slightly warm. But the metal was as cold as could be, only increasing his indignation.

"Calm down, Noakhail," his father urged from his chair. "You know you can turn the sword into flames," he added. He turned his head towards the tree he had burned the previous day. "The tree can testify in good faith to it."

"What if it was just a stroke of luck?" Noakh lamented as he shook Distra repeatedly.

"No luck. The sword woke up after tasting my blood," Lumio reminded him.

"Maybe the sword won't become engulfed in flames unless she tastes blood," Noakh suggested. He looked at Distra again.

"No," Lumio replied. "King Wulkan could engulf his swords at will." He himself had seen him do so on one occasion when he was not even a soldier. The king had marched surrounded by his escort, the Sons of Flame. In a show of power, he drew the twin swords and engulfed them in flames, causing his audience to burst into sounds of admiration. "If he can," Lumio said, "so can you."

Noakh looked at his father in confusion. "But how?" he said.

"I don't know," Lumio answered, shrugging. "What did you feel when you threw that flame?"

Noakh thought for a moment. What had he felt then? He had noticed how a thirst for blood grew little by little inside him, but that was after he had cut his father. *Then* the sword had engulfed itself in flames. No, he had to go a little further back, just before he had thrown the flame at that tree...

"I just wanted to test its power," Noakh answered. "I wanted to know if I could release a flare. I just didn't know how, until something inside me... a voice... then I just knew what to do."

Noakh looked at his father as if his words made sense.

Lumio nodded. "I believe you, son. And maybe that's the answer you need: You wanted to try it, and the sword listened to you. You wanted to unleash the flame, and somehow you learned to do it. Is it possible that it's as simple as your wanting the weapon to ignite?"

"What do you think I've been doing all morning, Father?" complained Noakh. "I've tried again and again, and no results at all!"

"You're right," Lumio answered. He considered another approach. "Why don't you just focus on attacking the scarecrow? You can try to vent your anger on him..."

Noakh gazed thoughtfully at the scarecrow. He and his father had tied it to the ground, burying part of the broomstick and covering it with earth so that it could withstand the onslaught of his swords. But there wasn't much fun to be had in facing an inert being who could not defend himself, he thought. Even so, Noakh thrust his swords against the scarecrow. Perhaps striking it would make him feel better.

The boy ran toward the scarecrow and feinted, lunging at the side of his lifeless opponent. His thrust struck the metal soldier with a loud *clank* that shook its structure. After that, Noakh took two steps back and then, with quick footwork, lunged at the opponent's chest, making two cuts with Distra's blade before throwing himself back and returning to the attack again. Noakh gasped from the effort, smiling as he lunged at his opponent anew. The training was becoming more fun than he had expected, the immobility of that metallic and wooden enemy allowing Noakh to perform thrusts and feints that he could not have tried against his father for fear of being too reckless.

Noakh launched a fierce attack, thrusting his two swords against the shield and causing it to shake intensely. Then he pivoted on his right foot and, taking advantage of the momentum, lunged powerfully with Distra. The blade of the fire sword clapped against the sword of his rival.

Lumio rose from his chair. Almost without Noakh's realizing it, Distra had become engulfed in flames. Noakh looked at the flaming sword, his face a mixture of surprise and joy. Somehow, he had done it—he had managed to engulf Distra in flames.

"Don't get distracted, Noakhail!" Lumio triumphantly encouraged. He had returned to sitting on the chair, resting his hand on his wound; the injury had seemed about to reopen after he had sprung from the chair.

Noakh looked up at his father. He nodded, blades once again held high against the scarecrow. Distra was in flames. Noakh's fire was reflected by his opponent's metallic armor, displaying undulating orange lights in the steel. The boy thrust his swords again—first the steel one, then Distra—cutting sharply into the soldier's side. Noakh retreated once more, remaining on guard, holding his swords carefully, simulating the moment in which it was the scarecrow's turn to carry out his attack. Noakh feinted then threw himself at the side of the soldier.

His forehead was covered in sweat and his breathing was loud and intense—a level of exhaustion that happened to him only when he trained all day. But today the hour was still early.

In his next attack, Noakh performed no lunges against the scarecrow, but he raised Distra in his hands. The fire sword's flames wavered intensely. Then Noakh lunged into the air, extending the sword in his hand. Flames leapt from the blade, rushing against the scarecrow and enveloping it in flames.

The scarecrow burned for a few moments. Then it began to crumble as the pieces of wood that made up its skeleton were consumed by fire.

"I did it!"

Noakh raised his two swords triumphantly. His voice faltered slightly from the effort. The flames continued engulfing Distra—though now they were less vivid than they had been even moments before, when Noakh had launched the attack. Noakh smiled. He extended the fire sword high into the air, pointing its blade toward the sky, trying to launch a new set of flames. However, Distra's flames suddenly went out.

"What?" Noakh asked himself, looking puzzled at his new sword. Moments later, he fell unconscious to the ground.

His body fell heavily. It raised a small cloud of dust from the dirt; Noakh's two swords fell at his sides. The scarecrow continued to rattle through the fire. What little wood was left was quickly consumed while the steel parts took on a blackish tone.

"Noakhail!" Lumio shouted as he ran towards his son. He reached the spot where Noakh lay on the ground then knelt before him. His son was passed out, his blond hair falling over his sweaty face. "Noakhail... are you all right?" he asked as he tried to awaken his son, shaking his body gently.

Seeing that Noakh would not wake up, Lumio went over to the bucket of water by his chair. He carried it back to his son's body, then threw the contents on Noakh even as he released a cry of pain. His wound was about to reopen due to his efforts. Noakh opened his eyes, completely drenched, looking around, disoriented. Drops of water slipped through his hair and down his face.

"Noakhail... how are you?" Lumio asked from his knees. He pulled his son's hair away from Noakh's face, while his son kept looking around.

"It wasn't a dream, was it?" Noakh asked.

He watched the remains of the scarecrow littered on the ground.

Lumio smiled. "No, it wasn't. What happened, Noakhail?"

"I... I don't know," he replied as he picked up his swords from the ground then touched the edge of Distra with his fingers. The blade was cold again, as if nothing had happened. "Suddenly I felt as if all energy had abandoned me. I felt I wanted to continue fighting, to throw more flares of fire... and I was about to throw a flare of fire into the air... and then Distra was not in flames anymore. That's the last thing I remember."

"I see," Lumio replied, considering his son's words. "You've done a great job, Noakhail. Let's take a break."

They sat down next to each other on the ground. Noakh was already feeling better; the fatigue had faded almost completely. However, Lumio's wound still hurt him.

"I'm afraid I won't be able to be an escort tomorrow." He ran his hand over his bandage. The effort to revive Noakh had caused the wound to open slightly. It was lightly stained with blood. "Noakh, I have to ask you to go see the merchant and inform him that I will not be able to escort him. I will tell you where you can find him and—"

"I'll do it," Noakh cut his father off.

His voice conveyed what he had immediately decided: He wouldn't miss the opportunity. He had asked his father to accompany him on many occasions, but his father had always refused. He wanted to imitate his father so much that on one occasion he had even approached a merchant, telling him that he was willing to escort him free of charge—in response to which the merchant, thinking that an escort who offered his services free of charge could not be up to anything good, had politely refused. "I'm ready, father," Noakh continued. "I'll show you that I can be a great escort!"

"You?" Lumio replied, unconvinced. "I don't know, Noakhail... You've never been an escort before."

"If someday I can be king, I have to show that I can at least escort a merchant without anything happening to him, don't you think?" Noakh answered, smiling.

"I see," said Lumio, with a similar smile. "You are right, Noakhail. Prove that you can protect a merchant, as you will soon protect your people," he added, rubbing Noakh's hair.

* * *

Reluctantly—and, of course, at almost half the normal rate—the merchant agreed to be escorted by Noakh.

"Remember, Noakhail," his father instructed, "you must not talk to the merchant unless he invites you to do so. Your job is to be alert at all times. You must make sure the road is as safe as it can be for the merchant and his goods. Do not rush. A good escort must avoid any potential danger, but he must also know how to judge properly what is happening around him at all times. When you are an escort, it is easy to believe that everything is a threat."

That night, his father's instructions echoed in his head again and again. Noakh couldn't sleep. A mixture of nerves and excitement prevented him from even closing his eyes. How could it be otherwise? At last he was going to be an escort like his father! If someone stood in their way while delivering the merchant's goods, he would give the thieves a lesson. Tired of staying in bed, his thoughts spinning, he got up and picked up Distra, which was lying on the wall next to his steel swords. Noakh left his room, trying not to make a noise, but the floor planks seemed not to want to assist his stealth. They crunched with every step he took. His father slept in the next room. If Noakh wasn't careful, he might wake him.

Noakh opened the bedroom door cautiously then began to walk around the house. He could hear his father's snoring. That was a good sign. He could go out to the backyard without waking him. He reached the living room then went out the back door, opening it as discreetly as possible.

Already in the backyard, Noakh drew Distra, watching her in the darkness. It was a clear night: a dark sky full of stars led by a beautiful crescent moon. What if he could not awaken the sword now? Noakh wondered. For a few seconds, his mind became flooded with doubt. Then his fingers tightened their hold on the grip even more forcefully, causing his uncertainty to dissipate. Noakh wished that Distra would engulf itself in flames, and the sword, after a second, lit up, as if weighing Noakh's command.

Noakh began to practice attacking with his sword of fire. He tried to launch a flare from a far distance, as he knew he could already do that. Then he launched a second flare, this time toward the front, and from the edge of the blade a powerful flame shot out, racing through the backyard until it gradually dissipated. He wielded his sword again, holding it vertically before him, then launched a new flare, this time with less power. A powerful flame emerged from the blade of the sword—a kind of fire disk that advanced through the skies, creating shadows in its path, until it dissipated into the night. He began to feel exhausted. Was it the sword that consumed all his energy? And not only that; it also felt as if the sword wanted to take control. It was a strange feeling, a feeling he had felt before, which led him to extinguish the sword's flames for a moment—to ensure that he was still in control. His face was once again varnished with sweat, not from the heat of the sword but from the effort he had made.

I must continue a little longer, he thought.

Flames engulfed Distra once more as he thought of other ways to use the sword.

As he practiced into the night, Noakh did not notice—for he was too engrossed in his new weapon—that Lumio was leaning on the doorframe of his house, watching his son all the while. A wide smile illuminated his face.

4. Misfortune

Today was an important day. Noakh was going to work as an escort for a merchant after all this time. Despite being awake almost all night practicing with his new sword, he had woken up immediately as the sun had risen. He had to meet the merchant at his home. He would have to walk for a few miles and it was too early, but the boy could not wait.

It was not unusual practice for a merchant to hire an escort. Some merchants, when they were loaded with valuable merchandise, preferred not to risk traveling alone, and they paid for an escort's services, ensuring the merchant arrived at his destination safely. Roads were not safe in those days; therefore, smarter merchants knew that at the end of the day, a bit less profit was better than none at all. In many cases, the hired escort was enough to make bandits decide to rob a less cautious merchant; others, however, thought that if the merchant's booty was so carefully protected it must surely be because it was valuable.

Because this was Noakh's first time working as an escort, he naïvely expected some bandit would be fool enough to assault them. He was enthusiastic about escorting the merchant, even though from Lumio's experience he knew that being assaulted was very uncommon, as escorts were merely a way to dissuade criminals and ensure they focused on easier targets. This, nonetheless, did not make the boy less happy. In fact, Noakh was smiling, imagining how he would face—and defeat—his opponents while he and the merchant were drastically outnumbered.

As night fell, Lumio was at home, lying in bed and reading a book by candlelight. The book told a story about knights and dragons, a tale that at least helped calm his boredom. It told how the knight had to defeat the dragon in order to save a princess imprisoned in a castle. Lumio kept wondering why anyone would confront a dragon. Dragons were huge.

They breathed fire and could fly—and depending on the story, they might be extremely smart and might even use magic. Why would anyone want to slay such a magnificent creature? Also, why would the dragon, being as smart as it was, waste its entire life guarding a princess in a castle? To Lumio, it was nonsense. Even so, the story was entertaining, depicting how the knight used his wit to slay the creature. It was nice to know the author was smart enough to be aware it made no sense for a human to defeat a dragon with only a sword.

Lumio tapped the cover of the book repeatedly. It was already dark and Noakh still had not returned. It would not take longer, Lumio hoped; the merchandise was to be delivered a few towns away. According to Lumio's calculations, Noakh would return in a couple of hours. He felt relieved after telling the truth to his son. For so long he had been wondering how he was going to face it, and what the best way was to tell him. Luckily, after a more-than-understandable initial confusion, Noakh had faced the truth decently; not only that, he was making a satisfactory progress with his new sword.

Lumio laid the book on the floor and walked over to the window, staring out at the yard. They already had everything planned. As soon as Lumio recovered from his wound, they would leave for the Fire Kingdom. They would arrive by following a secret path very few knew about. Then they would wait until the sky was dyed red once more. This time, Noakh would not be a helpless child, unable to choose his destiny; so many years living in whereabouts unknown had given Lumio and his son the advantage of surprise—the king and his soldiers would not be expecting their visit. Also, Lumio expected some of his fellow soldiers to help him. It had been a long time, and he had no doubt they thought him either dead or traitorous. But none of that would matter when they saw Noakh wielding Distra. They would listen then. They had to.

He had decided. He could not wait any longer. Tomorrow he would start packing. They would carry only the most basic equipment and supplies; a heavy load would delay them for no reason.

Lumio felt liberated. He had been awaiting this day for so long! He would help Noakh become the king, no matter the cost. Also, he could not avoid thinking about seeing his family again. He grew enthusiastic. Maybe he could see his wife, Flarelle, and his two daughters, Cosmille and Aenze. Would Flarelle forgive him for what he had done? Would his daughters remember their father? Would they understand why he had abandoned them? They would, Lumio thought, or at least he hoped. The idea of seeing his family again made him smile.

However, destiny apparently had other plans. The door began to rattle with taps that sounded increasingly louder. Lumio let out a curse and turned from the window. That damn merchant surely had wanted to celebrate the good luck of their trip with Noakh and had invited him for several shots in the local tavern, a pretty common habit of merchants. Lumio guessed Noakh had probably become so idiotically drunk that he could not even remember the key was under a stone in the entryway.

He walked with difficulty, feeling the sting of his wound, then he opened the door.

"Noakhail, how many times have I told you—"

Before finishing the sentence, he saw that it wasn't Noakhail who stood on the other side of the door. Instead, armed men with serious looks on their ugly faces stood outside. Six men were standing outside the doorway, all with weapons drawn. Most of them used swords, except for one who used a crossbow and was holding it tight, aiming at Lumio's chest. Even so, Lumio tried to remain calm while looking furtively around the interior of the hut, seeking the nearest sword. The closest one was leaning against one of the table legs. His shield, however, was hanging on the wall by the door. He looked back to the men. "Oh, I did not expect any visitors."

The men pushed him violently and entered his house. The candlelight made their shadows dance on the walls.

"Give us that sword, now," said the tallest of the men.

His appearance was as unpleasant as the rest of the group, with an eager look in his eyes and a nose that seemed to have been broken once or twice—no doubt in drunken bar fights, Lumio thought as he looked at them all. Blue eyes and blond hair—Aquos. It could be worse, he thought.

Despite the caution with which Noakh and his father had performed their training, they were watched by one of the soldiers of a rich merchant's guard, who was lurking between the walls watching the training with interest. When he saw what the young man's sword was capable of, he soon realized the value it could have. He had tried to convince his companions of what he had seen, but they had called him a drunkard and a liar, so he had to take them to the hut so they could see for themselves. The fear they had felt witnessing what had to be magic sorceries was easily surpassed by the temptation. At first they had thought about how much they would earn from selling such a peculiar and powerful magical weapon, but then, realizing what fools they were being, they realized that with such a sword in their power, everyone would kneel at their feet. Even so, knowing the risk they were taking, they became persuaded only when they were in the town's tavern, emboldened by alcohol, which quickly clouded both their fear and their judgment.

"My sword?" Lumio answered, shrugging. "It is a crude metal sword, like any other."

"You know very well what sword I'm talking about. The one the boy uses. The magic one," he said in a menacing tone.

Behind him, the rest of his crew nodded.

"I'm afraid I will not be able to do that," Lumio said, trying to keep calm. He and Noakh had been seen while practicing with Distra, he realized. They had been reckless... and this was the result.

With one quick motion, Lumio picked up his shield with both hands then charged the bandits with all his strength. He pushed them all out of his home. While the bandits collapsed on the ground, he seized the sword leaning on the table leg, preparing for battle. Every step he took caused a sharp pain in his chest; he knew the wound would soon open up again. But it was not as if he had any other choice. His opponents pounced on him, their weapons held high. However, they were no match for Lumio's abilities; he could fight all of them.

The bandits had not expected any resistance. They had superior numbers. They cursed, for even though they had been aware they would be fighting a swordsman, they had expected him to be frightened, and not to fight.

But Lumio not only loved fighting; he had a reason not to let the bandits get away. The destiny of his son was at stake, and in no way was he a gambler.

Lumio continued to face the thrusting swords of his rivals. Embattled as he was, he was nonetheless able to make them rush their attacks, using not only his skills with the sword but also the furniture of his house to take advantage whenever he could. He threw a wooden stool at one of the men, who stumbled and let out a curse. The man regained his footing and drew his crossbow. He aimed it at Lumio, who saw his intentions. He grabbed another of his attackers, whom he used as a shield and who received the bolt. He fell instantly.

The rest of the thieves were not intimidated by the fall of their companion. The fewer of them there were after the battle, the fewer to share the spoils. The taller man began to scream, advancing with his sword held high. Lumio threw his human shield at his attacker and, taking advantage of his momentum, quickly swung his sword at the feet of the other opponent, who fell to the ground, a prisoner of his pain.

Stinging with pain, Lumio's chest wound began to bleed, covering his bandages in black blood. It had been a long time since he had faced so many men. But he had been victorious as a soldier, as a Son of the Flame—and he would be this time, no matter what.

The thief with the crossbow again approached. Lumio threw a little table to distract him then gave him a firm thrust with his shield. His combatant's chest exploded in blood. Lumio grabbed him by the neck, preventing him from falling to the ground.

"Who sent you?" Lumio asked. An idea was in his head. He had to make sure of it, as he did not want to take any risks. He squeezed the bandit's throat tightly. He wouldn't show mercy.

The prisoner put his hands to his neck, trying to free himself. But he could only scream while choking. Lumio let the man bleed on the floor. The thief had said nothing, but his face was enough for Lumio.

The other bandits reacted quickly. Two pounced on him. The Fireo parried both attacks. Only four bandits were left alive. He could defeat them all.

Lumio thought of his son. How proud Noakhail would be. Although wounded and outnumbered, his father had been able to defeat all of them. The kind of motivation they needed before their journey to Firia.

The bandit who had received the cut on the foot was still lying on the floor. The marauder took advantage of his position and crept stealthily to his companions' crossbow; the weapon was already loaded.

Lumio could not react in time. The bolt crashed hard against his chest, soaking his clothes in blood. Aware of the seriousness of his injury, Lumio managed to end with the life of one of his opponents. Meanwhile, another bolt impacted his body, dropping him to the floor.

Death in battle. For a soldier, to die fighting was the worthiest manner in which to depart this world. However, Lumio instantly realized the error in his reasoning: Noakhail would soon return, and the bandits would certainly be waiting for him. The very thought made him regain his strength, and he tried to rise. The men were already on him.

"No... akhail," Lumio managed to say.

The bandits held their swords high and thrust one last time.

5. Awakening

It was already past midnight. The air was a bit cold and the moon was full. He could already see his front door. The merchant had had problems charging the purchaser for the goods; several hours had passed before he had reached an agreement with his counterpart.

Noakh kept walking while thinking. He was not happy. The merchant had not paid him any additional coins for the extra hours he had worked. Also, nobody had assaulted them. It had just been a journey full of babbling—no thrills at all. What the merchant had considered a great and profitable ramble, Noakh had found to be quite a boring assignment.

Not all the news was bad, though. His father had mentioned they would be traveling soon. To the Fire Kingdom. Noakh had received this revelation with both excitement and fear. The journey could be a great adventure, but how could he expect people to believe he was the heir to the throne? He had considered this question while enduring his boring work as the merchant's escort. Did he actually want to be king? Actually... no. It sounded like a lot of responsibility—too many choices to make, and in fact, it would be no fun at all.

Looking at his home, Noakh stopped for a moment, thinking. It was late. No doubt Lumio would remind him that warriors have to get up early, that he had to have an orderly life. He would also scold him for not having demanded extra payment from the merchant for lengthening the job. No matter what he said, even if he insisted he had demanded the merchant pay him for the extra hours, everything would remain the same; the truth was the merchant had given him no additional coins above and beyond the ones agreed to. Worst of all, Noakh knew his father was right to have expected him to demand extra pay.

At the door to the hut, Noakh was about to kneel to retrieve the key lying under the stone when he noticed that something was not right—the door was not locked. "Locking the door, protecting the home and oneself," Noakh said in a low voice, imitating his father in a mocking tone. "It is the least a warrior should do when he lowers his guard to sleep." Noakh liked to gloat in these situations, as they were not very common; he would remind his father of his oversight the next day.

After Noakh opened the door, a strange smell flooded his nostrils. Something was not right. *Blood,* he thought.

Everything was dark and silent. He began to unsheathe one of his swords. Just then, a shadow fell on him. Amid the blows that followed, Noakh fell to the floor. He did not stop calling his father's name, not wanting to admit what had happened. With a strong kick, Noakh discarded his opponent. After getting up, he reached for his two swords. Using Distra's power, he illuminated the room. Three armed men were charging him. He saw blood all around the room. Several bodies were lying on the floor; he recognized Lumio among them. With a leap, he knelt before him, calling to him. But Lumio did not answer. He had left this world.

"Father," Noakh said, sadness filling his eyes.

He was about to cry when a deep flush of anger seized him. His hands grew so tense they began to tremble. He pressed his jaw so tightly it began to hurt. His breath grew heavier and heavier. His brown eyes focused on the thieves who remained alive, his eyes as empty as his soul, his mind full of hatred and blocked with pain.

"You killed the only thing that mattered to me," he said in a terrifying tone. His hands held his swords as tightly as never before.

He roared powerfully—a last act of will before a second flush of anger and hatred imprisoned him. Distra began to blaze as never before. His jaw was disarranged. All the muscles of his face grew tense, and a murderous look appeared in his eyes. His face resembled more that of a rabid animal than of a human being. In his hand, Distra began to burn with ever more strength, eager to take action. At first the thieves recoiled. However, they had lost too many of their companions to cede defeat. And, seeing the sword again, they remembered how much they wished it to end up in their hands.

"The sword... Take it from him!" one of the thieves cried.

Pouncing towards the opponent who had spoken, Noakh began to lunge and thrust without discipline, quickly abandoning the teachings of his master. A flash accompanied each of Distra's thrusts. Little by little, the house lit on fire.

His technique was reckless. With every thrust, he left his body unprotected. The cuts he received seemed not to matter to him. His gaze was fixed on his opponent, his eyes not blinking. He had succumbed to madness.

Amid cries of panic and fear, his opponent tried to attack him. Each clash of their swords brought Distra's fire closer to the attacker's face, burning and blinding him. The intense red heat of the sword and the smoke from the fires around the hut irritated the attacker's eyes.

Noakh thrust Distra forward again, launching a powerful torrent of fire from the tip of the blade. Despite his attacker's attempts to deflect the attack with his sword, he was immersed in a hell of flames. Seeing this spectacle, the rest of the band panicked and began to flee the hut, running in the courtyard. Noakh, however, was not going to let them escape. He had no time to wait for the rain; he would wash away the bandits' sins for himself. Noakh followed them out of the hut, throwing a blaze off of Distra, he created a small wall of fire in front of his opponents, preventing them from fleeing.

Trapped, his enemies put themselves on guard, raising their weapons. One of them raised his crossbow and began to shoot, only to watch in horror as a slight movement of Noakh's sword turned the bolts into coal. Slowly, Noakh approached his enemies, dragging his two swords across the floor, leaving a trail of dirt and burned grass and earth.

The two thieves, aware of the superiority of their opponent, threw down their weapons. Then they threw themselves onto the ground, begging for mercy. Stopping a few meters away, Noakh fixed his gaze on them for what seemed an eternity. The sword emanated a flare in their direction. Both bandits screamed in unison.

It was then that Noakh recovered control. He was covered in blood. His wounds sprouted blood. However, none of that mattered. His eyes, full of tears, couldn't look away from his house, which was on fire. He ran to it, intent on saving his father. Between cries of pain and despair, he tried to clear the sundry debris, but it was impossible. Kneeling before his house, he broke down in tears, falling hard to the ground.

After a while, he realized that the smoke from the hut would attract the townspeople. They would see the bodies. Then questions would arise. He had to flee. Quickly.

He began to run. Away from roads, constantly looking back, his eyes still full of tears. He reached the forest and kept running.

He ran for much of the night, getting as far away from his home as he could. His face was swollen from his incessant crying, and his jaw hurt from the anger he felt from being unable to save his father. The thought of revenge was not useful for calming his pain; nothing could fill the emptiness his felt.

At some point he fell, exhausted. The sword had consumed all energy.

The next morning, he woke up hoping it had all been a dream. But it was not like that. He was surrounded by trees, his pillow the root of a tree of amazing proportions. He was dying of cold. He could feel the throbbing pain of his wounds, even though they had closed up while he slept. It was then that he began to wonder what had happened. His memory was blurry. His consciousness came up to the moment when he saw his father lying motionless on the floor of the hut. From there he recalled only blood and fire. But his village was ordinarily a quiet and boring place where nothing ever happened. Lumio had once told him this was precisely why it was the perfect place to hide: His life was very humble, they had nothing valuable. Then Noakh understood: It was not true. He looked down at his swords, staring at Distra. *Sword of kings!* he thought resentfully. Just when they had planned to return to the Fire Kingdom, this disaster had happened. It could not be a coincidence.

Noakh's head began to spin. Not only had the sword cost the life of the mother he had never met; it had also cost the life of his father, Lumio.

He rushed at the sword with a painful cry. Then, picking Distra up, he started thrusting fiercely against the tree of an old oak, as if he wanted his sword to feel as much pain as he did. He breathed heavily, his forehead soaked in sweat. Seeing that such punishment was not enough, he carried Distra over to the river. It was time to get rid of the thing that was guilty of killing his father, the one thing that had destroyed his life.

Noakh was standing above the river, his extended arm holding Distra very tightly. He was about to toss the sword into the slow current when a loud *"No!"* resounded. It was the voice of his father.

"This is your destiny... Noakhail"

Noakh looked around, with the hope of finding Lumio. But the voice had only been inside his head. Angered, he threw the sword into the water. He stared at his reflection from the shore as the sword slowly sank to the bottom of the river. "Down there you will not cause me more problems, you damn sword!" he cursed angrily.

Noakh washed his face to erase the tears. He looked again at his reflection in the river. He could see Distra resting on the bottom. He couldn't resist blowing on the surface of the water to make the vision of the fire sword disappear. He looked in his pocket. He had three silver coins and two bronze coins—the payment the merchant had given him. The coins were all he possessed, other than his other sword and his clothes.

Realizing that nothing mattered anymore, he went into the woods, hoping never to leave there again.

6. Lessons in the royal palace

It was one of the most boring lessons that the princesses had heard in a long time. Many of them were resting their heads on their fists in a crude attempt to try to pay attention.

As they did every morning after eating breakfast and getting dressed, they all sat in a room where Igüenza, their caregiver, taught them about the Aquadom: its customs, its history, and its traditions. The room was huge, and the girls were placed on a delicate carpet on the floor and supported on feather cushions. They had only to listen while their teacher taught them about the world. Sometimes it was difficult to pay attention, especially with those huge windows adorned with velvet curtains that filled the room with light. They allowed the princesses to see the palace garden, a huge place full of plants and trees.

Thirteen princesses stood in the room, all of them as beautiful as expected from the royal family, a lineage known both for the beauty of its women and for the lack of importance of its men. As it was known to all, only a princess would be chosen to reign someday, and as a result, any boy born in the royal family would be given to the Church of Water, an institution in which they would serve for different professions. The princesses, though, were taught about the world and the art of the sword. They all had, one way or another, inherited the beauty of the royal bloodline, despite the fact that each of them had a different father.

The older sisters, as always, toyed with the innocence of the smallest. This morning, Katienne had encouraged her smallest sister to ask about the queen's sons—a misdemeanor that had caused her little sister to be punished for asking inappropriate things.

Somehow they had split into two groups, with the older ones looking over their shoulders at the little ones. Katienne, the eldest sister, was in charge. Even her mother had said she was like her, and all of the other princesses assumed that she was going to be the next queen.

However, the Aqua Deus always chose one of the daughters from the queendom at his will; the mere fact that Katienne looked like her mother seemed to give her favor above the rest—but not over their god. Nonetheless, she took it for granted that she was going to be the Lacrima, allowing herself to threaten her sisters and servants, telling them they must fulfill her wishes or be punished as soon as she seized the throne.

That decision was not in her hands, of course. The ritual of the sword would one day decide which of them should govern. But today was not that day, nor was the previous one, nor the one before that. The ritual was the first thing they did when they woke up each morning. One day one of the princesses would be the Lacrima. The Queendom of Water, unlike their Fire Kingdom neighbors, only allowed the princesses to perform the ritual. Only one of them could be elected and become the heir to the throne. Some of the princesses took it as a challenge, the day they would finally arise with all the power and stop being merely one of the princesses, instead becoming the heir of the queendom, the one who would get all the attention. Others instead had gone along with the routine... Why dream of being queen when it was clear that it was going to be Katienne all along? It was just a mere formality until she was elected.

The caretaker's instruction had been interrupted by one of the princesses.

"I am not saying that our world is not a plane," Aienne began. She was the youngest of the sisters. Her long blonde hair was wavy and her face was sweet, with a small nose and big azure-blue eyes. Unlike most of her sisters, she was not restrained by doubt. She never questioned whether an inquiry might be inappropriate; in fact, for her, the inappropriate thing was to not know an answer. Unfortunately, not everyone thought as she did. "I am only asking how we can *know* it is a plane."

"We are Aquos, Aienne."

Igüenza sighed. She was an old woman, her hair already grey and her face creased. Despite her age, her voice never faltered. "Our naval fleet is undoubtedly the most powerful; our ships have sailed to the north, to the end of the world, where, as you will remember from our previous lessons, Finistia, the largest and widest waterfall you may ever see marks the borders of our world to the north."

"Yes, but—"

"It is called *planet* for a reason, you lubberwort!" her older sister Katienne cut her off. She had round lips, an oblong face with a slightly perky nose, dark blue eyes under very thin eyebrows, and curly long wavy hair. "It is called *planet* because it is a plane, obviously!"

Some of her sisters nodded, and so did Igüenza, but another sister, Vienne, sitting next to Aienne, frowned.

"That is a stupid argument," Vienne muttered. She was the tallest of the princesses, despite being one of the youngest, and was rather skinny. She seemed to have a permanent look of sadness in her electric eyes, one of them usually being hidden beneath her golden straight hair, and her face was oval, with small ears and a straight-edged nose.

Aienne snorted.

"What did you say?" Katienne said fiercely.

But this time Igüenza intervened.

"Time to get back to our lesson, ladies!" the old woman said sternly, then she reflected for a second. "So where was I? Oh, yes. Our queendom has more than five hundred vessels, both military and commercial. As you well know, girls, the Aquadom is full of navigable rivers that allow us to travel from one side of our cities to the other with relative ease. The Aqua Deus blessed us with such a paradise that the rest of the kingdoms cannot but admire. Likewise, the sea is one of our allies—and no wonder, because in the depths of the sea is our beloved God, who one day will welcome us to his lair."

While saying this, the teacher performed the typical posture of reverence displayed throughout the queendom, known as the Aquo reverence, setting one leg behind the other and placing the left hand on the chest while the right hand was extended. A small hand raised at the end of the room.

"Tell me, Aienne," the teacher said with all her patience.

All of the sisters' names ended in the suffix *enne*, a word that in Flumio, the original language of the queendom that was now in disuse, meant both *rain* and *gracefulness*. As part of the queendom's rules and traditions, when the queen chose a suffix for her daughters, none but the royal family was allowed to use it; thus this suffix could not be used by the subjects until the next queen was crowned. Therefore, citizens now were allowed to use the suffix *ia*, which meant *waterfall*, as it was the previous suffix used to name all the daughters of the previous queen.

"Has anyone ever seen him?" Aienne asked.

"What do you mean?"

"The Aqua Deus," Aienne replied, shrugging her tiny shoulders as she bowed badly, seeing that she was sitting down. Some giggles could be heard around her, as the other girls in the room were probably waiting for her question to turn into another argument.

"He takes care of us from the sea, Aienne," the teacher replied, "which is why, when we die, our bodies are thrown into the sea after the proper ritual is performed. But a sinner would get a worse destiny: being burned or buried."

The princesses' faces assumed a dreadful expression at being reminded of such a barbaric practice. How horrible a fate for those who were not thrown into the sea! As was said throughout the queendom, the families of those who were not thrown into the sea had lost the favor of the Aqua Deus, falling into the greatest of misfortune. At least that was what was said of the nobility who had fallen; among the working class, not many of who lived close to the sea, it was not so simple. They had to go to the nearest church to arrange for a more suitable ritual, allowing the deceased's soul to reach the sea and be welcomed.

After their morning lesson had concluded, the young princesses went out into the royal garden. "Look, Aienne, you will be this one," Vienne said as she showed her little sister a white flower. The garden was a broad courtyard of flowers of all colors and vast gardens. That day the princesses' games were accompanied by music, a young woman with long hair and bony hands was playing her lyre, filling the garden with a beautiful melody that mingled with her sweet voice. The royal garden was a place where troubadours from all around the queendom came. It was no mystery why this was so. After all, could there be a better and more profitable audience than the queen's palace? As a result, the princesses' games used to be accompanied by music—and in the case of the most daring and bravest troubadours, by compliments, as the royal women were known for their beauty.

"Then you will be this other," Vienne's sister said, pointing to a rose with blue petals. It was truly a beautiful flower, still wet from the dew of the night, with long, perfect petals and a delicious smell.

"Ha!" Katienne mocked. She had been listening to them while reading a book about a princess defeating a giant. "The roses are

64

beautiful—but they have thorns to defend themselves. Vienne could not defend herself from a simple fly!" she said with contempt.

Aienne could not see how the honor of one of her favorite sisters was tainted by her choice of a simple flower. "That's not true," she said, outraged at the comment from her oldest sister and unaware of the consequences of her words. "Vienne is very good with the sword. I'm sure she could give you a lesson!"

Katienne did not hesitate to accept the challenge. This would either be fun for her or instructive for her younger sisters. "A lesson, huh?" she said as she put her book on the bench where she was sitting and got up. Without even looking at them, she walked into the garden, where she tore off two branches from a tree. She then quickly removed the leaves and began to check that the two branches were similar in size. "This one is slightly longer," she said, throwing the branch at Vienne.

While Katienne approached her, Vienne picked up the branch fearfully. "Sister, no, please," she said, not wanting to face her older sister. Not only was Katienne older than her; she also did not understand the difference between a game and reality. Moreover, Vienne always acted a bit cowardly, and avoided conflict, even though she had always liked sword lessons.

"Too late, Vienne. The cards are already on the table!" Katienne said as she pounced, striking her improvised weapon at Vienne's.

"No, wait!" said Vienne. She closed her eyes to protect herself.

Both had received daily instruction in the art of the sword from a very young age. They knew very well how to handle a weapon. Thus Katienne did not stop upon hearing her sister's pleas. She struck the branch into her sister's ribs, causing her to fall to the ground and tearing her dress— which happened to be one of her favorites.

Before Vienne could get up, Katienne began to beat her with her weapon, brandishing it as if it were a sword. She did not allow Vienne to stand up. On the other hand, Vienne did not make the effort—she thought that if she did not move, Katienne would at some point stop hitting her. Meanwhile, tears fell down her eyes. She made an inhuman effort not to scream, because she knew that doing so would merely give Katienne satisfaction—another reason for her sister to keep hitting her. However, her sister Aienne could not contain herself. She interposed herself between the two of them, because she could not stand to see her beloved sister being beaten like that.

"Enough!" Aienne said while extending her arms.

But for Katienne, Aienne's intervention was little more than an excuse to continue her entertainment, so she moved into position to hit her little sister. Vienne, guessing her intentions, stood up and moved forward, blocking Katienne's blow and giving her, in turn, a blow to the cheek.

Katienne put her hand to her cheek. No blood. But she could feel a slight burn where her sister's blow had struck. After a moment, recovering her composure, she turned red with anger then tried to hit Vienne again. Seeing what she had caused, her sister dropped the branch. Grabbing Aienne by the hand, she led her away as fast as she could before Katienne could do any further harm.

One of the gardens had a hiding place where they could not be found: a small hole, larger than it seemed to the naked eye. Their sister Katienne would never find them here. It was a place Aienne had discovered once, while the princesses were playing hide-and-seek. Lately it had become a secret place for her and Vienne, with whom she had shared her secret. The hole was cold and dark, since it was well hidden by the trees. The air didn't carry the smell of flowers as it did all along the garden, but instead the place smelled like damp earth.

Vienne still ached from the blows her sister had given her. She could feel her back throbbing, and her eyes were swollen from crying. Even her lower lip hurt because she had bitten it so as not to scream from each blow she received.

Aienne looked at her sister. She smiled as she dried her tears tenderly.

"You see, Vienne, you have shown that you are the blue rose," she said with a look full of love.

7. Back to reality

He heard her screams while up in a tree, leaning against one of the top branches, trying to take a nap. Almost a year had passed since he had thrown that stupid sword into the river. Since that morning, he had not trained for a single day; instead, he had used the only sword he had left to overcome the adversities of the forest. Bears and wolves respected him now, after he had proven he was not easy prey.

At first, living in the forest was strange, but soon he was used to nature... It seemed that it had accepted him. His first days in the forest had been tough. He had been poisoned twice eating some yellow mushrooms he thought might make a good dinner, and animals ran away as soon as they smelled his scent. Now, however, he was used to the forest, and it seemed to him, the forest creatures were used to him.

Noakh thought he had found peace, a place where only survival mattered. He could spend the entire day traveling through the forest. Every time he did so, he discovered something new: a new fruit, some new animal. He was very respectful of nature and survived with having only the indispensable. He couldn't deny he had cursed more than once that he had thrown Distra, though. Her firepower would have proven useful in the forest. Instead, he had to learn to make fire himself, and such learning had not been easy. Many days had passed eating raw meat and shivering with cold all night. But, stubborn as he was, he ended up learning how to build fire. He had tried restlessly, eventually finding a way, and now he could make fire with two small stones. He had almost cried with satisfaction after managing to build a fire that the first time.

His appearance had become savage. An imperfect beard pocked his face. His hair was black again, although some of its tips remained blond.

Having decided to abandon the world, he saw no reason to dye his hair anymore. The forest seemed to care as much about his hair as his brown eyes.

Noakh snorted—a curse for his bad luck. He had chosen the tree because of its height. Few animals could climb up there—at least none that he supposed were a threat. The branches were thick, so he could remain lying down without fearing that his movements while he slept would make him fall into the void below. He knew from experience that such a fall could happen. Moreover, yellow fruits sprouted from the branches. He did not know the fruit's name, but he had discovered they were delicious. They tasted sweet like pears, only much more juicy.

His dreams were again interrupted by the screams. Noakh could not resist trying to find out what was happening. As he climbed down the tree, he saw that in the road below a woman was standing on her wagon. She held what looked like a pitchfork, which Noakh realized the woman would have typically used to move the straw atop the wagon. However, below her, several figures were encouraging her to lower her weapon.

An assault. This was one of the reasons Noakh's father had dedicated himself to being an escort. The assailants knew those were easy prey: bandits presumed the vehicles did not represent any danger, so many tried their luck by targeting them.

The woman's screams alternated with feints of her weapon as she tried to dissuade her assailants from approaching the wagon. She was in a disadvantageous position. She seemed to be alone, accompanied only by her mule, which did not seem willing to help her. Meanwhile, five thieves had strategically placed themselves around the wagon.

Noakh leaned on one of the lower branches, still observing the scene. He was so low to the ground that he surprised even himself: The assailants had not yet noticed his presence. So much time spent among the trees had made him stealthier than he had thought.

"Come on, woman!" said one of the thieves. His voice was calm as he waited for the woman to lower her guard. He raised his hands in a peaceful gesture. "We just want to see what you have in that wagon."

"Back!" the woman replied.

She wore her hair in a ponytail, but the expression in her eyes was as stern as any man's. She remained alert at all times, threatening anyone who attempted to come nearer. Her voice tried to convey anger, but somehow she could not hide her fear. Noakh knew that those ruffians were as aware of this as he was, and they were enjoying it.

"Back?" said a woman with curly hair and a bulbous nose standing behind the wagon. "Or what will you do?" She took two steps towards the wagon to see what was inside.

The woman atop the wagon tried to attack her with the pitchfork. This mistake led the rest of the ruffians to rush her, grabbing her feet and pulling her out of the wagon. The poor woman tried to strike out with her weapon, but her attackers anticipated her movements. They ripped the pitchfork from her hands and threw it several feet away. Then they pushed the woman into the mud. She stood there, soaked in mud and sobbing while the thieves ignored her. She watched as they climbed onto the wagon to learn what valuables she kept inside.

Noakh did not give much importance to a farmer who had been assaulted; it wasn't his problem. Considering the show finished, he climbed back up the tree, placing his body on his makeshift bed. *Running is the wisest thing to do,* he thought.

However, the farmer woman did not happen to share his opinion. Taking advantage of her assailants' absorption in their booty, she rushed over to the pitchfork. She drew it out of the mud then ran back to the wagon. Raising her arm, she stuck the weapon into the back of the largest and loudest of the thieves. Her victim gave a loud cry. The other assailants immediately turned to her, alerted to the attack.

The man who had spoken before got off the wagon first and shook his head.

"That is not right. You should have left when you had the chance," he said as he took out a short knife from his belt. After a slight gesture, the rest of his companions mimicked him. They wore knives of different sizes, small-time thieves who traveled simply. The one who had received the blow in the back demanded revenge and tried to move forward, but his leader just made a signal. He would be the first.

The young woman took a few steps backwards and lowered her weapon slightly, raising it suddenly again and assuming a defensive stance. Now that she had made the decision to fight for her wagon, she had to keep it up until the end.

Noakh was trying to ignore the situation. He reminded himself again and again that it was not his thing, as he was no longer part of that world. Why should he interfere? He was convinced he did not know anything about the woman; he did not owe her anything. He tried to convince himself of this using what he knew, on some level, to be the most stupid reasoning. *What if that woman stole the wagon? I don't know the whole story... Maybe she's no better than them,* he thought to assuage himself.

The assailants drew closer with smiles on their faces, enjoying the face of terror the girl showed as she hid behind the pitchfork. She had succumbed to fear. Her body had begun to tremble. She closed her eyes and prayed all the prayers she knew.

The leader approached slowly. He got so close the woman could smell his sweat mixed with a strong-smelling fragrance. The man showed a disgusting smile and snatched the pitchfork from the woman's arms, which were frozen with fear. Some subjects of the Queendom of Water enjoyed seeing the fear they could summon in other people; this man was one of those. He held his knife high. With his other hand, he stroked the woman's face. She was not even able to open her eyes; she just kept praying to her god. It was time for the Aqua Deus to make its move.

But it was not the Aqua Deus who made its move. Noakh was no longer in the trees. Then, suddenly, the man's hands had moved away. Not understanding what was happening, the woman again opened her eyes. She saw a young man with black hair standing between her and the group of heartless thieves, all of who seemed as surprised as she was.

"Go away!" Noakh said threateningly. He raised his sword with both hands. He did not know which was stranger: listening to his own voice after spending so much time in the solitude of the forest, or brandishing a weapon to face other men.

Noakh wished those fools would make the mistake of attacking him. Somehow they reminded him of the thieves who had assaulted his house. His eyes, full of hatred, seemed to reflect his thoughts. This time it was the assailants who took a few steps back. Although they understood they had the advantage numerically, the boy they were facing was armed with a sword—and he seemed willing to use it. The leader gripped his knife tightly, even as he looked carefully at the boy. His black hair and brown eyes were a disturbing vision. What was a Fireo doing in these lands?

"I will not repeat it again," Noakh said slowly as he looked at them. "Get out of here." He raised his sword, ready to fight.

The leader decided not to risk further action. He nodded slightly to his companions, and such a small signal was enough, as his crew sheathed their knives and drew away from the woman. Then they turned their heads, staring at the Fireo once more, as if they didn't believe their eyes, their eyes fixed on that strange-looking boy who had emerged from nowhere, and for no reason. They kept looking back until they disappeared into the forest.

* * *

When they finally left, Noakh sheathed his sword. His hands hurt, due to how hard he had held his weapon. He had not felt that kind of pain for a long time. He turned to look at the woman. She had backed away slyly after Noakh had appeared. Now she stood startled in the muddy road... Was she any safer than before?

Noakh realized that she was in fact a young girl—a girl of his age, or even a few years younger. Her eyes inspected him strangely, with fear. He realized that if his eyes and hair were not exotic enough on their own, they were accompanied by the look of a man who had spent an entire year lost in the woods. His clothes were totally ragged.

He looked into the girl's eyes for the first time. "Why did you not run, you stupid?" said Noakh with resentment. He was really upset about having to be part of a world he no longer considered his own.

The girl looked at him in surprise. She did not understand why he was asking her a question about something that was so obvious to her. "My parents worked hard throughout the harvest." Her voice somehow seemed indignant to Noakh. "I could not let those thieves ransack all my parents' work simply because of my fear," she said after a long pause.

This time it was Noakh who was surprised, not expecting such words. "I see," he said.

He turned and was about to leave, then the girl talked.

"May I at least know the name of my savior?"

Noakh didn't turn back to answer her. Instead, he paused before saying his name. He remembered what his name meant, what it meant to his father. That wasn't his name anymore, he thought. He had given up on life and become an outcast. "Akhail." He answered while lowering his eyes.

But a moment later, he left the girl again, returning the way he had come. The young woman did not even manage to thank him—not for lack of gratitude but because she was still perplexed by everything. First she was about to be beaten by those thieves and then that boy with black hair and brown eyes, a Fireo, no doubt...

71

Noakh began to climb the tree to resume his nap. But the girl's words kept repeating in his head. She had been brave. She was willing to fight until the very end for what had cost so much effort to his parents. He instead...

"Damn it!" he exclaimed.

Outraged, he swiped his hand at a tree branch. After all that had happened, it seemed *he* was going to be the stupid one. He started to climb down the tree to return to the girl. He wanted to thank her for opening his eyes.

The wagon was not in the road anymore. The girl had apparently continued on her way—a cloud of dust could be seen moving along with the wagon. But Noakh saw, on the ground where the wagon had been, some neatly folded clothes, and some food. He could not help but smile. Not only had the girl taught him a lesson; she had also given him new clothes and a decent meal.

Noakh paused for a moment to consider. It was curious how wisdom could be found in the most unexpected places... and the most unexpected people.

He kept running through the forest. He had avoided such paths during all that time. He panted heavily, but he would not stop running. Lower branches and bushes smashed his face, his hands, but he didn't care at all. He could already hear the water stream. He had arrived. Noakh stood in front of the river. There he was again, the same spot where everything had ended a year ago. Noakh dove into the water... the exact place where he had thrown Distra. He remembered the spot because, just before throwing the sword into the river, he had cut a particular tree several times with the sword, lashing out at it due to his anger. He kept looking under the water, desperately trying to find his sword.

The sword was not there. Probably the current had dragged it away. He came to the surface and gave a deep breath.

Noakh cursed his luck once more. Being fair, this time he deserved it. After all, he had thrown it into the river a year ago; he could not expect the sword to be there waiting for him with open arms. His Fireo temper wouldn't let him fail. He would search the entire sea until he found that damn sword!

He kept searching again and again, tirelessly, ceaselessly. The water was really cold but he didn't care at all. He tried not to think, because he knew doubts would begin to flood his mind. After a few attempts, he had to get out, take a breath, and dive again. The river's waters were crystalline and cold. The devoted citizens kept the waters pristine. No one would think of throwing things in them. And for those whose devotion was not motivation enough, they were convinced to keep the waters clean by the threat of death penalty, which would be imposed on them if they polluted the waters.

It was when Noakh's fingers were already wrinkled that he saw a shining object resting on the riverbed. The object was covered by a rock. Weeds were dancing around it. Noakh grabbed the hilt of Distra and pulled it gently, but the sword was blocked under the rock, as if Distra didn't want to get back to Noakh's hands. He pulled again, a bit harder this time, and got the sword out from under the rock. Noakh brandished his sword with both hands, admiring it for a few seconds, then pushed himself hard to the surface.

He was sitting on the riverbank, completely soaked, looking at his sword as if he hadn't seen a friend in a long time. He spent a lot of time contemplating it, distracted. His father had protected it for all those years, had sacrificed his life for Noakh, to the point where he had left his family... and Noakh had tried to throw it all away. *How stupid!* he thought. In the sword's reflection he saw what he had become. He looked horrible. He needed a haircut and a proper dyeing.

His father had trained him to be king someday, or at least to fight for it. While the other children had played, he practiced the art of swordsmanship, fighting with two swords. Now he understood why. He realized that he could not escape his destiny; sooner or later it would end up chasing him.

"I will face the world, and then I will face my destiny," he said sternly.

He had his sword and new clothes, although he had to do something about his black hair. This was not difficult at all. He only had to gather some white flowers whose stems contained a nectar that turned his hair blond. After all, that was how he and his father had done it for all those years.

He wandered through the forest, as those flowers usually grew in humid places. Being so close to a river, there would probably be some white flowers close to his place. Noakh frowned. He had usually seen some of those plants when he had meandered through the forest, and now that he needed them he was unable to find any?

Luckily, his knowledge of the forests helped him. Not far away, there was a meadow full of flowers of different colors. The ones he was searching for would surely grow there too.

He was right. There they were, growing between two rocks with moss. One would be enough to turn his hair blond for a while, but he picked another in case he needed it. He didn't like abusing nature.

He went back to the river, then he extracted the nectar of the flower pressing it with his own fingers. His hands were covered in a slimy whitish substance and then applied it, dyeing his hair and beard. He looked at his reflection in the water, making sure he had applied the liquid of the flower all along his hair and eyebrows, as his father had taught him long ago. His hair turned dark blond, as well as his beard. He really needed both a haircut and a shave.

He walked to the nearest town, Aquaterna, which was a short distance away on foot. Noakh had been there once with his father, but he did not remember many details of their trip. But today, walking through the streets of the village, he saw that everything was more or less as he remembered. It was a noisy place, with a large market where traders did their business. The stench from the accumulation of cattle and people... The stalls full of objects of all kinds, from vegetables to the strangest metal utensils... Lumio used to say that in Aquaterna you could purchase everything—even a woman. Being just a child, Noakh had not understood the exaggeration; he had approached one of the merchants to ask him to be his mother. Lumio had erupted in laughter. Recalling this memory brought a smile to Noakh's face.

While he was walking through the marketplace he met two City Guards, soldiers from the lower ranks of the army. He tried to avoid them but he was too late. One of the guards had noticed him and started talking to him.

"Hey you, Brown Eyes... Nice swords!"

Noakh had already grown used to being called Brown Eyes. At first he thought the nickname was meant to insult him; later he realized that it was often a quick way to address him when someone did not know his name. Even though the former connotation was the most usual, this time the soldier seemed to be employing the latter connotation.

Even so, Noakh instinctively extended his hands to defend himself. However, there seemed to be no hostility in the guard's words. Although the guard had put him in a bad mood, he knew enough to approach the guards if he did not want to have more problems.

74

"Thank you, sir," he lied while smiling. "I'm practicing hard to be a great soldier."

"Ha! Really?" said the soldier, pleased by Noakh's response. "Being a soldier is a hard task, boy."

The second soldier joined the conversation after letting out a snort. "Exactly, Aleas. It's hard for you to drink all the wine in the tavern!" He laughed.

"Don't be stupid, Treven." The first guard suppressed his partner with his hand; he had been trying to dilute the fun. "What do you say, boy? Would you like a practical class?"

Noakh did not know how to respond. The last time he had drawn his two swords, he had been engulfed in a murderous rage. He did not know how he would react to the opportunity to engage in a new combat, let alone a village in which so many people surrounded him. It did not seem the most appropriate circumstances under which to conduct such an experiment.

"On another occasion, my lord... without a doubt I would be honored! I still have a long way to go to understand the art of swordsmanship, in which you are undoubtedly well versed," Noakh lied again. He tried to speak with as much respect as he could, as he knew that sometimes making someone feel important is the best way to ensure he leaves you alone.

"Nonsense. On guard!" Aleas said joyfully.

Unsheathing the sword, he threw a trial thrust at Noakh, who drew both of his two swords instinctively and parried the thrust easily. The display caught the attention of the citizens, who drew closer to witness the event.

"Good parry... Let's see about this one!" Aleas said with a smile. He stepped back to gain momentum. Then he began to unleash a series of cuts that in his eyes were complicated. However, a soldier of the Fire Kingdom had trained Noakh since childhood. To him, such attacks were no more than a warm-up. Despite this, in order to extricate himself from the situation, he began to pretend he was having difficulty keeping up with the soldier, and he let one of Aleas's cuts disarm him of his steel sword.

This provoked shouts of admiration and applause from the audience, while the soldier, Aleas, bowed and his companion, Treven, affirmed with his arms crossed.

"Thank you, thank you," Aleas said, full of pride. Showing the people the skills of the queen's soldiers never hurt, he knew.

"You have beaten me, good sir. Your combat techniques are too advanced for a mere apprentice. I hope that one day I will be able to be as capable as you are." Noakh, too, accompanied his affirmation with a bow. He could not help but feel a certain discomfort at the falseness of his words.

"You have good basics, boy. You just need more training. I started like you, I did not know what a sword was. Hard work makes you reach the top, like us."

At this, the two soldiers inflated their chests, affirming their pride. They made Noakh bow while the audience applauded, and some of them even made the Aquo reverence. Noakh knew that he could not continue this farce much longer; his pride prevented him from continuing to praise the almost nonexistent skills of his rival.

"Then it would be better if I went to train as soon as possible, sir. It has been an honor to lose against you. Good luck during your guard!"

Noakh turned away from the people, saying goodbye as best as he could. He could not bear his defeat; although this time it was feigned, defeat was something that he had been unable to bear even as a child. In his first training sessions with the sword, there had not been a single combat against Lumio that he did not lose.

Lumio. He gave Noakh no leniency, although he had been a simple apprentice. "You must know which battles to fight, but you must also know which battles to win," he had pronounced. No doubt having left that soldier as evidence of which battles he could win would have caused him nothing but problems.

After leaving Aleas and Treven, Noakh passed in front of a tavern. He decided he needed to take one—or several—drinks. No better way to reintegrate into society.

He was about to open the door when a woman burst through the door and fell down to the street vomiting, while another woman, looking as drunk as her comrade, appeared from inside the tavern and tried to help her. When Noakh got inside, the tavern was crowded, and he had to push his way through the drunken crowd. The place reeked of alcohol and sweat, just as every inn did. He sat in a corner. Close to him, three men were bursting with bellowing laughter.

One tankard of beer followed the other, and he grew more confident. So what if king Wulkan had an army? An idea occurred to him. Why

76

had it not come to mind before?! It could work. He stood up on his table while pouring a half-full tankard of beer into his mug.

"Drink... ers!" Noakh began with some difficulty. "I am looking for brave soldiers who want to join me. I cannot tell you much, but it is an ad... venture, the likes of which you have never heard, with an un... im... aginable reward when we reach our destin... ation, a road full of dangers. What do you say? Who will join such an ad... venture?" he cried as he raised his beer, hoping that they all would do the same, toasting him.

All the people inside the tavern stared at him, surprised. Then they burst out laughing as they pointed at him and made fun of him. They were heard hurling all kinds of expletives his way. Seeing the little success he was having, Noakh decided to climb off the table, dodging some flying tankards as he did so. Crestfallen, he sat in a corner, waiting to be served.

"Very nice speech, brown eyes."

With a smile, a waitress poured Noakh another mug of beer. She laughed while winking at him. Noakh still had not noticed this third reason why strangers referred to him by the color of his eyes. "But I do not think an establishment such as this is the best place to find what you are looking for, adventurer."

She walked away from the table, turning back to give Noakh another warm smile. He returned it timidly, while swallowing his beer. Leaving the discouragement behind him, Noakh considered what his next step should be. A bunch of drunks were not going to end his determination, leastways not when alcohol flowed down his throat and filled his stomach.

At a nearby table, two men were arguing loudly, their beers no doubt adding more weight to their words. Their faces were red as tomatoes, so Noakh assumed both had consumed more than a sufficient dose of ale to engage in such arguments as powerfully as they could.

"And I tell you that the Kingdom of Air is the wildest of all! They subject their children to a barbaric ritual. They throw them from a cliff... and the one who survives will be the future king! It is the greatest brutality that can be done to a child, worthy of wild animals—that's what they are! Authentic and stupid savages!" His words echoed between hiccups and pauses, a result of his massive intake of alcohol. His narrowed eyes seemed to give no less indignation to his words.

"Blunders and fairy tales!" the other man said. "If it were like that and only the heir to the throne survived, the Aertians would not have survived as a tribe—they would all be dead but their king!" Despite the second man's drunken state, it seemed that at least a certain common sense prevailed. "Besides, what about the burned ones? Ha! I love that word. They take the newborns and they burn them alive to purify them. *They burn them alive!*" he repeated. However, it seemed that his logic was applicable only to the arguments of his rival.

The world of Alomenta was divided into four kingdoms. In the middle of the world was a vast location known as the Void, an enigmatic place where nobody dared to explore, since it was said that whoever journeyed there would never return. It had a reputation for suffering, paganism, and death. The four kingdoms were positioned around this grim area: The Aquadom was to the north, Firia to the east, Tir Torrent to the west, and Aere Tine to the south. The Aquadom bordered the Fireos to the northeast and the Earth Kingdom to the northwest. This was why the Aertian Kingdom, being farther south for the Aquos, was not as well known. The only way to get to the Aertian lands was to go through the territories of either the Fireos or the Tirhans. Nobody would dare cross the Void. As a result, the Aertian Kingdom was rife with rumor and speculation.

In a similar fashion, the Fireos had long since closed their doors to the world... and they had always had a raw relationship with their Aquo neighbors. So numerous rumors were spread about them. For the customs of the kingdoms were not usually shared; invariably, gossips who sought to belittle the traditions of their neighbors were always especially entertaining—as Noakh observed now once again.

A third man, at a nearby table, now joined the conversation.

"I have heard that the burned ones perform a ritual with one of their legendary weapons. They mark the newborns... and it's the weapon that chooses the heir," he said, shrugging his shoulders.

The other two drunks looked at each other and began to laugh. Noakh could not help but glance down at the palm of his hand, where the scar still marked the consequence of that ritual.

"Nonsense! Why would they do that? Everyone knows that their king is immortal. Nothing is more dignifying than the Dajalam family, a lineage chosen directly by the Aqua Deus itself! So pure that for generations it has always engendered a beautiful girl who will inherit the throne, just as it should be!"

"They say that if a man is born, he is locked up and raised in the palace dungeons," said the third drunk, shrugging his shoulders again as he sipped his beer.

"Sacrilege! Guards! Guards!" The man slammed his tankard against the wooden table, causing the beer to spout into the air, permeating his beard.

Luckily for the other drunk, no guard was nearby. Noakh looked around the tavern, making sure that this was the case. Seeing that nobody was listening to him—and that nobody was coming to put a halt to the insults of his opponent—the drunkard with the beard continued as if nothing had happened.

"Not to mention the children of the earth. They love those trees so much they actually look like them, with those dumb green eyes and their dirty brown hair! Just like the leaves and the trunk of a tree! Apparently, a tree chooses the heir to the crown. Ha! A damn stupid tree! Could you imagine a river choosing our heir?" The drunken man began to laugh as he again slammed the tankard hard against the wooden table. This time the beer splashed vigorously on his partner, provoking even more laughter.

"Guys, listen." Another patron sitting nearby made the entire tavern turn quiet. "I think I might be the heir to the Air Kingdom. Just listen quietly..." The man waited until everyone turned quiet, their stupid drunk faces waiting as if he really was going to prove his claim. After a pause, he farted. Noisily. The tavern burst into laughter.

Noakh had heard the rumors about Tir Torrent, the Earth Kingdom, although the information among kingdoms was scarce, especially as related to rituals and military tasks. The gossipers said that their king, Burum Babar, had been ill, so much so that he couldn't even move or talk. But he would remain king because the tree had to choose the new heir—and so far it hadn't. How capricious the gods can be! For as it had been told, when their king became ill, the Tirhans signed a treaty with the Aquos, the terms of which stipulated that the Aquadom was to provide military power in order to ensure the Tirhans' peaceful stance in exchange for a substantial sum of money.

Such an agreement supposed an antecedent never seen, since the relationships between both kingdoms had not always been in such good terms. Regarding the king, if he had been cured or not remained a mystery... and many years had gone by since then. The only thing known was that the Earth Kingdom was still very unstable.

As Lumio had told Noakh, each kingdom had its own particularities when choosing its heir, and although the four kingdoms were each a sovereign territory, the type of government by which each of them was ruled was as distinct as the colors of the eyes and hair of their citizens.

Seeing that his tankard was empty and that the drunks had moved on to much less interesting subjects, Noakh left a bronze coin on the table and walked out of the tavern. He decided that he had nothing to do in the village.

8. A collision

Noakh left the tavern still stunned. The laughter of the other customers had somehow ended the euphoria of the alcohol. At least he could walk without stumbling, or that was what he thought, anyway. He began to walk the streets of the city without having a particular direction in mind, thinking about what to do next.

His walk almost instinctively was taking place in the alleyways of the city. It was a way to get away from the noise of the merchants—and, conveniently, to prevent another encounter with the City Guards. He had been lucky once, having emerged gracefully from his earlier encounter with the guards. He didn't want to try his luck again.

While the main streets of Aquaterna were noisy, the alleys were quieter and less crowded. It was no coincidence; they were much dirtier, and swamped by nauseating odors. Noakh was sure he could smell urine mixed with animal feces. He grimaced at the smells impregnating his nostrils. At the same time, the people he met in the alleys seemed as interested in *not* being seen as he was. Even so, a couple of men had exchanged glances with Noakh then whispered to each another. Noakh's instincts were somewhat clouded, and he had not realized he might not be welcome in these alleys. One thing was shared by all the people he met: They frowned at the color of his eyes.

The young Fireo was absorbed in his thoughts. He had made a decision, but he had no idea how to carry it out. What would his father have advised him to do in such a situation? Noakh tried to rummage through his mind, trying to make use of the many lessons his father had given him, until he finally let go a snort as he kicked a stone with

81

indignation. So many years of lessons and training, yet he was unable to remember anything that had been useful to him at the time?

Without realizing it, he arrived at a small esplanade. A small pond stood in the middle of the park. Fish of all colors splashed in the bright water. At first glance, shades of red, orange, and blue—and even gold and silver—could be seen. Despite being a little far away from the main streets, the pond was well cared for and preserved. It was surrounded by steel bars painted black that allowed the villagers to observe the fish splashing in the water, and that prevented people from falling in.

Noakh stood behind the bars, watching the fish. The fish, meanwhile, began to crowd the water under his position, aware that a human was observing them and hoping that food would begin falling from the sky, exactly as it had fallen so many times before.

Noakh shrugged. "I have nothing to give to you." He breathed a sigh. "I'm sorry." The fish, as if understanding his words, swum in all directions, spreading around the small pond, creating a kind of rainbow.

"Many come here to find a moment of peace." Said a feminine voice.

Noakh couldn't help jumping.

Next to him stood a woman with straight hair and single-folded eyelids, gathered under a blue veil. Her tiny nose and thin eyebrows highlighted her face. Her clothes were also sky blue, and on her neck lay a small brooch in the shape of a mermaid. Even Noakh guessed that this woman was a novice, a woman who had decided to give her life to faith. Many families considered it an honor for a member of their lineage to give their life in pursuit of service to the church: It was a way to honor the Aqua Deus and, in some cases, a way for the family to have one less mouth to feed.

It was not until then that Noakh looked around. A church stood just behind him. It was tall, built of white rock, and beautifully ornamented with marine details honoring the Aqua Deus. At the top, a large copper-colored bell displayed myriad details that stood out in rusty green relief. The church was not a very large structure; in fact, it would be considered minuscule compared to other churches Noakh had seen—and especially with the church that stood in the capital of the queendom, which Noakh had heard was the largest of them all, competing in size with the palace itself.

The woman smiled, realizing how lost Noakh was. Several wrinkles appeared on her face, revealing an older age than one would have expected at first glance. Her smile was warm and full of tenderness.

"Your eyes," began the novice as she fixed her gaze on Noakh's brown eyes. He could not help but look away, something he had not done in a very long time. Again he stared at the pond. The fish had come together again, expectantly waiting for food, even more so than when Noakh had first approached.

"I know my eyes are brown," said Noakh grumpily, for he recognized he was being judged yet again for the color of his eyes. He had managed to keep the villagers' looks of contempt from bothering him in the slightest, but such derision still hurt when it came from people he didn't expect to exhibit it.

The woman raised her right hand and grabbed Noakh by the face gently but firmly, forcing him to look at her again.

"No, a faithful servant of the Aqua Deus is able to see beyond the color of the eyes," she said in a more serious tone before smiling again. Noakh tried to turn his face again when he heard her words, but now both the woman's hands held his face tightly. "We are water. Do not let doubt lead you in its direction. You must find faith not only in the Aqua Deus but also in yourself, and swim against the tide." She nodded and smiled again. Her hands caressed his face before releasing him.

Noakh smiled back. He was still as lost as before, but at least he was grateful that someone was trying to comfort him. "Thank you," he said, and after a brief pause he added, "sister." The woman's smile was enough to tell him that his response had been sufficient.

Noakh had never gone to church, so he did not know how to act or how to answer to one of the servants of Aqua Deus. The two remained watching the water in the pond for a brief moment, until the sister pulled out a loaf of bread from a small bag. She split the bread in two and offered half to Noakh. Both threw small pieces of bread into the water, creating small furrows in the water. The lumps of bread quickly disappeared due to the voracious appetite of the fish.

It was a moment of peace and tranquility, and for a second Noakh forgot where he was, absorbed as he was in the harmony he felt as he watched the fish move through the water, listening only to the slight splashing and bursting of the bubbles that the fish caused during their feast.

Suddenly a loud sound dissipated the moment: The church bell had begun to ring uniformly. The resounding *dong! dong!* of the bell continued energetically, although the fish seemed totally unresponsive to the noise, probably because they were already accustomed to it. The woman, however, threw her last remaining pieces of bread and started making her way toward the church while shaking her hands at her sides.

"Remember," she said, turning back to Noakh, "the doors of our church are always open to anyone who has lost his way." She bowed, paying the Aquo due reverence, then made her way to the church gate.

Noakh made a clumsy bow in response as he watched the woman disappear through the open gate.

For a few seconds, he stared at the pond again. Then he set out on his way. It took him only two more alleys before he was absorbed in his thoughts again. Before he was aware of it, he collided with someone, and as they both fell to the ground, he heard some glass shatter. Noakh could see that he had collided with a man—a man who was now looking desolate while staring at the glass object. Noakh assumed it had been a flask. The liquid inside, which by all appearances seemed to be simple water, began to spread over the ground, filtering down through the earth.

"Damn it!"

Lamenting the accident, the man pointlessly tried to collect the water with one of the pieces of glass. Noakh stood up and tried to help him, even if merely as a courtesy since the water had turned the earth into mud. "No, please, no," the man said.

Then the man, who thus far had seemed unaware of Noakh's presence, looked at him furiously. His face was desolate. His light blue eyes were swollen, the lids covered in huge purple circles. His straight hair was dirty, and a sloppy beard covered his face. The man looked pitiful—and that was saying a lot, considering that Noakh himself had just spent an entire year lost in the forest. He supposed he looked as pitiful as the man, except for his new clothes and his dyed hair.

"Sorry, I didn't—" Noakh began to say.

He didn't have time to finish his apology, because the man began to throw the shattered pieces of glass at him, even as he cursed him.

Then the man got up and tried to punch Noakh in the face. Noakh tried to stop him without putting up much effort, because the man seemed very emaciated and weak, but the strength of blow's impact forced him to remain on his guard. The man's fingers were thick, and his punch had been thrown with power: He was stronger than his appearance suggested. The man threw another blow with his free hand. Noakh intercepted this blow as well. Then after struggling, he butted his forehead sharply against Noakh's head. Both men were thrown back to the ground.

Noakh raised his hand. As he felt his forehead, which burned with pain, he heard the man's sobs. The blow had been hard, but Noakh had received the worst of it. It didn't seem possible that the man's sobbing was due to the blow's impact. Was that container of water so important to him?

"Listen," started Noakh again, feeling bad for the man. "I'm really sorry, I didn't look where I was going. I... Look, if that flask was so important for you, I can try to buy you another one."

The man was looking at the ground. He supported himself with his hands, but he stopped sobbing when he heard Noakh's words. His elbows began to tremble from his fury.

"Flask?" the man finally managed to say, though not without some difficulty. "You bastard unickey Aqureo!" Noakh knew *unickey* was a racist term used for those born as the result of intimacy between citizens of different kingdoms, producing a child sporting hair or eyes of a color different than that typically seen in the kingdom where the newborn child lived. Given that Noakh always wore his hair dyed, the ugly word was an insult he had heard more than once. Aqureo was what crossbreed Fireos and Aquos were called. They were also called Firquos, even though so far Noakh had only heard that term from his father. "It's not the flask that matters to me. That was holy water... and you've wasted it!"

"Oh," said Noakh, realizing the seriousness of the situation. The holy water was used in the funeral rituals of the Aquadom, a ceremony performed so that the soul of the deceased could reach the sea, where, deep in the ocean, the Aqua Deus welcomed them. If that man carried holy water, it was certain that a close relative of his had recently passed away. "I have seen a church near here. I am sure that they will give us a little more holy water."

"Surely they will give us a little," repeated the man as he put his hands to his head. "Can I know where you came from, stupid imbecile? You can't find holy water just like that; you have to ask the church and then they... Bah! What does a unickey bastard like you know!"

Noakh ignored the insults. For although it had not been solely his fault that they had collided, thereby breaking the glass flask, he could understand the pain and anger of a man who had lost a loved one.

"I can understand your pain, believe me. I myself lost my—"

"What do you know about pain? Don't say a word!" said the man as his eyes looked again at where the holy water had so recently been spilled.

85

"Of course I know! I lost my father recently! I know very well how it feels!"

"Your father? Ha!" the man mocked. "No matter how hard the death of a father may be, one grows up knowing that your father will leave you sooner or later, but..." A memory seemed to surface, the cause of the man's pain; he could not help sobbing again. Moments later, he regained his composure and pointed to Noakh as he looked at him furiously: "I hope your remains never find the sea," he said as he stood again then walked away. But suddenly he turned and added, "And let there be no doubt in your mind, the sin of spilling holy water on impure ground falls on *your* soul, not mine." After which he walked away as he spoke to himself in a low voice.

Noakh stood there for a while, shocked. Without knowing what to say, wishing that someone's remains would not reach the sea was a very offensive insult to any Aquo. For Noakh, however, it didn't matter in the least that his soul didn't reach the sea; in fact he didn't want to think about how. Being not only a Fireo but also having been chosen as the phoenix by one of the sacred swords, he might be received at the home of the Aqua Deus. Putting his thoughts aside, the Fireo began running towards the church. He didn't remember the way very well, because he hadn't paid attention earlier, but he wouldn't stop running until he found that church.

He ran with no rest, alley after alley. He heard the church bell ring once again. He ran faster. Panting, he finally found himself in front of the elongated church; after taking a brief moment to catch his breath, he entered through the gate. Noakh felt a shiver as he passed into the building itself. The air inside the church was much colder than out in the street, but the smell was similar to seawater. That was a good sign, he thought. If it smelled like the sea, there should be holy water somewhere in the church. His curiosity made him admire the interior of the sacred site. Daylight entered through the high arched windows, making the place more luminous than it might otherwise seem from the outside. Walking beyond the entrance, he found himself in a wide room, the walls decorated with ancient sculptures and paintings displaying marine details. Some of the pieces were severely damaged, the bright colors of the paintings being slightly covered in black soot and the statues having cracks through the hard marble, as if they had been created centuries ago. At the far end of the church, one could see an altar, on which there stood a table covered by a delicate white tablecloth. As Noakh began to

86

walk through the aisle, he realized that beneath his feet an enormous inscription had been carved into the floor:

Num diate numferae insto eure siel.

Noakh kept reading, trying to understand what the words might mean, until he realized that they were written in Flumio, the Aquo language. A language that was very much in disuse and completely unknown to him.

"Don't hate unbelievers, but weep for their souls," a familiar voice said, translating for Noakh.

Noakh leapt; the novice from the pond stood behind him. "A phrase that the High Priestess Ipsione spoke centuries ago. She thought our faith-filled tears could make those unwilling reach the sea. A very beautiful message, don't you think?"

"Beautiful, yes," Noakh said. He reflected for a moment then remembered why he was there. "You said the doors were open to anyone. Well, I won't lie to you, I'm not a man of faith, but I need your help. I need holy water! It's not for me, it's—"

"I'm afraid I can't help you," the woman said, looking sadly at Noakh. "We received the holy water a few days ago, but I gave it to a man not long ago, the poor being. He was totally desolate, my words and his faith couldn't comfort him," she said with sadness. She held her fist to her chest and her eyes were close to tears. "Not only did he lose his wife but also his daughter on the same day..."

"What?"

Noakh stared at the woman with a horrified grimace. He stood in the cold silence of the church, waiting for the woman to explain the man's tragic fate.

9. An apology

Leaving the village, he went through the countryside thinking about the best way to apologize.

"Look, I'm sorry," he muttered, trying to find the proper words. "It was my fault but you should be careful too..." Noakh wondered whether such an apology was good enough, shaking his head and trying again. "Okay, it was an accident. I'm sorry. Would you forgive me?" He touched his head, frustrated. "No, that is not good enough! How can an apology be so complicated?!"

The novice had told him where that man lived, in a farm, on the outskirts of the city. *Would that man accept my apology?* Noakh thought. He had to try at least. That man had wished him the worst, to never find the sea, but since Noakh had not long ago discovered he was a Fireo, never finding the sea seemed now more like a compliment.

He stopped for a second, trying to get oriented. The nun had said he had to walk only a bit to the south to would find the farm. Instead, he only saw trees and a river. Maybe he had gotten lost? He shrugged and kept walking south a bit more. The sun was setting at the west—his father had taught him how to get oriented—so he was sure he was walking in the proper direction.

Finally, in the distance he saw a small farmhouse and, next to a tree, a shadow. As he approached, Noakh spotted a man with a rope tied to a branch of the tree. Noakh guessed the intention of the man, so he started running towards him. The man had climbed onto a chair, and, having already made a knot, he passed his head through the loop in the rope, and with a hop off the chair, he began to hang in the air, swaying.

Noakh screamed. He would not arrive in time. In a last attempt, he unsheathed Distra and, while letting out a cry, instinctively drew the blade horizontally, cutting the air from right to left before him with all his strength. A disk of fire shot from the blade, rushing towards the tree. Although Noakh intended to cut the rope, the impact was directed against the branch around which the rope was tied. The branch broke off, and the tree began to burn. The man fell hard to the ground.

As Noakh approached, he saw the suicidal man writhing on the ground. The man clutched his neck, trying to loosen the rope so he could get oxygen. His face was red as a tomato and his eyes had widened. After freeing himself from the rope, he stood up then leaned his elbows on his knees and took in air with all his might. Meanwhile, Noakh had arrived at his side. The man, instead of thanking Noakh, averted his eyes. With a look of hatred, he rushed into Noakh while spilling all kinds of insults.

Noakh did not have time to anticipate the blow. He fell to the ground. With the man on top, the two started struggling. The man kept throwing punches while Noakh parried them with his hands as best he could.

"Bastard unickey! Bastard! Bastard!" the man shouted. "You again! Bastard unickey Aqureo! I was already dead! I was already... I was already..." His voice began to grow increasingly soft; little by little, between sobs, his blows became less aggressive, until he finally pulled away from Noakh and began to cry mournfully.

Noakh, still puzzled, stood up from the ground and brushed the dust from his clothes. His new clothes hadn't remained clean for even a single day. "Can you explain to me why you are crying? I saved your life. Would you rather die?" he asked.

"I was hanging from a tree! What do you think? Are you so stupid to think that someone who has just hung himself from a tree wants to be saved?" The man's words were accompanied by a look of rage. "What's wrong? Were there not any damsels to save? Is it that a man cannot even end his life without someone meddling? Why did you have to save me? Why?"

Noakh grew indignant at the man's reproach. "Because suicide is for cowards! It's the easy way out. Life is hard, but you have to keep going. Ending your life to stop suffering is not the solution. You have to keep fighting, no matter what obstacles you're facing in your life. If you surrender, it will be forever, but if you get up you will see the sunlight again."

As Noakh spoke, the man looked at the ground in silence. He remained on his knees, his eyes hidden under his dark blond hair, his mouth grimacing with pain.

"So it does not matter what obstacle, huh? Well, follow me."

Standing up without looking at Noakh, the man walked around the farmhouse and entered the backyard. On it, two gravestones could be seen, and two holes the size of a person both full of water. It was a ritual that non-rich people did for their beloved ones who had passed away. A small rag doll sat smiling at the edge of the smaller hole, along with a locket. "My wife and my daughter," the man said with a voice full of sadness. "They died two days ago. A disease took them, and they succumbed overnight. Aqua Deus decided not to take me instead... So kind of him to do so," he added with irony. "Until today I have not had the courage to end the ritual, and because of you, I couldn't perform it with holy water. My daughter was only five years old. Five years old... They were my sea... Now it has dried forever."

After this, the man fell to his knees, his eyes looking at the gravestones as he cried and lamented the loss of his family. Noakh, standing behind him, did not say a word. He was saddened by such a distraught vision of a man; also, he was remembering his own father, to whom he had not even said goodbye. His grave had been the rubble of his own home.

"I understand," Noakh said, as firmly as he could.

After that, he turned around and left. He had nothing more to do there.

10. Hilzen's decision

The man was still kneeling on the ground, lamenting, relieved that the stranger who had prevented him from meeting his loved ones had left. Then, shifting into a sitting position, he reached out and grabbed his daughter's rag doll, looking at it sadly and holding it while tears fell from his eyes.

He looked back, checking that the boy had really left. His reaction had been strange, no doubt about it. He had not expected the boy would leave that easily. In a way, he was disappointed. He had so much accumulated anger and frustration that he wished the strange boy would have stayed a little longer; what he most needed was someone to hit and yell at. His mind paused for a second to think about the way the boy had left, not saying anything, while he had been so talkative about not giving up... moving forward... And after all that, he had gone that easily. However, why did he care anyway? He had been so close...

He ran his hand down his neck, burned by the friction of the rope. No doubt there would be bruises the next day. He remembered the moment he had hopped off the chair: The lack of air... The kicks... The desperation of his lungs, gasping to take in some air... His hands clinging to the rope in order to free himself... And then that flash that had ripped off the branch in a single blow.

Then he that he had not considered something yet. The flash. Doubt flooded his mind. Where had such a fire flash come from? Perhaps the weird unwanted savior was a kind of magician? Couldn't be—he had never seen a wizard in his entire life. Then a fire arrow, maybe? No, that attack had been too powerful. But then what could it be? Also, he did not recall the boy carrying any bow, or a quiver with arrows.

Just then a voice interrupted his thoughts.

"Hilzen!"

Startled, Hilzen shivered. Then he looked around. The voice he thought he had heard was very similar—*too* similar—to the voice of Marne, his deceased wife.

"Who's there?" he said hesitantly, looking in all directions again, his hair bristling. On his wife's tomb a whitish shadow appeared. Hilzen, trapped by fear and fright, backed away from the graves.

"Marne, is that you?" he said. After a brief pause, he continued: "Of course it's you..."

"You tried to end your life, Hilzen. That's not like you..."

Hilzen did not know if his wife's strange tone was due to her transformation into an apparition, but her voice carried a certain sinister air. The white shadow flickered slightly.

"I am sorry, I am so sorry. I could not save you, I could not do anything..." Hilzen sobbed. "Without you here, the world does not make sense to me. I wanted to go with you, but the boy..."

"That boy has saved your life, Hilzen, and you know what that means..."

"No, Marne. Forget it," he said flatly. "He deprived me of being by your side. I cannot leave you and Lynea here, Marne, I cannot..."

"Hilzen, I'm afraid we will not go anywhere. Go away. Make us keep feeling proud of you. You know what you have to do..."

"But, Marne, I... I just want to be by your side. I cannot leave you two here, I do not have the strength to continue without you..."

"The pain is temporary, Hilzen. But if you surrender, it will be forever."

"You already talk like that boy," he said, upset.

"That means he was right..."

"My destiny is written then?"

"Enjoy your life, Hilzen. We will wait for you."

At that moment, a second smaller shadow appeared next to the other.

"Daddy, take my locket with you, so you will never be alone... Do not worry about us. My doll Rilay will protect us."

"I love you, both of you, Lynea, Marne, with all my heart... We'll meet again soon," Hilzen said sweetly, while tears fell from his eyes.

"We know," the two apparitions replied.

He knelt, grabbed the locket, and patted the doll's head.

"You better protect my two mermaids." Hilzen said. Smiling while looking at the doll, he kissed both gravestones, and gave turned his back to both entities of light.

"Hilzen, do not lose faith... Promise me that you will help him!"

With tears in his eyes, Hilzen nodded.

After that, the shadows disappeared.

A chill ran down Hilzen's back. The backyard appeared normal, as if nothing had happened. Hilzen wondered if it had all been an illusion, his own subconscious playing a dirty trick as a result of his pain and fatigue. He opened the locket. Inside, there was a small drawing of three faces that depicted Hilzen's family, smiling. For Hilzen, such a drawing was more valuable than the best work of Rubeliev, one the most notable painters in the Queendom. Then he put the locket around his neck and closed his eyes.

I must hurry, he thought.

11. The beginning of a trip

"So you're going to travel with me?" Noakh said, amazed. Hilzen had come to him while he was sitting on a log. "Without even knowing where I am going or what I am facing?" Noakh examined the man's square face, long nose, and large ears. His eyes looked more vivid now, but his lids were still covered in huge purple circles. He continued. "And this while not long ago you fought me for having saved your life? I wonder what could have changed your mind so drastically?"

Noakh had been plotting his journey when in the distance he began to hear cries. Fearing an enemy, he had prepared to brandish one of his swords. However, it had been Hilzen who had approached. He drew closer, stepping quickly, carrying a small bag that seemed to be his luggage and a crossbow hanging from his belt.

"That's right. From now on, I'll travel with you, my lord. I'm here for whatever you want," Hilzen said, bowing. "Even so, I would be glad if we didn't go to the south, you know."

Noakh nodded, heading to the south was a bad omen. Then he thought to himself. Hilzen was mocking him, but it didn't actually sound as though he was. Had he gone entirely mad?

"Okay, I want to know where that sudden change of mind comes from. First you try to kill me and now this. Can you explain it to me?"

"It's simple, my lord. You saved my life. Custom forces me to serve you in order to pay my debt. It is a debt sworn by blood. As dictated by the ancient laws, not to fulfill it would deprive me of reaching the sea with my two mermaids—that is, my daughter and my wife."

"A debt sworn by blood?" Noakh repeated. He was puzzled. "Isn't that one of those folktales, such as the right of parley in the pirate's code, that in practice isn't actually performed?"

Noakh and Hilzen stared at each other. Noakh's brown eyes were in complete contrast to Hilzen's light-blue pupils, which, in combination with his blond hair, made his features the stereotypical characteristics of the inhabitants of the Aquadom. But Noakh looked good with his dyed-blond hair. He was used to the disguise, because both he and his father had always dyed their hair. The combination of black hair and brown eyes would be too striking in those lands to avoid suspicion.

"It is true that those ancient laws were forgotten long ago. Even so, for me at least, those who do not comply with it are sinners who will never reach the sea," Hilzen said. "I cannot risk that fate, my lord. So tell me, in what direction are we heading?"

"Stop calling me *lord*," Noakh said, annoyed. "My name is Noakhail." He felt good saying his name again. True, he had given up once, but now he wouldn't. Never again, he would not forget his name. He would not forget what it meant.

"Noakhail?" Hilzen said frowning. "That really is a weird name."

"It is indeed." Noakh nodded. "Call me Noakh."

"As you wish, Noakh... Then tell me, which is our path?"

"Hilzen, have you ever visited the other kingdoms?"

Puzzled, Hilzen answered, "No, it never occurred to me. Why?"

"I have decided to face the world, so my goal is to reach the Fire Kingdom by traveling through the Aertian lands," Noakh said with determination. It was his decision, he had just made it; the idea of heading directly into Fireo territory did not appeal to him at all. Not only did he think the king's soldiers would be waiting for him, given what had happened in his house not too long ago—he suspected a plot had been hatched by King Wulkan himself, who had hired Aquo bandits to do the dirty job. He was also aware that with his current powers he would be no match for Wulkan.

His father had told him how powerful the Fireo king was. No matter that both he and Noakh would each wield one of the fire swords; Wulkan's experience not only far surpassed his own; he also knew the secrets of the swords, which he had inherited from his predecessors—an important privilege Noakh could not draw on. Facing Wulkan's powers, Noakh would not survive a single thrust! For not only was he able to control only a slight amount of Distra's power, but he also felt incredibly exhausted when using it.

Hilzen stared at Noakh incredulously. "What? Are you in your right mind? We'll die when we get there—if our soldiers don't kill us first!"

"Well... you desire death, and I'm afraid I have to tempt fate. I do not see what can go wrong," he said, full of optimism.

"I do see what can go wrong... everything! Besides, with what objective, boy? If you told me you wanted to go to the Fireo Kingdom, I would tell you that it is crazy—but at least I would understand it. Just go to the east and you'd get killed, I get that. But why head there through the Aertian Kingdom?"

"It's the decision I've made," Noakh said, shrugging.

Since he was at such a disadvantage, Noakh had decided to face the world; if he could do that and emerge victorious, Wulkan should be no match for him. He was aware how foolish his plan sounded, but it also seemed like the best alternative he had. Heading to the Fireos' lands with Lumio had been incredibly risky; going there on his own was perilous at best.

"I see." Hilzen understood that no matter what he said he wouldn't change the boy's mind. He accepted his mission, even though he had failed to understand his purpose. "Following your path seems to lead to certain death. I think you've found the right person... Those swords, do you use both at the same time?" he asked with interest.

"That's right. I'm a good swordsman. My technique is to use two swords. I have trained like that since I was a boy; it's a part of me." He gestured to Hilzen. "I see you're wearing a crossbow. Are you good with it?"

"I used it to hunt in the forest. I defend myself with it. I assumed it would be useful on the road. You could say that it is one of the few things that make my luggage." He paused for a moment then looked out into the distance. "If our goal is to go west, maybe we should go towards the Snowy Mountains. It is the shortest way, but not the safest route. The Snowy Mountains are full of danger."

"The Snowy Mountains, eh?" Noakh said thinking about it.

* * *

The wagon was filled with dust from the road. Its wheels were so worn out that it was hard to believe they would complete one more revolution

99

without breaking. The horse also showed signs of exhaustion. The trader himself was middle-aged. He wore leather clothes derived from several animals, giving him a strange appearance, and his red fox-fur boots were muddy. His name was Sigüen. His face resembled Hilzen's, though it was slightly older, with an aquiline nose. Also, he had a happier look in his eyes.

It had been a casual meeting. The wagon had reached Noakh and Hilzen while they were walking along the long, sunlit section of the road. Seeing that he was going the same direction, Sigüen had offered to take them.

"The Snowy Mountains are undoubtedly a particular place... and particularly dangerous, in my opinion." Sigüen loosely held the reins of the old horse. Noakh and Hilzen sat next to Sigüen, listening to his stories as they bumped along the road. "A village of taysees lies just before you reach the mountains and... well... you know what that means."

"That people... From our origins they have lived in this queendom and have never integrated. I say that when such people are here for so long in one place and is unable to live with the rest, then it is time to cut it off. I do not mean to exterminate them, but..." Hilzen scoffed. "It would be better for everyone if they did not exist. What have they contributed to the world? They live in shanties. Their culture is based on pagan music and little else. It's people from which nothing can be obtained, at least nothing good. Luckily our ancestors had the decency to isolate them. In every region that I have traveled to, they have lived away from town, on the other side of the river, behind a hill, under a ravine, or something like that. At least they have the decency not to get close to town and present us with their unpleasant appearance. They say a taysee can go years without taking a bath."

"The taysees, however, are required in wartime." Noakh gripped the edge of the wagon to soften the blows as they bumped along." Apparently they are skilled with various weapons and lack any kind of scruples—which in a fight many generals are grateful for." This last piece of information was something his father had told him.

"True," the merchant said, nodding while watching the road.

"At least they are worth something," said Hilzen while he spat over the edge of the wagon. "However, we must not forget that their motives are not precisely the noblest ones. War is just another way of pillaging for them—seizing the plunder of their victims, destroying villages, and ultimately releasing their wild spirit. You could say that war is paradise for them."

Hilzen laughed at his analogy. The merchant followed suit.

Noakh smiled at the irony. Hatred takes second place when you can be useful, and the taysees were more than useful on a battlefield. Unscrupulous, sacrificial, skilled in combat, and eager to finish off their enemy simply to steal their pretty boots—what more could you ask for?

"Speaking of the gods, look there."

Hilzen pointed to a small stand farther along the road. The stand was run by two taysees. Both taysees were short, which was a typical feature of the taysee people—along with their crooked noses. Their hair was as blond as the other inhabitants of the queendom, but they seemed to like quite peculiar hairstyles. One of them had shaved his entire head except for the front, the other one wore long braided hair.

The merchant passed by the stand without stopping, despite the insistence of the taysee to take a look at his herbs. Noakh, surprised by the merchant's lack of interest in a product that in many zones was very much appreciated, could not contain himself.

"How is it, Sigüen, that you are not interested in their herbs? I am not an expert merchant, but I understand that in some places they are very valuable. Taysees are said to be almost as expert in herbs as the Tirhans, after all..." said Noakh, rather upset. Taysees had wide knowledge of herbs, something useful and therefore, not feeding the myth of hatred, a reason not to comment such a feature.

"I am a merchant of another kind, Noakh," Sigüen replied. "Much more selective than those two taysees, judging by their miserable herbs." Sigüen's smile was one of superiority.

As he spoke, he gave the reins to Hilzen in order to search through his merchandise. He took out a bottle of wine and three tankards, passing each of them a tankard after filling all three.

"Speaking of precious objects, those swords that you carry look like good steel."

"Do not let appearances deceive you. They are mere trinkets..."

"I understand. I suppose then that they are swords of an apprentice. Are they not?"

"Something like that," Noakh lied. The less value he gave to his swords, the better. He should not forget that Sigüen was a stranger. His father had taught him not to trust people so readily; his experiences had only reinforced such lessons.

"Have you already killed someone with them?"

Noakh addressed the question by lowering his head. He took a long sip from his tankard, sadly remembering the incident the night his father died.

Sigüen nodded. "I see... At least you're not proud of it. And you, Hilzen, as I can see—you have a good crossbow, right?"

Hilzen pointed proudly at himself with his thumb. "I am a great shooter. I used it to hunt... and I have never failed!" He had lost all modesty after emptying his jug.

The merchant turned down a weedy path. A path full of weeds, Noakh knew, suggested that it was not very well traveled.

"We will rest here," Sigüen said, tugging the reins to halt the horse. "We will make a bonfire and continue talking. It's getting late; traveling on this old wagon is not exactly what I would call a pleasure."

It was indeed getting dark. Although the sky was cloudy—a condition that was quite usual throughout the queendom—it seemed that time was going to give a truce. Sleeping outdoors while it was raining was not the best feeling. They would sleep on the floor that night. Sigüen and Noakh gathered enough twigs and branches to make a crude mattress and also to build a fire, while Hilzen, willing to show his skill with his crossbow, had gone deep into the forest.

"We can sing songs. I can start. 'The Sailor and the Mermaid,'" Hilzen had suggested, seeming really animated. *"The mermaid was a real squid and ended up eating the sailor..."* He began to laugh as he pounded his stomach with his fist.

The fire lit, as Noakh could build a fire easily after his year in the forest. The night continued its pace.

They were surrounded by the forest, having ventured slightly off the road. This way was better, Noakh knew: It helped them avoid unexpected visitors. They roasted a rabbit over the fire. Hilzen, showing off his artfulness with the crossbow, had managed to hunt after they set up camp. Sigüen continued filling their glasses with wine. And as is the case with every self-respecting man, the intake of alcohol made these three men expert philosophers.

102

12. Attack

After nightfall, the three went to sleep. They had no difficulties falling asleep—they were helped, no doubt, by their intake of alcohol. Noakh slept with his swords, a custom his father had taught him long ago.

It was a cold night. The moon appeared in the sky when the clouds did not hide it. Shadows danced in the trees—the result of the fire—accompanied by the diverse sounds of the forest. Fortunately none of the sounds were disturbing enough to wake the travelers. Nonetheless, Hilzen, awakened by the call of nature, walked from his sleeping place. He went more deeply into the forest, looking for a tree that required a proper irrigation. Even though alcohol was still flowing through his blood, he had been sensible enough to take along his crossbow. One could never know when some nocturnal animal might decide to attack. It was true that he no longer cared to die, but even so. He had made a promise, after all.

* * *

In the camp, while Hilzen irrigated a young sapling, two shadows approached Noakh and Sigüen. When they were only a few steps away and hidden by a tree, they each drew a rope from their packs. Their shadows now dancing from the light of the fire, they jumped on their victim.

Noakh awoke, alarmed. At first he thought the two shadows falling on him were beasts. Reality was much worse. It was two men. The two, their faces covered, tied him up. He struggled, trying to release himself and straining to reach his swords. Realizing his intent, one of the men kicked the swords from out of his reach. The other man delivered a strong blow to Noakh's head, stunning him then taking advantage of Noakh's disoriented state to bind his hands and feet with rope.

"Sigüen! Help me!" Noakh implored.

The merchant sat on a log, eating a slice of peach with a knife while watching Noakh being captured. When he heard Noakh beg for his help, he stood up, keeping his knife and throwing the rest of the fruit into the fire.

"I'm afraid not, Noakh. I'm afraid not... Tell me, where is Hilzen?"

Noakh then suddenly realized that his traveling companion was not there. Perhaps he had run away? He looked around stupidly, searching for him. The two assailants then uncovered their faces. Crooked noses, short and peculiar hairstyles. They were both taysees—credits to their people's bad reputation.

"Hilzen knew your intentions from the moment we met you, Sigüen," Noakh lied. "By now he is surely arriving at the nearest village, looking for help. You still have time to reconsider your actions!" Buying some time while he talked, he began to consider his options. Given the shortage thereof, it did not take long for him to reach a conclusion.

He was tied hands and feet. His swords, though lying on the ground, were far enough away so that, if he broke free, the taysees would get there ahead of him. There were two of them and, of course, Sigüen... *You need not be a genius,* he thought. The situation was complicated. Moreover, he could not think clearly, not only because of the effects of the wine but also due to the feelings of betrayal that overwhelmed him by his abandonment of Hilzen.

Sigüen laughed at Noakh's words.

"In that case, we'd better hurry." Sigüen looked at the taysees. "Kill him and get in the wagon!" he ordered while he was wiping off his knife on his shirt and walking away from the fire. "Remember I said I was much more than a discriminating merchant, Noakh? The meat of human pigs like you is my merchandise. You will soon be part of a collection of skins purchased with some bourgeoisie's rotten money!"

One of the taysees approached Noakh from behind. He began to cover his nose and mouth, trying to choke him—his skin would remain untouched, allowing the merchant and taysees to obtain a higher price.

Noakh began to struggle. He tried biting the taysee's fingers. But the taysee, having acquired some experience in his task, avoided Noakh's attack. The air in Noakh's lungs soon began to expire. He was trying to

104

breathe, when it was obvious he couldn't. He started to shake his body hard, but the other taysee had joined his colleague in preventing Noakh from breaking free. His eyes widened. He began to sweat in panic. He tried to scream with all his strength, but the taysee's hands still covered his mouth, turning his scream into a low, drowned murmur. As he began to feel the effects of a lack of oxygen, he shook once again. He had to break free no matter what.

Suddenly the taysee choking Noakh screamed with pain. He turned back to the forest. A bolt buzzing from out of the trees had struck him in the back. Despite not knowing what had happened, Noakh took advantage of the opportunity. He knocked his forehead against the head of the other taysee, who had been distracted as he watched his partner. Then he jumped into the fire.

His hands held down to the fire, his skin began to burn—just like the ropes that bound him. Nothing the heir of the Fireos could not withstand. As the ropes on his hands turned to ashes, Noakh spotted his swords. He jumped towards them. Fearing Distra would awake again, he was sensible enough to reach for his standard sword. Weapon in hand, he quickly cut the ropes off his legs.

Seeing Noakh's intentions, Sigüen pounced on him, his knife held high. At the last moment, Noakh deflected Sigüen's attack. He kicked him fiercely, pushing him back toward the fire. Taking advantage of the distance, he lunged powerfully toward Sigüen, launching a powerful thrust that his opponent's knife could not block.

Maybe it was fate. Maybe he had made a mistake when looking at his two swords. It was dark. It was a matter of only a second. Maybe he still was stunned by the lack of oxygen, or maybe it was the wine that still flowed in his blood. But the sword that had pierced Sigüen was Distra.

As a consequence of the bloody attack, the blade turned completely red. It started to glow. With panic in his eyes Noakh tried to release it, but something kept his fingers clutched tightly around the hilt. He tried to command it—but it was impossible. The sword had shed too much blood. The weapon had become too thirsty. Distra took control again, ripping through Sigüen's body.

Noakh circled around the fire, gloating. Sigüen was really terrified, so he was that he did not seem to realize his clothes where all covered with his own blood, what he was witnessing was certainly not human. Noakh's eyes were full of madness. Distra's blade burst in flames, still dripping with blood.

With a malevolent smile, Noakh brandished Distra in both hands, drawing the sword vertically in the air before him. He launched a fierce slash, splitting Sigüen in two. The merchant's body collapsed to the ground, a mixture of flames, tears, and a pool of blood... inert... burning and bleeding in equal measure.

Still thirsty for combat, Noakh picked up his steel sword and ran in search of his other opponents.

* * *

The taysees, who had witnessed how Sigüen had died, hesitated to retreat. However, their ambition proved more powerful than their reason: Noakh's sword was too valuable to leave behind, and there were two of them to fight him.

Noakh approached them, deliberately dragging Distra on the ground, leaving a furrow of burned sand and flames in his wake. The vision of the madman approaching did not prevent the taysees from attacking him. One beckoned to the other and, thus positioned—one of the two always at Noakh's back—they did credit to their reputation.

The taysees' attacks were always quick and precise, and their guard was more than decent. Noakh's attacks, however, were abrupt—powerful but lacking in strategy, very different from his training sessions with his father, when Noakh was always in control.

While the taysee in front of Noakh dodged and rolled, blocking Noakh's attacks, the other taysee attacked from behind, causing the Fireo to turn around to defend his rear.

As the battle continued, Hilzen, from the top of a tree, could not move. He was frozen with terror. He had witnessed Noakh's fight with Sigüen: the rawness and brutality with which he had finished the merchant off. And that sword. He had never seen anything like it. What he was witnessing could not be the act of a human but that of an evil and ruthless demon; fire, in the Aquadom, was a sacrilege. Even so, his wife's words back at the gravesite prevailed.

He aimed his crossbow, trying to find a good line, but the frenzy of combat and the taysees' continuous movement prevented him from obtaining a safe shot—one that would not harm Noakh. Whether his desire was to not hurt his companion or simply to not be the next victim who died at the hands of that demon, he could not say. He knew only that making himself a victim of such a demon was not the best way to rejoin his family.

The taysees continued to gain ground. Noakh let out loud cries while making inaccurate thrusts with the sword that were easily diverted. The taysees had learned quickly not to be burned by his fire. Then, taking advantage of an opening, the taysee behind Noakh landed a blow to his back. He expected the blow to be lethal. However, Noakh shifted away, keeping the wound shallow. With a wild scream, he spun around, his sword held before him, creating a disc of fire that, shooting forth, impacted his two attackers. They howled at the burns they suffered. Noakh then charged the taysee who stood in front of him. Taking advantage of the distance by building speed—and holding the weapon with both hands—he launched an immense flare that immediately consumed the taysee. He died after a cry of horror.

The other opponent, furious at the death of his companion, rose and charged at Noakh. The boy evaded the attack by stepping to his right, leaving the taysee unprotected. With a scream of fury, he stuck the sword, wrapped in flames, between the ribs of his opponent, staring into his eyes. The taysee's blue eyes reflected his inner fear. Then a trickle of blood blotted his mouth, and he fell to the ground. After a shout of victory, raising his sword towards the sky, Noakh approached the flames of the bonfire.

With the crossbow against his chest, Hilzen pressed his body against the tree while praying and trembling with fear. He did not know how Noakh might react if he found him. He did not want to die, not at the hands of a demon, not as an offering to the fire god, or a sacrifice to whatever being such a creature worshipped. He remembered his first encounter with Noakh—the gallows, the flare that broke the branch—and now he understood how he had managed to free him from such distance. However, at that moment, the boy had seemed normal, maybe too meddlesome, but not even close to the blood-lusting beast that circled the fire.

Suddenly, Noakh fell to the ground, unconscious. The wound in his side was bleeding incessantly. The forest grew silent. Only the rattle of the fire could be heard. Hilzen waited a prudent amount of time before climbing down from the tree. He began get closer to Noakh, quietly, aiming his crossbow at the inert body of his companion, which still was lying on the ground. When he had drawn close to Noakh, he aimed the bolt at his head, intent on ending the life of whatever beast occupied

Noakh's body. He closed one eye to aim better, his index finger feeling the steel of the trigger. He quietly recited a prayer... and then he closed his eyes. But the next moment he lowered his weapon.

"Damn it, Marne, why are you making it so difficult for me?" he complained.

First he made sure the boy was completely unconscious by kicking him with his boot twice, just in case. He quickly picked up his sword then tossed it away. Finally he leaned down to check Noakh's wound. It was deep, although it looked like a clean cut. He ran towards Sigüen's wagon in search of objects that could be of help. Rummaging around in the wagon, he found a bottle of oak alcohol, a strong drink with a bittersweet taste.

"Perfect."

Hilzen picked up the bottle and gulped two deep gulps then continued to rummage through the wagon.

He covered Noakh's wound with alcohol to clean it. With the other hand he held the crossbow, pointing it at him, just in case. He washed the wound as best as he could and dressed it with mud and leaves mixed with water—a bandage that would not last long but that served to do what needed to be done.

"Look at you, Hilzen. Look at you!" he said, realizing what he was doing.

13. The sword under water

The sword lies under the waterfall. The water flows over it. It cannot rust, since it's the sword of the Aquadom: Crystalline. The water itself. One of the four sacred weapons of the kingdoms. It belongs to the royal family—and there it rests, in the palace, an entire room dedicated to it.

The queen alone has access to this room. And her daughters occasionally do too—but only during the ritual. One of them will finally be able to use the sword and become queen... eventually. Until now, none of them has succeeded, but this does not imply that one of them was not the Lacrima, because it was not the first time that Crystalline had selected the legitimate heiress only after several attempts, and after several years. Every day, the young women queued before the door guarded by ten soldiers from the Royal Guard. With them stood Igüenza, the elderly woman who had been granted the honor of the girls' tutelage—the same priestess who had witnessed the election of the current queen, Graglia.

The oldest were always the first to perform the ritual, as if to ensure the small ones would not be selected before the elders had their chance, always in the same order, from eldest to youngest. Their mother, the queen, had been the second of her sisters, and her grandmother the fourth, something that encouraged the older daughters to believe their chances were much improved compared to what might ordinarily be expected. One by one they passed through the doorway and went barefoot into the room, where, at the back, under a small waterfall, lay Crystalline. Today, as with every day, they each brandished the sword, and with its tip they touched the water, creating small circles, and today, as with every day, nothing else happened. They had not been told what would, in fact, happen should one of them be chosen—only that if they were, they would know.

All of them performed the act with some fear, something they each would not admit to their other sisters. A fear not for the act itself but for the moment in which one of them was chosen, in which one of them would become the main character whereas the rest would remain in supporting roles, mere sisters of the queen, with a relevance that was practically null. They only had to see their aunts. Women who lived with all kinds of luxuries, who had married into noble or wealthy families to strengthen ties and their own family's power—or, on the contrary, had become part of the queendom's army. A destiny that for many was not so bad, but that—for them, until now, raised as princesses with the illusion of one day possibly reigning—was no more than a consolation prize, more bitter than sweet.

The older women had sometimes commented that they preferred the way in which the heir was chosen in the other kingdoms. Some believed that the Fireos' ritual revealed a fairer system—partly influenced by the fact that they preferred to see anyone else as a monarch rather than as their own sister. If it was not she, then no one should reign. On the other hand, they seemed to be unanimous regarding the unsophisticated method of the Aertians, which they said consisted of throwing all the five-year-old children from a precipice, although they did not know how much truth there was on that particular point. In the Aquadom, meanwhile, only the daughters of the queen were allowed to perform the ritual.

One by one they performed the test without success. Then it was Vienne's turn. That morning she had fallen asleep and so was to be the last to perform the ritual, despite the fact that she was not the youngest. She approached the water with little desire to get her white dress wet, entering the shallow pool while walking towards the sword; her dress began to fill with air bubbles. On the way she yawned, something that would have caused total disapproval from Igüenza. Vienne walked with little affinity for the water. *It's cold. In the morning it should be forbidden for a princess to get wet,* she thought as she kept drawing closer. For her this was routine. She did not want to be a queen. She knew that she would not be queen anyway. She didn't resemble her mother at all and did not want to; her manners couldn't be less appropriate, as both her mother and Igüenza gladly pointed out. She did not hate her mother, but rather respected her in a way that most would define as fear.

Vienne approached Crystalline. It was a beautiful sword. Her blade was slightly, almost imperceptibly blue. The blackish grip was long enough to accommodate both of her hands. And the silvery quillons were short and perpendicular to the blade, while the wheel pommel was decorated with an interlaced ornament.

Then she picked her up, it was a light sword. She held her with her delicate little hands and, with a bored gesture, used the sword to touch the water. Without waiting, she shrugged while proceeding to leave the sword in its place, on the small altar, another day more. The worst thing about not having any princess chosen yet was that she would have to do the same thing tomorrow. She was about to turn around when something strange happened. Her eyes could not stop looking at the water. What ought to have been small ripples formed from steel touching water happened to become a whirlpool... which gradually grew bigger. Vienne turned away, but it was too late. The whirlwind had caught her. It was beginning to drag her to the bottom. The water was submerging her so she tried to stand on her feet, keeping her balance to avoid being drawn under while unsuccessfully looking for something to cling to. But the whirl did not stop its effort, dragging her harder until it finally managed to overtake her. Vienne tried to scream for help, but she couldn't. The whirlpool dragged her completely under. The water silenced her screams. This lasted for only a few seconds, which for Vienne seemed like years. It all ended with a thunderous explosion. The water shot out in all directions, revealing a clear path to the shore. Then, after a brief pause, the shoreline disappeared. The room had returned to normal.

Igüenza opened the door, alarmed. She had anticipated what had happened. With a cry of amazement and joy, she approached Vienne and hugged her while sobbing. Vienne was completely shocked and scared, too much to understand what had just happened, or perhaps frightened precisely *because of* what had just happened. Crystalline had chosen her heiress. The Lacrima.

"It's over, dear, it's over," Igüenza whispered sweetly as she combed Vienne's hair with her old bony fingers. Vienne returned her hug and tried to hold back her tears, without success.

The ten soldiers of the Royal Guard made the Aquo reverence and stood in position, motionless. Her sisters looked at her and exchanged glances between them, more than aware of what had just happened. The majority of them did not know how to feel, as something that had become their day-to-day routine—performing the ritual of the passage of water, as it was called—had come to an end. Many of them felt happy for their sister, Aienne looked particularly proud of Vienne, others envied her, some felt sorry. Not so in the case of her older sister, Katienne, whose nails were pressing so tightly against her palms she had started to bleed.

Her world of fantasy was crumbling in front of her. She had hoped to be the heiress, and not without reason. Her mother, the queen, had more than insinuated that she would be a *great* queen. How could she tell her otherwise? Katienne was the living reflection of her mother, not only in appearance, but also in her way of being, even her manners. This had led her to create her own fantasy. In fact, she had everything planned. She had chosen her first husband and had even known what palace rules she would change as soon as she was queen.

A feeling of repulsion ran through her entire body as she looked at the rightful heiress. She would not have forgiven any of her other sisters had they been chosen—but Vienne? It had to be a joke, the worst she had ever heard. Vienne's comportment was the complete opposite to Katienne's way of being. *She would be a terrible queen!* she thought. How could the Aqua Deus choose her? She was really trying not to think badly of her god since she knew it would know best... but believing in the good judgment of her god was not proving easy at all.

Katienne looked at the rest of her sisters, searching for any gesture to help her see that they were on her side, that they were as indignant as she was regarding the divine decision, but all of them were too busy kneeling before Vienne, something that Katienne was forced to imitate, though not without a certain reluctance.

While she was duplicating their gesture, she could not help but start biting her lower lip due to her rage, bearing her teeth down on it to such an extent that blood flowed slightly. *She isn't even happy!* she thought, frustrated as she watched her sister suspiciously. She was not mistaken. Vienne had not received the news very well, and she was not trying to hide it either. Until now, all the sisters had been treated like princesses, and her dealings with her mother had been merely cordial, since she, as the ruler of a queendom, had no time to take care of her lineage. Now, with Vienne having been elected future queen, everything was different. Her mother would assume her guardianship and teach her the performances and arts necessary to be a respected leader while simultaneously being loved by her subjects. Playing with her sisters and the lessons with Igüenza were *over.* For Vienne to be selected as the

Lacrima was a smack of reality. It was hard for Vienne to hide the tears in her eyes.

As soon as the queen found out, she gave the order for Vienne's selection to be announced. They removed Vienne's chambers from the common hallway, along which all their bedrooms had been placed. She was the heiress now; she deserved better: a larger room than the one she currently slept it—and much better decorated. If she thought that, as a princess, she did not lack anything, looking back now, as an heiress, the previous situation seemed to be that of a beggar woman. She had a huge bed, full of swan-feather pillows and a mirror as big as her closet, where all her new clothes hung, beautiful dresses of all colors. The queen had been very explicit about that from the moment she had Vienne's bedroom moved: Her clothes had to be different from her sisters'—until now they had all dressed the same—and of course all her new possessions (her shoes, jewelry, cloaks) had to be brand new.

The queen's reaction upon hearing the news had been as expected. One of her advisors gave her the good tidings. The queen received the novel announcement with her classic smile, hiding her disappointment because, for her, Vienne could not have been a more inappropriate choice. Unlike Katienne, who in her opinion would have been the most appropriate. But the Aqua Deus was capricious. The queen knew that better than anyone, and their god had indeed wanted one of the little ones to govern—someday. But there was still time for that. She still had time to mold Vienne to her will. If Crystalline had considered her the Lacrima, it meant Vienne should have potential—possibilities that she was not yet able to see in the tall skinny little girl with long straight hair that adorned her continuous displays of boredom.

Vienne was announced to the queendom. Couriers carried messages to all the cities to proclaim the news. Additionally, a dance was to be held in the following weeks in honor of the future queen. Only those who held the highest positions and who were the richest people in the queendom were invited. A perfect opportunity for Vienne to begin her sojourn in the world of royalty. For Graglia, the queen, Vienne was still far from being a fairytale princess—which would be ideal for the dance. *How simple it would have been if Katienne had been chosen,* thought the queen.

All of Vienne's classes were also going to be different from now on. Until now she had received lessons in the art of combat using the sword, like her sisters. This explained why her aunts, being so well versed in

113

fighting and strategy, were in charge of the Royal Guard, the River Guard, and the Sea Guard—the three most powerful military organizations that protected the Aquadom. Not to forget her aunt, Alvia, who was a Knight of Water. Some said that the aunts' designation as commanders was not only related to their skills with the sword, in which they all excelled, but also to their status as sisters of the queen, which allowed them to ensure the loyalty of these factions to a greater extent than would otherwise have been possible.

Now, instead of her regular sword lessons, Vienne had to learn how to use Crystalline, how to release all its power—knowledge that only the queen could teach her. Crystalline had the power over the water itself. How that power might work on Vienne's hands was still to be found, since Crystalline had granted different abilities to all of her previous owners. Her teachings did not end there. From now on, Vienne was to be the queen's shadow. She would be present at any event the queen attended and would be privy to any decision that the queen made, although she would act as merely a spectator, of course.

Queen Graglia stood in the middle of the pool, her hands on her back, watching Vienne wielding Crystalline. The queen's skin was perfect, as if her body had long forgotten it had to get older. Their bare feet were under the water, their dresses were wet.

"Focus," Graglia said. "Crystalline is at your command. She will obey you, and will show you her true power."

Vienne tried to focus, not knowing exactly what to do. *Please, do something, Crystalline*, she thought. She stood looking at the blade, waiting for the sword to do anything that would be sufficient for her mother. The sword failed to obey her pleading.

"Give me the sword," Graglia said dryly while extending her arm.

Vienne nodded and passed Crystalline to her mother.

"Using Crystalline is actually pretty simple. We do not require spells, or magic words of any sort. We are connected to the sword, we command and Crystalline obeys." The indigo-blue eyes of Graglia met her daughter's, and the queen drew Crystalline to the pool, its tip touched the surface creating small circles. Then, a burst of water emerged with an explosion, raising to the top of the roof. Then water fell from the sky as if it were raining. "What you have just seen is my blessing. I shall explain it to you later, since it might be too advanced for you yet. So let's start with something much simpler." Graglia then pointed to the blade of the sword, small droplets of water emanating from it. Vienne looked in

114

amazement. "Crystalline weeps—this is the most basic technique, so I hope you will not disappoint me and will learn it soon." She walked closer and gave Crystalline to her daughter. "You can enter this room whenever you want. You have been chosen, after all. You better come here and practice."

"Yes, mother," Vienne said while holding Crystalline. She looked to the blade of the sword, which was dry, with no water emanating from it now that the sacred weapon was in her hands.

"But not now, other matters require my attention. And I want you to be present."

* * *

Every day, while the queen sat on her throne, a counselor updated her about the rumors and facts that occurred throughout the other three kingdoms. Knowing the kingdoms' movements was crucial if she was to make decisions as effectively as possible, covering any type of information at her disposal. The queen had spies throughout the other kingdoms, which in turn made her suspect that her enemies' spies more than likely were in her territory as well. However, the queen was more than careful when appointing people to trusted positions, so she expected the information leaked to the other kingdoms to be the least valuable— or at least the least sensitive.

This morning, while the counselor was speaking in front of the Graglia and Vienne, the queen fixed her eyes on her daughter, who was standing on her chair, her head held by her fist, seemingly not enjoying the matters discussed at the meeting.

"Tell me, Vienne, how do you see our relationship with the rest of the kingdoms?" the queen asked.

The princess fielded the question, although she was totally unprepared.

"What do you mean, mother?" Vienne said hesitantly.

The counselor, in spite of being interrupted, continued standing upright, his eyes looking at the ceiling, his arms behind his back as he waited for the queen and princess to finish. It was not advisable to show one's feelings to the queen, unless one's goal was to be hung from a tree.

Given the condescending gaze of the queen, Vienne set her hand to her chin while saying out loud: "We have the Aqua Deus on our side. It provides us with the water and is so merciful that it also shares it with the other kingdoms." She beamed, proud of her response. She had actually recited a tidbit of information she had heard from Igüenza during some boring lesson. "That proves we are the good ones," she added, shrugging. Actually, she had no idea how to answer... How could she anyway? All she knew about those kingdoms came from what Igüenza had told her—and from gossip.

"The good ones... so innocent," the queen replied, visibly disappointed. "So for you this world is summed up in good and evil?" she concluded. "A simple way of seeing life, if you ask me. Tell me, Vienne, let's say that you want the last strawberry-and-mango cookie. You want it with all your might. You go to the jar where the cookies are, and there you meet one of your sisters. She wants the cookie as much as you do. Is your sister the good one? Or is it you?"

"We could split the cookie in half and share it," Vienne resolved.

"Share it? A queen? Oh, dear... we don't share. We take it, we fight for it. One day you will be queen, Vienne, so you better get this stuck in your brain: You will fight for something more than absurd cookies, and you won't be able to share *that*. In this world, there is no good and evil, dear—only sides. Master Meredian," the queen said, referring to the counselor, who was still waiting in front of them, "maybe you can help us with today's lesson. In a conflict, who defines the good and the bad?"

"The winners, my queen," the counselor answered firmly while still looking at the ceiling. Meredian was a tall skinny man with an elongated nose and thinning strands around the crown of his head.

"The winners, that's right." Then the queen looked again to Vienne. "Do you remember the war against the Fireos that was carried out by your great-grandmother, the Great Legan?"

"The Battle of the Blackened Mountains?" asked Vienne, after briefly recalling her lessons.

"Exactly. Those bastards wanted to take our mountains and make them part of their kingdom. Our ancestor did not allow it—and for good reason! They crushed the enemy's dirty army and made them sign the peace treaty that lasted thirty years. We won, and they signed whatever we put in front of them in order to maintain peace. Do you have any doubt who is considered the evil one in that conflict?"

"But they wanted to take away our land. That's the reason they are considered the evil ones, right?" Vienne answered, confused.

"See?" the queen said while she and Meredian looked at each other, complicit in Vienne's lesson. "That's only true because we won. The

116

reality is that this territory was not ours—nor theirs. Those were mountains that we appropriated for ourselves in the first place, something that the neighboring kingdom did not like very much, even though until that moment they probably did not even know the mountains existed. But after we got them, that location turned out to be considered the most important region of their kingdom..."

"I see. The winners write the story," Vienne repeated.

14. Awakening

Noakh woke up. He felt horrible, his skull felt as though it had been bashed in and his head was about to explode. The wound on his back caused by one of the taysees burned, and the muscles in his hands and legs had tightened. He was handcuffed, his hands tied so tightly his wrists ached. Then he began to remember. "Sigüen!" The merchant had betrayed them and had been about to finish them off, but then...

"I see you've awakened."

Hilzen's tone was serious. With one hand he held the reins of the horse, keeping control of the wagon, while his other hand pointed his crossbow at Noakh's chest. He turned the wagon off the road and stopped it. "Well, I think we have to talk." Hilzen then climbed out of the wagon, and helped Noakh to do so since he was tied, still aiming at his chest with his crossbow.

"Hilzen, I can explain," Noakh said, trying to speak calmly. Hilzen's attitude made him understand what had happened that night... which was exactly what he had feared had happened. Noakh also realized he was no longer carrying his swords. Hilzen probably kept them hidden, he guessed. "What you saw last night... It wasn't me... Well, it *was* me... but at the same time it wasn't. It's difficult to explain..."

"What I saw last night?" Hilzen was really furious, his right eye tickling nervously. "Last night I witnessed how a man... No... Calling *that* a man would be improper... A beast... Yes! How a beast confronted his enemies in the most cruel and ruthless way, brandishing the weapon of a demon from hell as if he had been born with it. Enjoying ending his enemies' lives by wrapping them in flames! Witchcraft! No, worse! Demonic arts. No sorcerer is capable of doing something like that. What happened yesterday was not human. Do you want to tell me what the hell that was?" He was out of his mind. He looked exhausted. His appearance reflected a mixture of anger and fear, and his forehead was drenched in sweat.

Whether he believes me or not, I'm lost, Noakh thought. *An oath is one thing, but to forgive the life of the heir of the Fire Kingdom? Someone like Hilzen? I'm dead, I cannot lie... No, I do not want to lie...*

Noakh did nothing but lower his head and snort. Then he smiled. *Time to see if destiny is on my side...*

He began his story. Hilzen's face showed nothing but disbelief. Then—as Noakh's story progressed—his eyes reflected bewilderment. After Noakh spoke of the scar on his hand, Hilzen's panic began to surface in his eyes. When Noakh mentioned his right to the throne, it was hysteria's turn to play on Hilzen's face. Finally Hilzen stood up and, glaring at Noakh with wide eyes, he began to throw curses and strike the air furiously with his fists.

Noakh sighed with relief. Hilzen's anger showed he had believed him. Another thing, a very different one, would be Hilzen's decision about what to do next.

"It must be a joke! For the Aqua Deus's sake! It cannot be! Please, Noakh, tell me... No! Better to not say anything. You've already said more than enough! And I... I'm helping you! I'm an accomplice! I'm a damn accomplice! I will never reach the sea, and I can't make up for my mistake... Or maybe I can?" He laughed hysterically. "I will send you to the authorities! To the City Guards... No! To the queen herself! She's the high priestess, too, after all! I'm sure she'll forgive me! She'll absolve my sins and then..." Hilzen again broke into hysterics. "Damn it! Why? Why did you make me promise it?" His hands were drawn to the sky. As he moaned, his face showed a mixture of panic and despair.

Noakh did not understand anything.

"Promise? What are you talking about?"

"I promised it to... It doesn't matter now! The point is that I can't kill you—and I should not help you either. It's a dead end!" Among his screams of despair, Hilzen came to see the light. "I know... What if I leave you tied in the middle of the woods? You would die—and technically I would not have killed you," he said, reflecting on his idea.

"It's not a bad idea." Noakh wasn't angry at Hilzen's attitude. The various pains assaulting his body weighed on him much more than his companion's hysterical threats. "However, you should pray every prayer you know, to any god you know. Because if, for some reason, I survived,

I would find you. I will make sure my inner demon, as you call it, tastes your blood."

"Shut up! Let me think," Hilzen said, sitting on the ground with his hand placed on his chin. Thoughtfully, he speculated about his choices. In his mind, the words *I promise* resonated heavily, causing such frustration that he hit the ground while cursing.

"Then—?"

"You know, you do not seem dangerous at all right now."

Hilzen looked at Noakh as one observes a piece of cattle in a competition.

"I already told you, it's not me... It's just that I still can't control Distra. Sometimes it controls me... that's all."

"Are you sure that... such a monst... such a thing can be controlled?" Hilzen said skeptically.

"Yes... No... I suppose." He shrugged. "Right now I'm unable to control it, but there must be some way, I'm sure."

"I admire your faith in that aspect. You know, one of the reasons I joined you was that I thought I would probably find a quick and somewhat dignified death, but this... it's too much, it's too dangerous! A lot of innocent people can die! And fire... blasphemy in its purest form! As you say, if it's the sword that holds the evil power, why keep using it? Why not destroy it?"

A chill ran down Noakh's back. "What? Absolutely not! I will not say it is because it confers power, not because it is proof that I am the phoenix, much less because it is a legendary weapon ... But"—he paused for a second—"my father died because of that sword, and I once made the mistake of abandoning it. I will not allow the death of my father to be in vain. I will control Distra, no matter what difficulties I might have doing so. I know I can do it," Noakh stated emphatically.

Hilzen, listening to Noakh's words, was still more amazed. He went to the wagon and took the sword. He had hidden it buried under all of Sigüen's merchandise. Then, returning to Noakh, he unsheathed it and held it in his hands, examining the sword closely.

"So you are not an unickey Aqureo after all, but a pure Fireo... which is much worse if you ask me," Hilzen said while reflecting. "You say that this sword is the reason why they killed your father, and yet..." Hilzen brought the sword closer to his face, so close that a large and deformed version of his own nose reflected in its blade. "Something so ordinary and mundane... It looks like a completely normal sword... barely adorned... and you say that only you can use it?"

"Any phoenix can, the ones chosen by the fire swords themselves," he corrected. "Not only me. Wulkan, the Fireo king, can also, obviously. You can try it yourself."

Hilzen's eyes opened wide.

"Can I? Won't it be dangerous? I do not want to turn into a demonic being. I saw more than enough of that, watching the sword in action. I'm also sure that just wielding this sword is a blasphemy of the highest order." But he thought about it again. "Maybe there is a certain religious vagueness. I mean, I do not think any other Aquo has ever tried before."

"Do it already or shut up!" said Noakh, starting to feel cold.

"Fine, fine," Hilzen said. "I only have to cut myself, true?" Noakh nodded quietly. Hilzen hesitantly cut himself on the palm of his hand. He closed his eyes, waiting for something to happen. He opened his eyes a few seconds later, looking at himself, verifying that there was no change in either his appearance or his attitude.

"If it were not a terrible blasphemy, I would say you had expected something to happen," said Noakh, jesting. Hilzen, for his part, had momentarily grimaced in disappointment. "I'm sorry to tell you, Hilzen, but I'm afraid you're not the Ascendant Phoenix." He was enjoying the situation, brandishing a smile while still on his knees, his arms tied. "And now, are you going to untie me? My wrists are killing me..."

After spending a moment considering Noakh's question, Hilzen sheathed the sword.

"All right, I'll do it, with one condition. I will not deny it is obvious that your destiny is linked to the sword. So I should not deprive you of it. In the same way, your meddlesome acts linked my destiny to yours until my death, so I will carry Distra. At least until it is no longer such a danger."

"I do not know, Hilzen," Noakh replied uncomfortably, his voice sounding slightly weaker than usual, while the wound on his back ached again, as he was probably falling ill. "That sword is a lot of responsibility. No," he corrected. "It's my responsibility." Noakh was obviously uncomfortable with the idea of not being allowed to carry Distra, not only because of the sword's significance, but also because his fighting technique was to always use two swords. However, he observed that he was still tied with the ropes. Hilzen arched one eyebrow, understanding the absurdity of his companion's refusal.

122

"Although, come to think of it, I do not think I have any alternative. But, Hilzen, promise you will protect the sword with your life."

Hilzen nodded. "And may this promise end my life end soon," he said with despair.

15. The clues

"I do not understand what we are doing here. Why do the soldiers of the queendom have to waste time on these things? A man who was in the wrong time and place—and two taysees who gave him what he deserved... Case solved, you are welcome."

The City Guard soldier snapped his tongue, visibly upset. He was a tall man with a small scar on his left cheek. Usually a case of accidental death was not important enough for the queendom to waste their time on. After all, it was just a run-in with a few taysees. However, this time had been different. Their superiors had ordered them to come to this precise place and wait for a higher officer. Their orders emphasized the importance of being present here as soon as dawn—a command the soldiers had received reluctantly.

"Shut up, Biveo. If he hears you complaining, your next mission will be the gallows—and mine too!" said the other soldier with a bulging nose and a scraggly beard. He slyly elbowed his partner.

Biveo, indignant, knocked the ground with the butt of his spear, frustrated. The two soldiers were standing side by side at the scene of the incident, anticipating their orders.

"I do not want to shut up," he responded indignantly—although he spoke softly now, in case their superior could hear him. "This man is responsible for us being out of bed, and all for some men with a few burns. It's absurd. In addition, he has not even introduced himself."

"You can't be serious. You're a bumpkin with a big mouth. That man is Gelegen! He is a legend in the army! He served for more than twenty years, participated in the Battle of the Flaming Beaches—they say his intervention saved his detachment from certain death. Now he is engaged in investigating matters for the queendom, having the favor of the queen... something only the Knights of Water happen to have, except for him! He is a blasphemous bastard son of a bitch, but his atheism is apparently useful enough; the queen has not taken him to the gallows..."

"And you, why do you know so many things about him?" Biveo reproached indignantly.

"Because on the contrary to you, I'm not a lousy goblin. Many consider him the fifth Knight of Water, although he does not officially hold the title," the soldier said. He looked at the man with admiration. Gelegen was standing a few feet away, inspecting one of the corpses with deep interest.

"That old man, a Knight of Water?" Biveo snorted with contempt.

A quarrel was about to start between the two soldiers when Gelegen approached them, causing them to immediately look forward and stand firmly. Gelegen's clothes were a dark blue. A purple cloak draped across his back and a bluish hat adorned with a white feather with a black tip, concealed grey hair. His face, though burdened with signs of age, was energetic. His sky-blue eyes radiated life. Two scars adorned his face—a pair of cuts across his right eye, memories of a duel in which he had almost lost his eye. These features, along with his robust bearing and his well-trimmed beard, still blond, endowed him with a much younger appearance. From his belt hung a sword and a two-bullet powder gun, a weapon of the most advanced technology.

Gelegen beckoned to the soldiers. While still observing the scene he questioned Biveo.

"Tell me, soldier," he said in a serious and calm tone, searching the corpses for any clue. "What is your analysis of the situation?"

Biveo was about to say what he really thought. However, guessing his intentions, his partner gave a sly nudge as a warning—an action that did not go unnoticed by Gelegen. But he ignored it.

"Three corpses, my lord. A squabble by the taysees that went wrong."
"I see."

Without yet turning to them, Gelegen gestured with his hand—*come closer.* He inspected one of the corpses while standing just above it.

As they approached, the soldiers grimaced at the state of the corpse. From the torso to the head, it was split in half, parts of the tear totally deformed by the burns. A horrible sight.

"Those two there show signs of burns that occurred at the same time as their cuts, but this one... has been torn with extreme violence. Besides, except for the burned parts it is easily observed that this man's death has been the result of a single blow. What weapon is capable of performing such a cut? And the burns do not seem to have occurred afterwards; they seem to be part of the same cut. But that's impossible."

"Black magic," Biveo murmured, feeling a chill. He had not spoken low enough that Gelegen did not hear it.

"Magic is simply what science has not yet been able to explain, boy. Keep that in mind. I will not deny, however, that this situation is at the very least atypical—a second incident involving deaths as the result of what looks like weapons using fire in such a short period of time..." Gelegen had been involved in the investigation of the first incident a year ago: a house on fire, its two inhabitants—a father and his son—dead, along with all of the bandits, dead too. "It is certainly not accidental. That is why it has to be investigated thoroughly."

Gelegen continued investigating the terrain, trying to reconstruct the scene of the battle, situating himself at the stake near Sigüen's body.

"Due to the presence of the fire pit, the battle must have taken place at night. Probably they were camping. The most logical thing is that this one was the first to die. The taysees are farther from the fire pit... yet they also have burns. So it must have been the same weapon that killed them— or a similar one..." Gelegen grimaced. "There is something that does not match, though."

The soldiers, who were absorbed by Gelegen's deductive reasoning, could not repress their curiosity.

"What does not match, sir?"

"Something I do not see the relationship between... These two taysees probably worked together. Perhaps they ambushed those who were at the fire pit? But then, what about the third man? He suffered a similar fate. It could be that it all happened by chance, being in the wrong place at the wrong time."

Biveo raised his head proudly as he looked at his fellow soldier. Vihaim, the other soldier, looked at him reproachfully.

"But no. Too simple," Gelegen concluded.

Vihaim nodded while smiling. He did not dare to look at Biveo, who was indignant. "Maybe the three were already here when they were assaulted? Although two of them were taysees, could it be that the three of them were the assailants and were simply paid their due?"

And how does this fit with the first scenario of almost a year ago? And yet the marks of fire and rawness indicated that the same means had been used to finish off their enemies—a kind of righteous vengeance perhaps? And also... fire? Gelegen was puzzled and frustrated. What was he missing?

While Gelegen walked around the grounds and through the burned grass, he realized something.

"Wheels of a wagon and horseshoes... They left by wagon!"

He followed the prints in order to make his calculations. "Judging by the visibility of the marks they must already be a few days from here. Soldiers! Collect the corpses and take them to the nearest mortuary; have the morticians examine the bodies for any clue that has gone unnoticed. I'll go out to the road to look for more tracks."

"Sir," said Vihaim, not without some hesitation, "should we not alert the defense counselor?"

"Not yet. Leave it in my hands," Gelegen answered impassively.

16. An unexpected encounter

"It's getting worse."

Hilzen looked worriedly at the wound on Noakh's back. Its color was greenish purple. Although it had stopped bleeding a strong fever had appeared, accompanied by chills. A yellow and purulent liquid with a strong stench emanated from the wound, a development that did not bode well.

This was not a surprise, after all; the taysees were known for using various poisons in their weapons, so that if a fight continued for a lengthy period of time, their opponent's forces would gradually be depleted; similarly, if they were beaten in combat, the venom would take its revenge.

"I'm... fine."

Despite his attempts to appear normal, Noakh could barely speak. His forehead was bathed in sweat, and in general he looked awful. His teeth chattered and his body did not stop trembling. The movement of the wagon did not make his condition any better. Although Hilzen tried not to be alarmed, he snapped the reins vigorously, urging the horse to go faster while he frantically searched for a place where he could find assistance, someone who could be of help. Hilzen had tried to use all his medical knowledge and herbs, which were rather scarce, to try to heal the wound. But he had been unable to stop the advance of the poison. It continued to tighten its hold on Noakh, provoking him to make mad ravings. He began to babble sentences that did not make sense. Although he and Hilzen could not know, the taysees called this poison *larva*. It initially showed no effect but the effects of the poison gradually increased, eventually causing death. Its use was rare, since the taysees used to prefer other toxins, whose effect during combat was faster. However, larva had some appeal to certain taysees: a slow and painful death... poetry to their ears.

With a groan, Noakh fainted. Hilzen stopped the wagon immediately, shouting the name of his companion in a panic. Seeing that his head was burning hot, Hilzen threw all the water he had on him, without achieving any results. Noakh's body was inert. His face changed from expressing pain to becoming totally relaxed. His forehead began turning yellow and brown.

Hilzen did not want to lose him. He had already lost enough. *Why did the Aqua Deus take everyone but him?* Hilzen thought.

Terrified not only because of his promise but because he had come to appreciate the boy, he began to pray, frantically imploring the help of the god of water. Then, realizing how absurd it was to ask for help from a god who, being benevolent, would be indifferent to the death of the Fireos' phoenix, he stopped.

"Fire," Hilzen said loudly.

He rummaged in the wagon until he found the rope. After tying up Noakh completely, he checked several times that he was tightly bound. He had wrapped the rope around him so many times that most of his body was covered by it, except his right hand, which still was visible. Brandishing Distra, Hilzen placed the pommel in Noakh's hand and tied the hilt to his inert fingers as best he could.

"I will die at the hands of a demon." He laughed hysterically, aware of the absurdity of his plan, something he never would have dared to carry out were it not for the drastic situation. "Look at you, Hilzen," he said aloud. "Who was ever going to tell you, years ago, that you would be in a situation like this?"

He took Noakh's hand—the hand brandishing his sword. He drew it closely to his own left hand, and he could already feel the sharp blade touching his skin. Then he closed his eyes and made a sharp cut in his left hand. In his right hand he brandished the crossbow, a bolt already loaded and locked in place, in case any unforeseen event arose.

"Let's see if you can be of any use, inhuman beast!"

Blood covered the sword completely. It ran along the blade's edge until it tarnished the rope that tied Noakh's body, turning it pink.

Hilzen looked at Noakh with disappointment. He was as inert as he had been earlier. He fell to his knees in disappointment. Everything was over. He started to moan, feeling sorry; his plan had not worked. It seemed he was going to be alone again.

"I guess I'd better get some wood and burn his body, a decent burial for a Fireo." Hilzen muttered with sadness. He started to walk into the woods.

Then a loud roar made Hilzen fall to the ground, his crossbow falling from his hands as a result of the shock.

Noakh had opened his eyes. He fixed them on Hilzen with hatred and fury. He writhed fiercely, staggering back and forth, trying to free himself from the ropes. He shouted cries of frustration.

Hilzen stood up and walked in front of Noakh. "Aha. It worked!" he said, pointing with both hands. "So you are the devil that lives inside Noakh, eh? You don't seem that dangerous after all!" he added mockingly.

Noakh responded by throwing himself forward, trying to drive his sword into one of Hilzen's feet. But his movement was merely a clumsy attempt. Hilzen responded with a mocking laugh.

"Ha! Stupid beast, your crude attempts to kill me are pathetic. They make me want to kill you. Who would say that you could be useful?" Encouraged by the strength of his knots, Hilzen grew proud that his plan had worked. "I could use my crossbow to end your deplorable existence, returning you to the hell you come from. You're lucky that I get on so well with Noakh."

Carrying Noakh back to the wagon as best he could, being careful to prevent causing him further injury, he set him in his place on the wagon's wooden seat then tied him to the body of the wagon. Then he climbed onto the seat and continued their journey. Anyone who saw them would have witnessed a real spectacle. The horse plodded along while Hilzen held the reins in one hand while he pointed his crossbow at Noakh with his other. Noakh kept throwing barbs at Hilzen while screaming in fury. The horse moved agitatedly, unable to ignore Noakh's behavior in the wagon.

"Behave at once, stupid beast! Enjoy the scenery," Hilzen encouraged. "I'm sure that in your region you do not have such beautiful views. Look at that river, how beautiful it is. I suppose that in your land it must be something strange, as it should be to get washed. Your water will come from mud and puddles of rain. The truth is that I'm sorry for you." Hilzen was enjoying himself. Insulting that monster surely was raising his spirit. "As soon as we find some help, I want you to get out of here—have you heard me, you evil and vile being? I wonder how ironic it would be to throw you into the water? Surely for you it is the cruelest death..."

A powerful roar ended the fun. Hilzen started to look towards the trees, trying to guess where the noise came from, for it had thundered all around. He did not know what animal had such a powerful roar. He pointed his crossbow toward the trees but he was unable to detect an approaching presence. However, the noise had left no doubt.

After a short pause, he put down the crossbow and let the horse resume a normal pace. Noakh was trying to free himself once again. Just when he thought that the danger had passed, a huge tree trunk fell right in front of the wagon, causing a loud *bang*—a hollow sound that echoed through the forest and caused birds to flit through the trees. The horse, frightened, began to whinny, rising on its hind legs. After recovering from the fright, Hilzen raised his crossbow without spotting anyone. Until he realized.

A huge moss-covered hand that had been holding onto the trunk in front of the wagon let go of it, and the body of a giant made its way through the trees. It stood in front of the wagon, its massive shadow covering the sun.

"Who dare disturb my sleep?"

In a voice that sounded hoarse and deep, the giant had started talking. It held the tree trunk in its hand, letting it hang from its fingers, ready for a second blow. Hilzen kept his crossbow steady, carefully avoiding brusque movements, realizing that a single blow from the tree trunk would be enough to crush them. However, Noakh, still restrained by Hilzen's ropes, did not stop shouting at the giant, looking at the colossus with the desire to kill him.

The giant, understanding Noakh's challenge, extended his huge hand and with surprising speed for a being of such size caught Noakh between two fingers, pulling him by the ropes and drawing him close to one of his eyes. Hilzen, without having time to react in any helpful way, simply put his hands on his head, hoping that even the spirit of Distra was sensible enough to understand the situation Noakh was in.

That did not prove to be the case.

While the giant still held him close to his eye, Noakh began laughing hysterically. He wriggled his body between the giant's two fingers, trying to thrust the sword in the giant's eye. Guessing Noakh's intention, the

132

giant drew him away in time, frowning angrily. Then, taking Noakh in the palm of his hand, the giant prepared to make him puree.

"Crush," said the giant.

Hilzen leapt from the wagon as fast as he could. He raised his hands over his head, running toward the giant and trying to stop it.

"Wait wait!" he implored.

The giant curled its fingers around Noakh. The fist gradually began to squeeze him, until all the blood ran from his head and he fell unconscious.

17. A new world

Their swords attacked incessantly, the taysees rotating around him, looking for any chance to finish him off. Noakh's defense was far from perfect: All his effort was dedicated to the attack, to injure or maim his opponents. The attacks with his left hand sought to destabilize the opponent, tocreate an opening, a place where Distra's steel could penetrate the soul of his rival and turn it into fire. He tried to recover control, to participate in a fight in which he saw that the aggressiveness with which he —or rather his body— fought exposed too many vulnerabilities for his rivals to take advantage of. He could only scream, trying to dodge the taysees' blows, unable to move his own body. Noakh, aware he was completely defenseless at his rear, tried to scream with all his might, hoping to alert his own body to the danger, knowing that no voice emerged from his throat. However, his body managed to dodge the blow from behind him; the taysee's blade left a significant wound in his side. He cried out in pain, falling on his knees.

Then he woke up.

The fire failed to illuminate the completely dark room. No matter how much he walked around, the room seemed to have no end. If it really was a room, it must have been part of an immense palace, run by a person with a particular taste for decoration.

After trying to walk in several directions without getting anywhere, Noakh stood in front of the fire, observing it. It sizzled and danced like any normal fire; however, despite the liveliness of the flames, it did not illuminate the room, as if it reserved all the light for itself. After a while, he also realized that no heat emanated from the flames, something that was certainly strange.

He tried to remember what he was doing there. The last thing he remembered was the wagon trip with Hilzen. His head burning with fever. A shuddering pain all over his body. All that seemed so far away...

Looking at his hands, he tried to understand what was happening. The idea that he had died crossed his mind. Not wanting to accept it, he closed his eyes and shook his head, clenching his fists and trying to erase his previous thought.

I have to get out of here, wherever I am—and, he thought, *some clothes would be great.*

Noakh was naked and disoriented. He began to walk around the fire, observing it again. He put his hand on the flames, wanting to check that the fire really did not burn by passing his hand through it. As his hand and fingers went through the fire, the flames became more vivid.

"This is your world now."

A hoarse female voice impregnated the room. It did not come from anywhere in particular; it was omnipresent. The fire, despite growing bigger, still did not illuminate anything in the chamber. Noakh looked around, trying to discern what the speaker was referring to.

"And that's the way it should be," the voice added.

After those words were spoken, the flames began to stir frantically, throwing off a hissing sizzle that ran through the room, making it so pure white that the light blinded his eyes. Noakh covered his head then opened his eyes again to face a too-bright light that did not come from the same fire—which now returned to its original size, dancing happily—but from the room itself.

"I... I do not understand," said Noakh, noticing the flames, the only area in the room that did not blind him.

"Aec ballah shinae aerneh!"

The voice seemed to make a reproachful sound at the puzzled look on Noakh's face. "Not even the old language of the progenitors is familiar to you? Pathetic!"

Without knowing why, Noakh understood whom he was talking to. That voice carried a feeling of reproach which was familiar to him, a mixture of sadness and hate. Despite that, he said nothing, waiting to see what else it had to say.

"Pitiful boy, aec ballah!" the voice said with fury.

"Your fighting technique is very wild, unprotected. You will kill us both," Noakh replied, seeing the voice had nothing to say but insult him.

"Besides, your thirst for blood, all that evil in your blows... I do not want to be part of this!"

The voice, amused by Noakh's discovery, began to laugh.

"So much time lying unused increases the appetite." It laughed again. *"You don't want to be part of this, you say? Aec ballah! The most embarrassing being that has wielded me in centuries! Where are the bloodbaths? Souls mowed down by fire! You're not the king, nor shall you be!"*

The voice was so full of anger that it sounded like a rumble. The flames flickered with dark vibrations.

"I do not enjoy killing like you do, so why choose me then? *I* did not choose this... this burden."

In response to Noakh's words the voice again began to speak in another language. In spite of hardly knowing a single word, it was easy for Noakh to understand the voice's words were not in the least bit pleasant. It was the Fireo language, of which Noakh hardly knew anything.

After a prolonged silence, the voice returned to a tone of greater composure.

"It is not in our power to choose; otherwise I would have chosen a better candidate, someone who had at least made an offering to the god! Is it that you do not know anything about the traditions of your people? How should you serve the one who gave you all this power, which you, with your miserable tongue, dare to call a burden? A power at the height of the gods, capable of protecting an entire kingdom! To turn your enemies into ash dust, aerb kallah!"

Noakh, ignoring the curses, which he did not understand, shrugged his shoulders.

"I haven't been instructed in our traditions as much as you seem to expect. However, I do not know if you are aware of the territory in which we are." He realized the absurdity of saying "we."

"I know exactly where we are. It has been so long since I tasted their blood. Do not dare to grimace, these creatures are pathetic! Ending their lives is rewarding; their blood is rejuvenating... What better place to pay homage than the lands of those who have been our enemies throughout existence? Let everything burn! All the queendom in flames, an inferno that those stupid children of the rain cannot extinguish, so intense that it makes our god proud!"

Noakh shivered. "I'm afraid not, I do not see honor in those acts." The thought of setting villages of innocent people ablaze while claiming his fervor for the Incandescent was a vision he would not accept.

"Oh, so now it's about honor... Since when is honor synonymous with cowardice? You do not speak like a king—you talk like a cowardly rat! The Fireos are condemned to die!"

"Do you dare to question the decision of the one who forged you?" Noakh said, remembering that the voice had said that it was not in its power to choose the heir to the Fireo throne.

"I do not," the voice replied after a while, far more calmly than before.

"I thought so."

Noakh looked at the fire. Still no light emanated from it. He turned away and started pacing around the room. The voice had reproached him but also seemed to acknowledge his power. That could be useful. He wouldn't burn down villages for no reason, but if the power was his, why shouldn't he claim it? Noakh assumed a serious pose, as much as his nakedness allowed him to. He began to speak, raising his chin. "You say I do not act like a king. Now I will. As the future king I order you to submit to my will! From now on you will lend me all your power, and it will be I who will mark my destiny."

The voice gave out a laugh.

"It seems you learn. So it will be, king."

Noakh caught a certain mockery in the voice's tone as it said these last words.

Noakh nodded proudly. "Good."

The fire began to die out. However, the room was still fully illuminated.

"One more thing," said the voice. *"Your friend, I will kill him."*

18. The cure

"Friend?"

In the palm of the giant's huge hand lay Noakh, inert again. A powerful squeeze of his fingers had forced Noakh to release Distra. The sword had fallen to the ground, impaling the earth. Having lost his bond with the sword, Noakh had quickly fallen unconscious. The giant, surprised at the sudden change, watched Noakh curiously. One of the huge fingers of his other hand gave what for him were small taps against Noakh's body. The giant's finger was the size of a child. His fingernail was yellowish, long, and broken.

The sight of such a titan was overwhelming. His appearance, though human, showed disproportionate features: very long arms and legs, a short neck, and a round head. His clothes were made with pieces of plants quite decently. On his arms hung bracelets formed from branches, which gave him a certain harmonic connection to the forest. His small black eyes and stiff nose made him look stupid. His head was covered with only a few hairs, which fell down his face. Other than that, he had a more than remarkable baldness.

"Yes, he is my friend, he is dying." Hilzen threw himself to the ground and cringed on his knees sobbing while tears fell down his eyes. "I can't go through this again..."

The giant turned his head, looking at Hilzen. Then he turned his head back to Noakh, nudging him with his fingernail again, making him roll onto the palm of his hand. With an ease that seemed astonishing to Hilzen, he undid the rope and began to observe it by grasping one of the ends with a finger and bringing it closer to his eyes. Noakh's wound in his back appeared to be turning increasingly yellowish, suggesting high levels of infection. The giant lowered his nose and smelled him. His nostrils showed irregular holes, as big as the entrance of a cave.

"Poison."

Hilzen raised his head in surprise.

"How do you know?"

"In my tribe I be a healer, I cure giants."

"Can you help him?" He jumped up, a ray of hope seeming to have emerged "Please... save him!"

"But... he attack me, he woke me up." The creature's words were sad, emphasizing the fact that Noakh's cries had awakened him, as if *that* were truly what had bothered him.

"Please!" Hilzen dropped to the ground, begging from his knees "Help him!"

The colossus paused for a second.

Then the giant drew his other hand down to snatch up Hilzen. The Aquo put his hands before his face as the colossus's immense hand drew him towards him. However, the giant took Hilzen gently and held him on his palm.

From the height of the giant's shoulders, the air was much colder. The giant's footsteps soon caused a roar to echo around the forest. Animals came out of hiding; birds fluttered, perching on the giant's head. Hilzen held onto the giant's fingers to see where the beast was taking him. He had to use all his strength to grab on to the fingers and keep from falling.

The giant's motion caused his palm to wobble, making it difficult for Hilzen to stand up. He intermittently turned away from the landscape before him to look at Noakh, who was still in the giant's other hand. Noakh's body protruded from the giant's closed fist, his little arms moving from side to side as a result of the oscillation.

The walk was rather short, partly because of the giant's huge strides. They soon found themselves in an esplanade, where the trunks of several uprooted trees could be seen. Leaves and branches were stacked on one side of the clearing. The giant's bed, Hilzen guessed.

The giant lowered his hand carefully, then opened his palm and let Hilzen scramble off. Then the creature took Noakh with him close to a tree. In it, there were several holes, in which, Hilzen realized, the giant had stored all kinds of herbs and utensils.

The giant sat down on the ground and crossed his legs. Still holding Noakh in one hand, he reached his other hand into the hole in the tree and took out some herbs. He set the herbs in a small pile at his feet then

140

took out a piece of thick tree bark and, digging his fingers into the bark, made a shallow hole in it. Then he dropped the mixture of herbs into the hole. He reached over and lifted one of the uprooted tree trunks and began poking a finger around in the dirt, then withdrew his finger, revealing a bunch of insects clinging to it. Carefully he dropped several of the bugs onto the crusty earth and crushed them between his fingers, creating a brown mass, which he drew up with his fingers and introduced into the hole he had made in the bark with the herbs. He then paused, touching his forehead with one of his fingers, as though trying to remember something.

"Missing flower."

He pointed to some flowers that were growing next to Hilzen. They were white with reddish spots—a species not very common in the area—so strange, in fact, that Hilzen had never seen them. He scurried around to pick them, intending to tear them all away.

The giant guessed Hilzen's intentions. "Only one!" he cried fiercely.

"Okay, it's okay!" Hilzen replied, raising his hands in peace.

He gently picked one of the flowers and placed it in the palm of the giant's hand. The giant crushed it and dropped the liquid that came out onto the bark. After removing the thick paste of herbs, flowers, and bug blood, he opened Noakh's mouth with one of his yellowish nails, introducing the mixture into his mouth.

Hilzen couldn't help but to feel repulsed, despite knowing that the giant's actions were beneficial. After he was finished, the giant set Noakh on the enormous bed of leaves and sat down next to Hilzen. When his buttocks hit the ground, they raised a cloud of leaves and dust, producing a soft *whoosh.*

"He will live. Lethal poison, but very slow."

Looking back at him, Hilzen could see an aura of wisdom in his eyes, an intelligence that he had been unable to see before, blinded as he was by his prejudices. Hilzen enthusiastically smiled and looked into the giant's eyes, then he made the Aquo reverence towards him. The giant deserved all his respect. The giant nodded with his head.

Likewise, the way in which he expressed himself was quite decent. The giants had their own language, which to human ears seemed like a cluster of meaningless screams but nevertheless, depending on the modulation and duration, helped the beings communicate. With their arrival into these lands, the giants little by little learned the common tongue—in many cases in order not to be attacked by humans, but also to collaborate with them in cases when they were fighting a common enemy.

The giants' language stood as a good example of all that had happened throughout the four kingdoms. Each kingdom possessed a language of its own that had nevertheless been replaced by the so-called *common language*, a language that thanks to *not* starting from any of the lexical rules of the other languages had extended to all the kingdoms, without any other territory imposing its language, a fact that had undoubtedly been part of the language's success, along with its lower degree of complexity compared to the others.

"Thank you, thank you very much!" Then Hilzen realized that he did not even know the giant's name. Standing up again while bowing, he said, "My name is Hilzen, and the boy whose life you saved is called Noakh. We both come from the Silvery Lakes region. What's your name?"

"Cervan." The giant looked at the ground. With one of his fingers he drew huge grooves in the earth. "From where I come I can't remember. Long ago... lands of giants."

Hilzen nodded. The giants were not a common sight in the Aquadom. Rather, they came from places far away. According to the stories Hilzen had heard, they had been attracted to this queendom by its springs of pure water, a strong contrast to their barren lands dominated by dust—or at least that was what the stories said. He remembered the story of the giant princess, a story that his parents had told him during his childhood. The giant king had had a daughter, Garlogian, who, within the giants' canon, was considered very beautiful. Their customs dictated that any giant who wanted to marry the young princess must emerge champion in a tournament. Several warriors of the tribe joined the tournament, a battle to the death in which the winner would win the hand of the princess. Borgan, considered the strongest giant of all time, respected and feared by the rest of the giants, joined the tournament too. When the other giants learned that Borgan would be joining, they decided not to participate, knowing they had no chance of winning. As a result, Borgan was declared the winner, as he was the only participant. The king, having been deprived of the spectacle of combat, reluctantly yielded his daughter's hand to the powerful warrior, well aware of the consequences had he not done so. However, Garlogian was not so eager to abide by the rules. She used her cunning to make Borgan understand that there was no honor in his victory. He proposed that the powerful giant embark on a journey in search of something so beautiful that it was worthy to give

142

a princess in exchange for her hand in marriage. Seeing the challenge as an epic adventure that would be forever remembered, Borgan accepted the challenge. Several giant warriors joined his cause, soon embarking on a journey around the world.

This story—with a few changes, depending on who told it—served as an explanation for many Aquos of how the giants had come to the lands of water; many added with pride that the water from their springs was undoubtedly the beautiful object the powerful giant had given as a present to the princess—a detail, Hilzen knew, that would certainly be replaced by the other kingdoms' most precious assets *if* similar stories existed in those kingdoms. It was a story that Hilzen especially liked, since, unlike most of the stories in which giants intervened, in this story the giants were not treated as simple monsters who loved to eat children and crush villages; instead, this story reflected a gentler side of the beings. And, looking at Cervan now, Hilzen could see how the human nature that the story conveyed was actually real. It was good, he thought, that at least one of the stories concerning giants mentioned such features.

* * *

"The way you knew how Noakh was poisoned was as impressive as how quickly you cured him. Where did you learn such knowledge?"

"Giants always know trees, they know forest. Cervan healer in the war, learn a lot to save as many warriors as possible. Because Cervan wounded in leg in combat, not able to fight but want to be useful, learn to cure burns, poisons. Horrible war." Cervan's tone grew mournful while he talked about the war and his giant colleagues.

"Burns..." Hilzen knew which war the giant was referring to, so long ago that only a giant could have participated in it and still be alive today. One of Hilzen's ancestors had fought and died in that war. A war where fire rained and the earth trembled. It was a bloody battle against the Fireos and the Tirhans, the Aquos being besieged by both sides. The Aquo Army had to divide its forces on two fronts; despite flooding their borders, the enemy armies had moved forward. Being aware of the situation, the queen at that time, Quarel—a woman as wise as she was beautiful—asked for help from the giants who lived in her lands, persuading them to fight at her side. This was one of several actions that led Quarel to repel the enemies' attack and thus endure the siege, pushing back both sides. That battle earned Quarel the nickname Giant Tamer.

Many warriors died in that war, and without a doubt many giants, who because of their strength were sent to the most bloody battle zones. But because of their size—and the humans' lack of respect for their lives—they were not treated by doctors. Cervan, after being injured, and wanting to help his fellow giants, had declared himself responsible for trying to save them.

Since the war had started, the population of giants had significantly decreased, both because many giants had died in combat and because many had decided to return home after the fight.

"My ancestors also fought in that war," Hilzen told Cervan. "Let's give thanks to what now seems to be an era of peace," he added, knowing that the Fireos and the Aquos were in the era of the Sleeping War.

Both stopped talking as they looked at the sky. Among the trees, the clouds advanced above the branches. Then from his position where he still lay on Cervan's bed, Noakh coughed and Hilzen ran on tiptoe to his bed, since after all it was a giant's bed. Noakh opened his eyes and looked sideways at Hilzen, stunned.

"Noakh! How are you doing?" Hilzen exclaimed while Noakh touched his own head. A sharp pain, accompanied by nausea, attacked him. The giant came quickly and pulled Hilzen away.

"Having to expel poison."

"Hmm? What do you mean by—"

Before Hilzen could finish the sentence, Noakh leaned over the edge of the bed and vomited on the ground.

"Exactly that. Medicine cures. But very powerful."

Noakh, who until then had been too ill to fully comprehend the scene around him, realized with dread that a huge giant stood next to Hilzen. Rather than back away in fear, Noakh found himself unable to move, frozen with fascination. Hadn't his father once told him about these beings? Hadn't he always wanted to see one in person? However, before he could say anything that might hurt the sensibility of the giant, Hilzen intervened.

"This is Cervan, a giant healer. If it were not for him... you would not be here."

Noakh was surprised at Hilzen's words. His prejudices regarding giants were not so very dissimilar from Hilzen's. Pushing himself to the edge of the bed of leaves, Noakh laid his eyes on the giant.

144

"You saved me?" Again Noakh looked the giant in the eye. Could it be true? What had Hilzen said? If it weren't for the giant, Noakh would be dead? He looked back to Hilzen, who simply nodded. Then he looked back to the giant. The intelligence. The compassion. He nodded. I owe you my life then..." Then he began to reflect. "Cervan, someday I will be king of the Fireos. I know it may seem stupid now, but such is my destiny, and then you will be rewarded. I will be willing to serve you, even to die for you."

"No need. You do the same for me."

Noakh was about to thank the giant, but then, with a lurch, he started vomiting again.

19. Separate paths

Early that night, a gigantic bonfire illuminated the giant's dwelling area in the esplanade. The three friends sat close beside it, with Noakh and Hilzen enjoying the dinner that Hilzen had hunted for them: a boar with large fangs. The giant, however, ate tree roots. This relieved Hilzen, who had feared that the amount of meat the giant would consume might be as gigantic as Cervan himself. Earlier the giant had gone to retrieve the wagon and the horse, both of which he had brought back to the esplanade with extreme ease. The horse seemed to have grown used to him, letting him caress him with one of his fingers without showing any resistance; on the contrary, the horse even seemed to like it.

Noakh had managed to get out of bed and, after drinking a huge amount of water, as recommended by Cervan, had begun to feel much better. Yet his face was still yellow, slightly swollen, and showed signs of fatigue. His appearance was horrible, but he was not going to complain, considering that the alternative was, apparently, death.

During dinner, Hilzen told him how they had gotten to the giant's dwelling, and his idea, which now seemed so brilliant while at the time had seemed demented, to use Distra to keep Noakh alive as long as possible. He told Noakh, too, of how Cervan, enraged by Noakh's cries when he was possessed, had blocked their way with a tree to scare them and leave him alone. Cervan then admitted that he used to do that as a warning, to scare off someone whenever they bothered him, even though he was not usually that close to the path. Such a threat was sufficient for the vast majority of travelers to quickly understand the consequences of bothering the giant; typically, they ran off at a rapid pace to let Cervan rest in peace. However, the giant admitted that he would not kill any man, because he had learned to live with nature.

Staring at the flames of the bonfire, Noakh remembered the conversation he had with the force inside of Distra and how the voice he had heard had promised to kill Hilzen. He wondered if the promise had something to do with the words he boasted to Distra when he was totally tied. He preferred not to say anything. It was better not to worry his friend, because as Hilzen had said on multiple occasions, although he longed for death, he certainly did not want it at the hands of a demon— least of all, if it was with fire. At first he thought that encounter was a dream, a simple madness, a consequence of the effect of the poison in his blood. However, now, holding Distra in his hands again, he perceived no hostility, only concord, as if they had reached a kind of pact. Perhaps it was a consequence of the conversations he had with Distra and because, real or not, he had come to perceive the sword differently, as if the fear of using it had vanished.

During their conversation, the sword had kept telling him that he was not a king. Noakh realized the harshness of those words. His father had sacrificed everything for a cause, one to which he had not given importance, without realizing he was tainting everything of what his father had fought, for what he had lived and finally died for. He wondered about the extent to which Lumio would be disgusted with him, letting Distra take control, being about to die without even starting to fight. Those thoughts bathed him in a sense of shame and embarrassment that soon became anger... anger against himself. Without realizing it, he was squeezing the hilt of the sword so hard that he was pushing the blade into the ground, little by little digging the tip deeper.

Hilzen, observing him, guessed his torment.

"Noakh, do you remember the story of the giant princess?"

"Yes, I think so... Isn't that where the giants search for the hottest flame?"

"I knew it!" laughed Hilzen. "I always wondered if this story was different in each of the kingdoms. Now I finally know the answer!"

Cervan, who had the horse in one of his hands while with the finger of the other stroked its back, asked about that story. After telling him, to the astonishment of both Noakh and Hilzen, reality was really far from any of their versions.

148

* * *

Once Noakh recovered, it was time for him and Hilzen to leave. Both of the men were sorry to say goodbye to the giant. He had revealed that he had a heart bigger, even, than his size. No doubt they would miss him.

As Noakh and Hilzen gathered their belongings, Cervan was very sad, continually crestfallen, and staring at the ground. He intertwined his fingers as he stood shifting his weight from side to side. Something tormented his mind.

"Noakh, you say willing to serve me. I only ask you one thing." Cervan was embarrassed at his request, although he had to at least try. However, Noakh interrupted him, guessing his request.

"The horse can stay with you. You have found a partner and he has been too long in the service of humans. It is time it has a better life." As he spoke he slipped the reins off the horse, stroking it on the back. Until that moment he had not paid much attention to the horse. It was brown, with powerful hindquarters as result of a life pulling a wagon. Although the horse was now in its later years, it seemed to have kept in shape.

Noakh looked at the horse's eyes. He seemed to see a special glint in the horse's expression. Perhaps it was merely his imagination, but he could have sworn the animal was genuinely grateful about his future destiny. A life in nature, without any burden to pull, and no master.

Cervan, as delighted as he was, started jumping with joy, causing the earth to rumble. Hilzen had to hold on to the wagon to avoid falling. Looking at the wagon, Noakh remembered Sigüen and his odious way of making a living. He realized the number of crimes the horse must have witnessed. Then, looking at the wagon, he saw it clearly.

"Cervan, I have a request for you. Destroy the wagon."

Although the giant did not understand the reason for Noakh's request, he did not hesitate. Cervan drew his arm back and then he threw a powerful punch that splintered the wagon. A powerful *crash!* thundered throughout the forest. The blow was so potent that it sunk the remains of the wagon into the earth, causing no damage to the colossal fist of the giant. Hilzen, understanding the symbolism behind that gesture, nodded with pride.

Hilzen observed Noakh. Something had changed in him. Perhaps it was the fact that he had been so close to death, an experience that would undoubtedly open the eyes of many. His attitude was different. Hilzen's respect for his companion did nothing but grow. Although Noakh was years younger than him, now he showed a resolution and determination that he, Hilzen, had not seen before in any other man.

After Cervan said goodbye to Noakh and Hilzen, the two friends started on their way again. The horse, seeing them go, stood on its hind legs and neighed loudly. And in that way, Noakh realized, he had saved two lives.

After a few minutes of walking through the forest, Noakh glanced casually at Hilzen. "You know, Hilzen, I think I should carry Distra. After all, it is my responsibility."

Hilzen turned to Noakh for a moment then turned away again. "No, Noakh, we made a deal. And we are going to fulfill it. Distra stays with me."

Hilzen carried Distra in a certain way... almost gloatingly. Noakh had not told him the sword had sworn to kill him; nevertheless it was unnecessary to reveal to Hilzen the little appreciation the sword seemed to have for human life. He merely accepted his companion's declarations reluctantly, seeing how Hilzen was the one carrying Distra.

20. Memories of a king

King Wulkan woke again from his nightmares. Something had been wrong for nearly two decades, but he had not yet gotten used to the dreams. His hand touching his throat, his body drenched in sweat, his heart pounding with cold and that feeling of... fear. A frailty he would never admit to in front of anyone, not even his wife. Wulkan lit a candle and approached the mirror in his room, where he started to examine his neck, as if expecting to find some kind of mark on his skin. When he realized how paranoid he was being, he clenched his jaw and looked sternly upon his reflection.

There was a wrinkle on his forehead, while on his head some greyish sparkles had begun to show. The nightmares, although varying, revolved around a common axis. Tonight's nightmare, though brief, had been particularly disturbing. While he was asleep —asleep in his dream— he felt the cold steel in his throat, and as he woke, his throat began to burn slowly, until the fire tore him completely. It was at that moment when he had actually woken up. Although he knew it was a dream, he could have sworn that his throat continued burning. His paranoia had advanced to such a point that he stood in front of the mirror of the royal room in search of some mark. Instantly he realized the stupidity of his actions, making him furious. He knew what was causing his insomnia.

Every day he remembered that fateful afternoon as if it were yesterday. He thought of how, after the ancient priest Thommes had not returned with his sword, and after the absence of his soldiers had been reported, the king had wanted to witness the scene with his own eyes, his personal guards had accompanied him to see what had happened. When they arrived, the red sun was already hidden, giving the Lava Sanctuary a yellowish color. From the beginning, he knew something was wrong. He entered the sanctuary alone, with a strange feeling. As he took his first step he saw how the floor was bathed in blood.

His personal guards, the Sons of the Flame, unsheathed their swords instinctively then spread throughout the room in search of any threat. After confirming all was clear, four of them went outdoors in search of enemies; the other two stationed themselves behind the king, their shields up, displaying the symbol of the phoenix with its wings spread. Wulkan approached Thommes's body, desperately looking for Distra. After seeing that it was not there, he looked at the other corpses: a soldier and a woman. He finally approached the corpse of the soldier, to see who he was, although he already knew the answer.

His eyes searched desperately for the inert body of the baby, hoping that that stupid soldier had at least done his job. However, nothing seemed to indicate that it had been so. The soldier, who was called Lumio, would have fled... along with Distra and the baby. In spite of the disturbing facts, Wulkan tried to remain calm; a king can never seem bested, no matter how events might threaten his reign or, better said, his head.

After gathering the guards again, he gave the order to hunt down the traitor. One of the royal guards had detected horse tracks leading away from the place, so they all rode off, following the fugitive. Wulkan, on the other hand, went back to the palace, trying to fathom the consequences. He began to consider the possible options. He was not very optimistic about the matter, even though the king considered himself a cunning being.

He called an emergency meeting with the only two people he could trust for such a sensitive matter. His eldest grandson, Minkert, and his counselor, Joher, who had assigned the task to the soldier who had fallen in the sanctuary. The king was quite upset, something that disturbed the other two present. Minkert and Joher had been informed of the meeting by the king in person; he had not wanted to involve any of the members of the court. It was held in one of the palace dungeons, a meeting place that was somewhat unusual but that had proven useful for meetings of a dubious nature.

Minkert was physically a younger reflection of his grandfather, with a hard look and broad shoulders. His attitude of superiority and overconfidence was his singular feature. Some years ago, Wulkan had sat with him alone, telling him that something tormented his mind. He began to tell Minkert how he feared the future king was not worthy of the crown, asking why he had to give up the crown when he had done such a good job, wondering if it really was so bad to want everything to continue as it was. Their kingdom was a strong kingdom, capable of causing fear in its enemies. Minkert, who had been a fervent servant of the Incandescent's dogma since childhood, was annoyed by the implications of his grandfather's words, trying to remind him of how the Incandescent chose the future king by way of the fire swords, and how the mere fact that they were discussing it could cause the divine fury to fall on him and his family, causing them to fall into absolute misery. However, Wulkan, trying to take the pain out of the matter, reminded him how unhappy his future would be when the Ascendant Phoenix was chosen. He would be adopted by the royal family until reaching the age of majority, instructed in the fighting arts, the war, how to govern a kingdom... and then the royal family would go through a beautiful ceremony to become part of the common people, with no more privileges than having a few lands in their name. Minkert, annoyed at the prospect of losing all the comforts and respect that the crown offered them, began to see with fresh eyes the implications underlying his grandfather's words. His doubts were completely silenced when his grandfather revealed that if Wulkan died in combat, not having a future heir, it would be he, Minkert, who could be named king. When faced with such a vision, Minkert could not help but agree with his grandfather's reasoning—and that is that dogma can occupy a secondary role as long as it was not in favor of oneself.

Down in the dungeon, the king walked from one side of the cell to the other, gesticulating wildly and with a lost expression on his face. "The sword is not there! That useless soldier has failed, and now he is nowhere! No trace of the child, no sign of the sword!" Despite the emptiness of his words, the rest of the attendees could guess what had happened. Red sky. The soldier Kodul had been manipulated by Joher with promises of gold and a more than relevant position in the Royal Guard; in exchange he only had to kill the newborn who was the phoenix—and obviously he had failed.

The situation caused a feeling of malaise in both the king and his grandson. Minkert threw his hands to his head, seeing how his world was falling apart, making him unable to think of anything other than the world of servitude in which he was going to live—an alternative that did not please anyone who, only one minute ago, had dreamed of governing the Kingdom of Fire one day.

Joher, on the other hand, tried to keep a cool head. The ability to do so was a very unusual quality among the Fireos—one that had undoubtedly made this humble citizen the most important counselor to the king. Many said that in a certain way Joher ruled from the shadows.

"My lord, although such facts are undoubtedly a drawback, I suggest we evaluate the situation with due dispassion." Joher, a man already in his fifties, had a deep voice that was somehow endowed with the power to calm those who listened to him. The way in which he timed his pauses, the care with which he chose each of his words, produced a sedative effect, generating calm at any moment, no matter how tense that moment was. However, for Wulkan *this* moment was an incredibly dramatic situation, so that even Joher could not calm him down and get him collected before the king interrupted him, presuming that his counselor's lips would pronounce no more than rough whimpers and protests even as Wulkan continued. "The loss of the sword and the baby are, without a doubt, an issue that we must resolve with the utmost priority; however, nothing seems to indicate that there were witnesses to the incident. This gives us a certain capacity in which to maneuver, although no doubt the families of the deceased soldier and woman will soon cause the alarm to be sounded, just as the clergy will demand to know about the priest Thommes."

Minkert was alarmed, infected by the nervousness of his grandfather. "If the incident reaches the ears of the citizens..."

"And it will, eventually," cut in Joher. "The important thing is how it reaches those ears. And that is just what we have to consider as our top priority. I think it is evident that the loss of Distra has to remain hidden. Outdoors, the disappearance could be seen as a symbol of weakness— our kingdom could be in danger if this were to become known. The swords of fire lead our armies; without one of them, the enemy could take advantage of the opportunity."

"On that we all agree," said Wulkan, who was listening carefully to his counselor's words.

"Well," continued Joher, "we will ask some blacksmith to forge an identical copy of Distra. We can tell him it is a copy that will serve in the event that future thieves wish to steal Distra, in which case they will steal the false sword."

"No, kill the blacksmith after his work is done," Wulkan instructed. "No matter if you then have to reward his family. I do not want there to be the slightest doubt as to the authenticity of the sword."

"So be it, my king," Joher replied with praise. "Well, then with this, the matter of Distra is settled. We will say that the sword was finally found in the sanctuary, among the robes of Thommes, who died protecting it. This will make the clergy proud; thus they will meddle less in the case."

Wulkan agreed, satisfied with the explanation that his adviser had given. That, after all, was why he was his trusted advisor.

Joher suddenly launched a chuckle—an ejaculation that upset Wulkan, as it came at the most inopportune moment.

"What are you laughing at, Joher?"

At such a reproach Joher lowered his head in apology, although it was difficult for him to suppress his smile.

"My apologies, my king. I just laughed at my stupidity and clumsiness. I realized how useful a false sword would have been from the first moment. There would never have been an heir!" At his words, Joher could not help but laugh again.

Minkert seemed about to join him, but was quickly besieged by one of his grandfather's stern looks, immediately ending his fun. Observing Wulkan's expression, the counselor realized he was tempting his fate too much. He was aware that his services were highly valued by his king, but monarchs had no problem ending the life of a henchman, no matter how useful he might be.

"That wouldn't work," revealed Wulkan. He looked at the wall, where there were some scratches on the surface, as if a prisoner had tried to dig a hole on the rock. A fool. "The fire priests feel the power of our sacred swords, even though they can't unleash their power at their will as a phoenix would."

"I see." Clearing his throat, Joher returned to his former composure and, with a serious demeanor, continued. "Sinistra will be used for the rituals from now on then. Therefore we will pretend Distra has not disappeared. This will be a temporary solution, while we solve our second priority—the disappearance of the soldier, Lumio, with the sword and the... newborn." Joher had been about to refer to the newborn as *the phoenix*. However, his many years in the service of the king, along with his cunning, had allowed him to use the precise words that would not harm the monarch's fragile sensitivity. This facility no doubt had been the key to his ascendency among the ranks of the king's servants. "I think it's obvious that the soldier, in a display of devotion, saved the baby and took the sword with him, fleeing the sanctuary. We have sent search teams hunting for him, and although we have not found him and the newborn yet, I am sure they are not far away."

Wulkan turned back, staring at Joher irritably.

"How many teams? And under whose orders?" Wulkan insisted, aware of the impact that the news of the search parties could cause. He did not want any information to leak—at least not before he had ensured everything was again under his control.

"Three teams—they were given minimal and sufficiently confusing and vague instructions in order not to raise the alarm, my king." Despite the counselor's attempt to duck the obligation to supply more information, Wulkan looked at him purposefully. "Teams are formed of four riders, all of them members of the Sons of the Flame and among them all those who accompanied you to the sanctuary. The instructions indicated that they are to hunt down Lumio, who has been described as a traitor to the kingdom—and it has been specified that after he is captured he shall be brought before me immediately."

"Well." Wulkan suddenly felt a great tiredness on his shoulders, yet there were still many issues to resolve. "About this man, Lumio... What do we know about him?"

"A soldier of the Sons of the Flame—as is obvious from his having been part of the ritual. Apparently he is well skilled in the art of combat. He was promoted to captain but he declined the post; he seems an exemplary soldier," Joher said, realizing too late it was not a good idea to praise the man who had caused all this trouble.

"Family?"

"Wife and two daughters, eight and three years old. Two infantry soldiers are constantly watching the house. If he contacts his family, we will know instantly."

"Watching? Seize them and kill them! Set them afire at the top of a scaffold! Force that rat out of his hole to save his dirty lineage!" Minkert raised his fist in order to give more force to his words. After speaking, he glanced at his grandfather, waiting for words of approval. Joher was about to talk, but Wulkan raised his hand to silence him.

"And then what?" His words were a mixture of anger and disappointment. "Use your head, Minkert! If we kill them, Lumio will not have anything to tie him to this place. If he manages to repress his desire to save them for a greater good, then surely we have lost the

156

opportunity to catch him. Instead, if he knows they are alive, if he believes that the danger has already passed, for sure he will try to get in touch with them sooner or later... and then you just have to follow him to his burrow."

"Not to mention that, after declaring him a traitor, their life will not exactly be comfortable. The citizens are not kind to the family of traitors. With his family devastated by shame and poverty, Lumio is even more likely to try to comfort them in some way. And then"—Joher made a gesture with his hands—"we will crush him."

Minkert began to laugh fervently. Wulkan, nevertheless, maintained his serious face.

"What about the newborn's mother?"

"Certainly little to tell. We know she comes from the region of Fallines, no known close relatives."

Wulkan raised an eyebrow, confused.

"Not even a husband?"

"Our sources suggest that is the case. That is, of course, there must have been a man to assist in the conception, but he is unknown to us."

"And what will we do if we find him?" Minkert pronounced, not daring again to propose severe punishment.

"I do not think it's a problem," said Joher. "This brings us, my king, to the key point of this whole issue, which is none other than how to approach this altercation. We must orchestrate a cover-up that does not expose us to any risk. The deaths, you will agree with me, cannot be hidden. A priest of fire has died and the clergy will certainly demand answers and ask that we hold those who are responsible accountable. Regarding the newborn," Joher began to reflect, "we have several options, actually; let's draw up some scenarios. We can create a martyr... The sword has chosen the new king, one of the soldiers of the guard turns out to be a spy for an enemy kingdom and ends the chosen newborn's life. King Wulkan, full of fury in light of the outrage perpetrated by his enemies, rides once again, renewing an age of fire and blood."

"No—although I admit that it is a good trigger to start a war," Wulkan said. "But without Distra it would be risky. I will reevaluate that option as soon as the fire sword has been recovered."

"So be it." After a curtsey, Joher continued. "Then I will pose the other possible options. The newborn survived and was kidnapped. The one chosen by the sword is in the hands of our enemies."

157

"Do not even think about it."

"I agree, my king. This scenario would leave us vulnerable and be a shame for our kingdom, an opportunity for our enemies to blackmail us. The next option would be to pretend that the baby died in the brawl, which seems to me the most advisable option. The only thing I can't visualize is if we should mention that he was chosen or not." Joher continued with his thought: "It might be more logical to say the trap was sprung after the baby was chosen. However, it is in turn more dangerous... saying that the baby was not chosen may be the best. An isolated incident?"

"Letting the phoenix die?" questioned Wulkan to himself.

"You are right, my king. How stupid of me. The mere news that a phoenix has been murdered..."

"The wrath of our people would be terrible," Minkert observed. "The vulnerability of our kingdom would be exposed..."

"Enough, Minkert," Wulkan cut in.

Minkert simply lowered his head, not understanding why he had to shut up when his words were sure to be true. Joher thanked Minkert for saying those words, as they were similar to the words that had fluttered through his mind but that his prudence had prevented him from saying aloud. He gave the moment its due, for maybe he had underestimated Minkert. No doubt his lack of caution could be very useful, a way to say what he would not dare to say to the king.

"What if"—Joher laughed— "a baby and a woman died at the hands of a soldier... Why have I not seen it before? Lumio secretly loved another woman. After discovering that another man had possessed her, he could not help himself—he killed her and the baby. Thommes and the other soldier tried to stop him, but they were unable to control the passionate act of Lumio; they both died in the act. Being a crime of passion, Lumio would naturally flee after having finished off their lives."

"Leaving behind the sword, as he just wanted to end the life of the woman he loved and the result of her relationship with another man... Brilliant!" Wulkan cheered, satisfied. "But what about him fleeing?"

"I know what you mean," said Joher, considering the options. "Lumio had to flee, so he decided to run in the only direction such a traitor would be welcome," he said with a smile of satisfaction.

The king nodded with satisfaction as well.

"Splendid, I will write a royal statement, my king, in which we will inform our people what happened. It is undoubtedly a much less disturbing version of events, leaving the credibility of the kingdom intact." Joher observed that relief could be seen on the king's face... No doubt this was only an arrangement until Lumio was found. Finding the baby and the sword would solve the problem completely, but at least this scenario gave them a certain margin of error, concealing a reality that was too crude to be revealed. "I will be in my chambers, my king. I will begin drafting the statement immediately."

Joher went to the door, allowing himself to conclude the conversation.

"One more thing... Why was that Lumio in the sanctuary?" the king asked.

Joher, with his back to the room, could envision how the king's eyes were fixed on his back. He thought he escaped having to explain such details, but he had underestimated Wulkan. He paused deliberately, considering the weight of what was going to say. After a moment he swallowed then continued: "It was he himself who asked to participate in the ritual."

At this, Wulkan raised an eyebrow. Joher noticed that his forehead was becoming moist. He was aware that his choice of words at that moment would be key to saving not only his position but also probably his head. "He was granted the honor only for this time, since Bravar, the soldier who was replaced, requested permission for his marriage. My king, as you know, it is customary..."

"I know very well about our customs, Joher," Wulkan interrupted firmly. His voice reverberated loudly against the dungeon walls. Joher was about to remind him that they were in a secret meeting and that raising his voice was perhaps not the most advisable thing to do. However, he decided that perhaps it was not the best time. The king paused for a moment to think, and neither Joher nor Minkert considered it an opportune time to interrupt whatever his thoughts were.

21. Livian

"All right, I'll say it—giving Cervan the horse was very nice, a very noble act, and so on and so forth. I'm sure Cervan will thank you eternally—my feet not so much." Hilzen raised one leg at a time so he could massage each foot through his worn brown boots.

"Do not complain, Hilzen. After all, we have arrived," said Noakh while he looked at Distra, which was buckled on Hilzen's belt after their agreement while they were with the giant Cervan.

Hilzen and Noakh entered the streets of the city of Livian. If the fact that they were armed was not enough to garner the citizens' attention, their homeless appearance did so. Noakh especially called attention. His brown eyes did not go unnoticed. As a child, when someone looked at him, he would quickly avert his gaze, believing that they judged him by the mere color of his corneas. Over time, he learned that looking away would not change anything, so instead there came a moment when he began to do just the opposite: hold the other person's gaze until they looked away. Although this had caused him more than one confrontation with other children of his town, he certainly preferred this alternative.

Livian was a city like any other in the Aquadom. It was a medium-sized city, with crowded streets that all seemed to lead to a river flowing straight through the middle of the city. The river, being navigable, was what the wealthiest merchants used to transport their goods. As a result, one of the main places in the city was the harbor, in which several sailors unloaded the goods and carried them to the main square, a crowded place that was home to several merchants shouting loudly about their prized, unique merchandise—of which they always claimed they were about to sell out. But the square was known for its curious fountain, in which several swans of white stone cast water in the shape of an arch. The water gently splashed on a jade mermaid reclining on a rock.

Hilzen stopped at one of the merchant's stalls, asking the proprietor about his leeks, and expressing interest in that year's harvest. Noakh did not feel quite so fascinated by the world of vegetables. He stopped at one of the nearby stalls at which a variety of amulets were sold. According to the screaming seller, the amulets each had the power to grant the wearer whatever he would like. Each amulet had a stone at its core: rose-colored tourmaline, dark-grey pentlandite, cream-white peridot, yellowish adamite. Depending on the type of stone, the wearer could achieve one objective or another. There were all kinds of amulets—some for luck, some to find love, and some even to attract money. Of course, the precious stone that represented the Queendom, the sapphire, was not present in any of those amulets. Sapphires were not only expensive; they were illegal. Because they represented the queendom itself, authorities considered using sapphires in mere amulets as a violation of the law. As a result, merchants would not dare to risk their business—or more importantly, their necks. For similar reasons, the other precious stones representing the other kingdoms—the ruby, the emerald, and the citrine—were also absent in merchant's collections.

The amulets' purveyor was a tall man with a very thin body. His nose was made prominent due to his tiny eyes and a shortage of hair on his head. Noakh wondered how the merchant, being in possession of so many amulets, was not the happiest man in the world. He supposed that this man simply wanted to share his good fortune in every facet of his life with the rest of the people... and do so at a reasonable price. Noakh could not help but smile—a gesture that was more than sufficient for the amulet seller to begin to entertain him by showing him several different amulets and how each could change his luck.

"Ah, young man," said he merchant with a sweet tone. "This amulet," he began while picking one of the amulets on the table, "with this beautiful peridot stone, will confer you luck whenever you throw a dice." Noakh waved his hand dismissively. "Luck is already on your side then? What about this one?" The merchant then showed Noakh an amulet with a translucent orange stone, "this beautiful mineral is called carnelian. It will make you feel stronger."

162

It was not until after several attempts that the seller finally gave up, focusing instead on a young girl with pimples, telling her about the wonders of the amulet of love and claiming that no man could resist her.

Noakh took the opportunity to escape and meet back up with Hilzen, who had already finished talking to the merchant with the leeks. While walking away from the merchant's stall, he began to open his sack to keep the leeks that he had bought inside—but not before holding them up so that Noakh could see them.

"Leeks! At a modest price and easy to cook in soup. They will serve as provisions during our trip. There is nothing like showing interest in a merchant's profession in order to soften the price of his products. Have you bought something?"

"I do not have any money. The little I had, I spent on our last meal."

"I barely have three coins—enough to buy some more food, nothing else. And we need much warmer clothes if we want to reach the Snowy Mountains. Who was ever going to make me believe that a shave would be an unnecessary luxury?" said Hilzen while he fingered his beard regretfully.

Their conversation was cut off by a loud sound of metal clanking in a nearby alley. A deep, rude voice spoke from the alleyway in a threatening tone.

Noakh approached the alley slowly. Hilzen followed him. They looked into the alley cautiously. They saw two men, one of whom was tall and corpulent, wearing a green vest. His arms were thick, and his hands were enormous, with fingers like sausages. The other figure was an old man of very short stature. He sported thick white eyebrows, the same color as the little remaining hair on his head. His eyes were hidden under huge folds. The man in the green vest had cornered the old man in the alley. Meanwhile, the old man reached his arm behind himself, trying to hold on to something strapped on to his back.

Noakh unsheathed his steel sword. Hilzen unsheathed Distra. Not willing to tolerate the situation any further, Noakh was about to intervene, but Hilzen grabbed him by the shoulder, urging him to hold off, in order to learn more about what was going on. The young Fireo was about to reproach his companion's attitude; to him it was more than obvious what was going on. But just then the man in the vest raised one of his enormous hands and pushed the old man against the wall. The old man hit the wall with a loud *clank*.

163

"Listen, old man," said the man in the vest, "that shield isn't worth any money and you don't want it at all. Why are you being so rude and won't accept my generous offer?" The man spoke with an aggressive tone. The shield he was talking about could be seen lying on the old man's back; that was the object that had collided against the wall to cause the metallic echo that had resounded through the alleyway.

"Do you call a copper coin a generous offer?" replied the old man defiantly. "It's not for sale anyway, I told you! And now, if I may, my wife is waiting for me at home..." He tried to brush the hand of his oppressor away. The man in the vest responded by squeezing the old man against the wall a little more tightly. With his other hand he hit the wall. Hard, producing a thunderous noise—the assailant's way of warning the old man that his patience was running out.

"Damn it, you stupid old man! You've had your chance and you've wasted it! So don't go around saying that Tugul is not a considerate man!"

Tugul grabbed the old man's clothes, lifting him off the ground with one hand. With his other hand he tried to grab the shield strapped to the old man's back.

At that moment Noakh and Hilzen entered the alley, both their swords held high.

"Hey... you!" Noakh shouted. He now was running toward the man in the vest.

Tugul turned to see who was provoking him. The old man took advantage of the distraction. Seeing that Tugul held him at an ideal height, he kicked as hard as his old legs allowed him to, striking Tugul in his noblest parts.

Tugul fell to the ground in pain. He released the old man, who fell gently beside him. The next moment, the old man took the shield from his back and showed it to his aggressor.

"Didn't you want this shield?" He held it high with both hands. "Here it is." Using both hands he brought the shield down hard on Tugul's forehead. Tugul moaned in pain. The old man set out to escape, but his blow had not been as hard as he thought. Blinded by fury and indignation, Tugul grabbed one of his legs.

"You will regret this, you old man!" Tugul roared. He raised his hand to where the shield had struck him: blood coated his fingers. "You earned it. Now you're going to lose more than your shield!

But just then Noakh and Hilzen were on him, both pointing their swords at Tugul. The man, blinded by his thirst for revenge, had not seen them approach.

"Let him go," Noakh commanded as he held the edge of his blade close to Tugul's arm—the same arm with which Tugul was holding the old man's leg. "One way or another you will end up releasing him," Noakh threatened as he held the edge of his blade a hair's breadth from the skin of Tugul's arm."

Tugul paused, then released the old man even as he glared furiously at the two meddlers.

"Don't stick your noses where you don't have any business," he grunted. He kept staring at them. Tugul's nose was bulging and thick. Pockmarks scarred the right side of his face.

"Shut up at once," Hilzen said. He sheathed Distra then helped the old man up. "Can you walk, old man?"

The old man nodded. He and Hilzen turned away and Hilzen helped the old man walk down the alley. But the old man had come out of the incident unharmed; so, after again hanging the shield on his back, he began to walk on his own.

Noakh, on the other hand, kept his sword pointed at Tugul, eyeing him threateningly.

"Attacking an old man like that," he said reproachfully. He spat on the ground in repulsion. "You'd better not follow us." He sheathed his sword then turned around.

Noakh began to walk down the alley, on guard in case Tugul wanted to vent his anger against him. Fortunately, Tugul seemed to have come to his senses, realizing that attacking an armed man wasn't the best idea after all.

Hilzen and the old man were waiting for Noakh at the alley's end. Hilzen looked at the old man with concern. The old man rested his hands on his knees while keeping his eyes closed and breathing deeply.

"Are you sure you are all right?" Hilzen asked.

"A man of my age... shouldn't be scared like this," said the old man with his eyes still closed.

"Seeing how you handled yourself, I could almost say that you could have finished him off," Noakh answered, smiling. The old man's performance had certainly been quite impressive for a man of his age. The old man opened his eyes and began to laugh.

"Thank you," he said, "but I'm afraid if it weren't for you, I wouldn't have come out of that alley." He sighed.

"It was nothing," Hilzen said, waving his hand dismissively. "Would you like us to escort you home?"

"Home?" The old man snorted. "What I need is a drink! It's what we used to do after every battle—celebrate our victory and honor the fallen!"

"After every battle?" Hilzen repeated.

"Of course. Do you think that at my age I did not take part in some wars? I was part of the militia, to be precise," said the old man proudly, somewhat more energetic after recovering from the shock of being attacked. Hilzen and Noakh nodded. Although the Aquadom had an army that was more than adequate to defend itself in the event of an attack, it was not strange that in times of need men and women were enlisted and trained for combat. "Well, what about a drink? You're invited, of course!"

Noakh and Hilzen exchanged glances. The Fireo shrugged.

"Isn't it a little early to drink?" Hilzen said, looking up at the sky.

"Under normal conditions yes, but a victory in combat always deserves to be celebrated, no matter the time of day," the old man replied, smiling as he drew his hands behind his back. "It is a bad omen not to do so."

"A bad omen, huh?" Noakh said. "Sure, why not, let's celebrate our victory."

"Wonderful," answered the man. "I know a tavern nearby. The pitchers aren't the cleanest but the beer is excellent."

* * *

"Three beers, lovely girl," ordered the old man, who was called Dleheim. The woman behind the bar nodded then diligently filled three sparkling mugs. They were filled so high that the beer foamed over the edges, leaving a foamy trail across the wooden bar. Hilzen was about to pay for the drinks, if only out of courtesy, as they had hardly any money left, but Dleheim shook his head. "I said I would invite you."

"Oh, thank you," said Hilzen, while Noakh nodded to Dleheim in gratitude.

Noakh's beer was so overflowing that he couldn't help spilling a little on the floor. The three men brought their beers out of the tavern and sat at one of the outdoor tables where they could watch people walking by.

"To our victory," Dleheim said as he lifted his mug.

"To our victory!" repeated Hilzen and Noakh as they also lifted their mugs. The three companions clinked mugs, causing beer to spill onto the table. The trio then had a good drink and set their beers resting onto the table.

"Well, tell me," began Dleheim, his shield resting on one of the legs of the table. He used the sleeve of his shirt to wipe the foam from his mouth. "What brings you to the village of Livian? I hope it's not because of our famed market? The merchandise exhibited these last few weeks has certainly been disappointing..."

"We're just passing through," Noakh said after drinking again. "We're heading west."

"I don't blame you." Dleheim shrugged. "Livian is a boring city, after all..."

"Yet it seems that the village is not spared from altercations with undesirables," Hilzen said, recalling the incident that Dleheim had had in the alley.

"Oh yes, Tugul," answered Dleheim, furrowing his white eyebrows. "That loathsome animal... I knew his father, can you believe it? A nice man... If he knew what his son has become..." He sighed. "Tugul is known for his problems with gambling; surely he wanted my shield to pay off his debts, but the shield would have caused him more trouble than good," Dleheim said, nodding his head.

"What do you mean?" Noakh said.

"This shield," Dleheim said as he picked it up and put it on the table, making sure that the wood on which he was about to rest it was dry. The shield was worn and damaged at the edges. It was a bluish wooden battleshield adorned with white sketches; a metal siren had been set as an ornament in the center. Hilzen and Noakh could not help but admire it. "It belongs—or rather, *belonged*—to a noble family, the Criven de le Dos family. An ordinary family of nobility, we could say, nothing to do with other powerful noble houses, of course. But even so, their coat of arms on the shield is more than recognizable," Dleheim said as he ran his hand over the emblem on the shield.

"I see what you mean." Hilzen nodded and drank.

"I don't understand," Noakh said, confused. "What's the problem?"

"Oh none, Noakh," Dleheim answered ironically. "None if you want to lose your head, of course. What do you think would happen if the authorities or some nobleman discovered that someone was selling a

167

shield that was the property of nobility?" Dleheim passed his finger from one side of his neck to the other as he raised his eyebrows and smiled.

"But then, Dleheim," Hilzen continued, confused, "why do you carry the shield on your back? Do you want the authorities to kill you?"

"Oh, yes... I understand that point may confuse you, Hilzen," answered Dleheim, nodding. "To answer that, I'll have to tell you a story... My battleshield..." Dleheim paused for a second. "No, let me begin properly. I, like many others, had to serve in the war. That shield belonged to a soldier of higher rank than I, of course. We militiamen did not have ornaments on our shields and armor—the queendom was not going to spend money on us," he added, laughing. "It was a hard battle," he continued, "I remember it as if it were yesterday... The enemy attacked our flanks, diminishing our defenses. However, we managed to recover and gain ground, forcing the enemy to retreat. When the battle was over, I found the shield next to the body of its unfortunate owner. As fond as I was of heraldry at the time, I could not let a shield like that be abandoned, simply left there on the battlefield. When I got back home, I thought many times about keeping the shield for myself—it was so beautifully ornamented—but that shield had a history. Armor often passes from parents to children; no matter how enthusiastic I was about keeping it, doing so did not seem right.

"After conducting a little research by rummaging through the books in my library, I identified the family to which the soldier had belonged; it was indeed a family of high position—the Criven de le Dos, which, as you may certainly know, is a noble family from the east. After traveling to their estate and being received by one of the servants, I was introduced to the noble house's leader, Eman Criven de le Dos, who turned out to be the soldier's father. After explaining what had happened, he told me to keep the shield, he did not want it back.

"Apparently the young soldier was the fifth in the family and never received recognition from his father. This led him to fight in the war, taking the family shield while understanding that no one would come searching for him, seeking in the war what he could not find in his own home—appreciation." Dleheim paused, leaving his mug on the table with his gaze lost. "Sad," he said quietly. "Very sad. I decided to carry the shield with me everywhere. At least this way the young soldier will have some humble recognition."

Noakh nodded while he stared gently at Dleheim's eyes and placed a hand softly on Dleheim's shoulder. "I'm sure the soldier is proud that his shield is with you, Dleheim."

"I think the same," Hilzen added. "And that father... how stupid. I'm sure that at some point he regretted what he had done."

"I do not have the slightest doubt of it," Dleheim answered. He picked up his mug and raised it. "For the fallen!"

"For the fallen!" repeated Hilzen and Noakh while raising their mugs.

"You know, Hilzen," said Dleheim after a long gulp. "I saw your sword in the alley. Would you mind showing it to me?"

Dleheim's words alarmed Noakh and Hilzen. Noakh grew very tense. Hilzen was still carrying Distra, following his agreement with Noakh.

"What do you want to know about his sword?" Noakh replied, perplexed.

"Nothing in particular. It's just that I could swear that I have seen an illustration of the sword's hilt in a book. I'd like to see it more closely... May I?" Dleheim noticed the two men had grown nervous.

"Oh, calm down!" he exclaimed. "My interest does not go beyond my fascination with literature and history. Yes, maybe I should have started from there. As I said before, I always loved heraldry, and although I am now retired, at one time I was responsible for the Livian Bookstore, one of the largest collections of books in the whole queendom! My work at the bookstore made me the happiest man in the world... having so much information at my fingertips, being interested in history—the history of this world, which of course implies the history of the four kingdoms." The old man turned his gaze to Hilzen's belt. "The hilt of that sword, I know I've seen it before; therefore, it must have belonged to a renowned family... or it may perhaps just be very similar to the drawing I saw. I just wanted to satisfy my curiosity."

Noakh knew that if he said no, he would sow doubts in the man. However, if he said yes and showed him the sword...

"I can sense your uncertainty." Dleheim laughed. "I do not care if it's stolen, I assure you that I just want to see it up close."

He was a bit confused, for it was Hilzen who carried the sword, sheathed against his hip, but it was as if Hilzen was asking for permission of the boy, staring ceaselessly at Noakh, as if he had the last word. He noticed Noakh's brown eyes, not giving them any greater importance beyond that which he would give any typical inhabitant of the queendom.

Noakh was still uncertain how best to proceed, but he had to make a decision.

"Fine," he said, "but not here."

Dleheim raised his hands in joy, thankful for his luck, while Hilzen breathed a sigh of relief.

"This is not the best place to talk about heraldry in any case," Dleheim chortled. "I live not far from here. I will be able to show you my collection! Come, it's this way."

22. Dleheim's house

With his energy renewed by his joy, Dleheim began to walk down the alley with his hands behind his back. The rhythm of the old man's small steps forced Noakh and Hilzen to jog to keep up with him. Taking advantage of the distance between them, Hilzen drew close to Noakh, as though in conspiracy, and spoke to him in a low voice.

"Are you sure about this, Noakh? Because I'm not at all certain! He looks like an innocent man—but why take the risk?"

Noakh nodded. "I know. At first I had my doubts, but something tells me I should trust him. Something similar happened with you, you know?"

"You mean the fact that you were utterly tied up and had a crossbow held to your head didn't help you to make your choice?" Hilzen said, frowning.

After crossing a couple of streets, they arrived at a one-story house. Dleheim knocked on the door. A moment later, an elderly woman opened it.

"Ogi, these are two of my friends, Noakh and Hilzen. They will stay for lunch."

The woman smiled at Noakh and Hilzen. She was stout, but her face was gentle and her eyes seemed kind.

Hilzen turned to Dleheim. "No, that's unnecessary. We don't want to bother you."

"You're not bothering us at all," Ogi said. "We're grateful for the visit—we don't usually get many visitors traveling here." She turned and

171

smiled at Dleheim. "I'll prepare my best dish—roast beef with vintage wine and oranges."

Dleheim smiled. Perhaps Hilzen had imagined it, but he could swear he saw the old man licking his lips when he heard Ogi mention the roast beef. He turned to Noakh and Hilzen. "You are lucky. Ogi is the best cook in the world... and I do not say that simply because she is my wife."

Ogi blushed. She began wiping her hands on the towel with some agitation. "Come this way," Dleheim said hurriedly.

After walking down a flight of stairs, they entered the basement. The large room was full of books. Scrolls were stacked on shelves, and maps of different regions of the world hung on the walls. Dleheim approached the front of the stairs and hung his battleshield on a large wooden hook before the stairs. On one of the walls, a huge worn map of the world could be seen over a dark wooden table. Together, Noakh and Hilzen approached the map.

The map was full of annotations and markings along the borders. The four kingdoms were labeled around the Void, which was depicted as a dark-brown spot in the center of the delineation: the Aquadom to the north, Firia to the east, Tir Torrent to the west, and Aere Tine to the south.

While the Aquadom had been drawn with perfect accuracy, the extent and locations of the other kingdoms lacked such exhaustive precision. Only the borders of Tir Torrent, the Kingdom of Earth, had been drawn with a bit more rigor. At every edge of the map there was a distinctive mark, showing the end of the world in that direction. A waterfall, Finistia, was drawn at the top, establishing the northernmost borders of the world. Dleheim noticed his guests' curiosity.

"On this map," Dleheim began as he approached the map and passed his fingers over it, "I like to mark the locations of all the battles that ever happened throughout the history of our world. And also, I fancy writing annotations of all the remarkable heroes of the wars and their astonishing feats." Dleheim put his finger on a particular spot on the right side of the map, where a set of mountains was drawn: the frontier between Firia and the Aquadom. "See here? In this precise location, General Riger won a decisive battle using his wits. I was there too, you know? That man was indeed a genius, a portentous mind and an imposing figure. Unluckily, that was his last battle..."

172

"But that's it. Let's leave sad affairs aside for now. You told me I could see the sword—I wanted to do so after lunch, but I admit that I can't wait another second!"

With Noakh's approval, Hilzen unsheathed the sword and passed it carefully to Dleheim. He took it with great gentleness by the hilt, then traced the entire blade of the sword with two fingers. His eyes rested on the hilt as he studied it. Noakh, despite having agreed to allow Dleheim to handle the sword, grew tense, seeing Distra in the hands of another man. But allowing the old man to examine the sword had seemed totally harmless. In all honesty, he did not expect the old man to know anything about Distra; it was a sword from a different kingdom, even if it was one of the two twins of fire.

"A very humble-looking sword," Dleheim said, "and yet so beautiful, its hilt not too ornate, its grip simple. It's funny because despite its simple design I can't stop staring at it. I do not remember which house it belongs to, but it's strangely familiar to me..." Looking more closely, his eyes focused on the pommel, where the tiny symbol of a flame and the D appeared on the dark copper plate. Leaving the sword carefully on the table, he took his glasses, which were laid over a dusty book, and set them on his nose and went swiftly to a shelf, from which he picked out several books. He brought the books to the dark wooden table and examined them energetically. "Do not say anything... I'll find out for myself!" he said as he turned the pages, pausing briefly at each illustration of a sword before shaking his head and quickly turning to the next page.

"As if he were going to believe us," Hilzen said under his breath. Noakh was still tense, his arms crossed as he stared at Dleheim. Hilzen was aware that the moment Dleheim discovered the origins of the sword, he and Noakh might be in peril.

Dleheim continued searching through the books. Having already taken up the second volume, he paused at a particular small image, stained with blots of ink, that appeared in the book. He glanced back and forth from the book to the sword, comparing the sword again and again to the image on the page. Then he turned, staring into the eyes of Hilzen and Noakh. Hilzen found the situation amusing, recalling his own reactions when he had learned of the sword's origins—and all that they implied. Noakh, however, maintained a firm expression on his face and crossed his arms expectantly.

"It's... It's a replica, right?" Dleheim's expression had changed dramatically. He picked up the book and showed it to Noakh. "It's... It's exactly like this illustration, but... that's impossible! But then... why carry a replica of one of the twin fire swords? Why only one and not both? What am I saying? Why would a citizen of our queendom desire to take a direct path to his grave?" The old man's eyes fell on Hilzen, who had carried the sword.

"Do not look at me, Dleheim." He pointed to Noakh. "He's the one who should answer you!"

Dleheim, surprised, looked at Noakh. Sternly, Noakh approached the table and took Distra. Dleheim stared at Noakh's brown eyes, guessing that he and the sword shared some connection.

"Dleheim," Noakh observed, "I do not think you would believe me if I told you..."

As Dleheim watched in astonishment, Noakh held Distra firmly by the hilt then snapped his wrist quickly to ignite the flames. Dleheim, at seeing such a vision, could not help but adjust his glasses while his mouth was open. Hilzen went to help him but stopped to see how the old man was looking at the sword, as if seeing a miracle.

"This is my story," Noakh said. "Let's start from the beginning..."

As Noakh told his story, Dleheim's face was as honest as an open book. At the beginning, his face contained a look of disbelief, a more than reasonable reaction when someone reveals to you that he is the exiled heir of a kingdom, but soon his face expressed absolute fascination. Noakh spared no detail, telling Dleheim everything he knew; as with Hilzen, he felt a huge sense of relief at sharing his story and showing his true self, albeit just like the previous time, when he had revealed his secret to Hilzen, the fear of rejection after this revelation, after something so radically different, was still there. Although Dleheim was full of questions, he avoided interrupting him before he had finished.

"And that's all I remember," Noakh concluded.

Dleheim looked into his eyes without blinking. Then, after a pause, he began to walk slowly around the room, finally staring at the shield with his hands behind his back.

"That explains everything... but why that fear? Did you think that if I learned the origin of the sword I would run to the authorities so they might delegate soldiers to arrange for your capture? Is that right? No doubt the trial would have been quick. Noakh, you would have been lucky if you were held prisoner—but Hilzen would have been treated as a traitor, and as such he would be lucky if he was thrown alive to the bottom of the sea while tied to a rock, but probably he would instead be burned or buried alive, a more fitting destiny for a traitor."

A lump arose in Hilzen's throat. As much as he longed to die, he certainly did not want to do so being judged a traitor by his people, even though he was aware the ballots had all been cast now that he had helped Noakh. However, he did not like to consider that. Noakh, on the other hand, weighed what it would be like to be captured by the Royal Guard. A public execution was the first thing that crossed his mind. But, thinking better of his prospects, he realized the queen might well know how to exploit his status as heir to the crown of fire. Somehow, he knew, she would take advantage of his claim, for the queen was well known for her cunning.

"You thought I would betray you..." Dleheim shook his head incredulously. "But honestly, who would have believed me?" He still was looking at the shield while shaking his head. But suddenly he turned abruptly. "Idiots! *Betray?* As much as I love history? The only thing I regret is that I'm not young enough to accompany you... But betray you? My debts to the queendom have been more than repaid by the battles to which I was recruited—the souls of my comrades no doubt paid for them! And besides, after seeing you here, I'm certain I'm doing the Aquadom a favor by *not* betraying you! You will undoubtedly prove a better king for us than that bastard Wulkan has been... Even his name sounds like that of a barbarian!

"So, Noakhail"—the old man continued staring directly to Noakh's eyes—"tell me, what is your plan? How do you intend to claim the throne? Surely you do not intend to tell me you will take the sword covered in flames to the height of the Fire Kingdom's power while claiming that you are the heir, right?" Dleheim began to laugh at his own words.

Noakh turned away to collect his thoughts. "I still had not planned to go there, at least not yet. After what happened years ago, it seems that they are still following me. I am sure that Wulkan will have soldiers and spies waiting for me to come back one day. After all, I have his sword..."

Noakh stared at the blade of Distra, seeing his own reflection; his look didn't convey contempt. He had blamed enough the sacred sword for all the disgraces that had occurred in his life.

Dleheim laughed loudly.

"I'm sure that bastard Wulkan can't sleep, thinking about when his time will come. And now that I think about it—of course! That explains why the Kingdom of Fire has been less... active. Yes, let's say it that way. Not long ago confrontations with his kingdom were practically constant; the Fireos are undoubtedly a warlike people—they love war, and Wulkan is its greatest exponent. Who would have thought it was all because of this?" He gestured towards the sword. "The fact that Distra is here, in Livian, is certainly very valuable information for the other three kingdoms... and you, Noakh, have to be careful. You say that Wulkan will have spies awaiting you in the Kingdom of Fire—yes, that's for sure... but have you thought that it is more than likely that he also has spies here in the Aquadom?" Noakh turned a bit pale, his expression sufficient for Dleheim. He laughed, realizing his innocence. "I see. Of course it's just an assumption, I can't say for sure there are spies in the Aquadom, but if I were king, I would certainly send spies to the other kingdoms. The loyalty of many is easily bought with a sack of gold—and there's no need to talk of the advantages that would hold for a monarch who wishes to keep aware of the movements of kingdoms seeking to rival his own. You do not have to be a genius to realize that the deeper the spy has infiltrated the citizenry of enemy kingdoms, the better the crown will be."

"Maybe that's the reason why those assailants..." Noakh's voice faltered. It was not the first time he had thought the incident at his home was more than a mere assault.

Dleheim guessed Noakh's thoughts. "Maybe you were being monitored under Wulkan's orders, or it was just mere assailants that thought of the price of such a peculiar sword. Who knows? But thinking about it again, that should not worry you—at least not here in this house. What was your way until you met me?"

"We were going towards the Snowy Mountains. We'll reach the Fireo Kingdom through the Aertians." As he stated his plans aloud, Noakh realized that many—including Dleheim—would not understand his motives.

"I see." Dleheim turned thoughtful. "Certainly not an easy way. It would be so simple to knock on the palace door and tell the guards who you are, so easy—and yet impossible... But life is not made to be that simple. For where would be the excitement if that were true?" Dleheim started to laugh again. "No. And even if you came and they sat you on the throne— Wulkan kneels, gives you the crown—do you think you would be a good king?"

Dleheim cocked his head, waiting for a response from Noakh. The boy lowered his head as he noticed Hilzen's eyes glued on him, waiting for his response. He did not need to weigh his response for very long before knowing what it would be.

"No," he said. "How could I be? I would not know where to start..."

"A humble and modest king," Dleheim avowed. "Qualities not very common among royalty." He let out a loud laugh. "Maybe you would not be a bad king after all! You have probably asked yourself what qualities a good king must have. I myself have been thinking about it right now, and I am afraid that there is no correct answer, precisely because our history has given us many kings—or *queens* in our beloved Queendom, of course.

"The sword may have chosen you, but that is only the beginning. What qualities must a king have? If you ask me, I would say that a king should have leadership, courage, wisdom, justice, the insight to inform proper decision-making—many attributes, which I am sure you will realize that you are still lacking. Noakh, you are too young after all. Even if you had been instructed at the palace, which the court probably would have ordered if everything had followed its usual course—it would still be too soon. It is unnecessary to go very far. In our queendom, it also takes a while until the Lacrima assumes the throne; it is a very hard burden to bear, after all." Dleheim laid his hands on the back of Noakh's shoulders. "I'm afraid there's no way to make a king; I wish it were as easy as that story..."

"What story?" Noakh asked. Although Lumio had tried to teach him everything he knew about the place where he had once lived, his father had certainly been unable to delve as deeply into popular culture.

"What was the name?" Dleheim rubbed his forehead, trying to remember. "Oh yes! It was the Four Pillars of the Crown."

"Oh! I remember it!" Hilzen replied. "It's that story written in rhymes about a king, isn't it?"

"That's right, Hilzen. It's a story written in verse. Many stories were once told like that, making them easier to remember—and they were more beautiful, if you ask me. That particular story tells the tale of a king who—one day before reaching the age of majority, when he would be crowned—decided to flee the kingdom in order to escape the panic he feels in the face of assuming such responsibility.

"The story describes how, on his journey, he travels dressed as a peasant riding to distant lands, so with his adventures he would gain the courage in the battlefield he would need as king, he would experience a thousand adventures, he would even find love—"

177

"Wait a minute." Hilzen cut him off, remembering more details about the story. "Did he not die just when he was going home?"

"That's right." Dleheim nodded. "The story says, 'Futata fell down looking at the sky, unable to dodge the ax of his murderer. He died remembering her hair... a king nobody would remember.'" Dleheim paused for a moment. "In your hands lies the ability to change that ending, of course! Even so, don't allow Futata's death to tarnish his story—he lived great adventures, learned much during his trip, and finally fell into disgrace. It's an old story, told before the beautiful stories were preferred, and it comes with a bitter end, precisely because of the lesson that lies behind it. In the story, Futata dies because he confided the truth about who he was, a king—a mistake enough to finish him off.

"Which leads me to give you this advice, Noakh. The sword that you carry no doubt carries a great power... a power that has been able to lead a kingdom for centuries. However, do not become overconfident; there are many gods out there, more than you might think..."

Dleheim's warning surprised Noakh.

"Many gods? What do you mean?"

"Dleheim," Hilzen added, "everyone knows that there are only four gods, one for each kingdom. That's why the legendary weapons exist..."

"Everyone knows?" Dleheim laughed. "Not long ago everyone knew that kings were immortal... and the ax that Queen Medus received made them change their thoughts. Until not long ago you knew that the Fireo Kingdom was a kingdom like any other... yet here is the living proof that it is not like that at all!" Dleheim pointed at Noakh with one of his bony fingers. "What we know changes every day. We just soon forget our own ignorance, and we adapt quickly to the new status quo... It's the way we survive, after all. So, I will ask this, Noakh: What is a god?"

The boy turned thoughtful in the face of such a tricky question, hoping to give a proper answer.

"An omnipotent being, with a unique power... Those who gave us legendary weapons to lead men and thus create balance in the world?"

"What a bunch of nonsense!" Dleheim snorted. "I really hope you do not believe your own words... What is a god? A god is simply a being that we worship. They are just our own creation. Do not look at me like that, Hilzen. I'm not saying that the gods do not exist—I said that we created them, which is different."

Dleheim sighed, seeing the puzzled looks both Hilzen and Noakh had on their faces.

"Look at it this way... If Noakh, with his flaming sword, traveled to an island where no one knew about our sacred weapons and then he demonstrated his power to the natives, how likely would it be for him to be praised as a god? See? We create the gods... A god is everything that offers us consolation, a being that protects and watches over us. They are the ones we worship. We want to have everything under control; since we obviously can't, we pray as a way of getting that control back... There are many gods in this world, Noakh. There is even a term to describe them: the so-called *living gods*—beings with such power achieved in so many ways, which made other creatures praise them in the same way that we pray to our beloved Aqua Deus. There are even some cults whose fervor for their gods make us seem like utter pagans by comparison... Look at you and me, Hilzen, helping the one chosen by the same Incandescent, and yet our beloved Aqua Deus has not sent a colossal wave to destroy our village as punishment—how soft-hearted, isn't it?"

Noakh paused a moment before answering. "I understand Dleheim, I won't rely only on Distra's power." He reached out and put his hand on Dleheim's shoulder. "You have my word." Then Noakh approached Distra that was still lying on the table and picked it up.

"I'm glad to hear it, Noakh."

"I was thinking about what King Futata did and even if he died, I can see why he did it," Noakh said. "He traveled to places he had never seen as king, he learned a lot and understood much more... That certainly made him wise, and surely it was fun."

Smiling, Dleheim nodded at Noakh's words. "I agree with you, Noakh. Futata may have died and regretted many things, but I am sure that undertaking such a trip was not one of them." He stopped, looking again at Noakh again. "I see that you have made a decision, Noakh—I can see the determination in your eyes. Nothing is going to change your mind. Stubbornness is in your blood, after all," Dleheim said, referring to the harsh qualities people presumed about the Fireos. He began to laugh while Hilzen crossed his arms at his waist and turned his back on Dleheim.

Noakh showed satisfaction. He had his doubts, but now he was convinced a trip similar to King Futata's was the best choice. He would visit the four kingdoms, learn from each of them, and see those landscapes that no one dared to see... He would face terrible enemies and learn from every victory—and even more from every defeat. He was sure that this, somehow, would help him to be a better king someday.

And if his destiny were similar to that of King Futata, at least he would die for something he believed in, a death based on his own decisions. Dying in the pursuit of a purpose he believed in would be an act he could endure.

Noakh unbuckled his belt, then slipped Distra's sheath—with Distra in it—onto the belt, then rebuckled it. It was time to carry the full weight of his destiny. Hilzen, even though not convinced of his friend's action, didn't say anything.

Ogi knocked on the basement door, indicating that dinner was ready. At the top of the stairs, when Dleheim opened the door slightly, the smell penetrated the stairwell, making the guests' belly growl. As Noakh and Hilzen approached the table, they saw a fountain full of potatoes covered in red sauce... beans roasted with ham... a loaf of crusty bread, and—as a culmination—the famous beef with oranges. The meat shone in the sauce coating it, giving it an extravagant appearance. The undisguised expressions of admiration in Hilzen's and Noakh's eyes made Dleheim laugh.

"I warned you—Ogi is a great cook!"

Ogi turned slightly red again.

It took little time for Hilzen and Noakh to push their manners into second place, behind their appetites, as they began to eat each dish. There was nothing that was not delicious. Dleheim smiled while eating at a good pace. Ogi, on the other hand, ate slower... and less. Her face radiated happiness, because there was no better compliment for a cook than to see how their guests enjoyed the products of their culinary skills.

During the meal, there was little time for conversation. Eventually Ogi grew interested in the guests, who, encouraged by Dleheim, explained that they were adventurers who had decided to travel the world, and that Noakh's sword had attracted Dleheim's curiosity, for he had recognized it in his books. Thus was their friendship established. As Dleheim had explained just before the three men had come up from the basement, he wanted to tell Ogi the truth—at least the part of the truth that did not hurt her, because she was a loyal devotee of Aqua Deus. Not sharing Dleheim's passion for history would undoubtedly have made it more difficult for her to understand the reason for his guests' trip.

After the meal, dessert was served, which their stomachs wanted to refuse, but which their eyes couldn't. A pumpkin pie wrapped in white chocolate and nut and cocoa powder, covered by a thin layer of cream—

its taste did not disappoint. The cake melted in their mouths, flooding the palate with its sweet flavor.

Such food, along with the heat of the fireplace, made all but Dleheim fall exhausted into their hostess' armchairs. Meanwhile Dleheim decided that he somehow wanted to contribute to the adventure his new friends were about to undertake. So he went back down to the basement.

When they awoke from their armchair naps Dleheim was waiting for them with his arms behind his back. "I see you've finally woken up," he said, laughing.

Ogi, to the contrary, was still sleeping. Both Hilzen and Noakh began to stretch. It had been a long time since either of them had eaten so well, and in such abundance.

"Come with me."

Dleheim led them back down to the basement. On one of the main tables there was a huge map that bared the world—or, at least, what the cartographers had come to decipher of the world. It was a yellowish parchment, cracking at the edges. The ink, although discolored, had nonetheless managed to last over the years.

"This map will serve you on your way. I have been trying to write some guidelines, but I realized that it is you who must write your own adventure. At least the map can serve as a guide.

"Hilzen," he said, turning to his friend, "I've been thinking about things... and this is for you." Dleheim approached the wall and took down the shield that hung there, coming back and handing it to Hilzen. Hilzen passed his hand over the detailed relief on the shield, observing the figure of the siren that was carved onto it.

"But Dleheim... I can't accept it. This shield is yours, it's part of your collection." In addition to his protests, Hilzen was aware that his combat weapon, a crossbow, would not allow him to make much use of a shield, which was a piece of armor more useful for fighters in close combat. However, he tried to avoid mentioning that part of his reasoning.

"Nonsense. It's a battleshield. It was not created to hang on the wall of an old decrepit like me! I'm sure you'll be able to make better use of it than the one I'll give him. Also, I want you to be aware of the risks of this present. This battleshield might help you sometimes, but have no doubt it will also bring you trouble; it belonged to a noble family after all, don't forget that."

"Okay then, thank you," said Hilzen, nodding his thanks.

"Noakh, for you I have nothing, but a simple word." Dleheim handed him a square piece of paper.

"A word?" Noakh, who did not expect to receive anything, was perplexed by such a gift. He fixed his eyes on the paper and read it aloud. "Akuhlun?" he read, looking at Hilzen as if to see if he had any clue.

His companion answered with a shrug.

"This word might not make any sense to you right now, and perhaps it is best that it remain so, at least until the time comes." Dleheim stared at Noakh's brown eyes. "Noakh, promise me you will not forget that word, no matter what."

"I won't, I promise." Noakh nodded. Then he put the note in his pocket while repeating the word in his mind several times to commit it to memory.

"Are you not even going to give us a clue as to what such a word, Akuhlun, means, Dleheim?" Hilzen asked, intrigued by the enigmatic word. "A powerful spell, perhaps?"

"Fools!" laughed Dleheim. "You'll see when the time comes. I hope it will also be helpful."

Noakh was full of enthusiasm. "Dleheim... thank you very much for everything. You could have betrayed us; instead you have done this for us. I do not know how to thank you," he said. For a moment he realized how many people in the world inadvertently offered nothing in return for an offer of help—even those who had taught them to hate from childhood.

"I do know how you can thank me, Noakh. If you finally reach your goal, and I am sure that it will be so, I hope you invite a humble inhabitant of the Aquadom, like me, and his wife, like Ogi, to your palace. I'd love to see you sitting on the throne.

"Oh, and that's not all, Noakh. In a way, I am forced to help you in your challenge. You can't leave the city in your present state of dress. You both need a haircut, a shave—and clothes that make you look like decent citizens. Besides that, you will need some armor. You can't face the world in simple cloth! It is true that the lighter the clothes, the better, so you will have to acquire the basics. Enough to protect you, but at the same time it must be light enough so as not to impose an obstacle in your travels, or attract too much attention."

"Dleheim, we thank you... but we can't accept it. You've done more for us than we deserve."

"Noakh, do not misunderstand my words. Do you think that I'm doing this for you? Or that this is just an act of generosity?" Noakh did not know how to respond. "Of course not. This is for a higher cause than you, as it is a higher cause for me. I do it for history! Do you know what it would mean for me to know that such a historic change was partly thanks to my actions? That I helped a king rise up and claim his throne? Call me selfish if you want, Noakh... I do this for me, not for you."

"I understand, Dleheim." Noakh nodded while smiling. "Even so, that does not change my words of gratitude in any way... We will be eternally grateful."

"I think so," Hilzen added as he hung his new shield on his back.

During the rest of their stay, Noakh and Hilzen visited the local barber, who promptly executed a half-decent haircut and a proper shaving. After that, they visited the village blacksmith and acquired several pieces of armor. Noakh purchased a chain mail shirt, which, although light, would provide good protection in close combat. Hilzen instead took leather armor, more practical and accommodating for his skills as a crossbowman. At Dleheim's insistence, they each also acquired overcoats that would allow them to withstand the cold weather they no doubt would encounter on their travels. They were finally going to the Snowy Mountains.

23. The Golden Tower

The Royal Guard crossed the square shouting, pushing people out of the way with their huge mounts. Their silver armor with slight bluish undertones flashed in the sunlight. Their helmets were ornamented with a golden relief showing the mermaid combing herself on the rock, the emblem of the crown. Citizens quickly gathered around the square. The Royal Guard could be there for only one reason: The queen was in the city.

The news spread like a whispered plague. In a short time, the square was filled with people who wanted to see either the queen or the coins that might fall from her chests as a result of her enormous generosity. Was it all that much to ask? At the end of the parade of horse guards, a stout-faced female soldier appeared, carrying the royal banner... and behind her a carriage pulled by two white horses. The carriage stopped. Accompanied by a fanfare of bugles announcing the queen's arrival, the door of the carriage opened. Queen Graglia drew her thin lips back, exposing her white teeth and putting a warm smile on her face, promptly exhibiting it to her lackeys—and looking beautiful, as always.

On her head the queen wore the traveling crown, as she was used to calling it, which replaced the original crown she used when she occupied the throne. It was a replica, smaller in size than the original and slightly less fancily ornamented. But like the original it was made of white gold set with sapphires that matched her eyes. A light veil covered the upper part of her face, and her smooth blonde hair peeked down her back, falling gracefully over her thin cloak. She had small hips and slender legs, and her face was round with a fleshy nose, big expressive eyes, and long eyelashes. Her light skin was smooth despite the fact that Graglia was close to sixty years old: it revealed no imperfections. If age advanced for the queen, her face did not seem to realize it.

With a proud smile she gracefully greeted the citizens of Hymal as she stepped out of the carriage, assisted by a member of the Royal Guard. After the queen, Gant Blacksword appeared, one of the four Knights of Water, a title that granted him the so-called forgiveness of the queen. The forgiveness of the queen allowed the four Knights of Water to freely perform any act in the Aquadom, assuming that their actions were performed for the good of the queen or her vassals. Although the Knights of Water were well known throughout the queendom, they each carried a pendant with a tiny flask adorned with a small sapphire in the shape of a crown. The pendants served to warn the most clueless about exactly whom they were facing. Although the four Knights of Water usually acted freely, it was not uncommon for the queen to enjoy their services, because they had achieved their title due to either their great ability or their usefulness for the queendom.

Gant was loaded with a suit of heavy blackened armor that, along with his broad shoulders, leant him an enormous appearance. On his back, he carried a black broadsword—a weapon so heavy that for a smaller soldier it would have been impossible to wield, even with both hands, and a blade so wide that a kid could hide behind it. The armor exhibited a worn look, having lost its brightness, and in its stead, displayed proud notches. Gant's head was completely shaved and displayed the hairy eyebrows of a very dark blond, which matched his mustache of the same tone that showed underneath his bulbous nose. Gant himself was a man of few words and quick judgment, which earned him the nickname the Queen's Executioner. He was not usually pleasant company because his seriousness and his lack of interest in practically everything unrelated to combat made him a somewhat soporific companion. For the most intrepid, seeing Gant with the queen was an easy way to realize that the reasons for the visit were, at best, delicate.

Despite having arrived with a grand escort, the queen's excursion to the square was not an official visit. Her gaze was fixed on the two buildings that dominated the square. On one side, the spectacular Hymal Cathedral, a building of apotheosic dimensions where the Aqua Deus was worshiped. Its huge marble pillars were adorned with reliefs displaying mermaids and marine motifs. The huge cathedral was until not long ago the tallest building in Hymal and the surrounding cities—

something that certainly the queen considered appropriate; worshipping temples had to rise above the mundane.

However, in front of the cathedral, a building had been built which acted both as a watchtower and a venue where the wealthiest merchants met to conduct business or hold auctions. It was known as the Golden Tower, precisely because it was the place where money often changed hands. Despite its insolent height, it had gone unnoticed until the boldness of the bourgeoisie had led them to place, at the top of the tower, a sculpture of a sea serpent engulfing a huge anchor. The monster was adorned on the sides with both a naked man and a naked woman, looking in opposite directions. Although horrific, the sculpture would not have been a problem if it were not for the fact that including the sculpture the golden tower was now slightly higher than the cathedral. After reaching the ears of the queen, she couldn't help but take part in the affair.

"All this trip for that simple piece of rock?" Gant murmured as he tried to observe the sculpture. He was employing his hand as a visor to cover his eyes from the sun and thus see with better clarity. He, just as a large portion of the Aquos, had problems tolerating the sun's rays, a condition that was related to the light color of their eyes in combination with the few sunny days, which prevented their eyes from adapting well to the light. He threw his shoulders back repeatedly in a circle, causing his pieces of armor to clash, generating a metallic screech. The road to the city of Hymal had been long—*very* long, in his opinion—*and* uncomfortable, even, despite the fact that he had been transported in the royal carriage, the most luxurious transportation in the queendom.

"Did you say something, Gant?" replied the queen, who had the ability to toss off the question in the sweetest way and, in turn, make a chill run down the listener's back, even for someone like Gant.

"No," Gant replied, and after a brief pause, he added, "my queen." It was a recurring oversight that he forgot to address the queen by her proper title, an omission he did not make on purpose or with evil intent. And the queen, although aware of it, could not avoid feeling irritated despite so much time having gone by without Gant having corrected the mistake.

The crowd did not have long to wait until the mayor of the city appeared in the square with his small escort. The Sisters of Hymal also appeared, the order of novices who were in charge of the cathedral. They had left the building and knelt at the door of the cathedral facing the

187

queen. For Graglia was not only the queen; she also long ago had been granted the title of high priestess of water, a position that had previously always acted independently—and with its own power. With Graglia, however, this was no longer the case. After the previous high priestess made a mistake leading the troops of the Congregation of the Church, Graglia interceded and was granted the title. Her wit had allowed her to dismiss the previous holder of the title, giving her, in turn, greater control over the church, a power that none of her predecessors had achieved. It was during this short period of time that the name Graglia the Usurper had sounded in the streets. A few beheadings served to ensure that title was easily forgotten.

The queen approached to the Sisters, walking in front of them so that they could touch her hand and kiss the ring of the Order—the one carried by the high officials of the church. The ring was the most luxurious and ornate object the high priestess had, a sapphire wrapped in gold molded in the form of a wave. After a brief bow, Graglia nodded slightly at Gant, after which they both headed towards the Golden Tower. The two passed through the huge oak door, with the Royal Guard standing on the sides, blocking the way. When Gant accompanied the queen it was known that the queen did not require the services of the guard. A Knight of Water provided more than sufficient protection... more so if it was Gant Blacksword.

The use of the Golden Tower was exclusive to the wealthiest merchants. It did not at all resemble a common market; not even raw materials or products could be found within its walls... no smells of farm animals or fishermen bellowing as they offered their products at the best prices to be found anywhere in the place. Instead, the room was filled with various spaces decorated with huge sofas where well-dressed men talked and reached agreements, with game rooms, with comfortable armchairs—all adorned with the greatest luxuries.

All conversation ceased when the merchants saw Gant and the queen enter: They froze, staring at such unexpected visitors, almost forgetting to get up and bow. The queen ignored the merchants, fixing her eyes on the details of the tower's interior, which was finished in darkened oak, golden filigree on the walls and rivets on the doors... walls adorned with paintings of the most popular artists of the time. Among them was a work of the renowned painter Rubeliev, in which a lady was shown caressing a swan. In truth, the tower was worth its name; all those details had cost a fortune.

The wooden steps creaked under Gant's weight, which did not seem to be affected by the number of stairs that he was going up, albeit with heavy armor. The queen walked behind him, eager to reach the top floor and see the faces of the guild leaders, those who had seen this pantomime through to the end. Graglia had no doubt that they had been alerted of their arrival. However, they could not do much to ward off their destiny. The thought drew a crooked smile to her face.

After climbing the last few stairs, Gant saw that the guild leaders were already on their knees, waiting for the queen to arrive. The guild houses represented the interests of the most important professions of Hymal; they had chosen a representative to watch over their interests and establish and respect a code of good practices. All this involved paying a fee that allowed only the wealthiest traders to participate in the guilds and, in turn, gain access to the privileges of the Golden Tower. The tower was not just used for trading, they said; apparently the best parties of the city were also held here—and the invitations were very restricted.

Three guilds were the most important guilds: the bakers, the bankers, and—of course—the fishermen, as fishing was the main activity of the queendom. Next in importance were the houses of the blacksmiths and the tailors, who little by little were gaining more influence. The three principal guild houses were those that had a more powerful representative in the Golden Tower. However, for some reason, the house of the tailors had managed to become part of that select group, the guild leaders then being four members.

Only three of those men were kneeling, the fourth member was not present. Although she had never dealt with them, the queen was well informed. On top of their ostentatious clothes, on the sleeves, the guild leaders liked to proudly wear an insignia that represented their guild. So, on the sleeves of all three men the queen could see the symbols of the wheat spikes, the two coins, and the fish.

It was Mormont, head of the fishermen's guild, who initiated the conversation.

"My queen, what a pleasant surprise! What do we owe such honor to? If we had known of your visit in advance, we would have celebrated it accordingly."

With a click, a servant appeared who, despite carrying a tray with a bottle of wine and several filled glasses, made a deep bow without spilling a drop. The queen rejected the offering with a quick gesture while Gant, skipping protocol, allowed himself to take one of the drinks. He knew that when he accompanied the queen, people offered them the most delicious delicacies. He had not been wrong—a blue wine with an intense flavor of fruit flooded his mouth. Gant did not understand harvests; he just knew that his palate liked what he was drinking. For that, if nothing else, the visit had already been worth it. And the fun had just started.

"I am sure you undoubtedly know how to hold a party, Mormont. You only have to look at what you have done with this tower," the queen answered acidly as she looked towards the ceiling, which was even more ostentatious than in the previous rooms. "The tower," she continued, "which as I'm sure will not surprise you, is the reason for my visit."

Graglia's words made a chill run down the backs of the three guild representatives. For a second their faces could not repress their fear. The queen did not allow a smile of satisfaction to appear on her lips. Observing how her mere words could make such important men tremble with fear was one of the powers that she enjoyed the most.

"Your Highness," the head of the banker's guild quickly replied, "we thought it was appropriate to create a sculpture in honor of the Aqua Deus, so that we might bless it with our praises."

"Our intentions were purely devout, Highness," added the third guild head, his voice slightly trembling while he put his brown-skinned hands together, while the other two concurred with his claim.

"Enough," said the queen firmly. "Save your excuses. I see this house full of ostentation, full of greasy merchants who show no respect, who have forgotten their faith, and who, with their lack of morals and intelligence, seek to overshadow our beloved cathedral. I see the Sisters very thin, feeding only on their faith... and you stupid bourgeoisie do nothing but rejoice before them. That monument is the last straw. You wanted to test your power in front of the church and you forgot that it has power and influence, and—above all—that this queendom is governed by the high priestess!" As always, the queen had not altered her tone of voice. Despite this, her speech was firm and full of emotion.

Seeing that their hopes had vanished, the three guildsmen did nothing but look down, sad and certainly regretful for having let their lust for power and ostentation lead them to this point. "Your ego has condemned you, gentlemen," Graglia continued. "You are hereby accused of treason against the church. All your property will be seized, and from now on your goods will become part of the royal property and the church of the Sisters of Hymal. Concerning yourselves, you will be arrested and locked in the ecclesiastical prison. You can act like

190

gentlemen and go downstairs by the power of your own feet, or else Gant Blacksword will surely be willing to assist you."

Hearing his name, Gant took hold of his huge and heavy broadsword. With a quick movement of his arm, he unsheathed it then, tossing it down, and pinned it to the marble floor, cracking it and causing a loud rumble. A not-too-subtle gesture that ended any idea the bourgeoisie might have had of escaping.

"One more thing—the head of the guild of tailors is missing." The queen, as well informed as she was, knew his name, Rivetien, but she did not want to give the others the satisfaction of showing them the slightest recognition. After all, they did not deserve it. "Where is that traitor?"

The three guildsmen looked at each other, worried. It was again the head of the fishermen who took the initiative.

"Your Highness, the leader of tailors has not come here today. We do not know the reason for his absence," the guildsman said, his voice conveying his fear.

"Well, I'm sure you can tell me where I can find him," the queen replied in a sweet tone.

"Mormont tells the truth, Your Highness. Our partner Rivetien has not appeared today... and we do not know where he is."

The queen glanced at Gant... a look that was just enough for him to take part in. With a powerful leap—his hand tearing his enormous sword from the ground—he pounced on the three guild leaders, setting the blade of his broadsword firmly enough across Mormont's neck that the man could feel its edge digging into his jowls. The other two guildsmen threw themselves to the floor, raising their hands to their heads in panic— a pathetic vision for the eyes of the queen. She hated weak men.

"Pathetic," she said. "I'll ask you one more time, Mormont. Where can we find Rivetien?"

"I do not know!" Mormont shouted between agonizing tears. "That bastard probably ran away from here! He's been smarter than we are!" Mormont said this with total sincerity, seeing that it did not make sense to continue with his politically correct talk.

"It's okay," said the queen, turning her back. "It seems that even the dungeon is too dignified for your ilk. Gant, you already know what you have to do... and bring me Rivetien's head.

The queen left the room while in the background she heard screams of agony and despair. From the stairs, she could hear them running through the room, trying to escape the fury of Gant's black sword. It was not long before the room fell completely silent.

Meanwhile, the queen went to the cathedral, where she took the opportunity to start her prayers and also to reflect on how well Rubeliev's painting was going to look in her room.

24. Gelegen and the giant

His prosecution of the evidence had led him into the forest. He led the way, the tracks of wagon and horseshoes allowed no reason for him to doubt. Judging by their freshness, Gelegen estimated the fugitives were two days away, perhaps less.

The order to stop and inspect every wagon or carriage that entered the forest roads had been given. Great caution was advised, and the immediate arrest of any vehicle arousing suspicion was ordered. For a generous radius, pairs of soldiers watched several roads. Gelegen's orders had been clear: If there was any hint of suspicion, an arrest of the crew of the carriage should be made immediately.

The soldiers, encouraged by the praises they might receive for capturing the traitor, and not having been informed by a description of the carriage crew, erred on the side of caution, stopping countless crews. When this news reached Gelegen's ears, he began to release such a torrent of blasphemy that the demons themselves would have turned red with shame. However, realizing that the soldiers had no descriptions of the suspects, he limited the detentions to carriages in which the crew carried weapons. With the majority of carriages and wagons being driven by merchants or itinerant families, the number of arrests would be drastically reduced.

Regarding the inspection of the corpses in the mortuary, the analysis had not led to any new clues. The report indicated that the victims had been burned before their death. The doctor was confused, since the wounds indicated that they had been made by a sword... but all other evidence seemed to indicate that the cuts and the burns had happened simultaneously, an outcome that the doctor indicated was very unlikely, as it was a capital sin to use fire in order to burn a corpse. Gelegen could not help snorting as he read this part of the report. It was obvious that the laws and principles that governed the queendom did not at all impress whoever was responsible for such carnage.

The report also noted that the attacks had been carried out with extreme harshness. Gelegen dropped the report to the floor, disappointed, as the report had not offered more than what was obvious to any minimally trained eye. However, there was one detail that was useful and that had previously gone unnoticed by him. One of the taysees seemed to have been hit in the back by a crossbow bolt. Did this mean that the man—or woman—was also a shooter? Or maybe there was more than one? Gelegen thought the last option was most likely. It was important to take such information into account when proceeding with his investigation. Again, he would have to follow his instinct if he were to solve this mysterious incident.

Although he was not going to admit it, this matter had undoubtedly stoked his spirit. It could not be said that the Aquadom was a quiet place—far from it, actually. In any case, for Gelegen the altercations were always mundane and predictable—to such an extent that, without realizing it, he had lost his passion for his work... He remembered how the moment he stepped on the first crime scene—a collapsed house with several corpses, marks of cuts and burns, a furrow of burnt land—it was more than enough to awaken Gelegen's curiosity, which had long been in a deep lethargy. He would get to the bottom of this matter—a challenge, finally, that would allow him to live up to his capabilities.

Prosecuting the search orders on the roads, the soldiers Biveo and Vihaim had joined Gelegen. As messengers of the reports of the various detachments of soldiers stationed on the different roads, they were the recipients of the anger imparted by their peers. These soldiers, no matter whether they liked Gelegen or not, took advantage of his popularity, bragging to their peers—provided it was not in front of him—about the special mission that they had been entrusted to: accompanying Gelegen as a result of their skills and experience as soldiers. But, if they had asked Gelegen, he would not have hesitated to replace them with others possessing a minimum of intelligence. Luckily for them, the carriage tracks were easy to follow. Apparently one of the wheels had a notch that left a very particular mark in the earth—and thanks to it, they could follow the track.

Gelegen increased the pace of the chase, as the crowns of clouds began to pile up. Their greyish color, along with the pain he felt in his right knee, where he had been wounded in a brawl several years ago, signaled that the rain would soon arrive. With its arrival, he would have to say goodbye to the tracks. The soldiers, believing that they were moving faster because the enemy was close, drew their swords, preparing for an altercation—a development that Gelegen accepted with resignation.

Within the forest they stopped immediately upon hearing Gelegen's order. It did not take an expert's eye to guess that something had happened there. The tracks of the carriage ended, and on the road lay a deep and thick mark that crossed it from side to side. The veteran lowered himself from the horse to inspect the cause of the mark. Approaching it, he observed that various splinters lay in the deepest part of the mark, indicating that a tree had once obstructed the way. However, the mark was too deep for it to be a simple tree trunk that bandits had used to cut off passersby and thereby easily assault them—a very common practice, unfortunately.

He looked around for the tree remains that might have fallen on the road caused this type of an impact on the earth. According to his thesis, the tree could have fallen from the wind and then been removed by some travelers who had to use the road. However, looking at the nearby trees, he saw no indication that would allow him to corroborate that this had been the case.

The soldiers dismounted their horses and stood on the road, looking around, armed with their swords and shields in case of an assault. Gelegen, unable to guess what happened, resorted to one of his old tricks. Discussing what might have happened with the other men was the best way to move forward.

"Tell me, soldiers, we have a tree that forcefully struck the road. The carriage tracks also end here; therefore, I think it is more than obvious that both facts are related. Any ideas?"

The soldiers made signs of thinking, not having thought about such connection before. These two soldiers were men of action. Again, it was Biveo who first answered, without long considering his response.

"Assailants, sir! It is a very common practice in this area. They chop down a tree and block the road with it, forcing the merchants to stop. Once they do, they launch their attack, coming from out of their hiding places, not giving the merchants time to react."

195

"I see," Gelegen said. "I confess, soldier Biveo, that that was also my first impression; however, the most logical thing would be if one of the trees used was cut close to the road, thus avoiding the need to carry it here. Nonetheless, it does not appear that this has been the case. There is no such trunk to see around here. No tree has fallen that might explain the violence with which it seems a trunk hit the ground."

"It sounds as if a huge beast threw it there," Vihaim quipped, somehow incredulous at his own words. For Gelegen, however, this did nothing more than reflect a theory that fluttered through his mind but that he did not want to contemplate as an option but that, being spoken out loud, he now could not help but confront.

"Yes, damn it." Gelegen drew his sword, looking towards the forest. "I am afraid you are absolutely spot on, soldier."

The deeper they went into the forest, the more evident the presence of a being of great dimensions became, although there was no destruction to the surrounding environment, which was something to expect in an area where a beast of such size lived. It was not difficult to follow the steps of a monster with such enormous footsteps.

The soldiers, finally realizing what they were pursuing, could not avoid reflexively lowering their weapons and shields, desperate, knowing that their weapons would be no rival for such a colossus. Biveo nudged his elbow into his partner, encouraging him to speak and make Gelegen come to his senses.

"Sir, should we not wait and ask for reinforcements?" Vihaim tried to make his voice sound firm but he could not help displaying a slight hesitation.

"We're not going to fight him, damn it!" Gelegen really did not know how he was going to react if he discovered that the beast had finished off his prey. His common sense told him he should conduct an inspection of the terrain, locate the beast, and wait after requesting reinforcements. In contrast, the forcefulness with which he gripped the hilt of his sword seemed to suggest the opposite. He himself did not know what was going to happen.

With each step they took, the sky continued to darken; it would not be long before the rains started. Although the rain was considered a blessing for the inhabitants of the Aquadom, Gelegen did not share their enthusiasm. Popular belief held that the water that dropped from the sky was nothing more than the Aqua Deus granting his disciples the liquid element that gave them life, allowing them to cultivate the land and restoring the full flow of the rivers. Many centuries ago, the inhabitants of the Aquadom thought the rains were a phenomenon that happened only in their queendom: a gift given by their god. When they discovered that this was not the case, the church, not retracting their doctrine, proclaimed that the Aqua Deus was so merciful that their god gave the gift of water falling from heaven even to its enemies, a fact that somehow explained why it rained everywhere. It was true that the Aquadom was characterized by a high frequency of rainfall, which for the church was a symbol of the preferential treatment the Aqua Deus bestowed upon its true disciples, making it blasphemy to complain about the rains.

The three men continued advancing. The first drops of rain began to fall on their faces. They advanced cautiously, Gelegen in front with his sword held high, the two soldiers in back, with shields held high. Never in their lives had they been as alert as they were at that moment.

Gelegen's footsteps began to slosh on the wet ground. The rain, little by little, was gaining strength. The men kept moving, more and more slowly... It was as if the rain were protecting them from some danger. The soldiers' morale gradually began to deflate, and their pace slackened and became less sure. Gelegen's urgency didn't slow, his pace continued without hesitation. He had to find the beast—and do so as soon as possible.

As if someone had heard their prayers, they suddenly came across an esplanade... and there, with his back against a tree, stood an enormous giant. Gelegen quickly grabbed Biveo and covered his mouth. The soldier had been about to scream in terror. Vihaim, meanwhile, was about to drop his shield and run. Aware of the sensitivity of the situation, Gelegen grabbed both soldiers by their heads and dragged them down to the ground to calm them.

"Listen, stupid soldiers, I don't know what they teach you in training school these days, but screaming or running in front of a giant is only an option if you want to end your life. So, you're going to stay here, with your heads down, and remain alert to the movements of the giant. Is that clear?" The soldiers nodded stupidly. Their blue eyes were a vivid reflection of their terror. Gelegen knew that if the giant saw them they wouldn't stand a chance. They had to be very cautious. "I shall go a little further and reconnoiter the area—do not move from here."

The soldiers felt a great relief knowing that at least they would not be getting any closer to the giant. Simply seeing him from their current faraway distance caused them chills.

Cervan sheltered quietly under one of the trees, not making any movements. Gelegen, however, moved stealthily, trying to hide among the shadows and heeding the slosh of his boots. As he drew closer, he realized that the giant held a dark object in his hand—but he was still too far away to see what, exactly, the object was. The water also did not help his purpose. It began to rain heavily, a flash of lightning illuminated the sky, and after a while there was thunder, given the time that had passed between the two atmospheric phenomena Gelegen knew that they still had time before the storm came.

Gelegen looked around for clues. Then he saw it. A jumble of broken wood. For a moment he lost all sense of caution and began to run towards it, exposing himself. Fortunately, the giant was distracted and did not notice any disturbance. Gelegen knelt down, making sure that the shattered pieces of wood were not, a short while ago, part of a wagon. The wagon he was chasing had stopped here, crushed by the enormous hands of the giant, it seemed. He came closer, more and more recklessly. From here he could see that the giant, in his open palm, held a horse. Surprised by their friendship, he nonetheless continued to look for the crew of the wagon, in case they were found captive in some corner of the giant's home. However, he had no luck along that line of inquiry.

Disappointed and furious, he returned to the soldiers, who had not moved a bit from their position. Gelegen did not know if it was due to his orders or out of fear.

"It's time to retire, soldiers."

As he spoke, Gelegen took a small map from one of the pockets of his coat and surveyed the approximate area where the giant lived. The soldiers could not contain their joy at the thought of leaving that beast. "We will seek shelter and ask for reinforcements. That giant has something that belongs to me..."

Biveo was responsible for requesting reinforcements to face the giant. So excited was he with the idea of getting away from there, that he did not realize that seeking shelter was a much more comfortable option. Gelegen began to move away from their hiding place, albeit reluctantly, but not before he took one last glance towards the giant, the same way a wolf stares at a crow trying to steal his prey. Vihaim followed him closely.

They retreated far enough not to be surprised during the night. After thinking over the situation, they decided to build a small bonfire. It was true that doing so was dangerous, but the water had left them soaked, and one night sleeping on the forest floor was hard, but it was even harder given the cold. The horses were located slightly further south, in the direction of the giant, so that if this or some other danger approached from that direction they would notice it, giving them time to react to the threat.

They sat together beside the fire. It was an uncomfortable situation for both Gelegen and the soldier. Gelegen was not very keen on conversation—and certainly not affected by social conventions. He could get up from the table in the middle of a conversation if the subject was not minimally interesting to him. Vihaim, on the other hand, never knew what topic to talk about. He was aware that the giant's presence for some reason irritated Gelegen so much that he was cautious enough not to use this as an excuse to begin a conversation.

After a long period of silence, against all odds, it was Gelegen who started talking.

"Why did you become a soldier?"

The question came as a surprise to Vihaim. He could not help but hesitate before answering.

"To... protect, sir. I am the oldest of five brothers. I have always been protecting them. I thought that enlisting was the best way to continue protecting them."

"You thought?"

Vihaim, realizing that his answer was directed at a superior officer, jumped from the trunk against which he was leaning, eager to clarify his answer.

"Do not get me wrong, sir! It's not that I do not like my work or that I regret my decision, it's just that I did not imagine it like that."

"Ah." His eyes closed, Gelegen nodded, understanding what he meant. "The dream! They all think that being a soldier is a life full of adventures, where everyone respects you—fight in the morning, sleep with young women at night... No, soldier, life in the army is hard. I remember my first year... just finished our instruction, they sent us straight to the front. We had not even been sent out on a single patrol and we were already fighting like a battalion! And I will tell you something, boy—there is no glory in war, only blood and death."

"Several of my companions enlisted in pursuit of that dream of yours," he added. "The few who survived their first battle did not take long to regret the choice they had made..."

Vihaim, taking advantage of the sentimentality, threw out a question that in no other moment would he have dared to even formulate,

199

certainly not to a superior, and certainly not to someone like Gelegen. But since he seemed to be in the mood, he tried.

"Do you ever... regret?"

Gelegen's gaze was fixed on the fire, as if he were looking through it, to the point that Vihaim did not know if he had heard him. It was not until after a long time, when Vihaim was not even thinking about it, that Gelegen dignified Vihaim's question with a response.

"No... For many years I believed I did have regrets... that I did not want to accept the bad decision I had made. But now, when I stop to look back, it may be because somehow you just remember the good things but... no, I would not dare to suggest I regret it, because it would not be true."

The way he said it, as he looked into Vihaim's eyes, Vihaim knew Gelegen was being honest. Without realizing it, Gelegen's answer had removed a burden the soldier had been carrying, because, knowing that someone like him, who had been at the service of the queendom for so many years, did not regret his decision helped him to believe his choice was the right one. He remembered, then, how as a child he had played at being a soldier, swearing with his childhood friends that one day they would train to join the Aquo Army. Finally, he had been the only one who enlisted; the rest had chosen different paths.

The next day, the reinforcements arrived at the meeting place. Gelegen observed the new soldiers. The nervousness in their faces was more than evident; they knew why they were there. As the moment of decision approached, the whisperings began, with the soldiers probably assuming that the assault was imminent. Feeling calmer after having slept, Gelegen had changed his mind. Initially his instinct told him to simply muster a group of soldiers in sufficient numbers then prepare to subdue the giant. However, after a long night of reflection, he reconsidered. Perhaps his original plan should be the solution only if things went wrong?

He also made sure that the soldiers had been instructed in how to confront a giant—a stratagem that, due to its lack of assiduity, no longer was taught during training. The approach was simple. The soldiers were to be divided into teams of four. The best archers would be placed at a far distance from the giant and would release a volley of arrows, distracting the giant. The rest of the soldiers would be armed with elongated pikes, which they would try to set between the giant's feet. The objective was to gradually wound the giant's heels, until he fell to the ground in pain due to the accumulation of wounds.

It sounded pretty simple, but in actuality it was not simple at all. Gelegen was aware that in the blink of an eye the giant could finish several of them off. That's why he divided the soldiers who were to attack with pikes into two groups. Some soldiers would get the giant's attention by attacking while trying not to get themselves killed, while the rest, approaching the giant from behind, were to attack the opposite heel as fiercely as they could.

He counted the soldiers at his command. Twenty-four. Twelve per foot. Not excessively numerous, he thought, but the number would have to do; he had no time.

"Give me one of the pikes."

With such an affirmation the soldiers cheered in surprise and admiration. It was atypical for a high-ranking officer to lead the attack from the front. The usual practice was to command from the rear—the farther in the rear, the better—so that the soldier with the superior knowledge of war could command the battle without suffering any injury, and if by some chance the battle did not proceed as expected, the high-ranked soldier would have the opportunity to retreat unharmed in order to be of use again in the next battle.

Gelegen did not share that philosophy. His was an approach that provoked admiration and contempt in equal parts, depending on the tolerance and rank of the listener. Fortunately, he had always given little importance to what anyone thought of him. And doing things his way was something that had somehow granted him the favor of the queen herself... which undoubtedly made the other soldiers' admiration and contempt stronger.

Checking that his pike was sturdy, he stood before the soldiers. It was time to give instructions. With a strong strike of the pike to the ground, the soldiers stood firmly before him.

"Listen, soldiers," Gelegen commanded, "divide yourselves into teams of four. I will lead the teams on the left... I hope that you at least know how to distinguish between the right and the left." This provoked some laughter among the soldiers, allowing them to release the tension that every soldier naturally has before a battle. "Well, do not try to be heroes... Listen to my orders and you will survive."

He walked in front of them, from one side to the other, his hands held on his belt. "The operation will be performed the following way. I will make an initial friendly approach to the giant. In this task I will be accompanied by the soldiers Biveo and Vihaim." At the mention of their names, both soldiers immediately became confused by their feelings. On the one hand, they were surprised that Gelegen knew their names, a bewilderment that would not have occurred if they had known the spirit of that man; on the other hand, it was not easy for them to contain what little pleasure they found in being among the few members of the group who would approach the giant. "If its words and actions comply with the laws of this queendom," Gelegen continued, "there will be no reason for combat. However, if it is hostile we will lure him to an esplanade, then the archers, at my signal, are to launch a volley that catches the giant's attention, so that we can regroup and reestablish our teams." After this speech, Gelegen gave his pike to one of the soldiers then climbed on his horse and gestured for his two companions to follow him as he began to head towards the giant.

Biveo and Vihaim exchanged looks for a moment, each sensing the other's fear. Fortunately the rest of the soldiers began to cheer them on, allowing them to gather their courage to mount their horses and follow Gelegen. With a little trot they managed to fall in line behind him.

"Fear is old, boys, and ugly. Even so, look it in the face as if it were your wife!"

* * *

When the three men rode into the esplanade, the giant Cervan was still leaning against the tree. His horse companion, whom he had named Orregahil, was trotting freely around the clearing. In the language of giants, the name meant *liberated beast.*

The soldiers with the bows stood on a hill, positioned distantly enough to not be attacked by the giant but close enough to aim easily against such an enormous target. The soldiers with the pikes held their backs against the trees, hiding and waiting for their turn, and some praying that turn would never come.

The three riders held their reins tighter, making their horses trot slower, so the giant wouldn't feel threatened. Suddenly becoming aware that men on horseback were approaching, Cervan instinctively took a huge rock from the ground snatching it out of the mud. Giants were known for their fine aim throwing stones. The problem—at least for humans—was that given the size of such creatures, the stones they threw were the equivalent of boulders hurled by catapults. So for Cervan, the stone signified a warning; to the victim it signified a deathblow.

The soldiers' hands were held aloft, the universal sign that their approach was friendly. Seeing this, Cervan walked towards them, still holding the huge rock in his hand, just in case. As he came closer he saw that the strangers were three soldiers.

Orregahil, seeing other horses he took to be his companions, grew curious. He trotted closer to the horses, welcoming them, coming up to Biveo's horse and nuzzling its nose with its own nose. Having been raised for war, these horses were much bigger and stronger than he.

When Cervan was at a short distance from the soldiers, one of them—the soldier in front—began to speak.

"Greetings, giant!" he said loudly so the giant could hear him. Gelegen was grateful that the giant carried a stone in his hand instead of a tree trunk. It was true that such a rock would still prove lethal if it impacted any members of his troop, but at least it did not provide the range and sweep that a tree trunk would have given him. This, along with the fact that the monstrous being had not attacked them at the first chance it had, seemed to indicate that fortune was on their side. "We come in peace, we just want to talk to you."

"Talk?" Cervan ruminated, with obvious annoyance at the visit.

"We want to ask you a few questions about some humans who came through here. They were our friends and we're looking for them," Gelegen lied, knowing that the giant's response would be crucial.

Cervan was suspicious of Gelegen's words. He did not know all the details of Noakh's and Hilzen's story, but it did not fit with the story of two men having some soldiers for friends. Also, the man he was talking to wasn't much of a conversationalist. Gelegen's words did not suit his gaze; his words certainly tried to be kind, but his gaze showed hostility. Cervan grabbed the rock a bit tighter.

"No one here passed by." Cervan also lied, only unconvincingly.

Gelegen lost his patience. "And what about that horse then? It is obvious that it is used to humans... and the wagon destroyed not far from here?"

As Cervan had guessed, the man was not very fond of talking.

Vihaim and Biveo shifted in their saddles, knowing that Gelegen's words could signify their end; even they knew that challenging the giant's words was not the best strategy.

Cervan was visibly annoyed at Gelegen's small display of empathy. However, he ignored it, though not without effort.

"Speak. Where is the crew? Did you eat them? Did you crush them against a tree?"

Gelegen initially wanted to end the encounter as soon as possible, always following his principles and experience. He was of the opinion that the simplest explanation was usually the correct one. In this case—in the case of a giant—the most obvious conclusion was that he had eaten the crew or ripped them apart easily, so he simply wanted the giant to admit what he had done in order to focus all his anger on him. However, now he knew that it was not like that; for some reason he could not understand, the stupid giant had not finished off the carriage crew. He swore he must be hiding them somewhere, so Gelegen had to force the giant to talk, one way or another.

Cervan now was fed up with Gelegen's bad manners. He stomped powerfully on the ground—a warning for the three soldiers to withdraw.

The war veteran had had enough too. Raising his right arm, pointing his index finger and middle finger towards the sky, he gave the signal.

Arrows began to fly toward the giant. The great beast covered himself. Taking advantage of the distraction, the three soldiers rode out to the meeting point, galloping as fast as they could. Their reconnaissance had not ended well, and it was time to move on to the alternate plan.

Gelegen regretted the outcome. He had wanted to provoke the giant; thanks to his interrogations, he had discerned that the beast was hiding the truth. The price that he, Gelegen, was going to pay for it would be high.

When the three soldiers arrived at the rendezvous, the teams stood at the ready. As they dismounted the horses they were given their pikes then separated. Cervan, unhappy with the rain of arrows, was advancing fiercely in their direction.

"Soldiers! For the queen!"

The soldiers repeated Gelegen's cry as they spread across the terrain. As soon as the giant approached, they would surround his feet.

Furious, Cervan threw the stone, and luckily for his human targets, he missed, the stone smashing several trees instead. Then he grabbed a nearby tree and ripped it from the earth. Employing it like a stick, he swept the tree powerfully before him. He did not strike any of the soldiers, but it was enough for them to realize that a single blow from the tree would be more than sufficient to end their lives.

Meanwhile, the team of archers were again launching a new barrage of arrows. Being such a big target, most of the arrows hit him; however, the giant seemed not to be aware of the arrows anymore. The team with the pikes surrounded Cervan's feet and delivered the first blows to his left tendon. It was Biveo who had hit the giant's feet first, followed by Vihaim, who stabbed his pike deeply into Cervan's tendon. Growing annoyed, the giant began stomping his right foot to expel the nettlesome soldiers.

One of the soldiers, a woman, unable to jump in time, was crushed beneath the giant's powerful foot. His teammates had no time to mourn this loss, as the giant continued stomping. Biveo and Vihaim ran heading to the woods strategically; it was time for the teams on the left foot. The soldiers on the other team, led by Gelegen, launched their attack, injuring the giant's tendon. But the beast did not fall. It did not stop moving... or throwing trees... or stomping.

More soldiers died because of the giant's attacks. The soldiers' arrows continued to rain down on Cervan. Wounds appeared all over his body. Ignoring them, the giant focused his attention on the soldiers closest to him. Biveo and Vihaim were again hiding behind a tree, waiting for their turn again, both panting heavily. They grabbed their pikes tightly.

"He's almost done!" Biveo claimed to his companion. "We won't last much longer, we have to do something. I'll end this."

"What? Don't be fool, Biveo! Wait for our turn!" Vihaim pleaded, but Biveo seemed not to hear his words, as he got out from his hide and headed to the giant's right foot. Vihaim wanted to shout his companion's name, he wanted to tell him his move was madness, but he didn't want the giant realizing Biveo was getting closer.

"Aqua Deus, protect your fool loyal soldiers," he prayed, a second after he also got out from his hide and went after his friend, with his pike held high.

Biveo got closer and stabbed fiercely on the giant's tendon, expecting his blow to be the last. But it wasn't. The giant turned his head. Vihaim was almost there too, but before he could join his companion, Cervan moved his foot and smashed Biveo as if it were an ant. Vihaim paused, unable to even talk or move.

"Get away, you idiot!" shouted Gelegen from the other foot of the giant. Vihaim regained his sense and went back while reminding himself what the veteran had told him the night before: *There is no glory in war, only blood and death.*

Gelegen calculated. Casualties were high... but they still had a chance. The giant's injured tendon was already very red and swollen; the cuts were bleeding deeply. The battle, now, was against time.

Despite the casualties, the troops' morale seemed high. Although they had watched their companions die, they continued to fight for the most basic principle of all. Survival.

With a last powerful sweep of the tree, Cervan sent several soldiers flying through the air. The tree itself had turned a sticky reddish tone from the accumulated blood; severed limbs were embedded in the bark.

Gelegen took a few moments to assess the attack underway on the giant's other foot. Watching the battle there, he realized he had miscalculated. Only two soldiers were still battling there—Vihaim and a curly haired woman—while five soldiers stood by his side, striking the beast's right foot.

Forgoing his earlier plan, Gelegen ran towards the giant's foot and threw the pike like a javelin, hitting the giant's tendon. Before the giant could raise his foot, Gelegen jumped and grabbed the pike. The giant raised its foot to stomp it again, pulling Gelegen along.

Gelegen unsheathed his sword. He began to lunge furiously, stabbing the giant tirelessly, causing more injury to the giant's shredded tendon.

Cervan focused his attention on Gelegen. Vihaim and the other soldier struck the other tendon fiercely; Vihaim wanted revenge. Finally, Cervan fell with a deafening roar. Everything happened so fast that Gelegen did not have time to jump to the ground.

A cloud of dust overran the clearing. The soldiers quickly carried out their orders, tying him with ropes then pounding pikes into the ground and into the trees so that he became immobile. But Cervan kept struggling. Finally the soldiers were able to keep him under control. When the dust cloud dissipated, Gelegen appeared. His forehead was covered in dust and blood. Despite the wounds, he stood on his own.

Soon it was time to honor the fallen. In the end, only five of the soldiers using pikes had survived, in addition to Gelegen. They searched the esplanade in case any wounded soldiers could be saved, but the giant's blows had been so devastating that whoever had had misfortune or insufficient skills had been turned into a pile of flesh and bones, full of blood. The tree the giant had used testified to this; more than one soldier vomited after seeing other soldiers' remains in the tree's thick crevices. The bark was entirely covered by a mixture of dripping blood and viscera, impregnating the forest floor. The blood turned the earth red. Little by little, the color darkened.

Gelegen watched sadly as Vihaim lay on the ground, crying at the sight of the remains of his friend. Biveo wanted to be the hero, he had been reckless, and had paid the price. He had died on the spot. Gelegen added his name to the list of soldiers who had died at his expense—a list so long, now, that it began to weigh on his conscience.

Cervan made a last attempt to free himself. However, he was exhausted. He had lost a lot of blood. All of the frenzy with which he had battled had vanished. In its place came the fatigue and pain he had not felt until now. His breathing was heavy. He began to sweat in fear... a feeling that a giant is not very used to. He had been captured, and it did not seem to venture any new promises.

Gelegen approached the giant. He lifted his leg then rested his foot on the giant's head.

"Too much spilt blood, giant. Now speak," Gelegen said, exhausted.

25. The Snowy Mountains

"There is no doubt why they named this place what they named it." Clinging to the ends of his coat, Noakh was having a very hard time. His boots were sinking into the dense snow and his vision extended only as far as Hilzen, a few steps ahead of him. The rest was eternally white. It was like a white dessert. The snow fell with an incessant softness and the wind continued to howl in their ears. "Are you sure it's around here, Hilzen?"

Noakh thought it impossible not to get lost in a place where, no matter where he looked, there was only one thing. Snow.

Hilzen had insisted on leading the march through the mountains, using the map that Dleheim had given to them. But he wasn't sure of the route. How could he be? Apparently, it was as simple as continuing straight on the road that climbed through the pass... something that was not so easy to do when the snow would not stop falling. According to his map, they should have already arrived in a village called Ograbh, but around them there was only snow.

Noakh, who was already fed up with the snow and growing cold, had an idea. "Why didn't this occur to me before?" Laughing, he drew Distra from its sheath. He made it burst into flames, providing the warmth he needed. He realized that the force inside Distra probably did not like the idea of acting as a torch. However, he hoped that it understood Noakh's actions were for a greater good.

Hilzen could not deny how practical the torch was, although at first he did not like it. He slowed his pace so that he might enjoy the sword's heat on his back.

"Don't worry, Hilzen," Noakh said. "If I see someone approaching I'll make the flames disappear... Maybe this is training, I've never tested how long I can keep the flame burning."

"What do you mean?" Hilzen asked.

"Somehow, the sword consumes my energy. At first I just could not even keep it lit without feeling exhausted." Noakh did not know how, but one way or another the flames were linked to himself. Perhaps this explained why only the phoenix could use it. Realizing how hard it was for him to keep Distra's blade engulfed in flames, he reflected, "I can't help but admire King Wulkan. Not only was he able to handle the two fire swords at the same time, but also, as my father had told me, he could summon the power to keep both swords in flames for as long as he wanted to."

Hilzen shook his head disapprovingly. *Now he's praising the man that killed his mother and made him become an exile,* he thought before returning to focus on his search for some place of reference. If the route they were traveling were the right one, they should not be very far from the mountain village of Ograbh.

The road seemed slightly more peaceful with Distra lit. Certainly, the light from the flames did not show the travelers their way, but its warmth, at least, was pleasant.

Being honest with himself, Noakh wondered whether Wulkan, although much older than himself, was a rival he could face. Not only did Wulkan possess the other fire sword, Sinistra, but he also had a lifetime of combat experience, not to mention the knowledge imparted to him by past generations. For, as dictated by tradition, each king had to teach all his knowledge to the new king, and among those teachings, of course, were all the secret techniques of fire swords. Noakh would probably never acquire such knowledge; the world would have to teach him.

His thoughts were broken by Hilzen's shouts. The snow had stopped falling for a moment, allowing them to see further ahead.

"At last!" In front of Hilzen lay the snow-covered town of Ograbh. It was a small village made up of stone houses and wooden roofs. As they drew closer, they saw that the streets were deserted, which did not surprise either of them. As the sun set, the town became too cold for the villagers to remain outside, so the great majority had retreated into their homes.

Hilzen turned back to his companion. "Noakh, stop it!"

210

When Noakh sheathed Distra he felt a sense of relief, realizing that he was still far from being able to control such power. He realized then, too, that he was once again somewhat tired, although he did not know whether to attribute his exhaustion to Distra's power or to walking up the slope of the mountain.

While they passed through the deserted town, they searched for an inn or some other place to shelter. The town was small. Though they searched every street, there did not seem to be any place where they could spend the night.

"We will have to appeal to the kindness of Ograbh's citizens." Noakh approached a door and knocked.

"Noakh, wait!"

Hilzen's warning came too late. While Noakh turned due to Hilzen's cry, the door opened. A huge middle-aged man behind it pushed Noakh firmly. He fell hard into the snow, hitting his head against a cobblestone that lay buried underneath. While trying to stand up again, holding his hands to his head because of the pain, a sharp stabbing sensation stopped him. The same man who had pushed him now held a pitchfork—and by his look, he would have no problem sinking the sharp tines into Noakh's chest.

Hilzen had tried to warn him. The sun setting... two armed men in such a small town isolated in the mountains. They could not expect anything good to come of it. Even so, perhaps the man's reaction had been somewhat disproportionate.

After a moment, the doors of the nearby houses began to open, revealing men and women armed with the same unfriendly expression. Large men whose appearance seemed even more formidable, as they were dressed in thick skins. They had long blond hair, blue eyes cold as ice, and a determination on their faces that made Hilzen and Noakh instantly aware that these men would not hesitate to end their lives. Life in the frozen mountains was apparently too hard in itself, the travelers realized, to also have to endure the arrival of undesirables.

Hilzen stepped forward with his hands up, trying to prevent Noakh from doing anything crazy. In addition, his more adult appearance would probably elicit a better feeling among the villagers. He knew that the people of the mountains were generally hard working. They put their family above all else, and a sense of community allowed them to survive in a hostile environment far up in the mountains—an element that had allowed them to become still more hermetic to the rest of the world.

Without a doubt, one false step and the two travelers would end up skewered.

"Citizen"—Hilzen tried to make his voice sound stern while still reassuring the man holding the pitchfork to Noakh's chest—"you are wrong. We have not come to harm you or anyone. On the contrary, we are simply looking for a friendly place to spend the night."

The man with the pitchfork stopped jabbing it into Noakh's chest. Instead he gave a grimace that in some way resembled a smile. Despite this, Noakh did not want to make the situation any more tense. He remained lying in the snow, shaking it from his hair.

The other inhabitants began to leave their houses and quickly surrounded Noakh and Hilzen. The two companions were perplexed by the evolution of events. The mountaineer who had thrown Noakh to the ground approached him, grabbing his arm. With a strong pull, he lifted Noakh out of the snow. Noakh checked his belt instinctively, making sure his swords hadn't fallen out of their sheath. Before he realized it, the big man gave him a hug. If he had not seen the man for himself, Noakh would have sworn a bear had hugged him.

The other inhabitants began to happily embrace Noakh while thanking the Aqua Deus for their luck. They all seemed unaware of the perplexed expressions the two newcomers displayed. Again, it was the man who had attacked—and subsequently embraced—Noakh who took the initiative. "Praised be the Aqua Deus for listening to our prayers!" Despite the joyful tone that the man used, his hoarse voice gave him a lugubrious air. The remaining inhabitants began to approach the strangers, surrounding them. The villagers' faces were filled with happiness. Noakh and Hilzen still did not understand what was going on.

"A minute ago, I thought I was going to end up buried in the snow—and now this?" Noakh tried to speak softly. He attempted to respond to the villager's happy expressions with a smile that sought to hide his bewilderment. "Do you know what is happening?"

"I had the same thought as you, Noakh," Hilzen replied. "I do not know what I said, but it seems to have worked!"

"You have a gift for public speaking, friend."

Their quiet conversation was interrupted by a murmur among the villagers. They made way, allowing an old woman of short stature to come through; she was using a tree branch as a cane. The woman looked down at them up and with a grimace of disapproval tilted her head, indicating that Noakh and Hilzen should follow her. The other villagers looked at the old woman with a mixture of admiration and respect. Noakh suspected she was their leader, some kind of spiritual authority who guided her people.

"This is not a good sign," Hilzen said, shaking his head.

"What? Why? What's wrong?" Noakh had not understood anything that had happened since they had arrived at Ograbh.

Hilzen was still watching the old woman walking away. She showed a dexterity and security in her step that seemed alarmingly agile for someone her age, and for the rugged terrain covered by the snow. By the time Hilzen turned to answer Noakh, it was too late. They had arrived at their destination: a worn wooden hut whose roof was covered with snow.

Inside, the hut was pleasant, but in a way disturbing. A bonfire in the center illuminated a single room covered with animal pelts on both the floor and the walls. Crammed onto tables were several smoldering candles, along with skulls of various animals. A strong smell of incense permeated the room.

The old woman gestured for them to sit down. "You are not the kind of help I expected," she said. "I told that pagan Vont and that whore he has for wife that their lack of faith would make the Aqua furious. Never underestimate the whims of a god..."

The old woman's murmurs did nothing but further confuse the already confused Noakh and Hilzen. The two friends exchanged looks of complete uncertainty, as if trying to find answers in the depths of each other's eyes. Realizing this, the old woman could not avoid letting out a dry laugh that was halfway between innocent and evil.

"Oh, Aqua," the old woman said as she shook her head. Her eyes turned towards them again. However, she seemed to ignore their presence, continuing with her murmurs of indignation: "I see that you like to play with destiny... These men do not even know why they are here. Even divine beings have both an evil and a playful side, it seems... Are these men the best help you could bring me? I wonder if this is just another of your challenges?"

Noakh raised his hand to clarify the situation. However, before he could mediate, the old woman stared at him. "Not a word, pagan. Nobody interrupts me when I'm talking."

"If you let us explain," Hilzen began.

"Silence!" the old woman interrupted. She raised a threatening finger, after which she returned to her absent conversation. "They do not even know about respect... and one of them has brown eyes? Oh Aqua, if it

213

were not because I trust blindly in you, I would have said that you were wrong to choose them."

"Choose us? Aqua?"

Noakh could not disguise the irony of his words. The response was a look full of hatred for his lack of faith.

"I'll explain, yes—but open your ears well, I would not like to have to repeat it." After a pause, during which the old woman began to pronounce expletives between her murmurs, she continued: "You have been brought here by Aqua Deus, to help us in our battle for survival." Her serious face could no longer counteract the grimace of confusion the faces of the travelers displayed.

With a sigh filled with indignation, the old woman tried to explain herself again. "She was beautiful, very beautiful, enough to steal the heart of that young man. Duranti, the count called himself, one of the many nobles who rested in our village on their way to the Sanctuary of the Lady, a place where there is a spring so pure that its waters are known as the Tears of the Lady, the prophet of Aqua Deus." After making sure that her listeners had a minimal knowledge of the world around them, the old woman continued with the story. "Duranti rested with his men here in Ograbh, and so he met a girl from the village, Anaril, the young man fell under the spell of her beauty. And although he continued on his way to the sanctuary and his adventures, he always found a way to send a letter to his beloved or visit the town again to see her.

"Anaril, to the contrary, had set her eyes not on Duranti but on a man from the village, a fact that the nobleman did not like, advising her that she would either go with him or regret it. Although frightened, her fiancé assured her that nothing was going to happen to her, that he and the entire town would protect her, believing that Duranti's words were nothing more than the empty threats of a broken heart. However, the nobleman had not ceased his efforts and visited the town once more— but this time he did not come alone. Taking advantage of the night, he and his men entered the town and forcibly removed Anaril, carrying out vile acts on her body before ending her life. The nobleman had demanded that his men also grab her fiancé to witness his revenge."

As the story progressed, Noakh could only squeeze his fists tightly and frown, wishing he could meet the nobleman and take revenge.

"But her beloved was right in one thing: Her people could not remain impassive before such acts, and armed with all kinds of weapons they offered resistance. There were several who fell on both sides. Our people

214

fought so fiercely that despite the casualties, the nobleman, already satisfied, called for the retreat, fleeing with his tail between his legs.

"But Anaril's story did not end here. Our people paid a high price for the girl. For their attack on the nobility, we lost the favor of the queendom, a reprisal that Duranti took advantage of by taking revenge on our people. This happened years ago, I was a child then. Count Duranti apparently died two decades ago, but his hatred did not; his son continues his legacy. Every year, the younger Count Duranti arrives with his noble friends and some of his troops, demanding a tribute for what they term the insult to the honor of Duranti House. We have to provide them a large portion of our winter reserves as a price to leave us in peace."

"And what if you refuse?" Noakh pondered with a serious face.

"Oh, we tried, the first time. They burned several of our houses and took everything they could carry as well. Since then, the town assumed that paying the tribute was something they had to do. They have assumed that it is part of their life now. They no longer curse the arrival of the nobles. They acknowledge it only with resentment, as if they had no choice."

"But I do not understand... Just a moment ago one of them did not receive me very cordially," Noakh remembered. "I would have sworn they were about to hang us."

The old woman laughed at his words.

"Oh that." She laughed again. "They knew you were not part of the nobles' army. One of our men had been watching you from far away for a long time. Traveling with a torch through the snow is not what is said to be discreet."

Noakh did not need to turn to notice Hilzen's gaze. He answered it with a shrug.

Thinking about what the old woman had said, Noakh figured that the man who had been watching them had been unable to tell from a distance that Noakh was not exactly using a torch. Grateful for his good fortune, Noakh recognized that in the future he would have to be more careful. The villagers' reception would have been much worse if they had seen that the fire came from Distra.

"But this can't be true!" Hilzen replied indignantly. "The queen surely would not allow this to happen. Is the crown aware of all this?"

The old woman sighed. "We tried. We asked for an audience with the queen, but she never answered us. We would have tried to talk to the

215

high priestess as well, but since the queen also assumed that position, we ran out of options."

"Why would the queen do something like that?" Hilzen replied, outraged.

The old woman couldn't help but let out a sarcastic laugh. "Because the Durantis are a noble family, of course. Why should the queen take sides in a matter that compromises her relationship with the nobility? She owns the crown, but the nobles are equally old families and a force to be reckoned with. No matter how she would have ruled on the matter, her act would have compromised her, in one way or another. By her lack of action, her reputation remains untarnished and her conscience can be at peace with itself, while our people are plundered by men who act like true barbarians!"

Hilzen said, "But—"

"We will help you," Noakh interrupted.

Hilzen turned abruptly, intending to tell Noakh that this was not his war, but after meeting Noakh's gaze he was unable to do so. His brown eyes shone with a mixture of determination and fury; it was almost as he could see fire in Noakh's eyes. The old woman nodded with satisfaction.

"They will not take long in coming."

"Today?" Hilzen asked, surprised at the timing.

"Of course not," snapped the old woman. The expression in her eyes made him see how stupid his question had been. "Soon... as soon as the snowstorm dissipates." Seeing that Hilzen was about to pose his question again, she added, "A couple of days."

"How many?" Noakh snapped suddenly, even as he stared at the ground.

"About six, probably. The younger Duranti seems to like to bring other noble families to enjoy the show."

"Then we will give them a show they will never forget"—Noakh turned to address the old woman directly, realizing he did not know her name—"venerable old lady."

"Dorein," the old woman corrected, not very happy with Noakh's way of addressing her. She began to utter insults in a low voice. Despite being aware of her advanced age, she did not like to be reminded of it. "I'm glad you're so determined. We'll wait for the rest of your men to arrive and—"

"Our men?" Hilzen said with a chuckle.

"We work alone," Noakh said, cutting him off.

216

Dorein opened her eyes, astonished.

Being aware of Dorein's newly formed doubts, Noakh continued: "If the Aqua Deus has sent us it is because she knows very well that we are capable, right Hilzen?"

Hilzen's response was a frown, which he followed with a look of indignation. Without reservation he did not agree with Noakh's agreeing to help. Despite this, he simply nodded.

Although she was still not convinced, Dorein could do nothing but assume Noakh's reasoning was sound. He could not help but grimace, aware that it was the second time that such a move had gone well.

Hilzen stood from his chair and went over to Dorein.

"Dorein, I would like to talk to my colleague Noakh about our plan," said Hilzen while staring into Dorein's eyes. "As you will understand, a confrontation in which he and I will be at such a large numerical disadvantage warrants a high level of preparation on our part. Might it be possible for you to leave us alone momentarily?"

Dorein simply nodded. Her eyes had started to exhibit some respect for her guests, even a hint of hope. No doubt that two newcomers fighting against Duranti's men was not a very enticing premise, but as Noakh had correctly pointed out, who was she to doubt the path Aqua Deus had chosen? If it were necessary, the villagers would no doubt join the fight.

Their prayers had been heard. After all those years, they could only have faith, since they had no other alternatives.

As soon as Dorein left, Hilzen peered out the window, waiting for her to walk away. Then he turned to Noakh, who sat looking at him with an amusing expression.

"Can you tell me what makes you think this is so funny?" Hilzen said angrily. This only further amused Noakh.

"We've been chosen by Aqua Deus to free the village... Do you not find it funny? At least recognize that it is ironic."

"Do not mock my beliefs, Noakh—do not do that!" Hilzen's face grew angry. He had always been a pious man. It was true that the whims of fate had led him to accompany Noakh in his travels... but that did not mean he was not a man of faith.

Noakh, realizing that he had broached a sensitive topic, knew how to quickly reconcile it.

"You're right. My apologies."

Noakh sat in one of the chairs in the hut, relaxing with his hands behind his back—a gesture that irritated Hilzen.

217

"You seem very calm... and it surprises me when you just accept that we're facing half a dozen men. Do you have a plan?"

"Well no," Noakh replied in a calm tone. "I do not think it's necessary."

For a second Hilzen doubted Noakh's intentions.

"What is that supposed to mean? Are you planning to escape?"

This time it was Noakh who was outraged at such a suggestion.

"Of course not!"

He settled further into the seat as his face turned more serious. "Chosen or not, these people are suffering. They have been waiting for years for someone to come to help them. I do not know if it was the gods, I do not know if it was luck, but fate wanted us to be here. We are their only hope, so it is our duty to help them."

This time Hilzen was the one who laughed—an outburst that puzzled Noakh.

"Look at yourself," Hilzen said. "The scourge of the evil men who defile the weak in the Aquadom... It would be better if this story did not reach the ears of your faithful peasants!"

"Oh shut up," Noakh returned. "The snow will certainly silence anything that happens here."

"A snow tomb." Hilzen laughed. "It's not what I had in mind, but it will work."

"You will not die here, Hilzen."

"It still seems like either you have a plan or you're out of your mind."

While he was talking, Hilzen kept shaking his head. He closed his eyes. As many times as he thought about it, he was unable to think of any trick that might successfully resolve the situation. There was Distra's power, of course, but using it would leave Noakh exposed. If that were the ace up his sleeve, he would certainly not have so much as implied it. Confronting nobility would be very troublesome; bandits were one thing, but if they fought nobility the queen's army would certainly interfere at some point.

Given Hilzen's repudiation, Noakh began to complain.

"Could you show me a little faith?" Noakh snapped. He stood from his seat. "I'll be honest with you. I do not have a master plan. I only think I know how that man is, the Duranti count."

"What do you mean?" Hilzen replied, puzzled.

"He is a coward! He comes here with his friends, aware of the impunity that his title grants him, shows his superiority to his

218

companions, gets what he wants, and leaves." While talking he began circling the room, gesticulating fervently. His face was the living image of his indignation. "At first I thought that only revenge moved him, but reconsidering it. I think revenge was left behind... *far* behind. It has become a test of his power. We just have to take that power away."

"Understood. But how do we do that?"

"Leave that to me," Noakh said, smiling confidently.

26. The night before the confrontation

Dorein was quick to tell the news to the villagers. So when Hilzen and Noakh left the hut, all the villagers were waiting for them, their eyes full of hope.

Noakh could not help swallowing nervously, realizing the enormous weight that had fallen on his shoulders. The words of the old woman—that he and Hilzen had been chosen—kept dancing in his mind. He did not reflect on the irony of that affirmation, but about how the desperation of the town had led them to blindly trust two people who they did not know anything about—and who, not long ago, had been confused for simple thugs. The villagers had been about to bury Noakh and Hilzen in the snow.

But now they were holding a party in their honor. They had built a great fire in the square, with meats of all kinds roasting in the flames. They had spared no expense in the provision of food. After all, Noakh and Hilzen had given rise to a hope the villagers had long forgotten. They had to celebrate the arrival of the heroes, who were going to release them from the suppression they had been subjected to for all these decades.

Everyone brought something: a freshly made cake, a soup of snow rabbits, anything was welcome. The music was not lacking either. Several members of the town had been encouraged to play, forming a small orchestra. They were playing "The Sailor and the Mermaid" now, which made Hilzen sing the merry melody too, his face lit by the fire while he held a bottle of blue wine.

It was an authentic celebration. The villagers seemed to be enjoying themselves as they had never done before. However, Noakh was not having such a good time. While sitting at a table near the fire, weighed down by his thoughts, two girls, each about five years old, timidly approached him. First they bowed down and curtseyed clumsily and then gave him a bouquet of violet flowers. Violets were a beautiful and small flower Noakh had seen growing in the area despite the snow. Grateful, he smiled at them warmly and smelled the flowers; it was a sweet scent that somehow comforted him. He tried for a moment to forget his reflections, he pulled two flowers out of the bouquet and slipped the stem through the girls' hairs, then he left the flowers carefully on a table and started dancing with the small ones in time to the music.

The longer he remained by the fire, the more numerous the signs of gratitude and affection became. Realizing how important his role for the villagers was, Noakh eventually moved away from the square. It was all too much for him. The wound he had received in his back during his confrontation with the taysees had begun to hurt him again... At first he had taken it as a game, as a stupid challenge. He simply had to defeat Duranti—to beat him. Now he realized everything that was at stake. Whatever he did would mean the difference for the villagers, who trusted him blindly.

Back at the fire, Hilzen seemed far calmer. Noakh had claimed he had everything under control—though if Hilzen were to ask him now, he might feel differently about the situation. Perhaps it was also the alcohol and the joy of the night... or because the outcome of the confrontation with Duranti's men could mean his wish for a sweet death might finally come true. Whatever the reason, Hilzen had temporarily put aside his minor concerns; now he danced beside the fire while holding a pitcher full of blue wine. The wine derived its name from the bluish color provided by the mixture of fruits used to make it, as well as by a much sweeter flavor than the traditional wine, which had a slightly bitter taste at the end.

* * *

Noakh looked at the stars. Without noticing it, he had walked until he had left the village. He bent down now and threw pebbles into the darkness around him. Even though he was absorbed in his thoughts, he noticed someone was approaching.

222

"I'm fine, Hilzen. Leave me alone," he said reproachfully.

"I'm afraid your friend is too busy with the wine to care about you," said a feminine voice which definitely was not Hilzen's.

Noakh turned his head. Dorein stood a few feet away from him, her cane stuck in the snowy ground, her eyes fixed on his. He anticipated that she would leave, but the old woman instead continued: "It is freezing here, Noakh. Why would you rather be here than celebrating with the villagers? Aren't you enjoying our party?"

"Yeah," said Noakh coldly. "It's just that I wanted to be alone..."

Dorein answered Noakh's insolence by muttering a curse. She stood there, looking at the dark sky full of stars. Noakh ignored her, throwing more pebbles that landed softly on the snow. Just when Noakh thought she was going to leave she continued. "Difficult, isn't it?"

"Hmm? What do you mean?" Noakh answered, confused.

"Knowing the people you must protect makes the task much more difficult," she said solemnly.

Noakh responded with a sigh.

"You do not need to answer, Noakh. I know it very well. I've been carrying the same burden as yours for a long time. I've been there." After a long silence the old woman resumed. "We are very grateful that you have agreed to help us, but I must also remind you that you are still the one to decide your own destiny."

"It's not my life I fear for, Dorein," Noakh replied. "It's the consequences... What if it all goes wrong? I could not stand that failure."

"You're too young for all this, too... inexperienced. I wonder why you were chosen for this task? Oh Aqua!" Dorein questioned.

Noakh clenched his fists tightly and took several deep breaths. Of course the Aqua Deus had not sent him here. However, he was soon able to control himself.

After a long period of silence, the old woman turned back.

"I'll leave you alone. But remember the saying, Noakh. We are owners of our destiny and slaves to our decisions."

Noakh stood there alone, absorbed in his thoughts.

* * *

The loud bells flooded the town, a means of communication once used to warn of attacks, or to announce the return of men after battle. They were currently tolled when announcing an unwelcome visit. The tolling made the whole village chill. It was a sound they had come to relate to sadness. The bells seemed to sound different this time, though: unfamiliar... happier, some might say, with a bit of hope instilled in them.

Fate had deemed the day should be cloudy, with no snow and little rain, which in a frozen wasteland such as the Snowy Mountains could be considered nice weather. The wind carried the smell of wet grass, which mingled with the scents of animals such as dark-brown pigs and goats roaming the widest streets of Ograbh.

It was early. Even so, Dorein had been up for a long time. Insomnia had long been part of her life, leaving on her face dark circles of purple and brown. The sound of the bells had interrupted her prayers. This time she allowed herself the luxury of finishing the prayers, a sign of defiance, before getting up, grabbing her cane, and heading towards the hut where Hilzen and Noakh were staying.

Dorein tried all possible ways to suppress her fear. She knew that such unpleasant emotion only reflected a lack of faith. Aqua Deus had heard her prayers. Finally, someone had come to help them—she had to believe in the two travelers Aqua Deus had sent to Ograbh. As she walked through town, she kept muttering all the prayers she knew, even as she came across other villagers who were already leaving their homes and stepping outside. Once she had reached the door to Noakh and Hilzen's cabin, Dorein took a moment to breathe deeply and calm herself. Then she tapped her cane against the door to alert them to her arrival.

"Noakh, Hilzen... it's time!"

Her firm voice hid her nervousness.

After a few moments of waiting, she opened the door indignantly, assuming Noakh and Hilzen were still sleeping. Then she began to curse them aloud when she realized they were not there. Her eyes searched the room, hoping to spot them in one of the corners the fours walls surrounded. She looked and looked again, hoping that her eyes were playing tricks on her. She was not wrong, they were not there.

She could not believe it. They had left, leaving the town to its fate.

Dorein squeezed her jaw tight. She tried to take a deep breath. This time, however, the situation overtook her, she was trembling.

She tried to review the matter at hand. The town had the necessary reserves to pay its tribute to Count Duranti; they had been stored throughout the year. But the villagers had used a large portion of them during the festivities to celebrate the arrival of their supposed saviors. Still, they should have enough. They had to.

She tried to make quick calculations, but her mind was clouded. Even if they could cope with making the payment, it would undoubtedly be a blow to the whole village. So many years tied to the yoke... then suddenly some hope, which had just as suddenly vanished. Being able to make the payment or not, it made no difference. The town would not recover from this.

At the door, a young woman rapped her knuckles, making Dorein aware of her presence. The woman had curly blonde hair peeking out from under a white wolfskin hood.

"My lady, the heroes are heading for Duranti's men. Shouldn't you also meet them?"

"What?" The news was a relief. With her cane she quickly hobbled her way to the meeting. The young woman tried to follow in her footsteps.

"Damn fools!"

Dorein could not help but smile as she walked as fast as she could. For a few moments she had given everything up for lost, her strength had vanished as had her hope. Even though she would never admit it, she had even almost lost faith. But only for a moment.

The villagers stood at the exit of the village, in an esplanade from which they could perfectly see Duranti's arrival. Villagers usually didn't like to witness such an event, but this time it was different.

Upon Dorein's arrival, she had to make her way through the crowd of people who, as prisoners of the moment, were not aware the village protector was trying to pass. In any other scenario, a brief interjection from Dorein would have been enough for the onlookers to clear a path for her, but now the villagers were just trying not to miss out on whatever was going to happen. Dorein could not blame them for that, since hope was a feeling that had slept inside them for so long—and it had awakened, voraciously.

Today they would start a new life.

When at last she broke through, she could see Duranti's horses approaching slowly in the distance. Approaching the horses, in turn, were two shadows. They were far away... How could she possibly reach them, even if she hurried? Dorein made a move to follow them. However, one of the men gestured with his hand.

"Back, Dorein, I beg you. Noakh has asked us to leave them both alone. We must respect the will of our saviors."

Several villagers around the man nodded, reinforcing his words. The hope in their faces, rather than any words, prevented Dorein from feeling offended. She simply nodded and watched as the two heroes walked on to face their fate.

"I wonder how you'll manage, Noakh," Dorein murmured.

27. The queen's lessons

Vienne stood with her mother in the sword room, the chamber where Crystalline lay. It was here where the queen had decided to teach her daughter the mysteries and techniques of the sword, the same place where her mother had taught her, the way it had been taught for several generations. Graglia withdrew the sword from underneath the waterfall then ran her hand lovingly over the blade.

"Vienne, what is it that makes Crystalline different from the rest of the legendary swords?"

Vienne tried to think of the answer. She knew that not responding correctly would disappoint her mother. "Her power over water?" she replied unconvincingly.

The expression on the queen's face was enough for Vienne to know her answer was not the one the queen was hoping for.

"It would be good if you stopped saying what you think I want to hear and instead said something with a minimum amount of common sense," the queen replied. She fixed her stern gaze on her daughter, a visage few had ever seen.

"Crystalline is a peculiar weapon. It certainly does not have the destructive power that its counterparts in the Fire Kingdom have or the absolute control that the Tirhans' swords provide over nature. However, its power is still something to consider. I'm sure that Igüenza has taught you about its many virtues; even so, words sometimes are not enough." While speaking, the queen extended her left arm and drew the blade closer to her skin before making a huge cut in her wrist, so deep that the blood began to fall on the water.

Vienne, not understanding what her mother was doing, watched in terror. Blood continued to emanate from the wound. In contrast, the queen seemed unaware of the seriousness of her wound. The extended arm still dripping with blood, she jubilantly observed the stupefaction of her daughter.

Then, Graglia laid Crystalline on her wound. Small drops of water began to drip from the blade, closing the wound within a few moments. The queen's wrist was perfect again, without any scar or spot that bore witness to the horrible wound she herself had provoked a few moments ago.

Vienne's face was pure astonishment, but Graglia could not help but let a smile form on her lips. She recalled when her mother had performed the same demonstration for her decades ago. The expression on her face had been exactly the same as the expression her little one bore now.

"No matter how often they speak of the water sword's power, it will never fail to impress," said the queen, quoting words her mother had once told her. "Crystalline has the power to heal all wounds... Yes, this is the reason why its wielder should never go to our army's frontlines. Those stupid Fireos have tried more than once to provoke us into carrying it there, because Wulkan and the Fireo ancestors always lead their armies from the front—a strategy they seem very proud of. We are smarter. Crystalline's powers make its wielder more useful mingling among our troops, from where the one who bears the sword can use all of its power. Crystalline's power extends over water in all its forms; it is not a defensive weapon, as many may believe. Its power when attacking can be equally enormous. It depends only on how you have been blessed."

"Blessed?" Vienne answered softly. She tried to review in her mind the many lessons Igüenza had taught her.

"Do not try to rummage through your head, Vienne," replied the queen, guessing Vienne's thoughts. "Your caretaker is a wise woman, and full of knowledge. However, these details are available only to the sword's legitimate carriers; neither your aunts nor even your sisters know about it—and that's the way it should be." Graglia's voice sounded at once resounding and peaceful. "The powers that the Aqua Deus grants to the sword's carriers are slightly different for each one. You have your great-grandmother Midalien, whose stories tell how she could summon the

228

beasts of the sea to fight by her side, and her daughter, Legan, who could control the rain."

"The rain?" Vienne answered, impressed. She wondered with which powers she would be blessed.

"Your grandmother argued that the powers varied from one to the other depending on the character possessed by the carrier, but in my opinion, I think it is a matter of the whims of our beloved Aqua Deus." The queen gave Crystalline to her daughter. "Test yourself. Let's see what path the Aqua Deus has chosen for you."

Vienne looked strangely at the sword, not knowing how to react. She tried to invoke the sword's power as her mother had taught her to do. We command and Crystalline obeys, she remembered as she commanded Crystalline to drop water as her mother had just done in order to heal her wrist, but again with no success.

She had learned some of her mother's tricks by watching her. Closing her eyes, slowing her breathing... somehow it was not working for her. But why? She kept wondering: What if the Aqua Deus had regretted his choice? What if she was not worthy of being the Lacrima? She really wanted to know what blessing the Aqua Deus might bring her. She closed her eyes, trying to focus all her concentration, trying to understand what was supposed to be done. She took a deep breath once more, trying to summon her inner strength. But nothing happened.

The queen was about to speak when a knocking on the door interrupted their session, announcing the end of the lesson. Vienne now, being the legitimate heiress, had free access to the sword room, so she began to familiarize herself with it and to little by little develop her power.

Outside the hall, three people were awaiting them. Among them, Vienne recognized her aunt, Alvia... The people standing there—two men and one woman—were three-quarters of the Knights of Water! A hasty short Royal Guard soldier appeared behind them.

"My queen, I am very sorry for their arrival with no announcement, but I was unable to stop them!" the girl said hurriedly, knowing the queen's temper.

"It's fine," the queen replied, dismissing her. "What are you doing here?" the queen asked, staring at her Knights of Water.

"We come to take an oath to the future queen," said the tallest of them. He knelt before the princess. "Her beauty is comparable to yours, majesty."

The other two knights imitated the first, kneeling by his side, their eyes looking to the ground. With their free hand, they each grabbed the necklace they wore around their necks—the same necklace worn by Gant Blacksword.

Vienne blushed at the comment. The knight who had proclaimed her beauty was the captain of the Knights of Water, the handsome Menest Casaniev, for many the most beautiful man in the kingdom. She was not going to disagree with this proclamation. Menest had strong, marked features that contrasted with his lively look and warm smile. When Igüenza told the princesses stories about princes, Vienne imagined them as Menest.

Kneeling beside Menest was Tarkos the Silent. While Menest radiated joy, Tarkos accomplished the contrary. A black hood full of tears and fraying covered his face. Very few people had seen his face, but the hood framed his small blue eyes. It was said that when Tarkos was named a Knight of Water he wanted to prove his faith and his fidelity to the crown, and thus he swore he would never question the words of the queen. And then he cut off his own tongue. The next time he was seen he was already wearing the hood—and since then, it was said, he had never taken it off. Vienne saw how his eyes peered at her for a moment, making her feel very uncomfortable.

The three knights remained kneeling on the floor until the queen gave them permission to stand up. Alvia looked at Vienne, her niece, then smiled and winked at her.

"Gant is not in the palace, so the oath will have to wait," the queen said. The fourth Knight of Water was in charge of hunting the fugitive Rebetien.

"Oh, my dear little sister," Alvia replied to the queen, amused. "Gant will probably die before completing his mission! Why make the rest wait?"

While Menest and Tarkos showed great respect for the queen, Alvia allowed herself to speak to her sister freely. She was, after all, one of her older sisters.

Alvia was slightly taller and slender than the queen, and her shoulders were also wider. Her face was as round as her sister's and they had similar lips, while her nose was aquiline, and her eyebrows were thick, with a strong arch. Although the two women were similar enough in appearance for a stranger to rightly suppose they were sisters, in temperament they could not have been more different. Alvia seemed to take almost nothing seriously, finding the humorous side of everything she encountered: dogs, combat, the fury of the queen. Vienne had heard rumors that several of her aunts—mostly those who led the various brigades of the Aquadom's guards—had not taken it very well when Alvia was named a Knight of Water. Although they were aware that she did not have the requisite virtues to be made responsible for an army, she was well versed enough in fighting to defeat all of them in individual combat.

"If Gant Blacksword dies, perhaps it means I simply should have entrusted the mission to another of my Knights of Water?" the queen replied, staring at her sister. Alvia's impertinence would have been punished long ago, had her abilities not made her more than useful on countless occasions. That was why the queen never questioned whether she had made a bad decision in appointing her. It was simply the price she had to pay for her sister's inhuman abilities. "I'm sure, Alvia, your presence here has not interrupted your mission. Is it not so?"

"Of course not, little sister—I mean, my queen," Alvia replied, amused. She turned to Vienne. "I see that Vienne carries Crystalline. Have her powers already awakened?"

"Not yet. She needs a lot of training," the queen replied. "She has not yet performed her ritual by the sea, in any case."

Vienne swallowed hard when she heard this, even though she had already been aware that this moment, the ritual by the sea, would come. The sea was revered by the Aquadom. It symbolized the queendom's power and immensity, its fury and its calm; all the queendom's waters ended up traveling to the sea. Therefore, the Aqua Deus was depicted as a sea beast of great power and beauty; the sirens and the most noble of the other marine animals cared for it. This was why the cathedrals, fountains, coats of arms, and, in general, numerous other emblems and insignia throughout the queendom were related to the sea. And it was also why the most powerful faction of the Aquadom army, the Sea Guard, carried that name.

"Oh, I see! Maybe then we can help her?" Alvia said, amused once again.

A small shrug from Graglia was enough for Alvia to take action. With one quick stride, she settled herself in front of Vienne and before she had time to react grabbed her by the neck of her dress, throwing her into the air and back into the Water Room. While Vienne fell on her back down to the floor, still holding Crystalline in her hands, Alvia clenched her fists and made a slight gesture with her wrists. Two daggers appeared

231

in her fists. With a powerful jump, she was on top of Vienne. Vienne tried as best she could to defend herself; however, she could not react in time, instead closing her eyes, hoping that Alvia would cease her attack. A rumble of metal caused her to open her eyes again. Tarkos stood between Alvia and herself; his sword had blocked the attack. If her aunt had intended to halt the attack it would only have been at the last moment.

Vienne tried unsuccessfully to contain the tears that began to flood her cheeks.

"Oh, come on, Tarkos. Do not be stupid!" Alvia said, annoyed by her partner's intervention. "Get out, Large Mouth."

Tarkos' little eyes flickered while they remained fixed on Alvia's.

"Is that a challenge I see in your eyes?" Alvia said, smiling. She had never fought Tarkos... Perhaps the time had arrived? Meanwhile, Menest was still standing outside the room. He let out a sigh, shaking his head with disapproval.

The queen casually strolled into the room, grabbed Crystalline from Vienne's hands, and then extended her arm so Crystalline's tip touched the water's surface. Before Alvia and Tarkos could begin to fight each other, a powerful spout of water threw each of them against walls on opposite sides of the room from each other.

"You are Knights of Water. Behave yourselves as such," the queen said calmly.

She returned Crystalline to Vienne. At her words, Alvia and Tarkos regained their composure, again digging their knees into the puddled floor but now being completely soaked. Vienne was still shocked. She was the heir to the throne and was supposed to be protected by the Aquo soldiers... So why had Alvia attacked her? The queen then addressed her.

"Vienne, they are sworn to protect you, but *you* must be the sword to defend the queendom. You are weak."

Her words did not contain even a bit of contempt or disappointment; they simply stated facts. Which did not make Vienne feel any better. "Your character is weak, and that is reflected in your skills with the sword. In the future, your lack of charisma may affect the queendom's power I'm here to ensure that does not happen, and I assure you"—Graglia's words resounded with firmness and determination throughout the room— "it will not happen. From now on, you will face me or, if necessary, one of the Knights of Water, every day."

They each received the news in a different way. Alvia tilted her head and smiled. Menest bowed in obedience to the queen's decision. But Tarkos was thankful, at that moment, for having no tongue.

"But... mother," Vienne whined, unwilling to deal with such monsters, "I can't face them. You've already seen what happened... I'll be harmed."

"Of course they will harm you." The queen turned to her Knights of Water. "Since all of us are present here, I'll announce that you have my permission not to restrain yourselves while you are training her!" She turned back to Vienne. "Do you want to survive, Vienne? You'd better learn to use Crystalline's healing powers as soon as possible."

Vienne looked away. She was terrified, finding herself in shock... Her mother certainly meant it. She was going to make her face the greatest military force in the Queendom of Water, after witnessing how Alvia grabbed her dress and threw her into the air before Vienne could react. She began to tremble, anticipating what awaited her.

"That's not all," the queen said in a crude voice. "Follow me."

* * *

Once the queen and the princess had left the room, the three Knights of Water stood up.

"Damn it, Alvia," Menest said furiously, "your nonsense has put us in a complicated situation again. This time you've turned us into nannies!"

Alvia's face flooded with a smile. "Oh, don't put on such airs, Menest. You'll have a chance to face Crystalline! The most powerful weapon in the queendom... Is that not what a white knight like you aspires to?" Her playful nature made her look much younger than the queen, despite that she was actually older. "And you, Tarkos, stop looking at me like that! How many times have I told you that it bothers me?"

* * *

The queen was walking through the cells, carrying Crystalline on her hand. She and Vienne were in the palace prisons, one of the most protected places in the queendom. The prisoners jailed here were the worst criminals in the queendom, prisoners from neighboring kingdoms to those who had committed the most unforgivable crimes. Only those who had committed attacks against the church were held in a different

233

area, where the Congregation of the Church, the main order of the church, guarded them.

The jailers had provided the queen complete freedom to walk through the prison, furnishing her with the keys to the cells of a particular section. Vienne realized that the jailers had not been very surprised by the queen's visit. Were her visits to the cells a common excursion?

The cells were very much a sordid place; it was dark since there were not a lot of torches on the walls, and it was also very humid, which gave the place a stale and fetid smell. Not only that, but there was something strange about the place that made its presence felt: the tortures to which the prisoners were subjected. Screams pleading for food could be heard... depraved sounds after seeing the figure of two women approaching. All those voices became silent as soon as their owners realized that one of those figures belonged to no other than the queen herself, the prisoners saw from their cellars how the queen was walking the prison grounds. While they were walking through the cellars, a dog— or better said, a horrid creature that resembled a dog but with dark-brownish flesh and red eyes—approached Graglia and started wagging his tail vigorously. The queen patted the animal on its head and then kept walking while the animal lied on the floor.

She stopped before one cell in particular. The wooden door creaked loudly as she opened it with one of the keys the jailers had given her. Sitting on the floor and leaning against the wall was an elderly man. He had a careless grey beard and was bare-chested, revealing a scrawny body. Each of his ribs was visible due to his extreme thinness. The man narrowed his eyes, struggling to his feet so he could better see who was there. After taking a few steps into the cell, the queen brandished Crystalline and, without a word, pierced the man's stomach. The man let out a muffled sound as he fell to his knees. Vienne put her hands to her mouth as she watched the man's blood begin to flood the ground.

The queen seemed not to show any emotion. Fixing her eyes on Vienne, she held out the sword, still covered in blood.

"Do you feel sorry for him? You have the power to save him. If he dies it will be because of your own incompetence. Perhaps this will be how you learn; otherwise we will have to try with your sisters."

Vienne's eyes turned to tears. She did not want to wonder whether the queen meant what she said.

28. An interrogation

"As you may have noticed, it is not my intention to kill you," Gelegen affirmed as he took a drink from the wine bottle. He was leaning on the ground, one hand on the back of his neck as he watched the stars. Cervan lay at his side, still handcuffed, the ropes nailed to the ground with pikes. Subduing the giant had been an arduous task. Many men had died during the fight so that there would be no further risk in capturing him.

Because of its size, the giant was being held in the same place where they had faced him. Gelegen had set the camp close enough so they could make sure everything remained under control. He had ordered his men to constantly monitor the giant in shifts consisting of three guards. However, it did not take long for Gelegen to realize that his order was unnecessary. Cervan was very weak; although the wounds on his feet had stopped bleeding, his spirit had not.

The giant had not eaten for several days. Gelegen's men had offered him food at his insistence. The soldiers had agreed reluctantly, since they did not have much empathy for the monstrous being. They were not to blame, having witnessed how that creature had shattered their companions and friends not long ago.

The giant was staring at the sky while breathing weakly, his gaze full of sadness. He had not made the slightest attempt to free himself. The only thing that indicated he was alive was his chest moving while he was breathing. His eyes were fixed on the stars; it was a beautiful night.

Gelegen sometimes wondered what such a beast was thinking. Until now he had not dealt with any giants, although he had seen one on another occasion, so he did not picture these creatures as being endowed with reason and intelligence, partly because of their way of speaking, which made them seem stupid.

Cervan continued observing the stars. According to his beliefs, when a giant died a new star rose in the sky. This was how Urrak and Kadoros, the twin gods of the giants, recognized each one of their brothers. When a shooting star passed by, it meant that the most recently fallen giant had been so important that he could travel the skies, announcing to everyone that he was no longer among the living. It was said that Urrak and Kadoros were represented by the sun and the moon, watching and protecting the giants every day and night.

"I just want to know who was riding in that wagon," Gelegen explained. "I know you know. Somehow, they managed to make a pact with you, and managed to escape from their encounter with a giant—something that many of my men cannot say, unfortunately."

"Me not knowing anything," replied Cervan, his voice weak. "Your men start... no, *you* start," the giant corrected. "Me respond same way."

"I do not remember it like that," Gelegen answered as he gulped another drink. It was true that his words had been a bit more hostile than he had intended, and this had caused the giant to put his foot down—figuratively speaking—issuing what might for him have been a warning. But at that tense moment, with Gelegen feeling he was being fooled by the giant, the giant's words had not served as a trigger for Gelegen to call for the attack. No matter how old he was, it seemed that he could always regret a new decision taken for the wrong reasons.

One lesson age had taught him was that everything was simpler when you blamed others instead of yourself. Luckily, or unfortunately, Gelegen had learned that, even if it was simpler, it did not mean it was either truer or more correct. At first he had blamed the giant for the death of his men, but every time he was more certain that it had been his fault. Besides, thinking about it, he really meant what he had said: He did not want to hurt the giant, not only because the giant had really only been defending himself but also because of his colossal figure... a magnificent and strange creature.

Gelegen had been fortunate to see giants twice in his life. Many people lived their existence without ever having seen any. He recalled the first time he saw one of those creatures; a mixed sensation of terror and admiration had flooded him. The giant had passed by his side, aware of his presence, without causing even a scratch. A being that could crush him at will... and he did not hold the evil to do it. Probably that first meeting explained why Gelegen did not want this particular giant to die. After being restrained, the giant didn't seem harmful; instead Gelegen felt pity for him. However, he had ended the lives of several of his soldiers. Not only did his remaining soldiers want blood, but if it reached the ears of the queen she probably would as well. He knew Graglia; she would want the giant's head.

At that particular moment, Gelegen was grateful to be Gelegen.

"Listen, giant, I'm sticking my neck out for this, but I just want you to tell me what you know and I'll leave you free, I promise. I'll assume full responsibility for freeing you. And to demonstrate that I'm acting in good faith"—he approached Cervan's foot and plucked out several pikes that held down the ropes restraining it—"now you are a little freer. The rest is up to you. This is what we call a bargain. Take the deal I'm offering you, giant..."

"I already say, my not knowing anything," Cervan answered without averting his eyes from the sky.

"These men go around with dangerous weapons. They have killed people, and do not doubt that they will do so again the next time they have the chance. You don't seem a bad creature after all. Why do you want to be an accomplice of criminals such as those who were riding in the wagon?"

"They are not criminals," Cervan said, slightly angry—and noticing too late he had revealed a crucial piece of information.

Gelegen was about to let out a triumphant cry for having guessed that the giant had not really killed them and that for some reason, which he could not understand, was protecting them. However, he knew how to contain himself, making a small gesture with his hand instead, as though to indicate it was not important. Nonetheless he closed a fist in triumph, not allowing the giant to notice, a private gesture of celebration.

He considered the giant's information. So, there was more than one. And he already knew something else too: He related the giant's piece of information to the report from the mortuary. *A sword and a crossbow,* he thought.

"The evidence points to the contrary," he replied as he walked around Cervan. He held the bottle of wine up high, grasping it by its neck. "Burned corpses, brutal cuts to all of the opponents—a consequence of a perverse and tortured mind—a disproportionate amount of violence against anyone who poses a threat... a crude way to kill. May I not accuse that of seeming to be the acts of a criminal mind?"

Cervan remembered his first run-in with Noakh when he had been about to die—his sword was blazing fire and he seemed possessed. Was it at that moment that Noakh had been able to perform such acts? he wondered. It was not strange, after all, to him... With Cervan being much bigger and stronger, Noakh had no problem trying to attack him. But then after recovering he seemed to have come to himself, being kind to Cervan. It had been Noakh who had given him Orregahil, his horse and friend.

"They not criminals, he cured, always be good now," Cervan confessed, thinking that Noakh's actions were a consequence of the effects of the poisons the taysees had used against him.

"Cured? How can you be sure?" Gelegen asked. He did not even know what he meant by "being cured." Was he implying those acts were committed due to an illness? That was nonsense.

"I cure, he be poisoned. I use healing pigment and now be safe and sound, he not attack anyone else, not anymore," Cervan explained.

Gelegen weighed the giant's words, unsure which aspect of his claim impressed him the most: the fact that a giant had decided altruistically to heal a human, or that he was an expert in poisons—or that there was a poison that would make people commit acts of such extreme barbarity.

Fortunately, he had not dealt very often with poisons; they were not to his liking, and he had somehow been able to avoid encountering them throughout his career. But poisons were more typical of the lifestyle of the taysees, who used them to provoke a person into a highly intoxicated state that resembled drunkenness. Was it possible a poison was responsible for the violent acts that had been committed back by the last crime scene? Why not? he thought.

"So now he's cured?" he said, following the flow of the conversation.

"He cured," Cervan repeated.

"Let's thank the Aqua Deus!" Gelegen said as he lifted the wine bottle towards the sky. "You know, although we are in the Aquadom, I will confess that I hold a secret devotion to the god of wine. He knows how to bestow happiness to his faithful worshipers." Gelegen then took a last drink of the bottle before tossing it to the ground. "Come on, giant. Help me get this over with! Just tell me where they are heading. I just want to know why they killed those people!"

"You hurt them," Cervan said with regret. Although he usually did not like to be mistrustful, it was true that his feet had been injured and he had been captured. Could he really trust this man?

238

"What about this?" suggested Gelegen, not knowing if it was madness or genius. "Come with me. You can see for yourself that I will not lay my hands on them. Otherwise you can easily prevent it. But, if it turns out that their acts are not as noble as you preach, if they really are barbaric criminals, then they will be arrested in the name of justice. Deal?"

The giant was silent for a moment, though for Gelegen it seemed an eternity.

"No. No trust in you."

Gelegen was about to let a curse fly from his lips, preventing it only at the last moment, knowing it would not help at all. He could not blame the giant. After all, his plan did not make any sense. Did he really expect that this creature he had fought and held prisoner would simply become his traveling companion? For a moment he thought that maybe he was even more stupid than the giant.

29. Duranti

Hilzen helped Noakh to walk, as the eyes of the Fireo were blindfolded, a ragged piece of brown cloth tied tightly around Noakh's head. Even though he had tied the blindfold himself, Noakh made sure he could still make out a few details of his surroundings through the cloth. However, he was very nearsighted. Objects and details that were close to him appeared with decent clarity, but all the details grew worse the farther he looked into the distance.

"You really aren't going to tell me why you blindfolded your own eyes?" Hilzen asked, once again growing nervous and upset. He was holding Noakh's right arm tightly, helping him to walk straight ahead. "If you have a plan, it would be wise to share it with me so I can act accordingly..."

"You will see, Hilzen. Trust me," Noakh answered. "Just give me a description of our enemies as they get close, please. You know, Hilzen," he calmly added, "it's more than likely that today you will find your long-awaited death."

Hilzen replied with a snappy retort as he stared at the sky: "I always thought it would be appropriate to die on a rainy day." He smiled. "What about you?"

"If I die here, it will be with Duranti's head in my hands," Noakh said, trying to fix his eyes on the approaching knights. "In one way or another the villagers will get their revenge."

The sky cleared periodically, allowing the two men to observe the odd ray of sun. Despite this, the light rain continued to fall, dampening the snow and making Noakh and Hilzen's footsteps resound loudly. Duranti's group of men could now be seen clearly, not far away.

"Seven men riding horses," Hilzen said. "One of the men rides slightly ahead of the rest. That must be Duranti, I assume."

Duranti's men rode in a wedge formation behind their leader. But then Duranti made a signal with his hand. Suddenly their horses' canter changed from a trot to a gallop. They had clearly noticed the presence of the two strangers approaching them.

"Here they come," Hilzen said.

Despite the situation, Hilzen now felt extremely relaxed—a strange attitude not only because of the tension embraced by the moment but because he knew nothing of Noakh's plan. That morning he had woken up at the first bell's tolling. Noakh was already dressed in his clothes, his two swords in their sheaths and buckled on his belt, and all of his winter clothes were on. He waited for Hilzen to get dressed then without a word headed off to where they had been told Duranti would appear.

When the knights drew closer, their leader raised his hand, signaling that his company should halt. Then he circled his horse around his men. One of the men must have made a joke, because they all started to laugh. Noakh and Hilzen remained where they were, their arms crossed before them. They were aware any unintended movement on their part would be considered hostile. The group of gentlemen opposing them were certainly perplexed by their reception, probably because they had been expecting Dorein rather than these two strangers, for Dorein was in charge of hosting all such welcomed visitors.

"Do not move, Hilzen," Noakh ordered. "Let them look us over thoroughly. That will give us time to do the same."

As Noakh stood there in the snow, waiting for Duranti to make his first move, Lumio's words, spoken to him during one of his many lessons during combat training, reverberated softly in his mind: *The hunter who fixes his eyes only on his prey is unable to see the ravine and so falls off it. A true hunter knows how to see farther. He does not watch only his target; instead he learns his surroundings, he learns the direction of the wind. He reads his opponent and defeats him. Thus before his prey notices, the hunter catches it in his trap.*

His father liked to teach him by using metaphors, since, as he had told Noakh, when he attended the military academy it was much easier for him to retain information if he turned it into a story. Besides, it was a much more entertaining method of instruction, in his opinion.

Hilzen looked at Duranti's men. All of the nobleman's horses were huge purebloods destined for battle, real fighting beasts that had

242

beautiful, elegant bearings. Their caparisons were blue and white, of different patterns, as unofficially directed throughout the queendom, displaying the coat of arms of the knights' respective houses.

"Three of them have the same coat of arms: a ship sailing on a wave," Hilzen told Noakh. "The man riding in the center of the others is one of the men with the ship, but his coat of arms looks golden. That must be Duranti, certainly." The other men who shared Duranti's coat of arms were much younger in appearance. Perhaps it was merely a result of the fur-trimmed coats they wore, but their aspect was certainly much more robust than that of the rest of the men. They also conveyed a slightly sterner demeanor. As these two men were located on either side of Duranti, it was not difficult for Hilzen to suppose they were both soldiers of Duranti House, probably escorting their master to ward off danger. Though he was not an expert in heraldry, Hilzen saw that the shield of Duranti House displayed golden details that were unlike those of his two escorts. However, the other men's coats of arms incorporated golden details as well. The different design elements, Hilzen realized, marked the difference levels of prestige within the same house.

Noakh nodded in agreement. He confirmed what he had already suspected. He could see only the men's shadows, but he had assumed that the man in the middle giving orders had to be Duranti.

Duranti was a man of medium height, clean-shaven, and, as his withdrawn hood allowed all to see, possessed an advanced baldness. He appeared to be about fifty years of age. His nose was pointed... as were his little blue eyes. He seemed really quite amused with the situation, though he was also somewhat perplexed, waiting for Noakh or his partner to make some kind of move that would serve as an excuse for he and his men to start their fun. While waiting, he looked at his colleagues and spoke a few words that did not reach the ears of Noakh and Hilzen but seemed to cause a fury to bloom in the others.

Looking at the men accompanying Duranti, Hilzen saw that each of their appearances was peculiar. One man had a long greyish beard, an elongated nose, and huge eyebrows similar in color to his beard. His brown horse with white spots was armed with an ax and a bludgeon. Beside him rode another strange-looking man. He wore a hood and a black cloth covering his mouth, but the portion of his face that was visible appeared quite red and bulky, lending the man a frightening appearance. The black cloth had the same markings as the caparison on the horse he rode, namely, a sea serpent twisting its body around a stone column.

243

The shields of the two men escorting Duranti displayed an eagle sailing the sea on a sun and four anchors adorned with rose bushes. The first of the two escorts had clear skin. His lips and face were very thin, and without facial hair. No matter how long he observed the man's face, Hilzen was unable to determine if it was that of a man or if it really was a woman, a prospect that although possible seemed incompatible with the enormous war horse the knight seemed to ride with ease. In any case, Hilzen thought it was a beautiful face. The second escort had a huge wart on one of his eyebrows—an enormous bulge that caused his eyebrow to twist, giving his aspect one of constant skepticism. His round face was adorned with thick, hairy sideburns of a very dark-blond color.

It was no coincidence that several shields of the House of Duranti made reference to the sea, since the sea was considered a symbol of strength. The Aqua Deus's raging waters pounded the earth forcefully, a fact that many citizens of the Aquadom loved, for it symbolized how water ravenously imposes its will over the earth, the symbol of the neighboring kingdom.

With a firm stride, Noakh began to approach the knights, his swords still sheathed. The men were distracted by Duranti riding in circles around them and making jokes. Hilzen stayed at his station, his nerves beginning to tighten. His instincts did not stop warning him that he should have his crossbow ready. However, he was aware that before he could put his hand behind his back to draw the crossbow, one of the men's huge horses would charge him.

Until that moment, Hilzen had not realized that he hadn't moved so much as a muscle in a while, and now, becoming aware of it, he had the crazy desire to change his position. However, he raised each of his feet only slightly from the ground, one after the other, making the wet snow rustle. He watched Noakh slowly advancing towards the knights, his step steady but deliberate.

It was the bearded, long-nosed man who noticed that the blindfolded man was walking towards them. With a slight inclination of his head, he pointed with his chin, alerting his companions, who stopped talking and adopted serious demeanors. Duranti turned his horse, which took a few strides, trotting out in front. The count's expression was bemused; it seemed that the change from the town's usual reception was a source of entertainment for him rather than a cause for discomfort. Noakh was not surprised. He assumed that this whole pantomime was for nothing more than the pursuit of entertainment and the display of authority for Duranti to put on before his noble friends.

At that moment, Duranti faced Noakh. The nobleman raised his eyebrows in defiance. But Noakh smiled, trying to show indifference, repressing his desires to unsheathe his swords and make the man pay for all the years of suffering he and his father had caused. He felt grateful that his eyes were blindfolded, because he was sure his look couldn't hide the contempt the man provoked in him.

Meanwhile, the rest of Duranti's men began to whisper... except for the two escorts, who stood firm. Noakh understood that they were probably hoping to attack him at the first sign of a threat to their lord. Duranti raised one finger in a white glove decorated with golden edges, at once silencing the men. After a brief pause, he finally deigned to speak.

"Well? Where is the old Dorein?" Duranti snapped in a stupid tone. "Why are we greeted by armed men? Has the town forgotten the effrontery to my father many years ago?" he said.

"The effrontery?" Noakh repeated. He tried to hide the indignation he felt upon hearing such words, but he noticed how his eyebrow trembled slightly.

Duranti responded with a shrug.

Hilzen began to approach slowly then. He advanced with tiny steps, hoping to go unnoticed. The rain was still falling on the snow, making small pattering noises; at this distance, Hilzen had been unable to clearly hear what Noakh and Duranti were discussing, and he very much wanted to know. Even though he trusted Noakh, he knew he was a passionate man. As Dleheim had said, he was a Fireo, after all.

The villagers couldn't contain their excitement. They had seen Noakh and Duranti finally meeting in the distance. The crowd turned completely silent. They were even breathing in unison, waiting for their heroes to make their move and rid them of Duranti's family once and for all.

"Where are my manners?" Noakh began again, trying to calm himself. He bowed. "My name is Noakileum, wizard of the Reddish Water Hills," Noakh invented. Until now, he had thought that using his real name was a good idea, so he had to improvise. Silently he cursed himself for his lack of imagination. "And the one who accompanies me is my assistant, Master Safarius."

"A wizard?" Duranti asked, arching his head. The character of the wizard was not completely unknown to him. However, wizards were

245

unusual figures. Very strange, in fact. Humans who claimed to have been endowed with supernatural powers.

Duranti's men showed the same uncertainty as their leader, exchanging glances, frowning, or pressing their lips together.

"Did that man just say he was a wizard?" one of them muttered.

Noakh kept facing Duranti with a smiling expression. Doing so wasn't difficult, because of Duranti's reaction... along with the response he imagined Hilzen must be having.

Hilzen, being a bit closer, had heard Noakh's words. By the Aqua Deus's stiff rod, what was Noakh doing? He cursed inwardly.

Noakh was aware that he was taking a risk. However, after much thought he had concluded that his options were not very numerous. He had considered fighting Duranti and his men, but this did not seem the most advisable course of action. It might be the fastest way to solve the problem, but killing several noblemen would probably only aggravate the situation. Engaging in a fight with Duranti and leaving him alive after teaching him a lesson in swordsmanship was another option, but after bringing a period of peace and calm to Ograbh, the consequences would more than likely involve a terrible revenge being enacted on the part of the battered nobleman.

We fight to protect; fighting is our last option, Lumio used to say to him, a saying Noakh was sure his father had made up since Fireos were known in fact for their love for combat. However, Noakh had had to accept this saying, because not so many years ago, when his skills in combat were far superior to those of the average swordsman, he had been able to solve any dispute with his swords. But Lumio put an end to such bravery by first disarming him verbally and then in combat; he had done so countless times. That had served to provide Noakh with humility and common sense in equal parts, understanding that he had to fight to protect, although many times he still forgot this, being carried away by his passion for combat.

"That's right. A wizard," Noakh repeated, nodding to Duranti. "I understand your skepticism, since we are not indeed very common in these territories. I come here on a mission, though. These mountains are full of magical power. I come to claim them. The villagers will be my slaves and will suffer under my power and my anger, as they have never done before. I have been told you have made them suffer; it was a marvelous job so I must congratulate you. Therefore, I am sure you will be happy to hear this: If you believe that you have caused damage to this village, the Aqua Deus knows that under my hand their destiny will be one of unparalleled horrors."

Duranti was both angry and confused. The blindfolded man before him had just credibly affirmed that he was a wizard. However, neither his appearance nor his age fit Duranti's preconceived idea of what such a being should be: an old man with a white beard, a tunic, and some sort of wand or powerful staff. Looking the man up and down, he snorted.

Although the idea that the town would still suffer had not seemed wrong to him, it was the fact that it would not occur under his hand that he didn't like. How could he show the rest of the noble houses the power of Duranti House? How could he prove he could subdue a rough and barbarous mountain town and tie it to his yoke for having risen up against his father, and for defending a soulless woman who had uprooted and despised the heart of his father—a heartless bitch, as his father called her?

"No, no. It can't be. My father took this town. They are cursed by the Duranti family, and that's the way it must be!"

For a moment he panicked and was about to draw his sword. However, Noakh's calm confused him. It was true that the wizard and his companion were only two men, and although armed, they did not seem to show any nervousness. Also, it seemed old Dorein had been relegated to the background, as she had not joined them. Everything was strange, very strange.

Duranti tightened his jaw as he looked at that man, Noakileum, with hatred and confusion.

"I can see that you don't like the decisions of the Aqua Deus," Noakh observed, "because my power comes directly from him."

"The decisions of the Aqua Deus?" Duranti repeated in a shocked tone.

Duranti did not know what to do in the face of Noakileum's strange words. His face was a mixture of anger and confusion. What kind of power was the wizard talking about? Finally, one of the men who had accompanied him, the eldest with the long nose, tried to put an end to Duranti's confusion.

"It's a bluff, Ribas!" shouted the man, the only one who allowed himself to call Duranti by name. "Look at him. He does not look like a wizard—and even if he was, there are no wizards in this world capable of facing the Duranti family!"

Noakh, having anticipated this, bowed.

247

"I understand that to your mundane eyes, magic is strange; however, it is true and I can prove it. Such is my power that I can create water in a place as cold as this," he stated, while remaining calm.

"Doubt it!" the old man snapped. Despite this, Noakh's claim had sparked interest in the other combatants. Hilzen, however, was not enjoying Noakh's performance. Did he really expect them to believe such a hoax? He began to feel a small tic in his eye.

In a low voice, the nobleman with the huge wart exclaimed, "What if it were true?" No doubt this Noakileum must be crazy, he thought; he did not seem to presage anything good.

The nobleman's question having been thrown to the wind, the others began to believe that it might be possible—the man before them might be a wizard. Some of them believed it because they had never seen a wizard, and some believed it out of their desire to break from the routine. As a result, they began talking to each other in low voices, wondering how a wizard should act, and what he should look like.

This time it was the man with the clean face who addressed Duranti, but with much more respect. "Count Duranti, do not make yourself beg before this sorcerer. If indeed he is such, let him dignify your nobility by showing you his powers."

The other men accompanying Duranti began to affirm their companion's suggestion, speaking loudly and requesting that Noakileum show them some magical power that would keep them entertained. Only the oldest man remained reluctant to affirm the request, keeping his arms crossed and shaking his head in disapproval.

Noakh could see why the noblemen followed Duranti in his conquest. It was not strictly for evil reasons but more like collateral damage; it was simply a way to end their boredom. It was as if, with Duranti decisively executing his position, the other men were mere witnesses, allowing them to believe they were not really involved in the abuses Duranti inflicted. Noakh did not think the same; to him, they were his accomplices.

After a second thought, Duranti began to nod. "Yes... You claim to be a wizard. Prove it!" the nobleman urged with a laugh. A gleam in his eyes suggested he believed this was a brilliant move. It was a simple task, to unmask a fraud, and after that, the town would see their tribute increased for bringing a liar to deceive him. Count Duranti rubbed his hands expectantly.

Noakh again bowed. "Magic is not something to play with, Count Duranti. You know it has a high price. However, it must be understood

248

that if I show you what my power is capable of, you will accept my conditions, and I will finally be able to torment these stupid inhabitants at my whim and without interruption?" Noakh prodded expectantly.

After a brief hesitation, Duranti accepted. He was encouraged by his companions, who did not stop screaming, asking him to accept. They did not mind either the fate of the town nor the effrontery their noble family might suffer. In order to witness something new, something different and unheard of, they would have challenged the devil himself.

"Okay—but no tricks!" Duranti warned with a threatening finger.

The soldiers in charge had their horses take a slight trot forward, preparing for any trap. Hilzen also slightly changed his position, in order to offer help in case Noakh's stratagem did not work.

"So be it," Noakh said while bowing once again. "It happens, my lord, that the Aqua Deus granted me some powers by unorthodox methods. I beg you, do not take it as a show of hostility on my part."

After having his say Noakh fell silent, observing how Duranti meditated until he finally agreed. Then, nodding and retreating, Noakh said, "I suggest you go backwards."

Paying attention to him, Duranti fell back a few steps with his horse, now standing slightly in front of his companions.

It was then that Noakh drew Distra. He began to swing his left hand around the sword. *"Aqua Deus Turiahim frostarim sehar! Aqua Deus Turiahim frostarim sehar!"* Noakh repeated these words again and again as if he were conjuring a powerful spell. These were the few words he knew in Flumio, the ancient language of the Aquadom. Whatever these words meant, he hadn't a clue; he didn't know if they had any meaning at all. It was a language that had fallen into disuse after the rise of the common language. However, Noakh did not know for sure if, perhaps, the nobility still used it. Whether or not that was the case, the faces of the nobles seemed quite impressed.

After repeating his words for a while, Noakh launched a last sentence, screaming in order to cause a more dramatic impact. The next moment, Distra was completely engulfed in flames. Noakh raised the sword up to Duranti and his men so that they might better witness its powerful magic. Their expressions of astonishment made it hard for Noakh to suppress his desire to burst out laughing. Duranti, in particular, stared with his mouth open, his eyes fixed on the flames, not saying a word. The remaining noblemen also displayed opens jaws. They had expected a cheap trick; this had exceeded their expectations.

249

Noakh, anticipating the accusations he might receive from the men, explained the reasons behind his power. "As I mentioned, the Aqua Deus granted me several powers—including the power of fire."

"Fire?" Duranti said anxiously. "You claim the Aqua Deus granted you the power of fire? But that... that is sacrilege!"

"I didn't want to believe it at first," Noakh replied. "The Aqua Deus, granting me the power of fire? That was not possible!" He shook his head and sighed. "I paid a high price for my lack of faith. The Aqua Deus grew furious at me for not doing his will and, as a retribution for my offense, I became blind," Noakh said.

He could hear Duranti gasping in horror. It was widely known that in order to be granted the power to cast a spell, wizards had to pay a price. This knowledge, together with the fact that the noblemen wouldn't find his story convincing at all if they saw his brown eyes, was the reason Noakh had decided to appear before Duranti blindfolded. Leaning down, he took a plentiful amount of snow in his hand.

"I know what you think... I didn't fathom this at first either. My lack of faith didn't let me understand," he schemed. "But the Aqua Deus, being such a powerful god, granted me magic beyond measure, even the power of fire itself." Then he threw the snow into the air, drew his sword up to it, and turned it into water. "Turns out, fire turns snow into water... What better power for an icy wasteland like this, right? Aqua Deus is wise..."

The noblemen were unable to respond. They were petrified by fear before the powerful wizard whom they had been about to battle. The long-nosed old man could not believe what he had just witnessed. Even Duranti was taken aback. He had been so sure that the wizard's claim was a bluff that he did not know what to do. The only thing that was certain was that he could not face him, although he also could not break the promise he had made to his father.

He remembered when his father was on his deathbed, he had ordered everyone to leave, including his wife, for his father had wanted to be alone with Ribas, his firstborn, his living reflection who made him swell with pride. It was then that he told him the true story of the effrontery to Duranti House. Ribas heard how his father told the story with hatred in his eyes—except when speaking about the woman who had provoked everything. Between strong breaths, the man spoke of that young woman, Anaril, and although his words sought to radiate hatred, Ribas could not help sensing the melancholy and affection in his father's voice. He truly loved that woman—and she had despised him. In spite of everything, the bitter memory of that day in which he had discovered her love for another man remained. His father made him swear an oath, a single promise. He did not even ask him to take care of his mother; he just wanted his son to continue avenging the effrontery those villagers had caused him—and therefore caused Duranti House itself. He had not left this world until his son had promised to avenge his memory against those who had dishonored him.

His father's words echoed in his mind once again. *Son, no matter what happens, promise me that Ograbh will continue to be tortured, they do not deserve forgiveness or rest, just fury.* Ribas promised his father that he would ensure that the town never found peace, eventually finding a way to put his promise to good practice. For what was to his father merely revenge was to him a way to demonstrate his power before the rest of the noblemen, to instill the fear of turning against Duranti House. In truth, the official version of the effrontery differed slightly from the actual one; it hid all the events that had signified humiliation for his father.

Ribas Duranti now found himself at a crossroads. He had promised his father that he would carry out his vengeance for the town's effrontery... so he must be sure, he had to be, that the wizard would do as he bid—although that indeed seemed to be the magician's intention.

Finally, after a long silence, Noakh simply stuck his sword into the ground, melting all the snow around him. He tried to make Distra blaze as hard as he could, though he was feeling weaker as every second passed. He wouldn't last long... What was the count waiting for? At this pace he wouldn't have the strength to fight him.

After a while, Duranti began to speak, staring Noakh up and down. "You say you're going to cause terror in the Snowy Mountains. But you do not have the look of being able to carry out your intention," he observed expectantly.

Noakh replied with a smile. "You also claimed that I did not look like a wizard..." Even talking was getting hard for him now; he would not last much longer. "And I must assume that my powers have left you no doubt about it. Do not be fooled by my appearance. The Aqua Deus sent me here for a mission, and in this case I'm afraid it brings pain for this town, for a greater good, of course. You think I care for the town or its stupid people? Fool!"

Noakh tried to look as evil as he could while smiling, brandishing Distra again. He turned back to the village, and with a fast move of his hand pulled the ragged cloth from his left eye just slightly—just enough to see—then launched several balls of fire from Distra's blade. The fireballs traveled through the air, arcing quietly through the rain until they struck the roofs of several houses in the town, bursting them into flames. The villagers, who until now had been closely watching Noakh's parley with Duranti, began to move quickly, turning back and running to their village, some to put out the fire, others to protect themselves against a second wave of attack, should it come. "Bring me that old woman you're talking about and I'll kill her in front of your eyes," he said with a tone full of hatred and disgust. Noakh could feel his face soaked in sweat.

Duranti was both amazed and horrified by Noakh's performance. The noblemen were also surprised. Even Hilzen had not expected such an act on his companion's part.

"I see you are serious," Duranti said, smiling. "That being the case, I think I can leave the responsibility for avenging the Duranti effrontery in your hands. Anyway, it was already becoming repetitive... having to travel for so many cold nights with so little to show for it." The nobleman snapped: "It's fine. You can torture these villagers in the name of Duranti House!"

With a gesture of his hand, Duranti wished Noakh farewell. It was only when he started turning his horse that Noakh spoke.

"Wait!" Noakh said in a stern tone. "My mission here is secret. I can't let anyone know I'm here, my existence should not even been known."

As Noakh spoke, Distra began to burn fervently, displaying her desire to thrust herself upon the stupid nobleman. Duranti raised his hands in defense. The other noblemen stared with terror; even the two escorts did not try to defend themselves, aware that there was nothing they could do against the almighty wizard who they believed they were facing.

"Do not fear, Noakileum. Your secret is safe with us," Duranti answered. He would have taken Noakh's words as an insolent threat if it were not for the fact that he knew it was better to heed them merely as a warning. Doing so would allow them all to remain alive. "None of us would want to interfere in the path of what seems a mission as crucial as yours. You will never see us again, you have my word."

He raised his hand and gestured swiftly, turning the noblemen back the way they had come. But their eyes still seemed unable to believe what they had seen; not a few times did they turn back to assure themselves

252

they had not gone crazy. Each time they turned, they saw Noakileum, still standing in the rain, his sword on fire...

Having shown great cruelty in his previous actions, Duranti was sufficiently satisfied to leave the town in the hands of the magician, knowing that he had no choice in any case; his pride and honorable name would remain intact. For his part, Noakh trusted Duranti's words. He was unsure whether it was his tone, or maybe his eyes, or perhaps his cowardly nature. Somehow he was sure Duranti would not bother the town again.

It was not until the count and his men were seen moving along the horizon that Noakh sheathed Distra. Greatly weakened, he nearly collapsed to the ground. Hilzen caught him by his shoulder. Without saying a word, he understood why Noakh had acted that way. The rain had stopped, and the grey clouds were moving away quickly, letting rays of sun fall on the snow.

"Let's go, Hilzen," Noakh said weakly while pulling the ragged cloth from his eyes. "I do not think we're welcome here anymore."

Hilzen nodded as he tapped his friend's shoulder, a sign of support, then helped him walk, putting his arm around Noakh's shoulder. Although Noakh's expression did not reveal much, Hilzen had come to know Noakh well enough to see that the actions he had taken grieved him. Even if that were the case, Hilzen had to admit that Noakh's most absurd trick apparently seemed to have worked. The nobles had left, and that was what mattered. Hilzen would wait a little longer to meet his destiny.

"So, 'Master Safarius,' huh?" said Hilzen mockingly, making both of them laugh.

The two companions started walking through the snow. It was time to continue their journey. They didn't look back. At the village, the fires at the different houses had already been extinguished. The fury of the inhabitants, however, did not allow them to view Noakh's actions as being quite so harmless. They cursed the two men whom they had offered lodgings to and who had celebrated with them. They seemed not to notice that Duranti had left without demanding his tribute—the first time he and his men had departed without taking any of the village's winter reserves with them. Only Dorein seemed to have realized it. Tears appeared in her eyes as Hilzen and Noakh disappeared on the horizon.

"Noakh and Hilzen... thank you," she said to herself, almost in a whisper. "Thank you, Aqua Deus. What a fool I was not to trust in your judgment!"

30. Vienne's obligations

Vienne bowed to the soldiers of the Royal Guard, who watched over the room where the sacred sword was kept. The soldiers lowered their heads slightly. Then, together, in a perfectly synchronized gesture, they struck one light blow directly on the floor with their halberds, their silver armor squealing from the movement. Two of the guards then opened the gate and allowed Vienne into the room.

After they let her pass, the gate creaked closed again.

The room of the sword was humid. Four torches hung on the walls. Even so, the room was fairly dark.

Vienne took off her shoes and put her feet in the water. A chill ran down her back as soon as her toes touched the shallow pool: the water was freezing. She began to walk towards the end of the room, where the sword lay under the waterfall, the water creeping higher and higher up her legs with each step.

When the water reached around her waist, the princess extended her arm and wielded Crystalline. She could see the reflection of her golden hair in the edge of the sword. When Vienne wielded her, she could not help but feel overwhelmed by a terrible sadness. She still remembered when her mother had taken her to the dungeons. In her nightmares, the bitter moment repeated itself with no rest: Her mother, for purely educational purposes, piercing the old prisoner with Crystalline then urging Vienne to save him.

Her hands began to tremble as she remembered the precise instant the man fainted on the floor. The moment was burned into her pupils. He had remained totally inert without her being able to do anything to help him. She had wished that the sword would heal the man. Her lower lip trembled in panic as her mother gave her a look of disappointment.

Her eyes fogged with tears as she remembered how it had all ended.

That fateful outcome was what had led her to visit the sword room so early in her training. She did not want to experience such a scene ever again; if someone was about to die, she had to be able to help.

Vienne pressed her fingers to Crystalline's hilt. She closed her eyes and tried to concentrate. *Drop water, Crystalline,* Vienne ordered. She squinted an eye, staring at the edge of the sword. It was completely dry.

"It's all right," she said out loud as she took a deep breath. "I'll try again."

Vienne closed her eyes and tried to concentrate.

"Crystalline, drop water! It's an order," the princess muttered.

Again, nothing.

Vienne sighed. The memory of the old man lying on the ground bleeding to death occupied her mind again. The princess shook her head, trying to banish the memory. She had to try again.

However, several shouts from outside the room interrupted her training.

"Vienne! Vienne, I'm here!"

Vienne waded back through the pool then approached the door, still carrying Crystalline in her hand. She had recognized the voice. She opened the door. Her little sister, Aienne, stood behind the guards, who had crossed their halberds to prevent her from passing. The young princess's arms were on her hips and her brow was furrowed.

"Aienne, what are you doing here?"

"Here she is, see?" Aienne said, staring at the Royal Guards with indignation. Through the open spaces of the crossed halberds, she looked at her sister, tilting her head with a mixture of a smile and a hurried face. "Vienne! They won't let me through! I just wanted to know how your sword training was going. But they say that only the queen and the heiress can now have access to the room," she added with an offended grimace.

"Could you please let her through?" Vienne begged.

The guards, after a brief pause, pulled aside their halberds, leaving the way clear for Aienne to pass. It was difficult to know if the soldiers had paused because they did not know if they should allow passage to someone unauthorized—even if the heiress had given the order—or if they hesitated because they had never been given an order in so kindly a manner. Aienne smiled and walked proudly through the guards, her head held high.

Once the two princesses were alone together inside, the door closed again.

"Those guards," said Aienne, frowning as she looked back to the door. Then, as she took off her shoes, she turned to look at her sister. "Did you manage to summon Crystalline's power?"

"No," answered Vienne as she looked away, again glancing at her reflection in the sword. "Mother says that making drops of water fall from Crystalline's edge is very simple, but no matter how much I concentrate, I can't do it," she replied.

Frustrated, Vienne kicked the pool's shallow water with indignation.

"How does it work?" Aienne asked. "I mean, do you have to pray in Flumio or something like that so that the sword will obey your will?"

Vienne sighed. "It is supposed to be simpler than that," she said. "I just have to order... and Crystalline will obey. That's what mother says."

Vienne sat on the floor, as the water was not that deep near the entrance of the room. She sat with the sword between her legs, her blue eyes reflected off the blade. Aienne approached and sat beside her, soaking her dress as well.

"Maybe it doesn't have to be that way." Aienne shrugged.

"What do you mean?" Vienne lowered her gaze to look at her sister.

"I mean, maybe that's how it works for our mother... giving orders, I mean. But that doesn't mean it's the only way it works, don't you think?"

"But I saw how mother was dropping water from the sword..."

"I'm not saying her way doesn't work. I'm just saying that if you've tried as she instructed and it doesn't work, it may not be the way it works for you. Our mother commands, to everyone. That's why it makes sense for her to command the sword as well; maybe that's why it works for her. But that doesn't mean that commanding the sword is the only way; if that was the case, why didn't the Aqua Deus choose someone more like our mother? If what you say is true, shouldn't Katienne have been chosen?

"You're not like our mother, Vienne," Aienne added, smiling. "And let it be known that I don't say that as a bad thing. Have you seen how the soldiers were surprised when you asked them so politely to step aside and let me pass? You should have seen their faces, sister. They didn't know how to react. I'm sure they've never been asked the way you asked today."

Vienne's face reddened.

In response, Aienne patted her sister's shoulder. "And yet, although after several decades of following our mother's orders, they also obeyed you, even though you asked them in the sweetest possible way. See? Just because it works for our mother doesn't mean it has to work for you. Or rather, it doesn't mean it's how it's going to work for you."

"I don't know," answered Vienne, looking again at the edge of the sword.

Her sister's words were more than convincing in some way. Vienne was reluctant to think that what her mother had told her was not true. After all, she had seen with her own eyes how her mother had used the sacred sword.

"You've tried the way our mother said, and it hasn't worked," Aienne said, shrugging her shoulders. "Why not try a different approach? The worst thing that can happen to you is that it doesn't work for you—which is the situation you're already in."

Vienne looked at Aienne, smiling. She had always admired how her little sister saw things differently from others. "You're right, Aienne." She stood up. "Let's give your theory a try."

Vienne walked to the middle of the pool, her feet hidden under the water. Aienne watched her from the distance. The heiress held Crystalline with both hands and closed her eyes. This time she did not order Crystalline; rather she asked a favor of her.

Crystalline, please grant me your powers.

Vienne did not have time to open her eyes to see if her request had worked. Before she could do so, she felt her energy go faint, and she fell with a loud *ploompf!* into the water.

"Vienne!"

Aienne shrieked in alarm as she ran to help her sister.

* * *

Vienne noticed the water falling down her forehead. She awoke stunned in her bed, around which all her sisters stood, staring at her. She could see how Aienne, who stood at her feet, seemed happy to see her awaken. The heiress saw that her little sister's eyes were red. Her older sister, Katienne, said something to the rest of her sisters, who burst out laughing.

At that moment, Igüenza, who was also in the room, made a space for herself among the princesses.

258

"Thanks to the Aqua Deus that you are well, Vienne."

The caretaker checked that the towel on Vienne's head was sufficiently wet then moved her index finger in front of Vienne's eyes to check that the princess's pupils could follow it normally. "Everything seems fine. You are a little pale perhaps, but nothing else. What happened to you, dear?"

"Nothing, I was trying to awaken the power of Crystalline and then..."

"Vienne the weak," Katienne mocked, causing the rest of the sisters, except Aienne, to burst out laughing.

Several of her sisters repeated that mockery, but their words were cut off as soon as the door was opened. They all turned to see who had arrived.

"I see you're awake." The queen stood at the door looking at Vienne. Then she turned to her other daughters. "I wish to speak with Vienne in private."

Without a word, the princesses and caretaker all made the Aquo gesture of reverence, then one by one they left the room. When it was Igüenza's turn, the queen gracefully grabbed her arm and smiled warmly.

"Thanks for taking care of her, Igüenza. She couldn't have been in better hands."

Igüenza smiled at the compliment. After a slight nod she left the room, closing the door.

Graglia approached the bed, her gaze observing Vienne. Whether she was angry or not remained a mystery to Vienne.

"I'm glad to hear that you finally seem to take your destiny with the seriousness it requires." Graglia stood next to the bed. "It seems it only took one weakling's death for you to give importance to your obligations. I'm afraid we're going to need more prisoners if that's the motivation you need to start taking an interest in your responsibilities."

Vienne realized her mother carried a scroll in her hand. She lowered her gaze.

"Aienne was there when it all happened. She told me everything," Graglia explained. "For the moment, I will overlook the fact that you allowed her into the sword room. You fainted when you were trying to summon Crystalline's power, didn't you?"

Vienne nodded, her eyes turned downward, her gaze lost amid the wrinkles of her sheets.

"You'd better look at me when I'm talking to you, dear," the queen snapped. Vienne then forced herself to look at her mother. It was incredible how severe her mother's gaze could be, despite showing the most absolute solemnity. "Before you fainted, what did you feel?"

The princess tried to remember how she had felt at that moment, how to explain it? It had happened so quickly. Even so, she tried to answer her mother.

"It was as if an enormous peace overcame me," Vienne replied. "I know it may sound stupid, but that's what I felt."

"It's not stupid." The queen corrected her, her face unmoved. "It is exactly the sensation that one feels when using Crystalline. You feel that you are at peace; it makes you stay calm. That feeling allows us to think clearly; it helps us not to rush our thoughts."

"So, was I able to invoke the power of Crystalline?" asked Vienne, surprised.

"From what Aienne says, you fainted before you did. However, it doesn't hurt to know that one way or another Crystalline obeyed you." The queen extended her arm, giving Vienne the scroll she carried. The princess examined the scroll with interest. "This parchment is guarded by the archivist of the Congregation of the Church's library. In this document, a scribe narrates the story of the queens who preceded us and their exploits with Crystalline. The Ritual by the Sea will be in two days. There, your blessing will be revealed to you. I hope you have read the scribe's words by then."

Vienne's heart turned. She had always been aware that sooner or later it would be her time to make the ritual, a ceremony during which the Lacrima had to jump from a sacred rock into the sea. She just hadn't expected the event to be announced with such short notice.

While the princess was absorbed in her thoughts, the queen left the room. If she had spoken any words in farewell, or if she had wished her daughter a speedy recovery, Vienne never knew.

31. Mistaken

The wind wailed loudly. Snowflakes fell ceaselessly from the sky. The fog clouded their vision. Noakh struggled to keep Hilzen's pace. After the effort using Distra in his ruse against Count Duranti, he had felt weak. The Snowy Mountains were not making his recovery any easier. The snows allowed them no rest, their boots buried in the cold drifts making the walking difficult. Hilzen didn't even carry the map in his hands, partly because it was absurd to attempt to read it in such fog. Instead, he simply relied on his sense of direction. Noakh followed him, striving to stop shivering.

"D-Damn the m-moment I agreed to go through the Snowy Mountains," Noakh cursed, striving to be heard above the noisy wind. His lips showed a bluish tone while his teeth churned without rest. "Why... Why couldn't they be the Hot M-Mountains?"

"Does that pl-place even exist?" Hilzen shouted without turning his head. His eyelashes were covered with the frozen remains of snow. His lips were as purple as Noakh's and the skin on his face had turned reddish. The snow squealed as they walked.

"Now I... I hope it exists! And I hope it will be the next place we are heading to!" Noakh tried to hold his balance after one of his feet sank into the snow more deeply than he had expected. "How... How long is it to get to that... stupid sacred place?"

"Don't mock my religion, Noakh!"

"Hilzen, I'm not m-making fun of your religion. Right now I would call any place *stupid*, even if it was my m-mother's home!"

Hilzen ignored Noakh's words as he tried to move forward along the trail with difficulty. He protected his eyes with his right hand as he tried to discern the horizon. After their encounter with Count Duranti, Hilzen had asked Noakh to visit the Temple of the Lady of the Mountain, a sacred place for the Aquos. The temple, in the middle of the Snowy Mountains, was a place of worship and pilgrimage for the most devout Aquos. Hilzen had vehemently insisted that they visit the sacred sight, and Noakh, after the incident at their first meeting—in which he had somehow deprived Hilzen's dead wife and daughter of the burial ritual—believed he could not refuse.

"I'm t-tired of this cold. I think I am recovered enough. It's time for some heat." Noakh unsheathed Distra and had her engulfed in flames. After a brief pause the boy breathed a sigh of relief. "Much better... At least this way I can stop shaking at once."

"Noakh," Hilzen scolded, "have you forgotten that the last time you used Distra to warm us, we were spotted by one of the lookouts of Ograbh?"

"Yes, but now it's different," Noakh replied. "Who is going to see us in the middle of nowhere?" he mocked.

Suddenly, as if his words had worked as an invocation, they heard increasing noises around them. Noakh hardly had time to sheath Distra before a vague dark figure in the distance transformed into three individual, giant black horses that began to surround them. Swords held by the three riders were aimed directly at their bodies. Noakh allowed himself to curse in a low voice. His teeth churned again.

The three riders were warmly covered in skins—including their faces. Their horses were as dark as the night and the beasts' neighing drew clouds of steam above their muzzles. Noakh saw the coats of arms of various houses depicted on the horses' caparisons. *Noblemen again?* Noakh lamented to himself. The Fireo prepared to speak, but as the three riders remained silent, the rider behind the two weary travelers hit Noakh's head hard with the hilt of his sword, rendering Noakh unconscious. His body fell into the snow with a soft *oomph.*

"Noakh!" Hilzen shouted.

Moments later, a second *oomph* sounded as the second body fell softly into the snow.

* * *

Noakh woke up with a sharp pain in the back of his head. Next to him lay Hilzen, who seemed to still be unconscious. Noakh noticed that they were sitting on stone ground. Snow was not falling anymore; they were not outside but underneath a roof. Instinctively, he drew his hands toward his belt, confirming what he had feared. He did not have his swords.

"Are you missing something?" said a woman in a stern voice.

Noakh looked forward and stared at their captors. The woman who had spoken held in her hands Hilzen's crossbow, which she held high while aiming a loaded bolt at Noakh's chest. The three riders—a woman and two men who looked to be in their late twenties, perhaps even younger—had uncovered their faces and now watched Noakh with interest. A man with a prominent beard, dark skin, and a wide nose carried Hilzen's shield—the shield Dleheim had given to him—under his armpit. His long curly hair fell defiantly across his eyes but was tied crisply in a ponytail in back. The other man, with a squared jaw and straight hair, carried Noakh's swords under his left arm.

The woman quickly realized that Noakh was observing them. She drew the crossbow closer to his chest. "What are you looking at?" she said. Behind her hostile gaze swam big sky-blue eyes and soft, distracting features. Her hair was cut short, reaching the top of her ears.

"Oh, come on, Laenise," said the bearded man on her right. "Are you going to talk to a mere servant now?" He fixed his gaze on Noakh's brown eyes, not without a certain contempt. "Or worse, talking to a unickey—an Aqureo, to be more precise... Think of your house's reputation."

Noakh couldn't help but frown, not because he had erroneously been called unickey once again—a term he had lived with ever since he could remember—but because of the previous comment. Had the man implied that he was a servant?

"Gorig, don't be like that," the man with the square jaw replied calmly.

The other two captors glared harshly at their colleague even as he seemed entertained by the situation. He was the one who carried Noakh's swords.

Just then, Hilzen began to move.

"Look, it seems that his master is already waking up."

His master, Noakh thought, understanding the conclusion the nobles had drawn.

Hilzen awoke, drawing his hands to the back of his head. As he lamented the pain he was feeling, he began to speak with his eyes closed. "I've had a horrible dream, some bast—" But just then he opened his eyes, discovering that what he had thought a dream was in fact reality. "Oh..."

"Continue," said the woman as she pointed the crossbow at him. "Go ahead, dig your grave."

The man carrying Noakh's swords reached out and lowered her weapon.

"Laenise, please... calm down."

He bowed his head gently, and the woman reluctantly complied, lowering the crossbow. The man with the ponytail, however, did not seem happy with his companion's performance.

"Have you forgotten, Dornias?" he said. "Fire! As they made their way to the Temple of the Lady of the Mountain! It's a sin, and you know it!"

Dornias answered his companion's gaze with equal severity. "I am as devoted as you, Gorigus, so do not question my faith in the Aqua Deus. Precisely because of that, I will not fall into the sin of hypocrisy. Do you think you are pure enough to blame these men? At least let them speak."

"All right," replied Gorigus, shrugging. "And what if we don't like their answer?"

"Then we will kill them with their own weapons!" the woman answered, bringing the crossbow dangerously close to Hilzen's head.

Dornias lowered Laenise's crossbow once again.

"If we don't like their answer, we will take them to the Church Court," Dornias said emphatically. "Based on the queendom's laws, they have done nothing wrong; they only carried a torch to protect themselves from the cold. Their offense is against God, and we, humble men, have no power to judge them in the name of the Aqua Deus. They shall be judged by the Church Court; for the court has the power to impose punishment in the name of God."

His companions seemed satisfied with the proposed plan. It was well known that those who committed any crime against the public were taken to prison—a punishment that could not be compared to what awaited those who had been judged guilty by the Church Court and locked up in the ecclesiastical prison. The prison's dire reputation made traditional prisons look like hostels with straw beds by comparison.

Hilzen grimaced. The idea of being judged by the Church Court did not appear to be to his liking. He was about to speak; however, Noakh was aware that Hilzen had no knowledge of their captors' earlier conclusions, and so spoke first.

"Wait, I can explain," he said.

"You shut up, unickey," the woman answered, now pointing the crossbow at him again. "Let your master speak for you." Laenise turned her head towards Hilzen, this time without pointing the crossbow at him. "You, Criven de le Dos, how can you have your servant so badly taught?"

Noakh pretended to start indignantly at the insult. He nudged Hilzen, hinting to his companion that by carrying the shield Dleheim had given him, he gave the impression to their captors that he was a nobleman belonging to the house of Criven de le Dos and that Noakh was his servant. Hilzen paused, as if trying to assimilate all that was happening. Then he raised his eyebrows, understanding the situation.

"You are right." He nodded. "My servant is a bit of a big mouth and seems not to learn his position." Hilzen's tone was indignant, taking some revenge on Noakh for having allowed himself to be discovered once again using Distra. "It's hard to keep him on the straight and narrow. I'll make sure he gets enough lashes as soon as we return home."

"A Fireo servant," replied Gorigus contemptuously. He spat on the ground to give additional weight to his words.

"Did you just spit on the sacred floor of the temple?" replied Dornias, amused. Gorigus turned pale. He threw himself to the ground, to wipe his spittle with his sleeve.

"Aqua Deus, forgive me," mused Gorigus with embarrassment, continuing his prayers as he rubbed the floor again and again.

"You see, Gorigus," Dornias said as he looked at his companion. He shook his head in disapproval even as he smiled.

Gorigus was too embarrassed to answer, but Laenise crossed her arms in indignation.

"Whose side are you on?" she said, frowning at Dornias.

Dornias sighed. "I'm only saying, I don't think what these men have done is that serious." He shrugged. Gorigus regained his composure and tried to cut him off, but Dornias lifted a finger to stop him. "I know, Gorigus. To use fire on the path to the temple is a practice many would consider a grave sin... but who are we to judge them? After all, these men were trying to get here on foot, and in fact they had almost arrived when we assaulted them! We, on the other hand, arrived here with our thoroughbreds, horses bred in the mountains and accustomed to riding in the snows, turning our route into a much simpler feat. Are we really going to judge these two men who have come here on foot, as was done in the old days? Just for a moment of weakness? The icy wind, the snow falling on their shoulders... I don't see such a serious mistake. Besides, I remind you that you weren't even able to find the torch they used." Noakh couldn't help but breathe an almost imperceptible sigh of relief upon hearing these words. "What evidence were you going to show to the Church Court?"

"Any torch would have served," Gorigus replied lowly.

"And lying to the Church Court, Gorigus?" Dornias answered in a tone of exaggerated alarm. "As I have already said, we are not the ones to judge these men, let alone judge a member of such a noble house that has as much history as that of the Criven de le Dos family."

After obtaining his companions' consent, Dornias threw the two swords he held to Noakh. Then Gorigus and Laenise returned the crossbow and the shield to Hilzen, though they did so with greater reticence than their companion and without looking Hilzen in the eyes. After that, Gorigus and Laenise left to tend to their horses, ensuring that their beasts were well protected from the cold.

After his companions had left, Dornias extended a hand toward Hilzen, helping him up. Noakh meanwhile hastened to hang his swords back on his belt.

"Forgive my companions, they are not normally so irascible." Dornias smiled. "This bad weather makes everyone grumpy."

"It's fine." Hilzen had strapped the shield onto his back once again. The crossbow hung safely on his belt. "This incident is already forgotten. Thank you, sir..."

"Dorniaseus Delorange," the man answered as he performed the Aquo act of reverence, after which he extended his hand. "But please, call me Dornias. Dorniaseus was my grandfather... and of the many gifts that I consider my ancestor to be endowed with, his given name was never one of them."

Hilzen and Noakh had a difficult time hiding their astonishment. Delorange House was not simply a noble house like that represented by the Criven de le Dos family. Rather, the Delorange lineage consisted of the oldest and undoubtedly most powerful noble family in the Aquadom.

266

This explained why his two companions seemed to listen to him. No matter how important their houses were, they could not be as important as Delorange House.

"A pleasure... and I am Safer Criven de le Dos," Hilzen lied, then bowed. "And this one," he added as he pointed to Noakh. "This is the scoundrel of my servant, who doesn't even deserve to have a name, but you may call him Servme."

Hilzen was satisfied, but Noakh couldn't avoid frowning. His friend was taking too much advantage of the situation.

Dornias could not help but burst out laughing at the name he had just heard. "A suitable name for a servant," he observed. He then looked around the entrance hall where they stood at that moment. Just then Laenise and Gorigus returned. "My companions deserve to be introduced. Before you stand Gorigus Emsier and Laenise Naudine, the heirs of their respective noble houses.

Both Gorigus and Laenise made a none-too-elaborate gesture of reverence. Then Dornias looked up at the roof and raised his arms, exclaiming: "May our troubled encounter not detract us from the value of our deeds. After all, we have arrived at the Temple of the Lady of the Mountain!"

32. The Lady of the Mountain

Dornias, Gorigus, and Laenise were the first to enter the hall, followed by Noakh and Hilzen. The room smelled slightly damp. The huge stained-glass windows were unable to provide light to the room due to the stormy weather outside. Gorigus approached the torches that hung on the walls and lit them one by one, each torch resting in a support that had been shaped into a spiral. With the improved light, the five colleagues admired the room where the statue of the Lady of the Mountain rested.

The hues of the stone floor were a mixture of grey and blue. In the middle of the room rested a marble statue that had acquired a yellowish tone over the years. Even so, the passage of time had not managed to diminish the astonishing detail of the sculpture. The marble was carved in the shape of a beautiful woman. Her head was turned to the ground while water flowed from her marble eyes, running down her face and along her entire body, until the tears fell to the floor. After such a long period of time spent crying, brown markings had appeared on the woman's face. Underneath the sculpture an inscription in Flumio could be read: *Lacma alem sinie. Lacma fortia.*

"Let my tears heal your soul. My tears are your strength," Laenise recited as she knelt before the statue. The others did the same.

"To be here," said Gorigus, unable to contain his emotion. "At the feet of the Lady of the Mountain..." Laenise ran her hand gently across his back as a sign of support.

Noakh and Hilzen knelt quietly behind the nobles. Noakh was about to ask Hilzen about the Lady of the Mountain, since he didn't know much about such a respected statue, but he realized Hilzen was holding back tears. The Fireo saved his questions for another time.

Dornias was the first to rise.

"Are we pure enough?" asked Gorigus, stepping back slightly.

"Nonsense, of course!" answered Dornias emphatically. "I think we've paid enough respect to the Lady of the Mountain," he added. Nonetheless, he approached the statue. "And if we are not pure enough, may the Lady of the Mountain give us strength with her weeping."

"Shall we?" Laenise suggested.

Dornias nodded. "Come, Gorigus. You first!"

Gorigus approached the statue cautiously. He ran his thumb over the cheek of the Lady of the Mountain and let his finger soak in her tears. Eventually he drew his thumb to both his cheeks and rubbed them with the water. After that, he turned back, looking at the others in the room, who seemed expectant.

"How do you feel?" Laenise asked eagerly.

"I feel..." Gorigus paused, trying to find the right word. "I feel as if my sins have been forgiven."

After his words, the others lined up to receive the Lady's tears. First Laenise, then Dornias. Noakh, not feeling that he should be part of the ritual, stayed behind at first. Hilzen, however, gave his companion a surreptitious nudge, urging him to get in line.

Hilzen took a longer time than the others to perform the ritual. He spoke quietly to the statue before passing his thumb over the aged marble. Noakh heard Hilzen mention the names of Marne and Lynea, his wife and his daughter, as he drew his necklace from his neck, opened the locket, and passed his wet finger over it. When Noakh's turn finally came, Gorigus raised an eyebrow while his face displayed a crooked smile.

"Are you sure, unickey?" he said just as Noakh's thumb was about to touch the water. Noakh paused at Gorigus's words. "If I were you, I'd think about it."

"What do you mean?" asked Noakh, perplexed.

"Isn't it obvious?" Gorigus replied, shrugging. "Fireo blood runs through your veins. The Lady of the Mountain forgives our sins, but even she is incapable of changing our origins."

"Who knows?" Laenise continued entertainingly. "Maybe the water will burn his unickey skin..."

"There's only one way to find out," Noakh replied in a more defiant tone than he intended.

Noakh brought his thumb closer to the Lady's face, as the others had done. Afterward, he ran his wet finger over his cheeks. He noticed a cold sensation as his cheeks came into contact with the drops of icy water. It was curious how similar the extreme cold sensation felt to the sensation of being burned, Noakh reflected. The Fireo realized everyone was watching him as if they were waiting for something to happen... for him to be punished for his Fireo blood, probably. Even Hilzen seemed expectant.

"I feel my cheeks burning," Noakh confessed with a shrug, "from the icy water."

"That's it?" replied Gorigus, disappointed. "I felt the same."

"I must confess that even I was curious to know what was going to happen," Dornias confided. "It seems that the Lady has not only purified us; she has also taught us a lesson, eh?"

* * *

After performing the ritual, they moved to a different room. It was a dark place, a kind of gallery, with one wall open to the elements. They lit a bonfire, aware that in such a chamber it was not a sin to do so. They sat around the fire, trying to warm their bodies. Gorigus had gone to the horses to get some food from their bags.

Dornias stared into the fire. "My father used to tell my brother and me that the Tears of the Lady of the Mountain could purify one's soul," he said.

"Really?" Laenise answered in surprise. "My mother said that from the Tears of the Lady of the Mountain originated the sacred sword of our queendom, Crystalline."

"The sacred sword, huh?" said Gorigus. He had just returned to the room. In his arms he carried some meat and a bottle of wine. Noakh and Hilzen stared at the food. Their provisions were almost entirely expended, and whatever remained was far less appetizing: Hilzen carried only a few radishes. "Is that why they say that the sword weeps, and that its lament can be heard when it is wielded by the queen?"

"That's right." Laenise nodded, drawing her hands closer to the fire.

271

"What about the House of Criven de le Dos?" Dornias asked, addressing Hilzen. "What stories do they tell about the Lady of the Mountain?"

Hilzen paused briefly before answering. "There is this story my mother told me when I was little. I used to tell it to my daughter before going to sleep." Hilzen's voice almost broke after mentioning his daughter. His eyes stared directly before him, lost in the storm. Then he began. "Before, long before she was known as the Lady of the Mountain, she was no different than any other maiden. She was not of high birth or even of a wealthy family; her origin, in fact, could have been no humbler." Hilzen smiled even as he snorted. "My mother, every time she told the story, gave the Lady a different job: soldier, merchant, baker. I used to tell my daughter that the Lady was a washerwoman. It didn't matter. One day the Lady looked out at a river, and she saw her pale face reflected, as on every other day, only this time, her reflection began to speak to her. Her reflection urged her to head towards the Snowy Mountains. This precise place." He tapped the floor lightly. "Her reflection had not told her why, not a single reason. Even so, the Lady left everything and headed towards the Snowy Mountains. It was a hard path, but her faith urged her to keep going. She suffered all kinds of calamities—she was robbed, attacked by wolves. It was as if all kinds of misfortunes were waiting specifically for her, and yet the Lady didn't give up. She arrived here, this very place, wounded and fatigued but proud to have fulfilled the will of the Aqua Deus. When she reached the top of the most prominent peak of the Snowy Mountains, nothing happened; it just started raining. The Lady was disappointed at first, but then accepted that her trip had been in vain. That rain, however, which looked like an ordinary drizzle, suddenly began to heal all the wounds she had suffered during her journey. It even seemed that her fatigue was dissipating..."

"And since then the Lady of the Mountain has been able to heal our people with her tears," Dornias said, concluding the story. He smiled quietly. "I hadn't remembered that story."

"What happened to the Lady?" Noakh asked. For he had never heard such a tale.

The fire cracked. "It's just a legend, but"—Dornias paused— "that woman is said to be the first ancestor of our royal family, the Dajalam, and the first queen of the Aquadom."

"Is that how our sacred sword received such powers?" Laenise asked. "The Tears of the Lady of the Mountain were transmitted to her blade?"

272

"Could be." Dornias shrugged.

The next moment, he offered Hilzen and Noakh some of their meat. They accepted the food, each man thanking Dornias with a nod.

"Wait a minute." Hilzen reflected. "That means that the Lady of the Mountain was..."

"The queen with the greatest power in all our history and the first bearer of the Sacred Sword, Crystalline. So it is." Dornias nodded. "In my family, it is said that none of her successors has been able to display as much power as the Lady of the Mountain."

Noakh nodded interestedly, wondering what Dornias meant by such a statement. No one had been able to display as much power as the Lady of the Mountain, so he could not help but wonder: Did the same thing happen with the Fire Swords? He could not know; his father had not told him anything about it. Yet he could not be entirely sure that it was not so. Noakh remembered hearing that the sacred sword of the Aquadom had power over water. Wondering exactly what powers the Lady of the Mountain had been capable of using that sword, his hand passed unconsciously over the hilt of Distra.

His thoughts were interrupted by Gorigus, who looked amused.

"You know, Safer Criven de le Dos," Gorigus said, his mouth full of food, "other noblemen have better taste when selecting the Fireos who accompany them."

Dornias could not help but laugh.

"Here we go again," Laenise said, as she snorted and squinted at Gorigus.

"You have to admit, Laenise, she has some charm," Dornias answered, smiling.

"Who are you talking about?" Noakh replied. Gorigus's words mentioning Fireo companions had aroused his curiosity.

Gorigus frowned mildly then sneered at Noakh. As eager as he was to talk about that woman, he knew how to put aside his contempt for unickeys. "Who else would I be talking about but the heiress to Rosswode House?"

"She's not that big a deal," replied Laenise, grumbling. "You're just attracted to her because her eyes are different..."

It was obvious from her attitude that this was not the first time they had discussed this subject.

"Oh, come on, Laenise," Dornias reprimanded. "Do you think a troll with those eyes would capture our attention in the same way?" He turned to look at Hilzen. "Criven de le Dos, what do you think? You surely have heard of the beauty of the Rosswode heiress."

"Beautiful, yes," lied Hilzen, who had never heard of such a woman. "She's not my type, though."

"If your type of woman is not the perfect woman, then I understand your words," Gorigus replied. He snorted, and Laenise twisted her mouth. "Her golden hair reaches to the small of her back, she is tall and slender, her face is sweet, and she has a thin delicate nose, round lips, and long eyelashes. Her features are adorned with a dazzling smile with perfect small teeth and large golden-ochre brown eyes... With those eyes she can melt the ice!"

Noakh tried to hide his surprise. Brown eyes and golden hair... Fireo blood ran through the veins of that woman, there was no doubt. But that meant one of her parents had to be a Fireo... So, an Aquo from a house of nobility had married a Fireo? Noakh wondered. It sounded utterly improbable!

Dornias laughed. "I don't know about her gaze melting the ice... but melting your heart, for sure!" He slapped Gorigus animatedly on the back.

"Gorigus." Laenise grimaced. "Would you really defile the nobility of your lineage? Humiliating your house by marrying someone affected by the Crossbreed Curse?"

Noakh had heard of that curse before. There was a saying about crossbreeding between kingdoms: *The gods are capricious.* They had therefore built evidence into those who were the fruit of what many considered a forbidden relationship. Consequently, the color of the eyes of the newborn would always be different from that of the kingdom in which the infant was born. In the case of the noblewoman who was the subject of the current conversation, given that she presumably was the fruit of a relationship between an Aquo and a Fireo, and having been born in the Queendom of Water, she would have been cursed by being born with brown eyes and blonde hair—which, according to Gorigus's description of the ochre color of her eyes, she had been. In that way, she was unable to hide that part of her blood. Of course, the Crossbreed Curse was a myth that could not be proved, since if a unickey born in the Aquadom had been born with blue eyes and a different hair color their parents might well have dyed the child's hair blonde, as Noakh did. *The eyes reveal what the hair hides,* a second saying related to the curse ordained.

274

"When did I say I would marry her?" Gorigus paused. "Wait. Did she tell you anything about me?"

"Aren't you being a little unfair to the poor girl?" Dornias complained.

Looking at her friend, Laenise went to answer indignantly, while Gorigus this time seemed to be on his side.

"Laenise, I know that Fireo blood runs through her veins, and that might not be to our liking."

Dornias turned to Noakh. "No offense, Servme."

Noakh waved his hand dismissively. Dornias turned back to Laenise.

"I know we've been raised to hate them as they hate us. I know. What I mean is, how can you think it's that girl's fault? In any case, her parents should be condemned, but her? She had no choice! What do you think she should do? Live a life of suffering for something that wasn't her fault?"

Noakh couldn't avoid smiling, feeling some appreciation for the nobleman.

"How can you say that, Dornias—in the very temple of the Aqua Deus?" Laenise said indignantly. Hilzen and Noakh watched the scene with astonishment, aware that it was better not to intervene in the conversation. "Not even you, so tolerant and modern, should say something like that."

"Laenise... the Aqua Deus displays benevolence towards the rest of the kingdoms. Our god is so kind, so gentle, that it even grants the other kingdoms the gift of rain. If our god is so benevolent, why not you?"

Laenise lowered her head without saying a word. Gorigus looked at both her and Dornias. The room fell silent for a while. Only the cracking of the fire could be heard.

"Where are you heading to?" Gorigus finally asked Hilzen, trying to relieve the tension.

"To the west," Hilzen replied vaguely.

Noakh nodded.

"Going away from home, eh?" Gorigus replied. "I don't blame you. It's the problem of the eastern houses. Who would want to stay there?" he added, laughing.

Noakh and Hilzen looked at each other. They had heard about this distinction. The most recognized noble houses were located to the north of the queendom, where the royal palace also stood. In fact, the royal building happened to be located at the spot farthest from the other three kingdoms, and thus it was the safest and most prestigious area. The noble houses of the east used to have less prestige, though Noakh was uncertain as to whether this was because they were closer to Firia. Some sense told him that the location of Firia had something to do with it. Dornias, Gorigus, and Laenise, given the prestige of their houses, were obviously from the north of the queendom.

"Yes," answered Hilzen. "And you? Where are you heading to?"

"We will return to the north," Laenise replied, not looking at Dornias. "But first we'll go back to Shaer, a small village of the Snowy Mountains, where we left part of our belongings for this last stage of our path."

Noakh was relieved to hear Laenise's words; it seemed that the three companions had not passed through the village of Ograbh, which had suffered for so long under the hand of the Duranti family. Thus it would be better if the village wasn't again visited by nobility, even though these three appeared to be far more kindhearted than Duranti.

"We will present our deed before the Congregation of the Church," Dornias said. "I know it is unnecessary, but my father insisted..." He rolled his eyes as though offended by his father's request. "It seems that our paths will then separate soon thereafter. We will depart again at the first light of dawn—if the snow permits, of course."

* * *

The next day dawned clear. The nobles drew out their huge black horses, grabbing them by the reins. They were leaving the place quickly.

"It has been an honor, Safer Criven de le Dos, Servme," Dornias said. He bowed his head after mounting his horse.

"The pleasure was ours," Hilzen replied, performing the Aquo gesture of reverence, followed by Noakh.

Gorigus also bowed his head, after which he spurred his horse. Laenise did the same, bidding farewell with her hand. Dorian was the last to leave. He smiled at them both before riding off.

Hilzen and Noakh watched them leave. In a few moments their horses had merged into a small black spot that moved away from them at great speed.

Still stunned as he watched them move away, Hilzen said, "Are you aware, Noakh, that we slept in the same room as three of the most important noble families in the queendom?"

"That Dornias, he's a good man." Noakh nodded. "The other two, though..."

"Don't take it personally." Hilzen looked up at the sky and the position of the temple, trying to orient himself. "They are noble after all... If Count Duranti had seen your eyes, he would have reacted the same way, if not worse. I think it's this way. Let's go," he said as he started walking, his boots immediately sinking and making the snow crunch once again.

"It's been a while since I've taken the comments about my eyes personally, Hilzen," Noakh said. He nodded then followed his partner. "Being called unickey may sound offensive to others, but to me it is nothing more than proof that my blond hair is still dyed well. Still, I disapprove of such attitudes."

Hilzen didn't respond. Instead, he turned toward the temple and bowed once more as Noakh watched him. Noakh could see in the eyes of his companion a sense of relief, as if the burden on his shoulders had once been far greater. They began to walk through the snow. This time, in spite of the cold, Noakh did not resort to the flames of Distra.

33. The dance

Princesses scampered along the common room, looking at themselves repeatedly in the huge mirrors that adorned the walls. They sported all kinds of ornaments, diadems, necklaces, handkerchiefs. They had to be radiant tonight, as their mother and their caretaker Igüenza had told them countless times. Igüenza was, in fact, in the room with them all, giving them instructions, making sure they all looked as beautiful, perfect, and elegant as the guests expected.

They had already been made up and combed by their maids. Only the small details were left: choosing which adornments and jewels best fit their personality, as well as selecting a perfume that would delight all those present for the dance.

They all wore the same dress: a dark-blue fabric that was simply cut and adorned with a tiny sapphire at the height of the neckline. Igüenza went from one side of the common room to the other trying to solve the small dilemmas that the princesses had to face regarding their appearance.

"I need to choose a beautiful necklace!" claimed Gisenne, one of the older sisters, in her high-pitched voice. She held five different necklaces in her hands, all adorned with pearls and small sapphires. She looked desperately in all directions, hoping that one of her sisters would help her choose, yet it seemed that her sisters were too busy with their own choices.

"Where are my earrings?" said Bolenne, a princess with a mole on her upper lip, just a moment before another princess, Eloenne, a skinny girl with a short haircut with bangs, set the earrings down in front of her.

Katienne stood at the back of the room. She had to make sure her appearance was perfect. She was the last of the princesses to have her hair combed, as she made sure none of her sisters copied her hairstyle. The blonde hair on the right side of her face was curled up, letting it embrace her face, while the left side had been kept straight and tucked behind her ear. Her asymmetrical hairstyle was daring, but Katienne was more than satisfied with the results; her sisters had looked at her with envy, wanting to copy her combing. But it was too late for that. Katienne had made sure she was combed with no more fanfare than necessary; having all the sisters wearing the same dress was shameful enough for her.

* * *

Vienne looked at herself in the mirror. She gazed at the bottom of her dress in the mirror reflection. It was a long cobalt-blue dress that accentuated her figure. Her hair had been gathered into a braid, her face bore a slight layer of makeup—just enough to enhance her beauty—and she wore two small earrings adorned with sapphire stones. Aienne was with her, her hair wrapped in a high ponytail, without adornment of any kind. She had been the first to dress and had rushed to her favorite sister's room to help her. The little sister hid her right hand behind her back.

"You look incredible, Vienne," Aienne said as she looked her sister up and down, smiling sweetly.

"Thank you, Aienne."

The heiress continued gazing at herself in the mirror. Apparently, something was bothering her. Aienne guessed what she was thinking.

"You're missing this," she said.

She revealed the object hidden in her hand. It was a golden necklace with a sapphire in the middle. Vienne looked at her sister with her mouth open as Aienne laughed with a naughty tone. "Katienne was looking like crazy among the jewels. I'm sure she was looking for this necklace."

"Oh, you little devil, Aienne," Vienne said mockingly as she tried on the necklace. "It's really beautiful... Are you sure you don't want to wear it, Aienne? You found it, after all..."

"No!" answered Aienne emphatically. "You have to wear it. You have to be *perfect* tonight... and with that necklace you will be."

"Oh, Aienne," Vienne answered happily even as she hugged her sister.

Vienne was a little nervous. The palace dance was to be held that night. All the houses of nobility and the members of the Congregation of the Church had been invited, and she would be the center of attention.

She adjusted the necklace and smiled again at Aienne.

Why me? Vienne thought.

* * *

Katienne was a little upset, still wondering where that necklace had gone. However, she smiled as she walked proudly and elegantly amidst the commotion of people in the Royal Hall. Even though she wore the same dress as her sisters, she had adorned it with a bronze brooch and had pinned a turquoise ribbon around her waist, making her dress appear slightly more charming and sophisticated than those of her sisters. The Royal Hall was a huge room, the walls adorned with great portraits of the previous Aquadom queens, battle scenes, or paintings praising the Aqua Deus. The smell of roast pork with vegetables flooded the room as servants went from side to side offering the guests the exquisite dish.

In a corner, a man played the harp while two women alongside him sung in a sweet tone. The music was decent, Katienne thought, but surely it would be better if they had some Aertians playing for them. After all, they were known for their natural talent for music. Maybe she could ask her mother to acquire some Aertian slaves someday? she reflected.

Katienne observed with suspicion how only one of the guests received as many looks as she and her sisters, and that was the heiress of Rosswode House—the young woman with brown eyes. Katienne knew, as all her sisters did, that the young woman was the fruit of the Rosswode House patriarch's relationship with a Fireo woman. The woman had long ago passed on to a better life... but her daughter reminded the world how far that house had fallen. Katienne passed through the crowd, trying to identify the members of the noblest families, not giving the slightest importance to those who were the least relevant.

"Princess Katienne, you look very beautiful tonight," a handsome young man from Hogne House complimented. However, his family was not important enough for Katienne to know who he was. She smiled politely and continued passing through the crowded hall.

The princess continued walking, even as she watched with disapproval as her little sister, Aienne, laughed wildly as she talked with two members from one of the eastern houses of nobility. The members were Aienne's age, but the house was the least prestigious in the queendom. Katienne turned away. Then she spotted a man, bent with age, with barely any hair on his head but an imposing ring on one of his fingers. He was one of the most important and respected members of the Congregation of the Church, the ecclesiastical organ that her mother controlled after having usurped the title of high priestess for herself. The priest was talking animatedly with a man from the House of Horin.

"Father Ovilier," said Katienne, with a smile announcing her presence.

"Ah, Katienne," said Father Ovilier, turning. "You look quite beautiful. You show off your family's reputation well, certainly." He smiled and looked Katienne up and down. The nobleman who was talking to the priest bowed and walked away. "A great feast, exclusive guests, and exquisite food," the Father said. "What else can an old and pious man ask for?"

"I'm glad you're having a good time," Katienne replied with her best smile. "You know, Father, I've been wanting to talk to you for a long time, about a matter that—"

The sound of cornets interrupted their conversation. The doors of the Royal Hall opened wide, and several soldiers of the Royal Guard advanced until they stood in position, posing in two lines facing each other, their halberds held high, creating a corridor between the two ranks. Behind them appeared three of the four Knights of Water adorned in their armor. They were led by Menest, the captain, displaying a stern gaze. Another knight, Alvia, seemed amused by the entire situation, while the blue eyes of their fellow knight, Tarkos, under his hood, seemed to show no emotion.

Soon the queen appeared. Graglia bore her crown and wore a beautiful, long, sky-blue dress.

Finally, after a second blowing of the cornets, Vienne appeared.

Katienne bit her lip. She could not avoid it. She could not deny that her sister looked impressive. The dress she wore was so beautiful that she couldn't stand to allow her to wear it. It was then that she noticed the necklace on her neck... How did it get into her hands? Katienne clenched her fists so tightly her hands began to tremble. She turned without saying goodbye to Father Ovilier and began to walk around the room once again, aware that the people around her were totally *un*-aware of her presence, a feeling that made her even more anxious. Everyone was admiring the Lacrima. The princess who had been chosen to rule. And it was not *her*. Katienne.

How could the Aqua Deus be so gravely mistaken in its decision? she wondered.

She had to do something. She couldn't simply give up.

She took a glass of blue wine from one of the servants' trays. The servant didn't even realize Katienne was partaking of his offerings, stunned as he was by the scene of the annunciation of the queen and her heiress. Katienne took a sip from the wine glass; feeling the silky, refined, and fresh taste of the wine on her palate. And she continued walking, this time without looking at anyone, focused on her thoughts. How could this be happening? Was it a nightmare from which she would never wake up?

The queen and Vienne joined the guests. Music started to fill the room again. Katienne stood in the middle of the great hall. She took a sip of her drink while her nails tapped the glass of her cup.

At that moment she spotted another man, none other than Filier Delorange, the heir of Delorange House. It was the house with the most power and wealth of all the Aquadom, in fact. Although Filier Delorange was not as graceful as his brother Dorniaseus, whom Katienne had not seen at the feast, the lack of beauty of the older brother was compensated for by his promising future as heir to his house—an asset that few would overlook. For a moment, Katienne could not help but feel sorry for that man. For it was widely known that Filier's father always preferred his younger son. She now could relate to that kind of pain.

But such thoughts gave Katienne an idea...

She continued walking through the hall once again, but this time her eyes kept close track of where among the throngs the heir to Delorange House was. Katienne also noted where her mother and her sister Vienne stood in the hall, so they wouldn't be aware of her movements. At the current moment, the queen was introducing Vienne to several of her guests, whom Katienne couldn't distinguish from that distance. She continued walking. Her gaze eventually met that of Minister Meredian, and she bowed her head to him while smiling.

The heir to Delorange House said goodbye to the group he was talking to, and then he began to walk aimlessly through the hall. Katienne made her move. The princess maneuvered around the room until she had positioned herself in front of him while he was still some distance away. Then she began to walk towards him. She approached Filier Delorange little by little, finally bumping into him intentionally and spilling the blue wine from her glass on his elegant and expensive clothes.

"Oh, I'm so sorry!" she said innocently. She set a hand to her mouth with the pretense of surprise. Meanwhile the blue wine stain began to spread over Filier Delorange's clothes. Their eyes met.

"It's all right, it's nothing," replied Filier Delorange, downplaying the mishap. "You don't have to apologize, Princess Katienne."

The princess smiled sweetly as she brushed her hand over his stained shirt.

"But, your elegant clothes," she said. "I'm sure we can do something." Her voice sounded worried, and even more innocent. "Come with me, please. I will clean this mess."

"Don't worry, princess. It's just a suit," Filier began, but he stopped talking when he saw Katienne's mournful gaze.

"Will you not allow a young woman to make amends for her mistake?"

Filier could not resist Katienne's beautiful face. She looked on him with sadness until finally he smiled and agreed to her request.

The princess led him to one of the palace balconies, where they found themselves alone. The moon shone round the sky. The perfume of the flowers in the royal gardens below them drifted slowly up to where the heir and the princess stood. Before leaving the hall, Katienne had asked one of the younger servants to bring a pitcher of water and cloth napkin out to the balcony. The servant appeared now and handed the items to her. Katienne took the napkin and the pitcher of water.

"Blue wine is not as strong as grape wine," she told the Delorange heir as she poured some water on the napkin then gently rubbed the napkin against Filier's shirt. "Excuse me for my clumsiness, but it hasn't been an easy day for me..."

Filier was perplexed. "Why, Katienne? It must be a beautiful night for your family—the night when the new heiress is presented to society and celebrated by friends and servants who remain loyal to the crown."

"Yes," Katienne answered in a low voice. She continued rubbing Filier's clothes, though now more lightly. Then she raised her eyes and they met those of Filier. The eyes of the princess were slightly humid. "It's just... Oh, it's nothing... A man so important as you, you must have more urgent matters to attend to, certainly, than listening to the troubles of a lady."

"Speak without fear, Princess Katienne. I can see something is bothering you," Filier said reassuringly. "And I'll be willing to help as long as it's in my power to do so. Delorange House has always been loyal to the queendom. Rest assured that your words are safe with me."

"Not only do you honor the good name of your family but you are also a gentle man, I'm sure any woman would be happy to be at your side," Katienne said, sobbing slightly—or at least pretending to. "Thank, you, Sir Delorange..."

"You may call me Filier, if you want." He smiled at her tenderly. "So, what is it?"

"I really don't want to worry you with my problems," Katienne said. "This is supposed to be a party, after all..." She lowered her head, pretending to be ashamed.

"I insist."

Filier extended his hand and touched the princess's face, causing her to raise her head.

"Have you ever felt that they didn't appreciate you as much as they should? I know I should be happy for my sister, but... I can't help it... I know, I'm so stupid..."

A tear ran down Katienne's cheeks, and not even she herself could reveal whether she was pretending or not. Filier grabbed her hands as he stared into her eyes.

"You're not stupid, Katienne. I know exactly how you feel," Filier said.

He grabbed her by the shoulders. Katienne embraced Filier tightly, and then she began to sob in earnest.

34. The tournament

After traveling several days through the last deserted slopes of the Snowy Mountains, they had finally reached the outskirts of Miere, a small city with no particular appeal but that in the eyes of Hilzen and Noakh, having gone through the hard conditions of the Snowy Mountains for what had seemed an eternity, looked like a warm and adorable place.

Noakh and Hilzen were now in a tavern, enjoying their beer with the money Dleheim had given them. They had deliberately chosen to sit at the table closest to the fire. After so many days in the freezing conditions of the Snowy Mountains, they were eager to feel the heat of the fire.

"Look at this, Noakh!" Hilzen said as he pointed to a sign pinned to the wall of the tavern. On the sign one could see some drawn swords— and an announcement. "The winner of the skills tournament will raise a trophy and earn a prize of two hundred gold coins," Hilzen read, with some difficulty. "Two hundred gold coins! It's perfect! We have almost nothing left from the loan Dleheim gave us."

Noakh also took a look at the poster. Apparently, the city was in the middle of its annual celebrations; the tournament was part of the city's festivities. There were several competitions: sword fighting, archery, horse racing, jousting.

"What about horse racing?" said Hilzen looking at Noakh. "Are you good riding a horse?"

Noakh shook his head.

"I've only ridden a couple of times," Noakh said. He reflected on his words, his father had told him he would have to learn to master riding before they headed to Firia. However, given the incident that had occurred before their journey had even begun, Noakh had never learned.

While Noakh and Hilzen reviewed the announcement of the tournament a second time, they tried to ignore several loud conversations being carried on in the tavern simultaneously. Soon, one conversation seemed to dominate all the others.

"They say she went to Hymal with Gant Blacksword and a thousand soldiers," a man related while he drank slugs of his beer. At least a dozen men sitting at both his table and the adjoining tables were listening to him. "He did not hesitate a moment to cut off the heads of each of those bourgeoisie!"

"I'm not sorry for them," another man added. "If the queen ordered it, it was certainly for a fair reason." He played with his empty beer mug, rolling it around the wooden table.

"Surely they did not pay their taxes!" another patron added indignantly. "Those bourgeois believe they can do whatever they want—and they do not pay their taxes!"

"They say it was because of something related to the Golden Tower," the first man continued.

"Fools!" answered another man, after a drink from his glass.

"If it's gold, they should give me a little!" said a fourth, with laughter. "For the queen!" He raised his glass; the rest did the same and took a strong drink.

Noakh and Hilzen were sitting at a nearby table listening to the conversation. As for their experience, it was one of the best ways to learn about what was happening in the queendom and all while enjoying a good drink of beer.

"Hymal," Hilzen said while thinking, *That city isn't far from here,* he recalled. *Maybe a couple of days on horseback.*

"Do you want to see the queen?" Noakh answered, seeing Hilzen's interest.

"Of course I would! One does not always have the opportunity to see her highness. It is not very usual for her to leave the palace. Besides, she must carry the weapon of the royal family. It would be curious to see her reaction if she met you."

"The sword of the Lady of the Mountain isn't it?" Noakh asked.

"Yes," said Hilzen while nodding. "The one that has the power over water, as the Aquos have the power to dominate the sea..."

"Dominate the sea, huh? I wonder how that works, exactly?" Noakh mused. But considering Hilzen's suggestion more thoroughly, he realized that perhaps seeing the queen brandish her weapon would provide him with clues about new methods to employ Distra.

Noakh's thoughts were interrupted by one of the drunkards at the next table.

"Hey you... Yah, I doth mean you... The one with the swords and those brown eyes!" said a man with a beard. He pointed at Noakh. His drunken state was so great that it prevented him from pronouncing his words clearly. "You intendeth to participate in the tournament, right unick... unickey?"

Noakh exchanged a glance with Hilzen.

"That's right, I plan to participate," said Noakh as he raised his glass.

The drunks looked at each other before they burst into laughter.

"Look at yourself. You stand no chance!"

"Of course not!" added another.

"And why not?" Noakh asked reproachfully.

"This year several bourgeoisie from the area will participate—an event unheard of until now! Apparently, they seek to win the favor of the maid of Trigonaldi House."

"So beautiful is that maid that she has encouraged them to participate?" Hilzen asked.

"Beautiful?" asked one of the drunks before they all burst into laughter again.

"Ugly!"

"Like a troll!"

"And with more of a mustache than myself!" added a third, who indeed wore a hairy mustache. "But she has money... *a lot* of money, and land..."

"*A lot* of land! You could solve your life, boy!"

"Look, Noakh," added Hilzen. "Not only can you win the tournament, but you can also gain the heart of such a desirable woman!" Everyone began to laugh at his suggestion.

"I think I better give the prize to one of those bourgeoisie," Noakh said, smiling.

"Noakh," Hilzen said quietly, once the drunks had lost interest in them. "Are you as aware as am I that you have a realistic chance of winning this tournament? We have to think about what you will do if that maiden decides to give her heart to the winner of the swordsmanship contest... and if that winner turns out to be you! The magician's trick will not work this time!"

"I know, I know. I do not know if I can win, but I do not intend to accept anything from that woman... I would completely deny whatever I won. Would it not be enough to serve her with a kind rejection?"

"It would be worth it if you wanted to have your head cut off... Think about it—rejecting a nobleman's daughter would embarrass the family. They could not stand such an offense!"

"I'm getting a little tired of the noblemen and the ease with which they are offended," Noakh answered indignantly.

"It's the reality of the world that we live in," said Hilzen as he began to cheer up. He gave a shrug and took a drink.

* * *

On the day of the tournament, the sun was shining strongly as it broke through the clouds. It bathed the pennons and standards swarming over the tournament venue in the sunshine. The stadium was a huge arena crowded with people of all sorts—peasants, farmers, craftsmen, and milliners stood together—while the bourgeoisie were separated, of course into different seating quarters. The best places to watch the contests were reserved for the noble classes. Not even the wealthiest of the bourgeoisie could occupy one of those seats. Instead, they had to settle for seats on the second level. The plebeians, on the other hand, did not even have seats, but instead crowded at the foot of the dirt track, trying to watch the show by peering between the heads of the audience standing in front of them.

Noakh and Hilzen were in an area reserved for participants, an exclusive section where all of the contestants in the various skills categories congregated. Among the contestants there was no class distinction. Participation was open to anyone; even the queen could participate, if she wanted to. Despite this, the nobility participated only in the jousting contests, a competition that required the contestants to bear the most equipment—and to provide a horse, of course, making the jousts necessarily more restrictive than the other skills contests; in fact, only nobility dared to participate. For who would dare to humiliate a nobleman but another noble family? Even so, given the distinctive rankings within the class of the nobility, some noblemen of a lower class would not dare to defeat a nobleman from a more prominent family. No amount of gold was worth that risk.

In the area where the participants had collected, the nobility had all gathered in the same corner, far from the rest of the competitors, who preferred not to approach them, just in case. It was true that merely watching the nobility was already a good show. The noblemen wore their best clothes for the occasion. It looked more like a beauty contest than a joust, all of them dressed in their battle armor full of color and excessively decorated, with their horse dressed faithfully to represent the family coat of arms.

"I've been wondering about something, Hilzen. You've signed up for the archery contest, but you do not even have a bow..."

"That's right. It seems it's unnecessary. They have spare archery accouterments in case you can't afford your own. Same goes for the swords contest by the way. Which reminds me, are you intending to use Distra in this tournament?"

"I had not thought about it," Noakh answered, considering his other choices. "I do not think I'll have any problem controlling myself in combat; it's not a fight to the death, nor anything similar. But you're right—given the opportunity, it will be better not to take a risk. I'll leave it with you when it's my turn. Do you think you have a chance to win your contest?"

"I do not know. It's been a long time since I last used a longbow. The crossbow is similar, but every weapon has its own technique. Who knows? Maybe I'll win and not you?"

Hilzen nudged Noakh while winking at him.

Noakh observed the other participants. It was easy to infer who would be participating in which tournament because each group of contestants had specific practice areas available to them while they were waiting. And thus, the archers had targets at which they could shoot their arrows. The swordsmen had straw mannequins and logs to brandish their weapons on. And the jousting participants had stables within which they could remain by their horses.

Focusing on the swordsmen, Noakh observed how the concept of what a swordsman might be was quite abstract, as the participants brandished all kinds of weapons. There were both men and women. This was not surprising in a kingdom such as the Aquadom, where women had historically occupied positions of high command. This had inspired them: Now, having been taken for granted by society, women learned the art of warfare in the same manner as men—and to such an extent that the Royal Guard was formed almost entirely of women.

Noakh noted several swordsmen who did not have the slightest chance of winning the tournament: contestants who had simply signed up because they were attracted by the prize. Others, however, seemed to be good fighters. It was easy to distinguish these, either by the accuracy and fierceness of their cuts to the straw mannequins or by how they patiently awaited their turn to sharpen their weapons. The types of weapons on display were diverse: axes, swords, clubs, spears, and even several flails.

The combat portion of the tournament had very simple rules. The contest consisted of one-on-one battles. Each contestant could choose his or her own weapons, as long as each weapon was appropriate for engaging in hand-to-hand combat. The fights would each end when one of the two combatants surrendered, was in no condition to fight, or was dying. This last circumstance was uncommon, but all participants were warned that there was a realistic risk it could happen.

Hilzen was going to start off the tournament. Apparently, there was a clear favorite to win the longbow portion: a lady who wore her straight long blonde hair in a ponytail. Her clothes were a mixture of yellow and bright-red design; she wore a matching hat adorned with a huge feather. Hers was an outfit that certainly called attention to itself, not only due to the combination of striking colors but simply by the atypical use of these colors in Aquo territory, where less aggressive tones were the custom. This woman was known as Dabayl On-the-Spot, so nicknamed because of her great accuracy with the longbow.

If the looks of the woman were not unusual enough, her eyes were honey colored—a feature that caught Noakh's attention, as such yellowish eye color, together with the red hair, was typical of the Aertians. Something did not fit, Noakh thought. It was true that sometimes the children of the kingdom were born of a different color, although this anomaly was very rare and served to reveal some infidelity committed with a visitor from distant lands. But it was not only the woman's eyes. Noakh saw that the archer's ostentatious clothes—and even her apparent domination with the longbow—all seemed to fit the description of a citizen of the Kingdom of Air. It was true that her hair was blonde, exaggeratedly long, and collected in a ponytail. It was as if she wanted to point out that she was not from there—was not a true unickey but was in fact an Aertian—as if she did it on purpose.

292

During the tournament, Dabayl immediately took the lead by shooting impossible shots. To make the longbow contest more entertaining, different obstacles—pendulums, mannequins—were placed in front of the targets then set in motion to make the contestant's aim more difficult. No matter what the obstacle, Dabayl On-the-Spot justified her name by managing to strike the target. Her superiority was such that she was always the first to shoot her arrows, approaching the next target without even checking to see if she had hit the previous one.

Noakh could not help feeling a little sorry for his friend Hilzen. Although he was not faring badly, his abilities could not compete with the absurd level of skill possessed by that woman. Her ability with the bow was just so impressive. Her arrows hit the ball of the pendulum as it swung to the left and then hit it again as it swung to the right—a feat no other participant would even dream of. Noakh had no doubt: She was from the Kingdom of Air. He no longer even considered the possibility that she had been born here in the Aquadom. Everything about her radiated arrogance. She clearly felt superior to the people around her. She wanted to stand out, and she did so in an improper way.

What was her goal? Noakh asked himself. If she were a spy, logically she would try not to attract attention to herself; she would instead mix in with the people around her and try to look like them. But she did not seem inclined to do that—although at least her hair was dyed blonde, indicating a minimum of caution on her part. Whatever the truth was, Noakh could not help but admire the woman's skills with the bow. It represented the heights that her kingdom's reputation boasted.

The audience seemed to adore her. All the stands cheered her name. Women saw in her a figure to imitate, while men noticed her figure with equal enthusiasm, especially those exotic eyes. Before they realized it, Dabayl had won the title, raising the trophy in her hands. Hilzen had finished in fourth position—and did not seem very happy with it. Everything had been fine until his last shot, which was aimed at one of the moving targets. He had failed to hit it.

"Good shooting, Hilzen," Noakh said, trying to cheer him up as he returned from the shooting grounds. "You did very well."

"Foolishness! Who could concentrate with that woman? Have you seen what she did? She didn't even aim before shooting!"

Although Hilzen said it figuratively it was true that the amount of time Dabayl had required to aim before releasing an arrow from her bow was significantly shorter than the time the rest of the archers required—a fact that ended up getting on Hilzen's nerves during the final rounds of the competition. He was well aware that there were much better archers than him, but such superiority became insulting, in part because of that young woman's arrogance.

"Don't you think her skills are too unusual?" Noakh hinted.

"What do you mean?" Hilzen replied, surprised.

"Come on. Haven't you thought about it?" Faced with Hilzen's odd expression, Noakh snorted. "That woman doesn't come from here! Her skills with the longbow are typical of archers from another kingdom. You know what I mean!"

"That's outrageous!" Hilzen replied indignantly. "So, according to you, as she is very good with the longbow, she can't be an Aquo—is that it? What a bastard you are!"

"It's not only that, it's everything. Her eyes, her attitude, her way of being... and yes, also how ridiculously skilled she is with that bow!"

"Nonsense. It would be very easy to concede that she's better only because she is an Aertian, but I will not concede that point! I lost and that's it. I just have to keep practicing with the longbow."

"Why would a dead man want to continue practicing?" Noakh said with a chuckle.

"It has nothing to do with that!"

The conversation was interrupted by the start of the one-on-one combat tournament. Noakh was not among the first participants, so he and Hilzen went to the stands to watch the tournament. As Noakh had predicted, there was a very clear difference between many of the participants, such that several of the matches ended very quickly, with one of the two opponents falling to the ground unconscious or kneeling in a corner, begging for their life. Unlike the longbow tournament, where practically the entire audience cheered for Dabayl On-the-Spot, in the one-on-one contests the screams were demands for blood. It was not unusual to hear someone in the audience call for a contestant to end the life of their opponent, or at least to crush him. The people clamored for blood.

"Noakh, I've been thinking," Hilzen said. He had not opened his mouth since his little brush up with Noakh. "Seeing all these knights with swords and escutcheons... I remember Ograbh, and our passage through the Snowy Mountains. Maybe you should consider covering your face during the tournament. It is true that we are far from that area, but it is better not to take risks, especially with the queen being so close..."

294

Hilzen is right, thought Noakh. It was not out of the realm of possibility that members of the nobility, perhaps even Ribas Duranti himself, had come to watch the tournament. The chances seemed minimal... but why take any risk?

Noakh and Hilzen moved down from the stands and went way back to the tournament ground. Looking around, Noakh found a worn helmet lying on the ground.

"Is this sufficient?" Noakh asked as he slid the helmet onto his head. His entire face remained visible.

Hilzen grimaced.

"No? What about this?"

From his pocket, Noakh removed a blue cloth he had purchased in town to use as handkerchief, which he then tied around his mouth, only allowing his eyes and nose to remain visible.

"You look like a bandit," Hilzen replied. "But it will do."

Back in the tournament, the crowd began to notice the first of the favorites. A man with a mace had been especially well received. He threw his weapon indiscriminately at his opponent, no matter what his ability was—a scheme that seemed to drive the audience into a frenzy. Likewise, a woman seemed to have caught the audience's attention. She wore a light suit of armor that hugged her body very tightly, and she wielded a longsword with remarkable efficiency. Unfortunately for her opponents, she liked to further ridicule them by disarming them while she was staring at the crowd, a skill that the audience received with applause and laughter.

Noakh went through his rounds in a simpler manner. In general he was lucky: Several of his opponents were no match for him, so he dispatched with them quickly. True, his performance was not as acclaimed as those of some of the other participants. However, Noakh had not registered in the tournament to strut. But not only was it a way to get money that could be useful during the rest of their trip; it was also a way for him to test his skills, including the handicap of being unable to use Distra, which would undoubtedly have afforded him a huge advantage.

Hilzen approached Noakh, who was sitting on a bench, resting and drinking water after winning his last fight. His face was now uncovered, the blue cloth resting at his thighs. His helmet rested alongside the cloth. From their position on the bench, they could clearly see the arena where the fighting was taking place.

"One more battle and you'll be in the tournament finals," Hilzen said, slapping Noakh on the back. "How do you feel?"

"I'm fine. Just superficial wounds for now." Noakh passed his arm across his forehead. "Any idea who will be in the finals?"

"No, but we'll know in an instant: Look!" Hilzen nodded towards the arena. There in the middle of the battle area stood a large man carrying a mace, his face as scarred as his armor was clumsy. A woman with a longsword stood some distance away, her shoulders confidently thrown back in spite of her slender frame. "That man is known as Vileblood... The public never ceases to cheer his name. But I have a bad feeling about him."

"So do I," Noakh replied, taking another drink of his water. His eyes were fixed on the combat that was about to begin. "The lady is very talented with the sword; her style of combat is very different... This Vileblood's strategy is brute force and dirty play, while she instead seems to rely on her dexterity."

While Noakh had been talking, the fight had already started. Vileblood's first move was to kick the ground, making the earth fly into his opponent's eyes. The swordswoman raised her hand to cover herself, but Vileblood took advantage of her brief incapacitation: He lunged at her powerfully. The woman dodged his attack at the last instant.

"Dirty. Really dirty," Hilzen said with disgust.

The public, however, seemed not to agree with Hilzen's opinion. They loudly cheered Vileblood's name.

The swordswoman tried to regain ground, using her agility to lunge quickly forward and thrust her blade at her opponent as fast as she could. But Vileblood, taking advantage of his greater physical power, drew as close to her as possible, causing his opponent's attack to pass harmlessly over his shoulder, and forcing the woman to retreat. Regaining her composure, she again thrust her sword at Vileblood, but the brute intercepted her cut by swinging his mace—a blow he delivered so hard the woman released her sword with a cry of pain. Vileblood then took a moment to enjoy the look of panic on the young woman's face, and then he extended his left hand, grabbing her face before using his handhold to throw her to the ground. The woman could not move: Vileblood set one foot on her chest, the weight preventing her from scrambling away. She was completely immobilized. Drops of his sweat fell on her fearful face. Vileblood bent down, placed his knees around the woman's waist and stood over her, immobilizing her, flashed a lunatic smile, and raised his mace, grabbing it with both hands. The tournament officials rushed over to stop Vileblood, but it seemed as though they would not arrive in time.

"No, I... I surrender," the swordswoman said, her voice broken. "Pl-Please..."

Vileblood disregarded her pleas, throwing his mace with two hands, striking the earth beside the woman's face as hard as he could. Terrorized, the woman fell unconscious. Sangrevil then stood, holding his mace, smiling and enjoying his forthcoming victory.

It was then that several officers grabbed him by his corpulent sweaty arms and pulled him away from the woman while a doctor rushed in and treated her.

Sitting on the bench, Noakh and Hilzen were indignant.

"You better watch out, Noakh," Hilzen said as he watched how carefully the officers carried the young woman from the arena.

Noakh nodded. He donned his helmet then grabbed the blue cloth and tied it around his mouth again. Then he rose and drew his two blades as he began to walk towards the arena. It was his turn. If he won, he would face Vileblood for the championship.

When he arrived at the center of the arena, his opponent was already waiting for him. He was a well-equipped contestant, adorned in shining armor. An ornate sword hung from his side and his helmet still lay in his hand. His light eyes looked at Noakh from head to toe. From the appearance of his armor and his sword, it was clear: He was one of the bourgeoisie they had been spoken of in the tavern, a wealthy man who was probably in search of a higher status in society.

Both contestants performed the Aquo act of reverence, so the fight could then begin. Noakh held both of his swords high, in a defensive position, while his opponent put on his helmet. However, he did not yet put himself on guard. Instead, without moving from his place, he said, "Are you aware that whoever wins will face that insane being they call Vileblood?"

Noakh arched an eyebrow. "Yes, why?" he answered, remaining on guard in case his opponent's inquiry was a trick.

"Do you think it's worth facing someone like that?" The public began to hoot and jeer them, bored by the lack of action. "Is it worth an almost certain death in exchange only for gold and land?"

Noakh shrugged.

"I don't fight for gold and land." He lowered his swords then looked toward the spectators. "Shall we begin at once? Our audience seems impatient."

The man stared at Noakh for a few moments, then he shook his head. "Monsters." He removed his helmet and walked out of the arena.

Noakh stood without moving, confused, watching the man leave. His two swords were still unsheathed, as if he did not want to admit that he had won the fight without even having thrown a single lunge.

Given that there had been no fight, the final battle began almost instantly. Noakh stood in front of Vileblood, both of them holding their weapons. The Fireo made the Aquo act of reverence, Vileblood didn't. All the public called the name of Vileblood as the man with the mace whirled his weapon above his head while clamoring that he was going to kill Noakh. His eyes remained fixed on Noakh while a wicked smile showed on his face.

"I hope you've come willing to die," he heaved, his voice hoarse and brusque. Noakh had no doubt that the man meant to carry out what he said.

Vileblood did not hesitate. As the trumpets signaled the start of the fight, he raised his mace and charged Noakh, roaring mightily. His armor was limited to a few metal plates that protected his chest, his back, and his wrists; the rest of his body was barely covered by his brown clothes. However, it seemed that the Aqua Deus had conferred him with a natural protection. He had wide shoulders and a broad back, and he was a bit portly, though in a muscular way. His equally thick arms were covered with a deep dark-blond hair that contrasted with the thin hair on his head, which was balding. His forehead had started to shine as a consequence of both the sun and the sweat that soaked his whole body.

While dodging his powerful charges, Noakh tried to design a strategy against his opponent. It was clear that he could not counter his strength; although he was athletic, Noakh seemed a child compared to that man, who resembled a bear. The blows from Vileblood's mace clashed with Noakh's crossed swords. He managed to at least deflect them. However, the powerful impacts Noakh had to endure caused great stress on his body, the muscles in his forearms weakening until he could barely raise his swords. Despite the incredible power of the blows, his opponent did not seem to exhibit any fatigue. His breathing still seemed even, and the blows of his mace were not weaker, although he did not stop sweating.

298

Vileblood did not seem happy fighting Noakh. The boy's strategy seemed to be based on avoiding his blows while trying to find an opening, albeit without success. At some point, Noakh's two swords parried his powerful two-handed attack, causing a metallic screech to rise across the arena. Vileblood began to shout at Noakh to fight like a man and stop being foolish. As close as he was, Noakh realized he had to fear not only Vileblood's strength but also his breath. The smell was so horrible and unpleasant that for a moment Noakh's strength vanished—time enough for Vileblood to take advantage.

He did not know the meaning of fair play. With a quick movement of his wrist, he threw a blow with his mace into Noakh's ribs. The blow had such strength that it threw Noakh into the air. He crashed hard against the ground.

Hilzen's shouts of concern for his friend were drowned out by the euphoria of the rest of the audience, which enjoyed Vileblood's hit almost as much as Vileblood himself. Noakh remained a few seconds on the ground. His chest was swelling rapidly. His light armor had absorbed part of the impact; even so, the pain in his ribs was searing. Despite that, he stood up, trying to get as much as he could into a defensive posture, unable to avoid wincing in pain. He was still stunned, not only by the pain but also by Vileblood's strong breath. It was so unpleasant he could not help but think it was a trick to gain some advantage. Vileblood, who was not one to overlook any opportunity, and who was aware that Noakh was still recovering from his earlier blow, again threw himself at Noakh. This time Noakh dodged him, finding an opening and drawing a cut on his opponent's arm: blood dripped to the ground. It was a shallow cut but it raised Noakh's morale.

Vileblood kept coming at Noakh, trying not to give him a chance to rest. His attacks were preceded by a series of howls and a smile of enjoyment. In a way, Noakh appreciated Hilzen's suggestion not to use Distra during the tournament, because the pride of his opponent was starting to get on his nerves. Each time was proving more difficult for him to dodge that smelly beast. The pain in his ribs was increasingly striking. He was sure that he had not broken a rib, but the blow had been very strong. He was aware that every time he moved slower, grimacing in pain, his reflexes barely able to divert Vileblood's strokes—and when he did, his body shook from the pain.

He had to end the fight soon or Vileblood would kill him. He had no doubt that Vileblood would not hesitate to end his life, to the delight of all present and himself. Could there be a better ending for a tournament?

Summoning all his might, Noakh launched himself at Vileblood, who received the attack with a grimace. He adopted a defensive posture, holding the mace before him with both hands. Noakh raised his swords as though to strike a high blow... but at the last moment it proved to be only a feint. Vileblood realized it too late. Although he attempted to deflect one of Noakh's swords, the blade sliced firmly into his torso, putting an end to his stupid smile.

Pleased, Noakh tried to withdraw his sword from Vileblood's torso. But he looked at it in horror, seeing how it had been caught in his ribs. Realizing Noakh was distracted, Vileblood took the opportunity to strike him hard with his right arm, causing his other sword to fall from his hand. It landed on the ground several meters away. Noakh made a last attempt to pull out the sword, but he let it go when he realized Vileblood was about to smash his head with a fierce blow of the mace. He drew his body back reflexively.

Vileblood realized his attempted blow had been thwarted. Instead, he kicked Noakh powerfully, making him roll on the ground until he fell backward.

Noakh's helmet shifted from the blow. While he tried to adjust it to regain his vision he saw his opponent moving quickly to strike the final blow. The sword was still stuck in his torso. The audience stood on its feet; several cries calling for his death were clearly audible. From his position on the ground, Noakh looked for his other sword, but it was too far away; his rival would rush him before he could even reach for it.

Noakh tried to stand. But he had spent his last ounce of strength in his attack with the sword... and that had not been enough. *I still have much to learn,* he thought. The pain in his side was increasing even as he watched his opponent advance, unaffected by his wounds.

He looked again at his sword, trying to move in its direction. But he was too slow. Noakh hesitated for a second, considering the surrendering words that would put an end to the battle. But he didn't want to surrender. He couldn't give up yet. He clenched his jaw, gripping the earth with rage.

"Ah, no, no," said Vileblood, approaching with a wicked smile, tapping his mace against his palm with every step. "Here you leave the arena when I say it!" he shouted, as if reading Noakh's thoughts.

His words were praised by the clamoring public.

He charged Noakh to finish him off once and for all. Guessing Vileblood's intentions, several officials jumped on him to try to stop him. The rules of the tournament dictated that if one of the participants was not in condition to fight, the combat was over, and Noakh clearly wasn't able. However, Vileblood easily dispensed with them by using his mace, screaming fiercely while returning to Noakh.

Noakh had no strength left. He was completely defeated. Needing to do something to stop Vileblood, he tried to at least rise, but couldn't. However, it was Vileblood who suddenly stopped. He collapsed to the ground, a completely stupid expression on his face, an arrow piercing his sweaty forehead.

The audience fell silent for the first time since the tournament began. Noakh looked for Hilzen among the audience, assuming that it was he who had shot the arrow, but Hilzen barely had time to jump the fence to try to help him. All the public also looked for where the arrow had originated. Suddenly a member of the public gasped.

"Look! In the tree!"

Leaning against the branch of a tree, a figure still held its longbow. The figure's long hair was flying in the wind, but the tree was so far away that one could not distinguish who it was.

"Dabayl On-the-Spot!" someone in the audience claimed.

The rest shouted in amazement. Then they applauded. Seeing the distance from which she had shot Vileblood, with so little time to aim her arrow at the moving target, it seemed impossible she had hit Vileblood so precisely. *Not for Dabayl On-the-Spot,* Noakh thought as he tried to stand up.

With effort and the help of two of the officiators who had been beaten by Vileblood, Noakh managed to stand up. A doctor was applying an ointment to his wounds. He had been badly injured but luckily none of his bones had been broken. While he was being treated, he drank some blue wine from a flask one the officiators had given to him. The wine helped him recover his strength and to relieve the pain. Hilzen appeared, running over to him.

"Noakh!" he said anxiously. "I thought that beast was going to kill you!"

"Me too, Hilzen. Me too!" Noakh answered while taking another drink, his other hand in his sore ribs.

"I tried to help you, but... she helped you first! No one saw that arrow coming!"

They left the tournament as poor as they had entered. The tournaments' marshals informed Noakh that Vileblood was the legitimate champion, so Noakh was not going to be awarded the prize. For Noakh, the prize was of no importance, but it held great importance for Hilzen.

Noakh relied on Hilzen to leave the tournament grounds. He would recover soon; other than pain and exhaustion, nothing was broken.

While they were leaving, a lady was waiting for him at the exit of the tournament grounds, escorted by two guards. The lady was dressed in a striking pink dress, and a huge hat covered her face. She approached Noakh and Hilzen. Anticipating what was to come, Hilzen made a great effort not to burst out laughing.

"Master Noakh, you are the winner of the swordsmanship tournament," said the woman.

She lifted her head, revealing her face for the first time. She was not as horrible as the men in the tavern had depicted her. Even so, the woman was in fact far from being considered physically graceful. Noakh was too exhausted to endure that, cursing his luck. For a moment he was speechless, until Hilzen gave him a sly nudge.

"No," Noakh said. "It's not true. It would not be fair, because Vileblood was the real winner of our battle. He's the one who should be awarded the prize," he said, repeating the words that the tournament marshals had told them.

"Oh, I see," said the girl, who had seen a noble grandeur in his response. "For me, you are still the champion," she added. After all, Noakh was more appealing to her tastes than that shameless Vileblood.

"I could not accept it," Noakh said again, trying to sound solemn. "It would not be honest of me."

"I understand," said the maiden of Trigonaldi House. "Then I will keep you in my heart."

Noakh and Hilzen walked away while the maiden watched them expectantly. As soon as he could, Hilzen began to whistle the "Song of Ermias," which told of a man who could cajole women by putting them under a spell. Then he started singing.

"He was a man, he stole their hearts... With only the spell of his charm."

He had not sung much before he burst out into laughter again.

35. Hooded

They walked down a few more streets. It was getting darker, but even so, given that it was Miere's festivities, people were still drinking and laughing together. In one of the corners, three Guards of the City were arresting two men who, judging by their swollen red faces, had drunk too much. Noakh and Hilzen walked among the people, trying to not draw attention. They had had enough at the tournament. For this reason, Noakh fixed his eyes to the ground as much as he could. He was not in a good mood and his body hurt, and he knew that seeing his eyes would be more than enough for a drunkard to start a fight.

They rounded a corner to avoid the main streets when Noakh noticed something: Someone was following them. It was a hooded man who had been walking after them for a while now. Despite fixing his eyes on the ground, he had seen that man more than once behind him out of the corner of his eye. Or maybe he was a bit paranoid? He wanted to make sure. He spotted a dark alley just ahead of them

"Let's go this way," said Noakh beckoning the alley.

Hilzen, who was still enjoying their encounter with the maiden of Trigonaldi House, nodded while helped Noakh walk towards the alley. At the alley, Noakh hid behind one of the pillars pushing Hilzen beside him. Upon Hilzen's faint cry of protest, Noakh covered his mouth with his hand and unsheathed Distra, a gesture that alarmed Hilzen. The Aquo tried to free himself from his companion's grasp.

Before Hilzen could break free, the suspicious man appeared in the alley. When he had advanced far enough, Noakh took advantage to jump him. He kicked the man, who fell to the ground on his back. Noakh approached him, pointing with his sword.

"Who are you and why are you following us?" Noakh said with anger, his body hurt because of the effort.

The hooded man, still on the ground, raised his hands defensively. "I'm glad to see you can walk. It's certainly a relief. I'm sorry that you have not earned that money. Judging by your appearance, you very much need it."

"I asked you a question—answer me!" Noakh replied, having had more than enough entertainment for a day. He was not in a good enough mood to put up with the nonsense of a man hiding his face.

"You've asked two." The hooded man giggled. "Look, it's obvious you're not bullies, or else I'd already be dead on the floor. I can almost feel how uncomfortable you are in this situation. Why don't you sheathe your sword so we can talk as civilized men? Not only is it two against one, but I am sure that a man like me would not be a problem for one of you." He laughed heartily this time, amused with his predicament. "Do you mind if I get up off the ground? These clothes are rather expensive, you know."

Noakh nodded.

The hooded man, seeing that he was about to ask him again, kept talking. "Do not feel guilty and have no doubt—yes, I was following you."

"Why?" asked Hilzen.

"You see, my name is Rebet, and—"

"And can you tell me why you were following us, Rebet?" Noakh interrupted him.

"A man who gets to the point, a great quality to have in the business world... on certain occasions, of course, sometimes it's better to hear what the other has to say and take advantage of it." The hooded man's tone was somewhat strange; he put extreme emphasis on particular words. He continued speaking while facing the ground and his hood hiding a large portion of his face.

"Can you tell me what you want?" Noakh said again.

"You know," the hooded man said in a rather upset tone. "It's a custom that when someone introduces himself, others return the favor."

Noakh sighed. "My name is Noakh, he is Hilzen. Can you tell us what do you want? It's been a long day."

"I want you, boy! Or, why not, maybe both of you, although I suppose there will be a discount then." He let go of the hood while laughing. "Vileblood was my first choice, but now that he isn't of any use there's no choice. You can fight, right?!"

304

"Thanks for the kind words," Noakh replied sarcastically. "And yes, I can fight. I recover quickly."

"I also feel very loved," Hilzen added.

"We're not for sale," Noakh concluded as he started walking away.

"You would not listen, at least to hear what it is about?" said the man. He raised his hand to prevent them from leaving. "A businessman always listens. It's the best way to find a good bargain..."

"Yes? Well, a hooded man should not mention a profession so often if he does not want to reveal what his profession is," Noakh said.

The hooded man was silent for a few moments, realizing that he had been reckless.

"A smart man. I like it. Good job, hired!"

Noakh and Hilzen exchanged glances, not understanding the man's attitude. Hilzen shrugged.

"Can you tell us what you're talking about? Hired to do what?"

"Oh, you'll thank me later. There's no time to lose! Follow me!"

Noakh and Hilzen followed him for a few steps until they realized that he had not even given them a simple reason for them to agree to follow him.

"Wait! Stop playing with us," Noakh said. "Tell us what it is or we won't go anywhere with you!"

"But we are close." After seeing their faces, the hooded man reluctantly said, "You are a hard nut to crack, huh? I guess it's fair. I'll tell you, but not here. Cities have ears."

After following him for a while, they arrived at a carriage in the middle of a square. Upon seeing the hooded man, the driver in the carriage, also hooded, bowed and opened the door. While the three of them climbed inside, the mysterious man withdrew his hood. Underneath was the face of a middle-aged man. His hair was blonde. A few grey hairs protruded from various pores. His chin was perfectly shaved and his eyes were small, as was his mouth.

"Very good! Much better, right? I have to say that accepting an invitation to follow a hooded man is not the best of ideas. Thank goodness that I am an honest man," he said while laughing at his own words. "Let's see, where to start... Two hundred pieces of gold! For both of you, yes. I had not thought that the two of you would come together, but a little extra protection never hurts..."

"Two hundred pieces of gold? It is a considerable figure," Hilzen replied, reflecting on the matter.

"Everything depends on what you intend for us to do to earn it," said Noakh. He nudged Hilzen for being so easily convinced. "Come on, what is it?"

"Hard to crack," said the man, nodding. "It is certainly a very simple task. I simply need you to escort me out of the queendom. I am heading to the east, to Tir Torrent. Yes, I intend to get into Tirhan territory, and I need a good escort. As you can guess, my world is that of business. No. Nothing like that of a merchant. What I do is an art that goes beyond screaming in a marketplace like a goat. As I say, I perform the beautiful yet profitable art of negotiation."

Noakh was not listening to his words.

"Two hundred pieces of gold is too much for a simple escort to the Kingdom of Earth," Noakh said, letting the man know he had discerned he was hiding something. He was aware of the escorting rates. After all, his father had served in that very profession for years.

"You mean maybe I should pay less?" The man laughed. "If you think it's a lot for the work, I can offer half, if you believe that would be more in line with the price of the mission."

"I meant to say that maybe it would be better to tell us the reason for the trip, the one that makes you have to wear a hood in the streets so that nobody recognizes you," Noakh answered firmly.

It was true that reaching Tir Torrent was not contrary to his own plans, but he did not like the real reason for their trip to be hidden from him. Even though, ironically, he had been the first to hide certain information, in this case it seemed that the work entailed a risk that the man did not even want to mention.

"It's okay," the man said with a sigh. "I'd better tell you the truth." He paused, looking guilty.

"Well?" Hilzen said.

"I had a little run-in with someone important. Apparently we had very different points of view, and that led to this conflict..."

"How serious is that conflict?" Noakh asked. No matter what he said, the man did not seem to be honest enough.

"Pretty serious," he acknowledged while shrugging. "Hence the high price for your services. Also, I do not intend to go on busy roads. I assume they are looking for me, so I have drawn up a secret route that will take us into the lands of Tir Torrent in a hurry and without inconveniences." While he was speaking, he pulled a folded and wrinkled piece of parchment from his clothes.

"May I take a look?" Hilzen said curiously.

"Of course not," the man replied with a snort. "You are in charge of the escort. I'll take care of any small details that are unimportant... Well, what do you say?"

Hilzen was about to answer for both of them, but Noakh spoke first.

"Give us a moment to talk about it, please?"

As they walked away from the carriage, the hooded man stood inside waiting, his hands crossed.

"Enough, Hilzen. Your eyes are shaped like gold coins. So I do not need to ask your opinion, right?"

"One hundred gold coins each!" said Hilzen, unable to hide his excitement. "Do you know how much that is? You could hire an army with all that money!"

"I knew you would say something like that," Noakh said. He turned to the carriage. "You know he's not telling us the truth, don't you?"

"Who cares?" Hilzen replied while shrugging. "To be fair, though, we aren't telling the truth either. Probably his secret is totally ridiculous compared to yours."

"You are right there, but even so..." Noakh reflected.

"In addition, we have to get to the earth kingdom on our own. We have the opportunity to be accompanied there, with an alibi—and also get paid for it. What could go wrong?"

What could go wrong? Noakh thought. Hilzen's words were true, although traveling to the earth kingdom on their own was equally risky; in fact, crossing the border would be very difficult. Maybe traveling with the odd man would make it easier.

It seemed that they had made a decision. The man was in his place, waiting for them, drumming his fingers impatiently.

"Rebet, we accept the job."

Noakh could not help but think about the irony of his destiny. It would not be the first time he would be escorting a merchant. He could not avoid the bitter memory of his last assignment, replacing his father.

"Fantastic!" Rebet allowed. "In that case, you can already meet our other traveling companion."

Before they could ask, the hooded figure who had opened the door of the carriage appeared and took the hood off. Her yellow eyes were watching the two new arrivals with an expression of disapproval.

"Dabayl On-the-Spot!" said the two in unison.

"Of course, I do not put my safety in anyone's hands," Rebet said, waving his hand.

He continued to regret that Vileblood had died, although he suspected that even if he had not won the tournament's gold prize, he still would not have accepted being his escort. The two men he had hired seemed much more malleable, and they had both shown more than worthy skills in their respective tournaments.

Deep down, Rebet did not expect them to be confronted by anyone, although he had no doubt that they were after him. He very much trusted his map: a route used when his men had been transporting very valuable merchandise and which now was going to be his escape route. After learning the fate of the rest of the guild leaders, however, he could not take any risks. Fortunately for him, a contact had informed him in advance of the forthcoming arrival of the queen in Hymal, along with that of her escort, both with unfriendly intentions. Even for someone who was used to paying for information, those were the best coins he had invested in his life—so much so that even in retrospect, fifty gold coins were a bargain in exchange for still having one's head in place.

"You shoot like a farmer," Dabayl said, looking at Hilzen with a mocking smile. Her voice had a joking tone that perfectly fit her haughty attitude. Her eyes seemed to sparkle, looking for a fight.

"Well... I was a farmer."

"Oh," Dabayl said, not expecting such an answer.

"But isn't that appropriate? Because you don't shoot badly for being a cow," Hilzen answered, returning the jab.

Dabayl crossed her arms. After a few seconds she looked at Hilzen seriously then suddenly burst into laughter.

"And you," Dabayl said, resuming her serious expression while looking at Noakh. "Stop looking at me so much... Don't think I don't know what you're doing!"

Noakh did not know how to respond. The only thought that ran through his mind was that the woman had turned from being completely happy to being utterly serious in a matter of seconds. Then he remembered what he had heard about inhabitants of the Air Kingdom: their countenance was as variable as the wind. Even that fit.

"I'm glad to see you get along so well," Rebet said. "Because you're going to be spending a lot of time together."

Noakh was in charge of steering the carriage, a very modest carriage, rather old and worn. Rebet had emphasized that this transport was very different from the one he was used to, which was much more luxurious and ornate—so much so that if they were to travel in it they would not go unnoticed, which was crucial for his mission. On the other hand, the horse, a pretty mare with a brown coat and a white spot on its face, looked energetic and full of strength. Rebet knew that the horse's condition contrasted significantly with the carriage's appearance, but a fast mare could save him if his precautions proved not to have been sufficient.

Hilzen and Dabayl shared the surveillance work, one of them always looking ahead and the other always looking to the rear. Rebet had insisted on always being alert to any danger. However, the guards were constantly tense, not knowing when an attacker might appear. To make matters worse, Hilzen and Dabayl could not wield their weapons, as they needed to avoid raising suspicions. The carriage was loaded with food, which would serve not only to feed the riders but would also be their alibi for the trip. At least they would not go hungry.

Unlike the others, Rebet rode inside the carriage, except when he appeared using a door connecting to the interior of the carriage on which Rebet could climb out to ensure that the route he had instructed Noakh to follow was strictly enforced. It was true that the direction they had taken was not the shortest—it was far longer—but they were avoiding the main routes the merchants used to travel with their merchandise. Instead, they took a much more rugged route, where the traffic was much lighter... so light, in fact, that an assailant would not waste time waiting for a traveler to pass by, as he would fall asleep waiting.

While Hilzen was keeping guard at the front of the carriage, he and Noakh talked to each other. Meanwhile Dabayl rode in the back without calling out to them. They did not know if her silence was due to the fact that she did not like to talk, or simply because she was very focused on her duties as an escort.

Despite the descent of night, they continued on their way. Rebet insisted that the darkness would allow them to travel more securely, without fear, so the three escorts turned their gazes back and forth to follow the route as much as the meager light of the moon allowed them. Meanwhile, Rebet's snoring competed with the sounds of the other animals of the night. That night, Dabayl stood next to Noakh while Hilzen was at the back of the carriage.

Noakh turned to Dabayl, briefly observing her small pointed nose, her thin lips, and her big honey-yellow pupils under long eyelashes. She had big ears, pierced with several rings of different sizes and shapes.

"You know, Dabayl," Noakh observed, "I still have not thanked you for saving my life in the tournament. If it were not for you, Vileblood would probably have finished me off!"

"That stupid oaf? He was a problem the moment he arrived at the tournament. It was only a matter of time before it got out of hand." Then, in a sweet voice, she said, "Don't think I did it for you, you idiot. You were lucky I was ready to shoot after seeing what that idiot had done to his previous combatant; that bastard simply did not deserve to live." Seeing that Noakh did not understand what she was saying, Dabayl snorted with indignation. "You must be joking... You fought him without knowing who he was? Do you think a baker would have the nickname Vileblood? The man was a mercenary, Noakh. A soldier who was expelled from the army a few years ago."

"Expelled? Why?"

"Some say he killed a member of his platoon for some boots. Others say he hung his captain from a tree. Who knows which story is true? Perhaps both. Or neither. Even so, all do honor to Vileblood's bad reputation. So yes, do not have the slightest doubt that the man would have killed you."

Noakh had no doubt. Vileblood's eyes had radiated a small spark every time he launched an attack on Noakh, accentuating his desire for slaughter and pain. Noakh grimaced, reminded of Vileblood's breath, how horrible it had been.

His thoughts were interrupted by a scream of terror that flooded the night. Rebet appeared from inside the carriage, alarmed. Hilzen and Dabayl pointed with their crossbow and bow respectively towards the night, waiting for someone—or something—to assail them at any time. Noakh was limited to trying to calm the mare, which was very disturbed by the screams.

"What was that?" Rebet said, terrified.

"That... That sounded like a child screaming to me," Hilzen said terrified.

Another howl could be heard, this time sounding like the scream of a woman.

"We have to help those people!" Said Noakh while flicking the horse's reins.

36. Volcanite

Vienne and Queen Graglia were standing as still as statues, wearing their best clothes. Vienne was wearing a light-blue high-low dress that was longer in the back and shorter in the front. The queen was wearing a cobalt-blue wrap dress, its fabric tied at the waist. Vienne was holding Crystalline while Graglia stood behind her, wrapping her arms around the princess. They were not allowed to move an inch. The famous painter Derodoy had agreed to paint a portrait of the queen and her daughter, though not without imposing several of his many conditions, one of which was that he be granted complete freedom to portray them at his will. The queen's only requirement was that she and the princess be dressed with dignity instead of being naked—a way of posing that seemed to be the artist's favorite. After all, they would not be allowed to view the painting until it was finished. The only detail they knew regarding the portrait was that it already had a name, "The Legacy." The title symbolized the rise of Vienne to the monarchy, as guided there by her mother, Queen Graglia.

"Why are we making them wait?" Vienne asked, trying to move her mouth as little as possible. They had been posing for the portrait for a few hours and Derodoy, who did not have much patience, had already twice called her attention to the fact that she was not remaining still.

"The counselors wait for the queen, not the other way around, darling."

The queen, more used to posing than Vienne, maintained her posture while speaking perfectly. And, anticipating her daughter's next question, she added, "Just imagine how embarrassed one of our advisors would

311

feel if he made the queen wait. Trust me, you would not want to be in their shoes."

"I see," Vienne replied while Derodoy, a plump old man with a crooked nose and a moustache so big that it covered his upper lip, looked at her, frowning.

"During this meeting, you will stand as a mere spectator. The issues that we are going to address are more than a little bit delicate. Any question you have, hold it for later."

Vienne nodded. Derodoy again frowned at her. They had gotten up very early to pose for the painting. Now, what Vienne wanted most was to go back to bed. So the idea of having to be a mere listener at the meeting reassured her. Apparently, it was a very important meeting; at least, her mother had claimed so. The queen herself did not have the slightest idea what topics might be discussed at the meeting.

In the Hall of the Crown, the three most outstanding ministers were waiting for them. Vienne had made sure in advance to know their names, because her mother had taught her that recognizing people in this way was important, especially for those who expected it. There was Meredian, the queen's tax advisor, with whom she had already spoken; Galonais, the defense counselor; and Lampen, the director of research. All three advisors were of advanced age, a quality expected of everybody who occupied the prestigious position of adviser to the queen. Galonais was a tall and stout woman whose skin was light brown and whose wide lips never smiled but only gave orders. Lampen, on the contrary, was a short and plump old man who usually smiled brightly. Observing Queen Graglia and Princess Vienne entering the room, the three advisors performed their curtseys while standing on the carpet, holding their positions until the queen, sitting on her throne, gave them permission to straighten up. Sitting on a chair next to her mother, Vienne noticed how the advisors looked at her discreetly, observing that her mother had not informed them she would be present. It was not until the queen and Vienne occupied their respective seats in the royal room that Graglia began to speak.

"It's fine," the queen said, waving dismissively. "She's here as a listener. If she's going to govern one day, it's better she learn as soon as possible," she added, silencing their thoughts. They nodded, assuming the princess had every right to be there. "According to your letter, you had important matters you wished to address. So, who would like to start then?"

The three counselors looked at each other for a moment, wondering who should speak. They knew in advance that this meeting was going to be, at a minimum, tense.

"My queen," Meredian began. He was the advisor with the most tact. "I'm afraid that the three of us are here as a kind of common axis, so let me speak for now on behalf of all of us."

Galonais and Lampen nodded at his words.

The queen made a face. The counselors' approach was out of the ordinary. Normally each of her advisors announced the changes in their policies and their proposals, to which the queen gave or withheld approval. It was merely routine.

"Save your kindness, Meredian. Speak."

Meredian began to interlace his hands nervously, a tic that began to visibly irritate her majesty.

"It is a conflict of interests, my lady. The coffers of the queendom begin to feel the great expense that our armies require. Maintaining such a large army for so long imposes difficulties even for a queendom as prosperous as ours. I am aware that King Wulkan declared war almost two decades ago, and yet his threats have proven far different than any conflict worthy of his words—"

The queen raised her hand, a gesture that was sufficient for Meredian to fall silent and the three councilors to stand firm.

"I do not like the way this conversation is going, Meredian. Wulkan was very clear with his threats. It is true that his attack has been delayed, but knowing that stupid bastard, I am sure that he will attack when it is most unexpected, and we to have be prepared. It is well known that the ferocity of his people is overcome only by their stupidity."

That was a peculiarity of the Fireo people. Whereas the Aquos maintained an immense army in order to defend themselves, the Fireos' army was far less numerous. However, whenever the battlefield called, the ranks of the Fireo army were countless, outnumbering the Aquos. It was a matter of attitude. The Aquos had an army to defend their citizens; the Fireos, instead, had their citizens to defend themselves—and their kingdom. From man to woman, from child to old man, if they could handle a weapon they would join the war, and do so with pleasure. Ironically, this mentality was said to cause trouble when trying to convince the Fireo citizens to remain in their homes. After all, King Wulkan had to make sure the majority of the population remained alive.

313

As if this were not enough, Fireo steel was the best ever made, allowing the Fireo army to carry the deadliest swords.

"Yes, about that," Lampen began. He was in charge of the investigation that had resulted in this meeting. "We have news, my queen. During the last weapons assignment, our men discovered something by our borders—"

"Something?" The queen tilted her head curiously. "Be more specific, Lampen."

"Volcanite," Lampen said as he lowered his head.

Vienne let out a small squeak as she put her hands to her mouth. Volcanite was a scarce mineral with explosive properties. The Fireos had a working knowledge of it. In one of their last bouts, they made good use of it over the Aquo troops. Entire platoons had died under a huge explosion—a vision that had made many of the surviving soldiers who had witnessed the slaughter go mad. Even the queen had nightmares remembering such a horrific scene that she had once seen.

"How much are we talking about?" the queen asked with a worried look. Her nails dug into the throne's armrest.

"Enough to endanger the queendom," Defense Counselor Galonais put in with a stern look.

"Any indication that the Fireos know about it?" the queen asked, fearing the answer.

"It is located in a remote place, close to one of the routes by which our purchases of illegal weapons are transported. So that everything seems to indicate that they do not know; otherwise, it would not have been possible for us to have received the last load."

Vienne blinked, trying to remain calm. She had heard about the illegal weapons operation but had never known how it worked. It was no secret that the best steel was obtained from ores in the mines of Firia. According to what people said, in the Kingdom of Fire dwelled the best dwarf smiths, an almost-extinct breed with a supernatural talent for forging weapons. The Aquadom had proven the superior quality of these weapons on countless occasions, witnessing how Fireo blades pierced their armor without difficulty. For that reason, the Aquos, leaving aside their pride to make use of their intelligence, had obtained a contact who illegally provided weapons of the highest quality at the most affordable price.

"I see," the queen answered, understanding why the three counselors had approached her together. Certainly seeing the same synergy that she saw. "Lampen, how long might it take to extract all of that volcanite?"

"Under normal conditions, and with a large enough team, two months. But in this case, considering the difficulties posed by the location and the implicit need to act with the greatest secrecy, we might consider... a year," he said, making calculations in his head.

"And if our miners work knowing that their services are under the strict orders of the queen, with the promise of triple their usual pay and rations?" the queen said with a smile.

Lampen began to redo his calculations, trying to formulate a reasonable answer that in turn would please the queen.

"Let's say... five months?"

"Four," the queen replied. "Have the extractions begin immediately—and in the meantime, I want your investigators to focus solely on this issue. Making volcanite operational in combat must be their highest priority. Not having an answer if the volcanite can be rendered operational in the next two months would be an absolute disappointment. Is that clear?"

"Very clear, my queen," Lampen said as he continued to redo his calculations.

"Galonais, our actions may have consequences. Summon the Sea Guard and the River Guard. Strengthen their positions on the borders of Firia... Send more frigates to the east!"

"I will do so, your majesty. Will we also have the Temple Guard?"

"No, the Congregation of the Church won't want to know anything unless we go to war. For now, our guard will be more than enough. If war ensues, I will use my position as high priestess. Meredian, war may be imminent. How long can our coffers hold with the current army?"

"A couple of years, my queen. Collections have not covered the expenses of the queendom for a long time. Fortunately we have the Tirhans' payments to use for maintaining our military services, but even so, I fear our policy of becoming increasingly indebted will be a problem if the situation continues much longer."

"The war will come soon, and with it I fear that the ranks of our army will be considerably reduced, although the Aqua Deus knows very well that I wish it were not so. Any donation from our houses of nobility perhaps? A new tribute that allows us to raise funds?"

315

"Delorange House does not seem to be willing to lend more money, my queen. In general, the houses of the highest nobility have made more than generous contributions to the crown, the highest since our records began. As for taxes, the people will be unable to face more tributes, Your Grace. The rates have already been doubled, and we have created two new taxes on trade and the use of our waterways." Meredian acted as though he were considering a suggestion that he had wanted to propose for some time. "You know that the church is exempt from the payment of any tribute... Perhaps we could implement some kind of payment?"

"Do not even think about it," the queen answered flatly. "Come up with a better solution, Meredian, and do not bring the church's business into this matter. It will be better to have the church on our side when war resumes."

37. Night meeting

The shadow was walking practically blind along the park. The moon was not very bright that night. She couldn't risk carrying any source of light. Luckily, she had wandered those paths several times before. She was in the Cloistered Park, so called because decades ago it could be accessed only by the cloistered nuns who lived in the nearby convent.

However, that had changed long ago. The place was deemed too beautiful not to be open to the public, so finally the convent agreed to allow everyone to enjoy its beauty, although its name remained unchanged.

It was a huge park full of large trees and paths adorned with beautiful flowers and statues to praise their god. So large that every time someone visited, they could get lost along its paths or even discover something new: a new statue, a good seat on which to enjoy the sunset, or maybe even an inscription that had been carved in adoration of the Aqua Deus. It was common for many families to come spend the day in the park, even to eat there while the children played on the grass, especially during the warmer months. Many musicians liked playing in the park, where young and old alike could listen to them and give them some coins if they enjoyed their performance.

It was curious how a place so full of life and happiness during the day could become so sinister once it turned dark. Her footsteps were accompanied only by the sounds of the animals that lived in the trees and the whisper of the leaves that howled due to the force of the wind. Such was the silence that she could hear her strong breathing and the rapid beating of her heart. These symptoms were not, however, a consequence of fear, but of the importance of that night. The most important day of her life—and for the Aquadom, if she was asked.

They had agreed to meet at the lake, a beautiful place where everyone could take a boat ride at a decent price. It was a favorite place for lovers, being considered a romantic rendezvous—a timeless spot that many painters had decided to immortalize in their works.

The lake was guarded by the shadow of an imposing monument to General Riger, the famous soldier whose actions during combat had on countless occasions led to the glory of the Aquadom. A semicircle of spiraling pillars curved behind the general, providing a backdrop to the monument's principal focus. Atop a huge block of stone, General Riger assumed his battle posture, riding his steed headlong into the fury. At his feet was the inscription *Aq Rictum*—Flumio words that in the common tongue meant "All this water is at your feet." It was a phrase that symbolized the Aquadom's citizens' thanks and respect for the services General Riger had rendered to the queendom.

The lake was impressive even at night, the moon reflected on the water. For her, it had seemed the ideal place for her secret meeting, a quiet place where no one could interfere with their affairs. Even the inscription on the statue denoted a certain symbolism that nicely fit the issues that had brought her here.

She took a small silvery bell out of her pockets and made it sound loudly, just two tolls. Those had been the instructions: toll twice and wait for the response. She could feel her pulse accelerate gradually as she waited for the other bell to ring. For a brief moment, questions arose in her mind: What if he had not come? Would she be able to convince him?

Finally, the second bell answered in the same way: two tolls. Then a small raft made its way across the lake until it reached the shore where she was standing. A hand offered to help her step on into the wooden boat.

Everything had been prepared with absolute secrecy; nobody would know that they were there, let alone why. She had arrived early, impatient to get on with what this meeting could mean for her, while he had accepted it simply out of sheer curiosity.

The two shadows observed each other in the darkness for a moment, which seemed an eternity to her. He began paddling towards the center of the lake, while she beat her fingers nervously against her thighs. Both were hooded. He had opted for a dark-brown tunic while she, displaying much more flair, had decided to wear a navy-blue tunic with fine green details.

"I take for granted that you are aware of the risk you are taking," said a masculine voice. The man didn't take off his hood, his face remaining hidden in the moonlight.

"I am, Father. However, it is a risk that I am willing to take. Everything I do is in the name of the Aqua Deus and the queendom," she said.

As the man extended his arm, showing his ring of the Order, she leaned forward in the darkness of the boat and lowered her lips to kiss the ring.

"That's right, my daughter. Even so, I can't help but wonder why someone in such an advantageous position as yourself would want to meet in such an... atypical place, and under such secrecy."

"Even the most minor precaution is of great importance, Father. For the matter of which I intend to speak is most delicate." Her voice sounded full of worry.

"Ah yes. That important and necessary matter which requires us to speak in a place well removed from all living beings," he recalled. "I admit that all this secrecy has left me intrigued. Well? What is it about?"

"The queendom is in serious danger, Father," she said with a grievous tone.

"In grave danger?" he repeated curiously. "But tell me how, please!"

"You know how important it is for the queendom to have a strong ruler who is respected? A leader who is self-confident and possesses the necessary leadership skills? A weak figure on the throne would pose a risk to our sovereignty and to the security of our entire queendom."

"I see," the man said in a disinterested voice. "I expected something more from you, my dear. You have always been known as an ambitious person, the living image of the queen, after all. I guess our princesses are not good losers. Accept it, Katienne—your sister will be queen. This has been the choice of the Aqua Deus and we must respect it."

The man made a move to start rowing back to the shore, while Katienne clenched her fists in anger.

"Even if she questioned the will of the Aqua Deus?" Katienne replied in anger. "I wonder what our people will say when an insecure young woman without any talent becomes overwhelmed with the responsibilities of governing the queendom and makes it falter in front of its enemies. Do not forget that we continue to endure our position in the Sleeping War. Wulkan will wake up one day. My mother will lead

319

our armies again—and if something happened to her, god forbid, my sister shall reign, and with this, disaster will devastate the queendom. You have met her, Father Ovilier? Or do you hold your words only in good faith and hope?"

"Your mother introduced her to me in the dance," he admitted. "A shy girl, I would say. She kept looking down while your mother talked. After such a brief encounter, I can't say I know her."

"If you knew her as I do, you would see how my words are not enough to describe my sister's faults. She is unstable, she is weak, and worst of all, she does not care!"

"Such words make me uneasy, Katienne. But what can an old man like me do about events that are scheduled to happen very shortly?"

"You are the most respected member of the Congregation of the Church, Father," Katienne observed, knowing these were the words he wanted to hear. "I am sure that if I explain my reasoning and you lend your support, the rest of the congregation will follow your wise judgment. Who would not pay attention to the pious Ovilier?"

"Well it could be, yes," the Father said in a tired voice. "Even so, I do not know if your arguments carry enough weight to condemn a poor girl. I do not usually agree with decisions that contradict the Aqua Deus. Besides, even supposing that princess Vienne never occupies the throne, what makes you think that the crown will be yours?"

"The queendom needs power. The Sleeping War has made the queendom waste a lot of its resources; our coffers are being emptied despite the monies we receive from the Tirhans. We need more power—and I can provide it to them." Katienne paused to heighten her companion's interest.

"Oh, please continue." Whereas his tone had before sounded skeptical, now Ovilier was intrigued by Katienne's words. "Explain to me in detail!"

"The House of Delorange, the noble house with the most power and wealth in the queendom, as you well know, is one of the few houses whose members do not have any kind of conjugal relationship with the royal family. Somehow their heirs have always been able to escape the charms of my ancestors. I can change that. A position of power such as that could very well carry me to the throne, even while Vienne, the stupidest of my sisters, gives birth to descendants as if she were a rabbit until one of them is chosen to occupy the throne. But there is still much time left for that."

"The House of Delorange, eh?" Ovilier reflected. "Cunning, very clever. It seems that you have everything planned. A woman of your lineage, backed by all the power of nobility... with their support you would undoubtedly occupy a high position as regent, I have no doubt. You only have to convince the Congregation of the Church to carry out your plan."

"Tae ferae, Father. I think you are not seeing this in the proper perspective. Allow me to explain. My mother, the queen, as you well know, usurped the title of high priestess... Do not doubt that she intends for her daughter to also inherit this title. If that daughter who occupied the throne were someone with... better qualities... and if she were in the good graces of the Congregation of the Church, I am sure that this title could be granted to someone in that chamber. Someone wise enough, who I could trust implicitly," she hinted.

"You are indeed as cunning as your mother, my daughter," the man said, smiling. Then Father Ovilier started rowing the boat back to the shore while Katienne stared at the statue of General Riger.

Aq Rictum, she thought.

38. Howling

The screams did not stop, heartrending cries of what seemed like women and children. Wherever they came from, it seemed to be a slaughter. It was dark. Fate had dictated the moon be hidden behind the clouds, and for some strange reason, the cries did not seem to come from any specific place. It was as if the screams were all around them.

Noakh continued trying to calm the horse by tugging its reins. As he did so, the wound on his back began to sting him. Although he had recovered, his injury sometimes seemed to want to remind him that it was still there, as if warning him how close he had come to death. Another cry, this one sounding closer to them.

"I can't stand this anymore!" said Noakh, trying to look through the dark. "I will go help those people!"

"I'm going with you," answered Dabayl.

"Hold on!" said Rebet. "Where do you think you are going?"

Everyone on the crew was willing to go and lend a hand, except for Rebet, who advocated more for his own protection. They would not have hesitated a second to run to help those people whose cries made shivers run down their backs.

"We have to go help them. They're dying!" Noakh said.

"No. The only one who you need to help is me!" Rebet replied indignantly and fearful from inside the carriage. He drew the candle closer to his map, his eyes restless, reviewing the map for any clues that could help explain where they might have taken a wrong turn; occasionally his eyes looked up to see if anyone was approaching. Although he checked the map time and again, it did not seem to him that they had deviated from their intended path. The roads through the forests comprised the route usually used to transport his most valuable merchandise, and his men had never warned him of any danger. Hilzen, who stood next to Noakh, and Dabayl, who was over the carriage, looked indignant upon hearing Rebet's words.

"You can't be serious!" Hilzen answered, surprised at Rebet's selfishness.

Dabayl was the only one who knew how to stay calm. "Rebet, if that slaughter continues, we'd better help whoever is still alive before the savages come for us. It's more than likely they know we're here," she added.

Instead of heeding Dabayl, Rebet continued to look at his map, as if he were going to find the answer there, and as he did so, wax fell on the parchment but he was too worried to care. No matter how long he looked, he could not find a nearby town. They were too deep in the forest; even if he told them to escape, they would probably get nowhere, as the sounds from the horse would have already alerted whoever was doing the killing.

Then, for some reason, the sounds were heard incredibly close to the carriage... yet there was no movement around it.

As if that was not enough, it seemed to be Rebet's misfortune that his three escorts were showing too much concern for the problems of others, beyond the one man who was paying them to protect him. He could not ensure that they would not take justice into their own hands by going to help those people, leaving him alone in the middle of the forest at the mercy of all danger. He had to act smart or he might find himself alone.

"Okay then," Rebet said as he tried to regain his composure. Another scream flooded the night, making him curse his bad luck. "We have to know what's going on around us. I'll appoint an explorer to investigate and let us know what's happening. Then we can act accordingly." Noakh stopped the carriage.

Rebet pretended that he was reflecting on the situation when in fact he knew from the beginning who he was going to appoint for that task. He had a swordsman, an archer, and an arbalist. He needn't be a genius to make the decision. "You, Hilzen, you look like a good explorer. Go into the woods and find out what's going on out there."

Hilzen reluctantly agreed to enter the forest. He held his crossbow high. Dabayl and Noakh watched him, their weapons drawn and ready for any unexpected visitor.

For a moment he thought about how easy it would be to die in these woods. He realized he did not want to die there. He was not a very inquisitive man, nor had he even planned where he wanted to die; the forest simply seemed a rather unfortunate place to do so. Yet as each step took him deeper into the forest, it became more and more likely that this was his destiny. For a moment, he remembered his wife and daughter, somehow unconsciously trying to avoid remembering their deaths. It seemed to be a way to put aside all the pain and loss. Ever since he had started his travels with Noakh, in times when his faith had failed him, he had put his hand on his chest where the locket of her daughter was, remembering her words that had urged him to continue. *I'm not going to die here!* he thought decisively.

The moon was now visible through the clouds, allowing Hilzen to see slightly better. Around him there were only trees and bushes. The ground was soft and the breeze carried a smell of fallen leaves and damp earth. The screams did not stop. Even though Hilzen tried to discover where they were coming from, he failed. Instead, on several occasions, he changed position suddenly, pointing his crossbow toward each new scream.

It was a very silent night, as if the rest of the night's inhabitants had been silenced by the heartbreaking slaughter happening nearby. Only the snapping of the dry branches on the ground as Hilzen passed by, and the brushing of leaves against his legs as he found a passage between the bushes, interrupted the silence that buried the forest when the screams of pain ceased.

He could not help but feel that someone was watching him. The cries continued from time to time... He'd swear they were only a few meters from where he was, though when he looked there was nothing. No evidence, nothing. After a cry, again silence for a moment, until another of those unpleasant cries flooded the forest. The next shout was right behind Hilzen, so close that he was aware that if he turned around he would see where it came from. It was so strange and supernatural that Hilzen began to believe that perhaps his end had finally come. He tried to turn slowly, avoiding quick movements. For the first time he could hear sounds around him. Something was moving, very fast, incessantly.

Suddenly several reddish flashes began to appear among the bushes around him. This time, several heartbreaking cries sounded in unison.

Hilzen swore. He turned around and tried to run towards his companions. The shouting and running behind him made him not have

325

the slightest doubt. He tried to see how many they were. Dozens. Maybe hundreds. It was difficult to know for sure. A wave of red eyes was behind him. He had to run.

Hilzen shouted with all his might so that his companions knew of his return—and the company he had brought with him. When he got back to the carriage, he could see how everyone had climbed up onto the vehicle, probably hoping to see better. While he ran, he could see his companions' faces lose all expression at the sight of the beasts swarming after him. Noakh jumped from the carriage, with his swords ready to protect the flight of his friend; Hilzen had already drawn close to the carriage. Dabayl had already started firing off her precise volley of arrows, shooting at a frantic pace. She hit her targets with an overwhelming level of accuracy considering the darkness and the dark skin tone of the beasts. The horse, even more aware of the danger, began to rear up on two legs and whinny, as if possessed.

Noakh began to confront the beasts, lunging at them tirelessly while arrows continued flying around him, fired from a very short distance away. He hadn't engulfed Distra in flames; he had decided he wouldn't use the power against those beasts unless it was strictly necessary. When Hilzen arrived safe and sound and climbed atop the carriage, Rebet leaned down and extended a hand to him, pulling him up. After helping Hilzen, Rebet knelt on his knees and continued to immerse himself in his prayer. After recovering his composure, Hilzen joined in the shooting. No matter how many beasts from the forest died, it seemed that more and more emerged. For every beast that they killed, two took their place. The screams continued sounding nonstop. Hilzen cried out even as he shot another bolt. At least they had discovered what was causing those horrific screams.

Little by little, Noakh retreated, because although the beasts were not very strong, it was hard for him not to lose ground in the face of such numbers. The soil at his feet had turned into mud because of the amount of blood that had been spilled, making his movements more difficult. He was aware that if he lost his balance and fell, all would be lost for him. But from the forest the beasts did not stop coming. They came more and more. Seemingly seeking revenge on their dead brothers, the creatures kept pouncing on Noakh, completely oblivious to the rain of arrows falling on them.

As if that were not enough, they were slowly being surrounded.

At close distance, the beasts were the size and appearance of a dog, but they had longer claws, their bodies had no fur, and their skin had a dark-brown tone mixed with black. Their appearance was fierce, in large part because of the reddish tone of their eyes, and their heartrending cries. Noakh wondered if their cries were a way of attracting their prey, imitating the cry of a child or a woman, making someone come to their aid. Whether this was the case or not, the cries were incredibly sordid; were he to hear them through much of the night, he knew he would still not get used to them. He felt chills every time he heard them.

"What beasts are these?" Dabayl asked as she launched a pair of arrows at two of the beasts trying to surround the carriage. The two creatures let out cries of pain before they fell dead on the ground.

"Dogues of the woods," Hilzen answered while firing his crossbow. "I have heard of them. I knew that they hunt in large packs... but I could not imagine something like this."

"If we continue this way..." Dabayl said, fearing the worst. "Hilzen, aim better, you bastard!"

More and more dogues appeared from the woods. Noakh retreated farther and farther, trying to block the beasts' teeth and claws as much as possible, while answering with steel, swinging his swords wildly in front of him, trying to discourage the dogs from attacking. Despite the frenzy of battle, Noakh noticed how Distra, despite tasting a large amount of blood from those creatures, was not trying to regain control. It was as if the sacred sword was not very interested in taking part in a fight against mere animals. Could it be that Distra only found joy in tasting human blood?

The cry these beasts uttered when they were dying was no more desirable than the one they proclaimed in life. One of the dogues managed to dodge his thrust and launched a bite on his shoulder. Noakh responded by cutting its head. He could feel his own blood staining his shirt.

"Rebet!" Noakh shouted, making himself heard above the beasts' screams. "If I am going to die here, I'd like to at least know the truth!"

Rebet continued with his hands on his head, trying to isolate himself from all that was happening around him. He looked around, searching for any way to be of use. Instead, he cursed the moment he and his stupid fellow guild leaders had decided to pit the queen against them. Certainly, they had not acted with bad intentions, but they were aware of the risks. What they had done could be considered an act of rebellion against the crown. But their actions had seemed innocent enough; in any case, the punishment, they thought, wouldn't be severe. But the mind of the queen—or more likely, the minds of the sisters of the cathedral—had not considered it so. Their arrogance had put a price on their heads.

"Rebet!" Noakh shouted again as he tried to stop the dogues.

He had to use Distra's power. He could not face the beasts' attacks anymore. The wound on his shoulder continued bleeding, since he continued using the strength in those muscles to fight the dogues. Fortunately, the frenzy of combat seemed to render him immune to pain.

"The queen!" Rebet said between sobs. "The queen herself! How stupid we were!" he lamented, again throwing his hands to his head. "To give her a chance to take everything from us... It was just a tower! A stupid golden tower!"

Noakh turned around. Hilzen and Dabayl stopped firing for a moment too. The three were stunned. Had he said the queen? They had expected that whoever was after him was someone with power—probably one of the most powerful of the noble houses—but the crown itself was something that had been beyond their imagination.

The dogues took advantage of the distraction. They pounced on Noakh with more force, while they also took that moment to surround the carriage. Now Noakh could be attacked on either side. The horse kept neighing incessantly, trying to defend itself from the dogues. Hilzen tried to help the horse by shooting all the dogues attacking the poor animal. Dabayl tried to cover Noakh. Rebet was on his knees atop the carriage, his face hidden under the hood, tears soaking the wood.

Noakh tried to put aside his feelings. Rebet had revealed his secret; it was time to unveil his own, if he wanted to save their lives. The blade of the sacred sword started to turn orange and to emanate heat, an act that was enough to scare the beast that was then in front of him. But before he could light up Distra, Hilzen shouted.

"Noakh! Wait!"

Distra began to shine slightly, his blade turning blazing orange, but Noakh stopped the attack in time. Noakh suddenly held Distra tightly. He could have sworn that Distra was not happy to stop the attack. Probably the sword was eager for battle. A long time had passed without it displaying its power.

The first rays of light appeared in the sky, and with them the night gave way to dawn. Realizing this, the dogs looked around, bewildered.

Then they ran to shelter in the forest. Apparently their thirst for blood had made them unaware of time.

Exhausted, Noakh threw himself to the ground. His shoulder began to burn. The injuries he had received during the dogues' incessant assault were beginning to make themselves known. His eyes closed with fatigue.

Hilzen went to check if Noakh was fine while Dabayl tried to calm the horse as best she could. The animal seemed not to concede that the danger had passed. It had managed to survive without the slightest scratch, thanks to Noakh's and Hilzen's efforts to ward off the beasts.

Around him lay countless corpses of dogues. Their dark-red blood—almost black, in fact—created small puddles on the ground. Hilzen was responsible for ending the life of any dogue that was still clinging to what remained of its existence, and for setting aside the corpses that stood in the carriage's way. All of them wanted to leave as soon as possible.

Rebet was slow to realize that they were safe. He was unable to believe that his prayers had been heard. It seemed to him that his confession had given way to the sunlight—and to his salvation. Even for a man as unruly as Rebet, at a moment like that, he could not help but doubt... Would Aqua Deus really be upset by their tower? Either way, they had been saved at the last moment, and Rebet did not even regret having confessed the truth. In fact, a huge burden had somehow been lifted.

After calming down the horse, they set off. Hilzen had suggested that some of the dogues could be taken for their meat, in case their supplies ran out. In spite of Dabayl's refusal to consider Hilzen's suggestion—her denial was accompanied with a gesture of disgust—Hilzen took several dogues, asking Noakh to help him carry the bodies to the carriage, claiming that they should be delicious, having been raised in the forest. Dabayl, meanwhile, was collecting her arrows, pulling them from the inert bodies of her ugly victims, and putting them back in her quiver.

Hilzen drove the carriage this time, moving at a good pace to get away from that nightmarish place. Noakh sat inside the carriage, along with Rebet, who had regained his composure.

"The queen herself, huh?" Noakh said with a smile as he grasped his shoulder. His wound had stopped bleeding and had been wrapped in bandages, but the pain remained. Those dogues knew how to bite.

Rebet answered Noakh's question with a snort.

"Did you know what was going to happen?" Rebet asked softly, his blue eyes peeking out from under his hood. "That they were going to leave at sunrise?"

"No," Noakh replied sincerely. "Thinking about it now, it makes all the sense in the world. It's more than obvious: Everything about them is characteristic of any nocturnal animal. Their red eyes, their color... Now I'm even realizing that we first began to hear those cries at night. We were very lucky..."

"Lucky?" Rebet laughed. For him it had been more than luck. It had been destiny. A signal. Maybe a last chance. "You know, I thought I was going to die... and that's the moment when you understand everything you've done in your life... and what you *have not* done," he confessed in a melancholy tone.

"What do you mean?"

"I've always been good at business—no, *exceptional*. I'm not bragging, Noakh. It's just a fact. I could count a million things I'm bad at. My mother used to say that since I was little I had a gift for negotiation, that I always went to bed later she wanted, thanks to my ability to bargain. In one way or another, I always got my way.

"That gift grew bigger and bigger. My achievements in the textile market did not go unnoticed by the rest of the guild members, and little by little I gained a prestige such that not even my youth could overshadow it. I ended up becoming the youngest head of a guild—any guild!—at the age of twenty-seven. And that was now fifteen years ago." Rebet let out a sigh full of melancholy. "I made a lot of money. I earned the respect of my colleagues. No competitor overshadowed me..."

Rebet continued to tell his story, his eyes hidden under his hood, which he clasped in his hands as he was shaken by the movements of the carriage.

"Last night I assumed I was going to die. My whole life went by in my head. That's when you realize... I wasn't happy, Noakh. A life based on greed and money... I just felt remorse."

"Remorse?"

"Yes. For all things I didn't have. No family, no friends, even my parents... I always thought that everything personal was only a barrier that hindered success. Now I realize that my pretensions came at the cost of my happiness. Success catches you. It turns you into an ambitious person. You close a deal and you feel a happiness that little by little fades away... You need to close the next deal, and do it more cheaply, and for more profit!"

"It's still not too late..."

"I try to make myself remain aware of that... If we manage to reach the earth kingdom, I will look for a business with few pretenses, something that doesn't attract much attention, in order to live without fear, knowing that the queen's dogs will not come after me... who knows? I might even be able to have a family, a little Rivetien to learn the family business..."

Rebet's words served to relieve his pain. His idea of a future life for himself seemed more plausible when translated into words. At that moment, he realized that he had spoken his real name—Rivetien—and discovered what little it mattered now.

39. Ruins

In front of them stood a small church in ruins. The huge roots of several trees had found their way around the structure and entangled the walls of stone and marble: The building had succumbed to nature.

As they entered the church, a swarm of bats fled out of the church and swooped down on Noakh, making him fall to the ground. Hilzen and Dabayl held their weapons at the ready, thinking they were being ambushed.

"It's fine, it's fine," said Noakh dismissively while still standing on the ground. "Only bats welcoming us." Both Hilzen and Dabayl lowered their weapons. Rebet extended his arm and helped Noakh get back on his feet.

The grounds of the building were decorated by statues of white stone that were severely damaged, missing several pieces, and being eroded by the rain, giving them a somewhat fragmented appearance. It smelled of moss, while the air was slightly colder than it was outside. Hilzen was kneeling at the foot of one of the statues, reciting his prayers. His fist was set in the center of his chest.

"What happened here?" Noakh asked, surprised as he walked along the church, his steps resounding on the walls. He ran his hand over a white marble statue. The statue's head was missing, but its remains allowed him to guess that it had once held the form of a mermaid. "This place seems to have been swallowed by nature."

"That's a fairly accurate description of what has actually happened," Rebet said as he dipped his head back down to his precious map.

"What do you mean?"

"We are close, very close!" Rebet replied, turning his gaze away from the map and exhibiting a smile that reflected his joy. "This is a sample of what awaits us... contemplate the powers of the Earth Kingdom! Or, better said, the powers of his king, Burum Babar." He raised his arms and stood up, looking at the cracked roof above them. The four companions all admired the damage that the roots had incurred to the building: huge cracks shown in the walls and columns. The earth seemed to have embraced the marble feet of the statues, while a dim light went through the holes of the roof. It was as if there was still evidence of the greatness of something that had long ago become extinct but that refused to stop shining in all its beauty... a beautiful symbiosis.

"Did Burum Babar do this?" Dabayl asked, kneeling at the foot of a statue. Only a part of its marble torso remained. She raised her hand and moved some earth, revealing a hidden prayer carved into the stone beneath it. "Show mercy and listen to our humble praises," she read. It was written in the common tongue, which meant the statue was not as old as the church itself; otherwise, the words would certainly have been written in Flumio.

"So they say," Rebet replied. "The Tirhan monarch found himself in front of this church decades ago, where the Temple Guard and the Divine Protection fought him. The victory was not enough for him; he wanted a reminder of his triumph. This is the result of his work."

Hilzen, Noakh, and Dabayl contemplated the reach of Burum Babar's power, looking silently at the tree-shattered walls and the gigantic roots that entangled them. *This is the power of a king,* thought Noakh astonished. "Why do they not restore it?" he asked. "Isn't it shameful for the Church of Water to have one of their temples continue like this?"

"On the contrary," Hilzen said as he stood up. "This church shows the mistakes that were made in the past and teaches us how to learn from them. It is a way of teaching us humility."

"That's right," Rebet affirmed. "The church army ignored the queen's instructions—and as a result their sacred army, the Temple Guard, and their elite soldiers, the Divine Protection, were crushed by a higher power. Even soldiers with as much faith as those who form the ranks of the Temple Guard fainted before Burum Babar's army and his power over the land and nature.

"Shortly after that defeat, they say, the queen took control of the church, acquiring the title of high priestess then locking her predecessor in the prison that not so long ago she had governed... As a merchant, I must say that it was a masterful move by the queen. As a citizen, well... that's a different story. She took advantage of the weakness of the only organ that could overshadow her and subjected it to her wishes... a great scheme!

"I admire the queen," said Dabayl with fascination. "She wants something and she takes it."

"You needn't tell me," Rebet said softly. "Well, after this church we come to the place known as the Valley of the Fallen—there, a brutal confrontation against the Tirhan Army unfolded, and countless soldiers died on both sides. I'm sure you've all heard stories about that place; they say that the souls of the soldiers continue to wander around it, fighting tirelessly, unable to return home. Dimwitted fairy tales, in my opinion."

"If we are near the Valley of the Fallen, that means that the North Sea is not far away. Is that the direction we are headed towards?" Hilzen asked.

"You know what they say: One sails out of the Aquadom by sea... but one does not return," Rebet recalled. "The Sea Guard controls the seas, getting to the Earth Kingdom through the sea is not an option. Even if we obtain a boat, they would detect us before we reached the open sea. Believe me, I have tried. A boat that does not have to pay taxes for its merchandise and can use many of the routes throughout the queendom? Of course I've tried!"

"So what is the plan?" Noakh asked. "Go over the border and hope they do not stop us?" It seemed a plan that was meant to fail.

"Not at all. Don't worry, Noakh. Leave it in my hands. That reminds me..." While talking, Rebet searched among the merchandise stored in the carriage, which was standing behind him.

Finally, he found a small can. "This is a high-quality dye," he said, showing it to the others. "It will allow us to color our hair as brown as mud, and the dye will last so long that we won't have to worry about being discovered. This way we will look like unickeys, having brown hair but not green eyes. When we are in the Earth Kingdom, they will think us simple merchants returning to our homes. The Crossbreed Curse at its best." He paused and looked at his companions. "Two Tirhquos, a Tirheo and a Tirhtian. I must say, Noakh, that because your eyes and Dabayl's are a different color, they lend great credence to our story," Rebet said, smiling, but Noakh gave him a curious look. "Oh, come on, you know why!" He turned to the others. "So, who wants to start?" he said as he offered the can to his travel companions.

40. A ritual

The wind howled loudly, making her white dress flinch and her hair flutter back. She was about to perform the Jump. The queen wanted Vienne's powers to awaken as soon as possible. The Jump would allow Vienne to know her blessing. Some heiresses had shown enough talent to discover it for themselves before performing the ritual. Vienne was not among them. Different blessings had been granted to her predecessors as she had read in the manuscript her mother had given to her while she, Vienne, was lying in bed recovering after trying to summon Crystalline's powers. She had read about the different blessings, summoning the beasts of the sea, making it rain, or summoning a torrent of water from the floor, as her mother did, were some of the blessings her predecessors had.

In her bare feet, she could feel the cold rock, the little stones breaking into her toes. The moon was before her, as round and large as she had ever seen it, as if it wanted to witness the ritual that Vienne was to face. She looked down, trying not to feel dizzy. She could see several ships. As usual, the queen had invited the Congregation of the Church and the noble houses to witness this act. *The Lacrima must embrace the sea,* the books instructed... Vienne thought of her sisters, who were also present at the event, protected by the Royal Guard and the Sea Guard, in addition to the Knights of Water, with the exception of Gant.

Igüenza had told her that the act was simple. She just had to jump into the vastness of the ocean, together with Crystalline, which she held in her hands, and let the sea accept her as another of the Aqua Deus's subjects. Vienne did not stop wondering whether Igüenza had once been in a similar situation, thereby causing her to call the ritual Vienne was to perform *simple*. The rock on which she was standing was high above the sea. The great Rock of Salt, one of the queendom's sacred places. Behind her stood two Guards of the Temple, who watched over her safety. The Guards of the Temple, along with the elite troops called the Divine Protection, were led by the Congregation of the Church instead of the queen herself, as was the case with the rest of the guards who protected the queendom. With Graglia, as a result of having also acquired the title of high priestess, the Guards of the Temple were also under her power, but not as firmly as the rest of the guards, since the Guards of the Temple obeyed the Congregation of the Church as a whole, not just the high priestess.

Vienne lowered her head, staring at the rock on which she stood. The rock had different inscriptions in the Aquadom's native language, Flumio. Vienne tried to remember her lessons. Flumio was a language whose use was very limited; she had not used it herself except on occasions such as this. With effort, she managed to read one of the inscriptions: "Welcome in your bosom the one who gives everything for you and with his humility faces the wrath of the ocean." Finally, realizing there was no going back, she knelt on the rock.

She was about to jump, but first she had to pray, as Igüenza had told her to do. She paused for a second, realizing she had forgotten the prayer. It was not her fault; it was in Flumio, she thought. Luckily, she remembered what the praying said in the common tongue. "Aqua Deus, I, heir to the throne, chosen by your servant Crystalline, give myself to you. As your most humble servant," she said, hoping the Aqua Deus wouldn't care she had not said the praying in Flumio.

Then, as she approached the edge of the rock, a few pebbles fell to the ocean above her feet. As she held Crystalline tightly with both hands, she could feel her blood pounding in her head. Then she threw herself into the ocean, her eyes closed.

In an instant she fell, buried in the water, the force of the fall driving her toward the bottom. She tried to orient herself, but it was tremendously dark. Even with her eyes open, she could not see anything; soon, her eyes began to sting from the salt. She had Crystalline, but if she was unable to use it, how was she supposed to know about her blessing?

She stood there, under the water, not knowing what to do. Nobody had explained what she had to do once she jumped. Nothing happened. Maybe she would not be blessed? It made sense, she thought; she was not like her mother, after all. The Aqua Deus had probably made a mistake choosing her.

Then she suddenly felt as though something had surrounded her. With difficulty, she saw fish of all sizes and colors swimming around her. She tried to touch them, but as her hand approached they swam out of reach. Then she heard something under the water, a kind of singing in the distance. It was beautiful... breathtaking. At first she thought it was a single voice, but it was not like that. Several voices were singing in unison. Suddenly something wrapped itself around her leg. Before she could react, it had grabbed her tightly and began to pull her down into the depths of the ocean. She tried to scream and swim upward, back to the surface, but the water silenced her cries for help. Around her, the fish began to swim in all directions, frightened, ignoring her. Vienne kept sinking deeper and deeper...

She tried to free herself, but whatever was grabbing her was pulling her down with such strength that it was impossible for Vienne to loosen its grasp. It was a tentacle of immense dimensions. She tried to hit it with all her strength, reaching her arm down, making a fist, and pounding her fist against the tentacle. She also held Crystalline tightly with both hands and tried to cut the tentacle, but her blows, muffled by the water, seemed to go completely unnoticed. Even so, after a moment, the tentacle released her, leaving her motionless under the water. It was so dark she could not see anything. She began to tremble with fear. No matter how much she tried, she could not see anything. She could only hear how something immense moved around her in circles. Then, she heard a voice:

"What is this feeling that floods my home? It is not only fear, it is not anger—feelings I could regard with understanding... Is it indifference that I perceive?"

The voice spoke in an irritated tone, with a strange and fluid accent; Vienne had a hard time understanding it. After a pause, it continued:

"You have surrendered even before you started... You think you are weak, and that justifies everything."

It's just that I do not think I deserve any power. I'm not as strong as my mother or my predecessors! Vienne thought with sadness. Despite Vienne being underwater, tears formed in her eyes, her tears becoming part of the sea.

"The Lacrima must not be like anybody else," the voice rumbled. It was a firm voice without any emotion. *"She has only to be as unique as she is."*

In the distance, at the bottom of the sea, Vienne thought she saw two small yellow eyes gleaming. They were very deep down. Their gleam reflected off the rocks that spread across the sea floor.

Vienne still had a hard time clearly understanding the creature's words. She felt she could stay underwater as long as she wanted, though anyone else would have run out of oxygen by now. After a moment of silence, the voice resounded again:

"You have been blessed..."

Vienne felt a chill. Somehow, she had come to consider herself unworthy of receiving even the smallest, weakest blessing.

What blessing has been given to me? she wondered. She wished it were to be able to control the creatures of the sea. She had dreamed that it was to be that blessing, so she could play with the fish.

"Absa Poestas," the voice said in Flumio.

The words of the being resounded forcefully one last time before a strong current emerged from the depths of the ocean, driving Vienne to the surface. After she appeared above the waves, the boat where the queen and priests stood on deck sailed closer to pick her up. One of the soldiers from the Royal Guard threw a rope ladder over the side of the boat. Vienne swam and then climbed up it.

When she was on the boat's deck, she approached the crowd. Her mother nodded at her, Aienne stood with her other sisters smiling. The Knights of Water stood around the queen. Alvia seemed entertained by the situation. Menest looked solemn, while Tarkos' eyes stared uncomfortably at Vienne. Vienne could not see Katienne, since she, unhappy about the ritual that was being celebrated—or, better said, unhappy about who was performing the ritual instead of her—stood as far back as possible for a woman of her position, standing close to where the noblemen stood. Katienne's eyes, continuously and unconsciously, stared at Father Ovilier, who stood leading the priests. Ovilier, meanwhile, seemed to avoid her gaze. They had advanced that Vienne, if she received any blessing, would get a lame one, and this would help them in their plotting.

As protocol dictated, Vienne knelt before the high priestess as she put Crystalline on the deck's wood. She had to announce what had happened during her blessing. Despite feeling quite cold, Vienne would not cover

340

herself. She had been welcomed by the water and now had to stand firm. Her sisters, the rest of the priests and representatives of the highest nobility, waited expectantly. It was an important and solemn moment for everyone present.

"High priestess, I have been blessed," Vienne said, pronouncing the exact words Igüenza had taught her to say just before the ritual. She remained kneeling with her eyes fixed on the wooden deck of the boat, her hair spilling around her head, water shedding off her dress, creating small puddles around her.

"So be the will of the Aqua Deus," the queen said as she bowed to the sea. The rest of the boat's crew imitated her. Meanwhile, the Knights of the Water kneeled to show their respect. "Tell us, Lacrima, what blessing has the Guardian of the Oceans granted you?" Even Queen Graglia was intrigued to learn what power her daughter had been granted. She was not expecting a powerful blessing, because the guardian had probably seen in her the weakness that she herself had perceived.

"He did not grant me any particular blessing," Vienne said, shrugging as she continued to fix her gaze on the deck. Cries of surprise arose among the spectators. Katienne had to repress herself, so as not to let out a shout of victory. Even the queen was perplexed by such a result. Seeing the reaction of the people around her, Vienne realized that maybe she had not been accurate enough in what she had told them. "The guardian said only two words: *Absa Poestas,*" she added, not understanding what kind of blessing that might be.

The reaction of all the people could not be suppressed this time, sounding even louder than before. People shared astonished looks and open mouths with amazement, accompanied by cries of admiration. The Knights of Water, who until now had still been kneeling, could not help but stand and look at the princess in shock. Even Alvia's usual smile had been suppressed, her face showing astonishment instead.

Katienne looked at Ovilier, their eyes meeting for the first time. His eyes under his hood returned her gaze with a mixture of disappointment and concern. She gave a small nod. *We have to act fast,* she thought. She dug her nails into the palm of her hand with such force that blood began to flow.

Even the queen could not help losing control for a second... It was hard for her not to remain as calm as always.

"Absa Poestas," the queen repeated. "Absolute Power," she translated, even though almost everyone, given their reaction, had

341

understood what such words meant. "Are you sure those were the words the Guardian of the Ocean said Vienne?"

"Yes," Vienne said, perplexed. She hadn't read of any of her predecessors being granted with such blessing in the manuscript her mother had given to her.

Absolute power! Graglia thought. Only one of her predecessors had been granted such a blessing, and she was considered the greatest queen the Aquadom ever had: the Lady of the Mountain.

41. The fall

Vihaim went into the woods. He had volunteered to go and collect the firewood. Any task was a good excuse to occupy his mind; otherwise, the image of his companion Biveo being crushed by the giant was repeated relentlessly. It was early in the morning. Horrible dark circles marked his face, and he had been unable to sleep all night. Every time he closed his eyes, he memorialized once again that unfortunate moment when he saw his friend Biveo turned into a lump of blood and viscera.

Why had his friend tried to play the hero? Biveo was stupid, but his silliness didn't mean he deserved to die.

The soldier crouched to pick up a tree branch from the ground. As if having seen their companions die was not painful enough, Gelegen had ordered those who remained alive to watch over the one who had so cruelly killed them all: that stupid giant. At this thought, Vihaim tightened his fingers around the branches he had collected, making them crack. Why was Gelegen waiting to torture the giant? The veteran had ordered them to do nothing to the colossus, only to watch him—no matter how much the soldiers insisted on giving their due to the cruel beast that had claimed the lives of their companions. Gelegen's obsession with the whereabouts of those criminals and his relationship with the giant were allowing the monstrous creature to *not* pay for their deaths, Vihaim fiercely believed.

Vihaim ducked down and took another branch from the ground. It was entangled among the grasses, so he pulled a rusty knife from his pocket and cut the grasses then picked up the branch. Just then, he heard a whinny a short distance from where he stood. He looked around the woods.

The soldier advanced a couple of steps toward where he thought he heard the sound. After a few steps, he found the creature that had whinnied. There, looking into his eyes, stood a horse. Vihaim recognized the animal instantly. It was the horse that lived with the giant.

"Well, well," Vihaim said, approaching the horse slowly. The animal was accustomed to humans, so he remained in his place. Vihaim rubbed the horse gently on his loin. "Maybe you can help us..."

The soldier threw the wood to the ground, then he extended his arm and set his hand on the horse's back, guiding him back to camp. There, the rest of the soldiers stood around a bonfire, some still mourning their loss and others trying to forget the massacre they had witnessed some days before. Behind them was Cervan, tied up so he wouldn't escape, his chest swelling slightly with his breath.

Seeing Vihaim approach with a horse instead of the wood he had gone to look for, the soldiers watched him curiously.

"Vihaim." A female soldier with short hair called to her colleague. "Where did you get that horse?"

Vihaim did not answer. He passed behind the rest of the soldiers, heading towards Cervan. His gaze was completely lost.

Happy to see Cervan, the horse tried to approach him. But sensing the horse's intentions, Vihaim restrained him, grabbing ahold of the beast's mane, making the animal walk at a slower pace.

The rest of the soldiers looked at each other, exchanging looks of confusion in light of their companion's strange behavior. What did the soldier intend to do?

Vihaim continued walking, guiding the horse. The soldier stopped when he was only a few meters from the giant. Cervan was thoroughly bound and constrained; Vihaim had nothing to worry about.

"Hey, giant," Vihaim called, his voice emotionless.

Cervan opened his eyes. His massive black pupils contracted, surprised to see Orregahil, the animal companion he was so fond of. Vihaim, seeing that he had caught the giant's attention, pulled his knife from one of his pockets and set it against the horse's neck. "You'd better start talking about the whereabouts of the criminals..." The soldier pressed the knife more firmly into the animal's skin, drawing blood.

"No, stop!" begged Cervan.

"As you stopped when you saw our friends die, right?" Vihaim answered, his voice almost broken, his eyes red and full of hatred.

Orregahil's neighing sounded full of anguish and agony.

344

"No more!" Cervan again beseeched. He tried to free himself, twisting his body left and right, but the ropes merely tightened.

"Talk then!" said Vihaim.

His knife was now soaked in blood. He again cut it into the horse. Orregahil gave a second painful neigh.

The rest of the soldiers approached, drawing their own knives and swords. They also wanted revenge. Cervan begged once more; the soldiers didn't seem to hear him. The horse tried to escape, tried to gallop away, but several soldiers were holding him now. Orregahil let out another cry of pain... such a painful neigh that Cervan winced.

"To the west!" Cervan confessed, in what sounded almost like a cry. "Kingdom!"

But the soldiers were not listening anymore. They didn't care what he had to say. They only wanted him to suffer as much as they had, having witnessed their companions die.

Orregahil neighed again. Cervan knew the horse was dying.

The giant clenched his jaw. He had had enough. Every trace of a civilized being that might once have streamed forth from his pores vanished. His agony and fury transformed into a new strength: He tried to extend his right arm with all his might, with all the energy that only rancor and hatred can provide. The ropes began to strain. He pulled once more, harder... The ropes strained one last time and then broke. He had freed his right arm. Then before the soldiers could prevent him, the giant yelled with fury, raising his arm then drawing it down in a powerful blow, smashing half of all the soldiers who were standing there watching him. Before the bodies had fully collapsed to the forest floor, the giant landed a second blow, and then a third.

* * *

His head was spinning as his stomach burned. Too much wine last night, he thought—and the night before too. Gelegen put on his leather boots and left his cabin in search of the giant, determined to use a new strategy this time to make him talk.

He approached the river beside which they had set up camp. He washed his hands and face, slightly relieving the vague discomfort that harassed him. Time was running out. Two days had passed. By now the distance between them and the crew of the carriage could be insurmountable, but he should still try his best.

Upon seeing him leave the cabin, one of his men came running up to him with a careless smile on his face.

"Commander, we have come up with a way to make the giant talk. We found a horse that seems to be his pet. Our men are torturing it to make him talk. They've just started... If you hurry, you can still see the show!"

Gelegen's jaw clenched with a mixture of terror and fury.

"Damn idiots!" he blurted as he ran towards the giant. The soldier who had given him what he thought was good news ran after him, not understanding what the fuss was about.

As they approached the area where the giant still lay roped to the ground, screams of terror could already be heard. A chill ran down Gelegen's back as he cursed the previous night's drinking: running was proving much more difficult than usual.

When Gelegen arrived, the giant had gone mad. He had partially freed himself from his constraints.

"Damn you idiots!" Gelegen shouted again as he unsheathed his sword. Close to the giant there were several mutilated corpses, including the corpse of the horse. Gelegen looked at the soldier who had followed him. "You! Search the area for survivors!" Gelegen ordered. The soldier did not need further instructions. He moved away to look for survivors.

The giant affixed his crazed eyes on Gelegen. He gave a loud cry and tried to grab him, but the veteran was cautious enough to stay out of his range. Cervan's mouth was full of slobber, and snot ran from his nose. Apparently the giant had been crying shortly before he had entered his state of madness. Gelegen looked at him with consolation.

"So it's true... The great Gelegen has captured a giant!" a female voice behind him said in a mocking tone. "It's huge! And it seems *very* angry!" But the woman's tone quickly turned mischievous; it seemed to suggest the situation was humorous despite the dramatic nature of the scene. "So many dead soldiers... My dear sister will not like this at all!"

"That voice... Why just now?"

Gelegen turned around knowing who he was going to meet—a person whom he would least want to meet at this time. Alvia was sitting on the grass with her legs crossed, eating a very red apple. Behind her was her mount, a white stallion. Her face was beautiful like her sister Graglia, but Alvia's face was always smiling, while her sister's was more serious. Alvia was quite a peculiar character. When people heard of the legendary Knights of Water, they imagined fearsome-looking fighters. Fighters with

346

expressions so hard and challenging that they seemed able to beat their opponents without so much as unsheathing their sword. Alvia shared none of the traits of those fighters.

"Alvia!" Gelegen said, annoyed. "Now is not the best time!" He turned his eyes towards the giant... He had to find a way to end this.

"Oh, I don't think so! It's *the perfect* moment, right at the climax of the show!" she said enthusiastically. She took another bite of the apple without moving from her spot.

Cervan continued to scream. He hit the ground hard, pounding his fist into the earth while looking at Gelegen, blaming Gelegen for everything that had happened.

"You," the giant's voice resounded full of fury. "You kill Orregahil. I kill you all!"

The worst of it was that Gelegen could not deny what the giant said. He had to take down the giant, but he could not even get close. He thought about shooting him with arrows, but not only would killing the giant that way be difficult; it would also be far too cruel. Even tied down, the giant had killed nearly all his men.

"Oh, for Aqua Deus and the rest of the gods!" Alvia said indignantly. "It's really boring to think too much! Just finish him off! Are you afraid?"

"Would I not be foolish if I were not?" Gelegen replied. To him it was obvious: Facing an opponent so absurdly superior in strength required a foolproof plan.

"Anyway," she sighed. "I thought that for once you were going to express a little emotion." Alvia got up while throwing the apple to the ground.

Gelegen shuddered, seeing what she was about to do.

"Wait!"

Even before he had spoken, Alvia was already charging the giant, her steps swift and long. Her daggers shone with the sun. Cervan, still crazed, saw her. He tried to crush her with powerful blows, but Alvia's agility and skill far surpassed his brute strength. She amused herself by dodging the giant's attacks, making faces of surprise or mockery—something that only further angered the frustrated giant. In Cervan's eyes, Alvia was a fragile creature; he should have been able to crush her.

In one of her advances, Alvia jumped onto Cervan's huge arm. Leaping with a quick and graceful gait, she landed on his head before Cervan realized it. The giant made a last attempt to crush her, but his hand was incredibly slow compared to Alvia's leaps. Spurred forward,

Alvia advanced towards the giant's temples, where she drove her daggers so hard into Cervan's skin that it sounded as if a tree had cracked in half. Cervan fell instantly to the ground, motionless. Drool from his mouth impregnated the earth.

"Knight of Water," Gelegen said in a low voice.

He recalled when Alvia was named one of the Knights of Water. Many accused the queen of favoritism for having endowed her sister with such an important title. However, Alvia didn't need much time for silencing those voices... Just like the queen, she had been trained in combat since childhood, as all princesses were skilled in the art of the sword; Alvia, however, had gone further. Her interest in combat had led her to learn the use of all kinds of weapons. When she realized that her teacher could not instruct her any further, she left her tutelage in search of an instructor who could teach her combat techniques and styles that she had not already learned. Her physical condition had also become far greater than that of any of her opponents. Some even described her speed as inhuman, as she was able to move so fast that some of her opponents died even before they realized Alvia had shifted from her position, drawn her daggers, and stabbed them to death.

Her favorite fighting technique had always been using the daggers. Although they were not considered the most lethal weapon, Alvia saw a certain charm in being able to finish off a rival with a weapon that her opponent believed, a priori, would seem to place her at an absolute disadvantage. But her talent and dexterity more than compensated for the weapon's shortcomings. Years later, she would become the most veteran of the Knights of Waters, surviving battles and dangers in which many of her companions had succumbed.

Gelegen began to feel a great sadness for the death of the giant. He did not know why. Was age softening him? No, he realized. The deaths he had left behind in his life had simply begun to weigh on him too much. The giant's death haunted him in particular... and not only because of the giant's size. All his soldiers had died, except one. Many would have tried to blame the soldiers' stupidity in order to feel better, but not Gelegen. He blamed only himself.

Alvia jumped off Cervan's head, landing on the ground, then she approached Gelegen. She was using a silk handkerchief to clean the blood on her dagger. Her face bore a smile, as always.

"I expected giants to have harder heads," she said with a shrug.

"Why are you here, Alvia?" Gelegen said, unable to rid the giant from his mind. In a way he was grateful that Alvia had finished his work for him; he did not know if he could have done the deed himself.

"Do you think hearing that the great Gelegen had captured a giant is not reason enough?" she said. "Vienne has been chosen as the legitimate heiress; I thought you would like to know."

"Vienne, huh? I guess nobody expected that," said Gelegen, interested. "How did Graglia take it?"

"You know how my little sister is—queen first of all!" Alvia replied, laughing. "Also, as it so happens, Vienne has been blessed with absolute power."

"Are you serious?" Gelegen said, impressed. He was aware of what that meant. Whereas some heiresses could use only some of the sword's abilities, whoever was blessed with absolute power had utter control of Crystalline. She could use all of the weapon's powers...

"I believe I have nothing more to do here," Alvia said. "This is getting very boring, without a giant roaring and killing people." With a smile and a gesture of mocking reverence, she proclaimed: "For the queendom!"

Alvia climbed on her white horse then left by the same path she had come. Gelegen had always seen her on a horse of that color, as far back he remembered.

It was only when Alvia had gone that he began to weigh her words. The Aqua Deus had made his choice... and in such a curious way. The girl must be around fifteen, Gelegen thought, so in five years the throne would be hers. He could not avoid wondering what the Aquadom would be like ruled by a new monarch. Graglia was no doubt already busy carving Vienne in her likeness.

The soldier whom Gelegen had sent in search of survivors stood behind him, waiting for Gelegen to become aware of his presence.

"Commander Gelegen..." The soldier's voice was full of despair. "All dead—or about to die. None will survive the night."

"I see," Gelegen answered, lamenting the news. "Thank you, soldier."

"One more thing... Just before dying, one of the injured said something of interest: They are traveling west, to the next kingdom. I do not know what he meant."

Gelegen was surprised. Were they leaving the queendom? He must overtake them as soon as possible.

42. Gant Blacksword

The four traveling companions still seemed to find it difficult to adapt to their new hair color, which was brown and dark as the earth. Noakh had laughed when he first saw Hilzen with his new hairstyle. To Noakh's eyes, his friend had looked quite odd, but seeing him now he would say Hilzen looked rather stylish. In general, Hilzen's and Rebet's blue eyes contrasted much more starkly than they had before. Dabayl, meanwhile, kept complaining about her new hair color, even though Noakh suspected she was used to dyeing it.

"Are you sure we're walking in the right direction?" Noakh asked Hilzen, who stood at his side on the carriage.

Noakh, having recovered from their encounter with the dogues, held the reins.

"We are following Rebet's instructions," answered Hilzen, shrugging. "But it's true that according to him we should already be seeing the river..." He held a hand to his forehead, shielding his eyes, finally seeing the river in the distance. "Look! There it is."

They had come up on the River Peond, one of the mightiest rivers of the Aquadom. Although the river was known for its strong current, they had now reached a stretch of the river that seemed much calmer. Noakh looked to the horizon, trying to find a bridge, there was none. He shrugged, not having the slightest idea of how they were going to get to the other side, not only were they still riding in the carriage, swimming across the river would be suicidal. Moreover, the rivers of the queendom were flourishing with fish... and enormous predators patrolled alongside them. Noakh stopped the carriage.

"We are already here, Rebet!" shouted Hilzen. Noakh and Hilzen got off the carriage, while Dabayl and Rebet opened the carriage's door and joined them, with Rebet carrying his map. They all looked at the River Peond.

"Well, Rebet?" Noakh said. "What is the plan?"

Rebet had his head trapped in his map once again. He raised a finger, urging Noakh to wait while he tried to figure out what they had to do. His instincts told him that the map must indicate some way to skirt the river, but instead it seemed to indicate that they had to cross it: No matter how long he looked at the map, he did not see a sign of a bridge. Instead, the map showed only a drawing: a mark of a tree. He began to feel nervous. Was the map outdated? It was true that none of his men had traveled this route for several months, but that did not seem like enough time for the route to have changed. Still, there was no hint that a bridge had ever been there.

Hilzen, who until then had not participated in the conversation, simply extracted from the carriage one of the bodies of the dogues he had taken as provision, pulling it by its legs. The dogues' meat had proven delicious; only Dabayl had refused to try it. But the bodies had already begun rotting, so Hilzen threw one of the carcasses into the water. The next moment, a loud murmur started up. Huge bubbles heralded an impressive din of fish. Their enormous jaws fought to tear off pieces of meat. After a short while, the dogue's dead body had disappeared completely from the surface.

"Yes, I think swimming is not an option," Hilzen said.

Rebet tried to ignore his companion's words. Instead, he was walking by the river and began to study the trees that bordered it. He understood nothing of what the map was trying to tell him until he found a tree marked with a small cross. It was the same drawing that appeared on his map.

Rebet began to observe the tree, trying to solve the mystery of the map. It seemed that his men had forgotten this small detail; thinking Rebet would probably already know what to do, no one had told him what actions he needed to take.

The rest of the travelers gathered around him, trying to understand what features that particular tree had to make Rebet so passionate about it.

"This tree," said the merchant, "seems to be the key... We are supposed to cross the river over here."

"Shall we cut down the tree to cross the river?" Dabayl asked.

"Even if we did, we still would not get close to the other shore," Hilzen judged. The River Peond was so wide that it was indeed difficult to see the far shore.

"Rebet, there must be some kind of instructions," Noakh said.

"There is only a small inscription, but it is in Flumio," Rebet replied. He cursed. "Tae ferae... that's what it says."

The four companions looked at each other, all of them apparently sharing a total ignorance of the Flumio language. They had been taught the common language, after all. Although at the beginning the common language had many detractors, the language soon proved to be useful, thus opening the doors to trade and treaties. A common language undoubtedly greatly facilitated understanding of these transactions, and with the adoption by the traders of this language, its reach was greatly extended. The disappearance of the original languages occurred by different means, depending on the kingdom and the language; the Earth Kingdom's attitude, however, was notable for its eagerness with which the merchants adopted it, gradually extending the common language's reach to such extents that at present the majority of books were written in this new language and few were those who spoke their kingdom's own original language. The respective rulers of each of the kingdoms were aware that they could not fight against progress and practicality. It was a war that they knew none of them could win. Finally realizing this, they decided to let progress go its way.

"But surely it's just two words," Noakh said, who hated feeling as though they had failed when they were so close to their destination.

"Tae ferae," Hilzen repeated to himself. "This is not the first time I've heard that..."

Hilzen tried to rummage through his memory. Where had he heard those words? For some reason he associated them with Marne, his wife... but why? She knew as little Flumio as he did, but something told him that the words were related to her. Then he remembered the day of his wedding.

"Tae ferae... Have faith," Hilzen said in a low voice.

It was what the priest had said! Hilzen remembered. The priest at their wedding had spoken in Flumio... He had talked about how, in every marriage, the husband and wife had to have blind faith in each other— *Tae ferae posi etem,* he had said. And then he had translated that part of the ceremony into the common language.

353

"Have faith!" Hilzen said aloud. "The inscription means we must have faith."

"Have faith?" Rebet said as he cocked his head.

"And what is that supposed to mean?" Noakh said, as confused as the rest.

Rebet reflected on the words. *Have faith...* What did that mean? Could it be? It was crazy, but why not give it a try?

"Hilzen, walk from the tree to the river... and keep walking. Have faith!"

"Oh no," Hilzen said, having learned his lesson from his encounter with the dogues. "This time it's Dabayl's turn."

In spite of everything, he still held some loyalty to Noakh.

"Damn you, Hilzen," Dabayl said while she crossed her arms. "I do not intend to do it." She raised her eyebrows. "I'm a lady, after all."

"I'll do it," Noakh said.

From the tree, he began to walk towards the shore. But there he stopped, reconsidering. He bent down, picking up a stone as big as a frog. Then he threw it into the water before him. Surprisingly, the stone did not sink to the bottom of the river.

"A surprise, to be sure," he said.

Carefully, he set one foot into the water and then the other. Incredibly, he was floating over the water, to the amazement of the others, who were still standing by the tree with the mark. His feet had sunken slightly, just below the waterline. He had the feeling that the river's depth was little more than three fingers deep. "It seems that I am a man of faith after all," he said jokingly.

"As I thought," Rebet said. "I had heard of this, but I did not know if it was true. It is an escape bridge—bridges whose structure is made of a resistant and transparent material. They are usable only by those who know where they are. According to old sayings, there are more of them throughout the queendom. Not many, of course. They say that the bridges have not been used for so many years that not even the crown knows where most of them are. My grandfather told me once that they were created to establish routes only the Aquo people could use, but they were so undetectable that finally a time came when even the Aquos themselves did not know where they were. Ironic, right?"

After Noakh verified that the escape bridge was long enough for all of them to cross, one by one they entered the river—not without some reluctance. As Dabayl stepped carefully across the bridge, a vague anxiety told her that it shouldn't be possible to ford a river in that way, no matter what her eyes were telling her... But the most difficult part of the crossing was getting the carriage into the river.

They started guiding the carriage across the river, with Hilzen and Rebet pushing it from behind. Dabayl held the reins while Noakh was quietly whispering to the mare's ear in order to calm her.

When they had almost crossed the river, Hilzen stumbled, his right foot falling into the river.

"Hilzen!" said Rebet, extending his arm and helping him to get on the bridge again.

"That was close!" Hilzen said, luckily coming out totally unscathed.

After crossing to the other side, they soon entered a forest. The route Rebet's map told them to take was unmistakable: They had to travel slightly south, where they would enter the Valley of the Fallen. After crossing the valley, they would arrive at the Cold Wood, through which they could finally—hopefully—enter the Tirhan Kingdom without being noticed.

Rebet, already more relaxed after getting of the bridge, proceeded to tell them what his reason for traveling in the Tirhan Kingdom would be. It was very simple. He was a merchant—which made sense as far as his plan was concerned, because he was the only one among the travelers with sufficient knowledge of the merchandise. Hilzen would act as his brother, and Noakh and Dabayl would be his children... who were also his escorts.

"That's all?" Hilzen said, somewhat disappointed. Having crossed an invisible bridge, this part of the plan seemed mundane.

"That's right. We're not at war; both kingdoms benefit from trade. I always say that trade is what a modern society does," Rebet noted. Much relieved after crossing the river, he took off his hood, finally feeling a free man. "This kingdom is fascinating in its own way. The Tirhans are different from us, certainly, but their way of living life is at least beautiful."

"You say that now that you don't live there," Dabayl said. She crossed her arms, laughing. "If they call them tree lovers, it is for a reason."

"Oh, yes, they love nature above all," Hilzen confirmed. He, like Noakh, had never been in the Tirhan territories; each man knew only what little he had heard from the histories. "Their crops, from what the histories say, are impressive."

"Their warriors," quoted Noakh, "fight with the strength of the black bear. Their spies move among the shadows like spiders." It was an old saying that Lumio had taught him. Noakh had always loved learning about the warriors of other kingdoms.

"Yes, they treat nature with an enviable respect. It will be difficult to get used to praying before eating a good piece of boar!" Rebet added while laughing.

They didn't need to walk much farther to reach the majestic Valley of the Fallen. So impressive was its scenery that Noakh and Hilzen could not help but gasp in amazement. Rebet smiled as he contemplated the spot once again. It would probably be the last time he saw it.

The valley was steep, covered with trees whose roots cling to the abrupt cliffs. On the mountain, there was a huge crumbling grey stone statue. Two giant figures fighting each other, each wielding a sword that had pierced their opponent, one with a mermaid tail and the other that looked like a living tree. Under the statues was a huge esplanade of stones and moss. The ground there was strewn with fallen tombstones.

Although the valley was a place of passage, few did not stop to admire its beauty, or at least that was the case before it was said that the place was full of ghosts. It was a place endowed with mysticism... A place that had known much pain but that, despite the tombstones and the bloodshed, had known how to remain beautiful.

It was Dabayl who with her privileged view realized that they were not alone in the valley.

"Have you seen that man kneeling on the tombstone?"

With effort, the others managed to see him. As they watched, the man got up. Gradually he approached the travelers, who were again in the carriage. The wind began to whisper, and the sun hid behind the clouds.

A hooded man in a black robe stood in front of the carriage. A huge sword was on his back. A pendant was visible among his clothes, a tiny flask adorned with a small sapphire in the shape of a crown. Hilzen gasped with terror, recognizing the pendant as an ornament only a Knight of Water would carry. Noakh and Dabayl got their weapons ready.

"You taught your men well, Rivetien," the hooded man said. "Of all of them, only one confessed after being tortured. Only one... So close, right?"

Reaching behind his back, he withdrew his enormous sword as black as his clothes. Rivetien covered his ears with his hands, trying not to hear any more of the hooded man's words.

Without further delay, Gant charged the carriage. Noakh jumped out to meet him. He drew his two swords, parrying Gant's thrust. But the attack was so powerful that despite firmly planting his feet on the ground, Noakh was thrown several meters back. Even though Distra had not tasted his opponent's blood, as only their blades had met, Noakh could feel the sword's lust, as if it were impatient to face such a formidable foe. Noakh had to fight to maintain the control.

"Get out of my way, worm," Gant said, annoyed. "I'll take care of you later."

"No," Noakh said resoundingly, then he turned and addressed his companions: "What are you waiting for? Go!"

"But..." Hilzen said hesitantly. He knew Gant Blacksword was a Knight of Water; not only that, but he also had a reputation for death. It was true that Noakh had Distra, but still...

"Go!" Noakh said again, parrying another powerful attack from Gant.

But Hilzen and Dabayl could not simply watch Noakh fight Gant with their arms crossed. Instead, both drew their weapons. Dabayl slipped an arrow for her quiver and drew back her bowstring, while Hilzen loaded a bolt onto his crossbow. When Noakh lunged at Gant, pushing him backwards, Hilzen and Dabayl released their shot. Gant's black sword flashed in the sun, deflecting both Dabayl's arrow and Hilzen's bolt, which fell harmlessly to the ground.

"Infected cockroaches!" Gant said as he spat contemptuously. With a strong kick, he threw Noakh into the air. He landed hard against a tree. Taking advantage of Noakh's incapacitation, Gant ran onto the carriage, leaping between Hilzen and Dabayl.

He hit Hilzen roughly, knocking him out of the carriage. Then he grabbed Dabayl by the neck and lifted her from the carriage with one arm. She tried to free herself and stop Gant from choking her.

"Ladies first!"

Gant squeezed Dabayl's neck. A smile played on his face—he was obviously superior. Dabayl tried to break free without success. She kicked her legs desperately, but Gant ignored her. Rebetien drew a wine bottle out of a box at his feet and approached Gant, but Blacksword was faster. He struck the businessman so hard with his steel gauntlet that the merchant fell to the carriage floor.

Dabayl was still struggling. Her eyes reddened with tears of rage. Her fury seemed to amuse Gant. He lifted her higher from the carriage floor to commemorate her last moments.

357

Suddenly a gust of fire swept in Gant's direction. The blaze rushed by so fast that he barely had time to step out of its path. The distraction caused him to release Dabayl; she fell to the floor, trying to catch her breath. She breathed as hard as her lungs allowed.

Gant rose from the ground. He was slightly stunned. Frowning, he tried to find an explanation for what had happened. He saw Noakh, standing in the direction where the gust of flames had come. One of his swords was completely engulfed in flames.

"So you are something more than a common insect," Gant acknowledged. What had seemed like the most boring mission had just become more interesting. He did not care how Noakh made flames arise from his sword; he cared only about the challenge he was facing.

Gant resumed the fight.

"Hilzen! Get out!" Noakh said, parrying Gant's sword by pinning it between his two swords. Then, he avoided one of Gant's kicks.

Under other conditions, Hilzen would have refused to obey Noakh, but the determination in his voice made him heed his request this time. Helping Dabayl to her feet and taking Rivetien back to the carriage, he grabbed the reins and began to march with them towards the path that led to the Tirhan Kingdom. Gant, unhappy with this, made a feint that then allowed him to thrust his sword at Noakh's neck using a single arm, an incredible feat considering the weight of his weapon. Had it not been for Noakh's quick reflexes, he would have been beheaded. Instead, he deflected the blow by forcing Gant's sword up into the air until he released it. It fell and rolled onto the ground.

"No!" the Knight of Water exclaimed. He picked up his sword from the ground and charged at Noakh again, launching a thrust so hard that after being blocked by Noakh's blades the boy gave a cry of pain as he rolled backwards due to the force of the blow. Gant walked away from Noakh and ran after the carriage. Dabayl shot her arrows precisely while urging Hilzen to go faster. Gant again avoided the projectiles, using his sword to deflect them; each stride brought him closer and closer to the carriage. When he was at a sufficient distance, he held his blade high with both arms as he kept running. With his strength, his attack could split the carriage in two. He was very close to the carriage.

* * *

"What is this sword capable of? What kind of powers does it have?"

358

Noakh ran his hand along Distra's steel edge. He was sitting with his father in their small hut, having come in from one of his first sessions practicing with Distra

"I do not know," Lumio said. "Many are the legends about the power of the twin fire swords. I suppose the techniques are transmitted from bearer to bearer... although something tells me Wulkan will not be willing to show them to you." He laughed. *"I never saw our king use his swords in combat, but I do remember hearing something in one of the legends about him."*

"Which one?" Noakh asked anxiously.

"How did it go?" He tried to remember. *"The enemy was trying to escape, but Wulkan was thirsty for blood and revenge. So many dead soldiers, so many inhabitants of our kingdom. No, they could not escape, not this time. Brandishing Distra and Sinistra, Wulkan raised a huge wall of fire, preventing the flight of his enemies..."*

"Wall of fire?" repeated Noakh, stunned. He looked at the sword, wondering if he could one day do something like that.

Lumio seemed to guess Noakh's thoughts. *"The power is inside you, Noakh,"* he said as he took him by the shoulder. *"Never forget that you are the phoenix... You are its rightful owner..."*

Noakh was standing in the road. While he was recovering from the blow, he saw Gant Blacksword closing in on the back of the carriage by leaps and bounds. At this rate, he would overtake them soon. The carriage turned down a sharp bend in the road, and Noakh pointed Distra between the carriage and its pursuer.

"Wall of fire!" Noakh roared.

Fire began to pour forth from the sword, creating a wall of flame that prevented Gant from moving forward. The wall was not as spectacular as the one Noakh imagined Wulkan had been able to summon, but it was more than enough to stop Gant in his pursuit. After a few moments of watching the wall of fire blocking his way, he turned to look at Noakh.

"I'm afraid I can't allow you to chase my colleagues," Noakh shouted. "You'll have to settle for me..."

Gant turned back to the carriage. It was moving away quickly. Before he could consider whether to jump through the fire, he sensed Noakh was behind him. He turned again. A powerful flare rushed his way. He blocked it using his broadsword. Immediately, the weapon began to warm.

359

Their swords met again. Gant blocked Noakh's cuts, taking special care to parry his fire sword, trying to keep it as far away from his body as possible, as he had realized the sword's blade could release a flare at any time. Noakh's cuts were fast, but they lacked Gant's strength; with each parry and thrust, Gant moved Noakh off of his position.

When Galt held his weapon with two hands, Noakh tried with all his efforts to get away from the attack, because from what he had learned from his battle with Vileblood, such powerful attacks involved enormous damage to his muscles and he could not endure them for long.

Gant's fighting technique was the opposite of what Noakh expected from a Knight of Water. His technique was dirty... He looked for any trick that would allow him to gain an advantage. There was no honor in the way he fought. Despite this, Noakh had to admit that it was very effective. Gant showed more than remarkable skill with the sword, and even more surprising dexterity, considering the heavy armor that his body had to bear. His enormous strength and experience combined made Gant a more than fearsome rival.

Noakh noticed that with each attack, Distra gradually tried to break through. He tried to prevent it, but again and again sought to gain control. His heart was pumping frenetically.

Gant parried another of Noakh's attack with his broadsword. Then he bent down slightly to grab a handful of earth. He threw it into Noakh's eyes, blinding him. Gant swung his sword again. The powerful two-handed attack violently struck Noakh's chest. Noakh's light armor was not enough to stop the force of the attack, almost completely shattering it. A deep wound began to impregnate Noakh's clothes with blood.

Gant kicked Noakh, who fell to the ground, shuddering with pain.

The Knight of Water approached Noakh to execute the final blow. Noakh was trying to rise up.

"Why don't you give up already, you pathetic unickey?" he said as he drew closer, raising his black sword two-handedly.

Give up? Noakh thought.

"Because I already gave up once!" Noakh said with all his might. He lunged forward, thrusting his sword at Gant's feet. The knight blocked it with his broadsword, and at that moment Noakh struck his side with Distra, where his armor was not as thick. Gant instinctively grabbed the sword with his hands, forgetting that it was alive with fire, causing it to burn despite his steel gauntlet.

360

With the strength that he still had left, Noakh made a feint then launched a counterattack. But his eyes began to cloud... The loss of blood from his wound compounded the fatigue from using Distra so long and so fiercely. His movements began to slow, and his breathing became heavier. *Give me a little more time, Distra,* he thought.

Noakh stuck his other sword into the ground so he could stand up. His wound continued to bleed quickly, red drops bathed the ground. Gant was still recovering from the pain in his hand. Noakh launched another flare. Gant tried to block it again with his broadsword. Noakh tried with all his soul to increase the fire's intensity as much as possible.

"Your turn, Distra."

A malevolent smile emerged on Noakh's face. Distra's flames were as strong as he had ever seen them before.

"Aec kallah!" his lips spoke. His smile turned wicked once again. From the edge of the sword the powerful blaze continued to emanate against Gant.

Gant half kneeled while he stuck his huge sword on the ground. He stood behind it, covering his head and part of his body, a defensive posture to avoid the flames as much as he could. The flames wouldn't last long, and then he could land his final blow, the Knight of Water had thought. However, the flames didn't stop, but instead increased in intensity while the boy kept shouting words that, to Gant, made no sense at all. His weapon began to burn—and with this, his armor also began burning. He tried to free himself, but the fire continued to spring from Noakh's sword tirelessly, growing ever stronger.

Gant's screams of pain mingled with Noakh's effort until he finally stopped the flame. Noakh struck Distra also into the earth beside him to stay on his feet. A trickle of blood fell from his mouth. He had regained control of his body again.

Gant remained hidden behind his sword. His clothes were engulfed in flames. His armor and sword had gone from black to red-hot, but nevertheless he continued in his defensive posture. Noakh continued looking at him, panting, waiting for Gant to get up and finish him off.

Instead, the knight fell to the ground, raising a cloud of dust around him. Noakh crawled in the direction in which his companions had fled towards the Earth Kingdom, as far from that beast as possible. He could feel some kind of presence around him.

Join the ranks of the fallen, Noakh heard.

"Leave me alone!" Noakh said as he tried to push away the presence with his hand and kept crawling, leaving a trail of blood in his wake.

Meanwhile, Gant pulled from his neck the small flask that all the Knights of Water carried. He opened it and emptied its contents onto his head and body. Drops of water covered his torso and face. An instant later, he fell unconscious.

43. The defeat

Vienne put her hands to her mouth when she heard the news. Someone had beaten Gant Blacksword. As she understood it, Gant had managed to crawl back to the Aquadom, where several Guards of the City had found him. The young princess could not stop wondering what kind of monster could have beaten a Knight of Water.

The queen, on the other hand, had more important matters to deal with at that time. She was in the Hall of the Crown, sitting on her throne. In front of her stood the priest Ovilier.

It's war then, she thought, once again, as she looked at the floor, trying to weigh everything that conflict involved.

An emissary had arrived that morning on a black horse with grey fur, carrying a statement—a message stained with the blood of the poor extractors of volcanite, who had been discovered by the Fireo troops. The message was concise.

We will make your walls dry. Your temples will be ashes. Everything will burn. Your entire queendom will evaporate. Beware the Incandescent.

It had been months since the queen's counselors had informed her of the volcanite deposit; almost all the precious mineral had been extracted. She would have to talk to Lampen as soon as possible... but that was not among her foremost priorities. The meeting she was attending at that moment required her full attention. The other four members of the Congregation of the Church had unanimously made a crucial decision for the queendom, and she, despite being not only also the fifth and last member of the congregation but also being its representative, due to being the high priestess, could do nothing but accept their decision.

"Graglia, do not look at me like that," said Ovilier, who had been selected to inform the queen about such a decision. "You know it's for the good of the queendom."

The words had been carefully chosen. They were the same words Graglia had used long ago when she managed to win the position of high priestess. This did not go unnoticed by the queen.

"If I die," the queen said, quoting the words of the priest Ovilier. "Katienne... Why her?" Graglia said. She knew the real answer; she just wanted to learn how the priest would reply.

The old man just shrugged. "She's like you, Graglia. Who better?" he said with a crooked smile.

"Vienne deserves the opportunity. There is still time. She is the legitimate heir. She was the sword's choice."

"A few months, Graglia. Admit it's the best option."

"If Vienne controlled Crystalline, if she awakened her power, it would prove she is of some worth to the queendom," Graglia suggested. "She has been blessed with the absolute power of the sword, Ovilier. You were there."

"There is no time," the priest said. "The future of the queendom is at stake."

"The Aqua Deus gave her absolute power," Graglia said again. "Something that only one of my ancestors had the honor to possess. Absolute power—you understand what that means? The Aqua Deus itself granted her all the blessings. Isn't that proof enough that the Aqua Deus trusts her as a worthy heir?"

"I don't know, Graglia... Other members of the Congregation of the Church, me included, think precisely the opposite: that the Aqua Deus granted her all the blessings because she needed all the help our god could provide her, proving she is not worth to the queendom..."

"Swear it, Ovilier! If Vienne controls Crystalline she will not be denied her right to the throne. If she fails and I die in battle, which I assure you won't happen, Katienne will rise to be the queen in any event."

"So be it," Ovilier said, satisfied, aware of Vienne's low chances of success.

The queen left the assembly with a certain taste of defeat in her mouth. She was aware that Katienne would be smart enough not to be in the palace. A pity. The news seemed to have reached the church as soon as he, the priest Ovilier, the oldest member of the Congregation of the Church, had appeared before her, announcing a contingency plan in case she died in combat, just after she had read the declaration of war from the Fireos.

Vienne was seen in the eyes of the clergy and the nobility as someone weak—unable to reign. Graglia felt helpless knowing that her title neither as queen nor as high priestess would be enough to prevent Ovilier's plan from becoming a reality: Katienne would be queen. She had apparently achieved the favor of not only the church but also the noblemen, thanks to her relationship with the heir to Delorange House. Vienne was now her only asset.

As if that was not enough, she had to face another problem: the defeat of Gant. The news of his defeat had surprised the queen. It meant not only that the ingrate Rivetien had managed to escape, but also that someone had been able to defeat a Knight of Water. The Earth Kingdom also happened to have powerful knights, some as strong as a bear, Graglia knew. But if what she had heard was true, he had been defeated with a weapon of fire. What was that kind of madness?

"Is he awake?" she said, addressing the other Knights of Water, who were all eager for the queen to arrive.

"Awake, my queen," Menest replied with a bow.

"Although not for long," said Alvia with a laugh. She had received the news with a very different attitude from her companions. While they had worried over Gant's condition and over who could have caused him such injury, she had preferred to boast about his defeat and show interest in who could have caused the fire wounds—and to such a formidable opponent. His defeat had shown weakness. Alvia could not respect someone weak.

Vienne was also there, simply because something told her that she must be there, waiting for news of the soldier's improvement. She was sitting in a chair, holding Crystalline vertically while she rested her head on the sword's hilt. She had been training when she was informed of Gant's arrival. The news of the war had not reached her ears yet, much less the plans of the church.

Gant was being treated with the blessed water—water that had emanated from Crystalline, and that, thanks to the arts of the priests, remained pure enough to heal the knight's wounds; otherwise, once stored, the water would lose its healing properties.

Graglia took Crystalline from Vienne. Then the queen entered the room where Gant was being treated. The room was dark, illuminated by only two candles. The smell was repugnant. Gant's wounds were infected, and he was lying in the bed with pillows, almost naked. One of the healers stepped up, thinking that it was again one of the Knights of Water who wanted to harass him with questions.

"For the last time, I told you that he is very weak and that you must let him rest..." Her words broke off once she realized that the visitor was no other than the queen herself. So she knelt, performing the usual bow. "My queen, he is very weak—"

The queen raised a hand to prevent her from continuing to talk.

"Can he talk?" she said softly.

"He is barely conscious..."

"Leave us alone."

With a gesture from the healer, her two assistants stopped applying the healing water on Gant and left the room. Then the healer followed them.

As the door closed, Alvia leant her ear to the door to more clearly hear the conversation inside. With a mischievous smile, she pointed to Vienne, inviting her to join her. Vienne did so, approaching the door with a timid smile. Menest joined too, shrugging, while Tarkos remained in his kneeling position. A gesture of his head indicated his disapproval for his companions' attitude.

Inside the room, Graglia walked around Gant to observe his condition. He had no wounds from knives or the blades of swords; instead he exhibited burns around his body in addition to scars produced by having to remove pieces of armor that had been stuck to his body due to the heat. Graglia stood in front of Gant. Then she examined his wounds from a closer distance. The burns were severe. The queen thanked the Aqua Deus it had been Gant who had been wounded so mercilessly. She was aware that, of all her soldiers, he alone, with his inhuman physical strength, could survive such injuries.

"Oh Gant, who has done this to you?" said the queen sadly.

Gant breathed with difficulty. Seeing that it was the queen, he tried to stand up but not even his pride allowed him to do so.

With her hands, the queen urged him to calm down.

"Gant, answer me. I have to know..."

"A... worm," Gant said with great difficulty. The wounds prevented him from breathing normally; it was hard for him to speak more than two words in a row.

"Take your time," Graglia said. She was aware of how important the information was. "This will hurt you, but it will speed up your recovery."

"Brown... eyes," Gant managed to say. "Brown hair."

Graglia frowned. A Tirheo? They were not very common, given the distance between both kingdoms. Even so, why would a Tirheo wield a sword of fire?

Brandishing Crystalline, she made a thin cut across Gant's body while drops of water fell onto his skin. Although the stored blessed water had healing qualities, it was nothing compared to the water dripping directly from the sacred sword.

With the first drops of Crystalline's water, Gant felt a great relief wash over his body. Graglia, however, frowned again. Gant's burns were not healing. She only knew of one kind of burn that Crystalline was unable to heal: the kind inflicted by the sacred swords of fire. But those swords were in the possession of Wulkan, obviously. What was she missing then?

The water from Crystalline revitalized Gant. He felt his blood pulse through his veins, giving him the strength to tell what had happened, although still with difficulty.

While he was telling his story, the queen could not believe it. Judging by his words, the power he had faced was indeed very similar to Wulkan's. But that was impossible. The twin swords of fire were in his possession, and there was no heir. In fact, if that weren't the case—if an heir had indeed been chosen—Wulkan would have passed away or would soon, according to the barbarous customs of his people. No, it could not be. There had to be another explanation. If it were not for Gant's wounds, which fit the description of the facts, she would have thought he was delirious.

As the queen left the room, an idea had crossed her mind. She was wondering if it was madness or genius.

"He was defeated by a brown-eyed boy!" Alvia said, enjoying the humiliation. If the mere fact of Gant having been defeated were enough to joke about for months to come, the fact that it was a unickey Tirheo boy who had beaten him would keep Alvia mocking him for years.

"Silence, Alvia. This is serious," the queen replied. "Apparently whatever power defeated Gant could have reached the Earth Kingdom."

"Gant's sword is lethal, my queen." Menest saw no reason to conceal that they all had heard it. "If that boy was injured as Gant says, I'm sure that he will be dead by now. His corpse might be lying on the valley floor, if it hasn't already been devoured by the beasts."

Tarkos took a step back. The Valley of the Fallen was known for its ghosts.

"As captain of the Knights of Water, I offer my services to bring you his corpse," Menest said as he knelt down.

"No, I need you here, Menest. War threatens us. The lack of the captain of the Knights of Water would cause fear to rise up among our troops. We have enough of that already with the fall of Gant; we do not need any more of it."

Vienne frowned at her mother's words. Had she mentioned war?

The news did not please Menest. Although he saw logic in the queen's words, he did not like the idea of remaining on the sidelines. Even so, he nodded. "As you wish, my queen," he said with a bow.

"Alvia, you will take care of this."

Alvia jumped for joy at her sister's words. Although surprised, she was anxious to face the power that had been able to defeat Gant... if he was still alive.

"You will escort Vienne," the queen continued. "She will be the one who will face the power of that boy. It will be her last opportunity to unleash all of Crystalline's power. For some reason, the Aqua Deus granted her absolute power. It is time for her to awaken it. She has no time other than now to prove herself."

Alvia's face turned from joy to indignation. Both Vienne and Alvia were not very happy hearing the queen's words.

"Oh come on, little sister, Are you telling me I am now to be called Vienne's wet nurse," Alvia answered indignant.

"You will take the *Merrybelle*," the queen replied, ignoring her sister. "Find the boy... and if he is alive, make him fight Vienne, whatever it takes." Her tone had become very serious. Graglia was aware of the sensitive nature of the situation. Vienne had been chosen and she had to reign, even if she was not Graglia's favorite. She had to respect and protect that decision—not to mention that she did not like becoming the target of anyone's blackmail.

The *Merrybelle*, Vienne thought. She was the fastest ship in the queendom. She was not the most modern one, nor was she the one with the greatest number of sails. In fact, she was actually a small boat of simple construction. But for some reason that the sailors could not understand, she was faster than the rest.

Some said that inside the *Merrybelle* was the spirit of a sailor who loved to sail, and that was what made her the fastest. Whatever it was, the *Merrybelle* was used only in instances of extreme urgency. If the queen was willing to use her for this mission, it meant that the mission was exceptionally grave and important.

Vienne considered her mother's words again. She was to fight the boy who had been able to defeat a Knight of Water, one of the most powerful fighters after the queen herself. She started to tremble, knowing she stood no chance against such a monster.

— END OF BOOK 1 —

Thank you for reading the first volume of The Sword's Choice!

I hope you liked The Sapphire Eruption, and this is just the beginning! The second book in the series is on its way, and I assure you that it will have some great surprises for you! Several of your favorite characters will appear again, new alliances that you don't expect will arise, and, mostly, we will finally discover Tir Torrent, The Kingdom of Earth.

Now, it's **time to ask you a little favor.** I want to know what you thought of my story: if you liked it, if not... if you would recommend it. Anything. So, could you leave a review on Amazon? It would be a great help for me, and I love to know your opinions.

Leaving a review is very simple, as easy as this in fact: Search for The Sapphire Eruption, go to the reviews section, and press "Write a Customer review".

Also, if you want to know before anyone else when the next book will be published, you can also follow me on Amazon (next to my author's name on Amazon you will see the "Follow" button), so you will be notified as soon as my next book is published.

The journey has just begun. The story continues in...

The Emerald Storm

Made in the USA
Las Vegas, NV
03 September 2022

54630123R00217